About the author

I live in the Midlands with my very successful and handsome husband, who I am incredibly proud of and our two younger children.

I am a married, working mum of three; the oldest is twenty-eight years and the youngest is seven years. I also have two adorable granddaughters. I spend my time looking after the children, the hens and my adorable cockerel, and last but not least, the two hamsters.

I found my love of writing later in life and have drawn upon many personal experiences when creating each of the characters; I have fallen in love with them as I've written their stories.

I love 'happy ever after's' and spend my spare time writing about them. My inspiration comes from 'life'; living and experiencing the full spectrum of emotions then transferring ideas from this to the make-believe worlds I love to invent and explore.

LUCIA'S LOVE

Paula Dennis

LUCIA'S LOVE

Vanguard Press

VANGUARD PAPERBACK

© Copyright 2019
Paula Dennis

A CIP catalogue record for this title is
available from the British Library.

ISBN 978 1 784654 50 4

*Vanguard Press is an imprint of
Pegasus Elliot MacKenzie Publishers Ltd.*
www.pegasuspublishers.com

First Published in 2019

**Vanguard Press
Sheraton House Castle Park
Cambridge England**

Printed & Bound in Great Britain

Dedication

To Elise and Alice, with love

Chapter 1

"It's good to have you home, little sis, even if it is only for the weekend." I return my sister's enthusiastic hug; I'm as pleased to see her as she is me.

"Yeah, but it's an extra-long weekend though, Em. I'm not going home until Tuesday." I tried to get the week off work but, Will, my boss, was having none of it. The new winter ranges will be ready for publishing next month so he wants me back at his beck and call as soon as.

I pull back from my beautiful sister Emilia and we check each other out. She looks gorgeous as ever. Living by the sea gives her such a healthy glow. I miss it here more than I'd like to admit. Em's dark eyes are glistening as she grins at me. We share the same features and colouring. Brown, almost black, straighter than straight hair and dark brown eyes with skin that permanently looks sun kissed, which some people describe as olive skin. We definitely take after our mamma, Sofia, who is Italian.

I drop my bags on the floor and follow Em through her flat to the living room. Em is an artist but prefers to describe herself as a 'painter'. She has a sea front gallery here in Layton on Sea where we grew up. Her flat is over the gallery and is quite small. This doesn't bother Em as she's just happy to have her work just a staircase away.

"So how's my beautiful niece? I take it she settled OK with Mamma and Dad? They've been so excited, Luce. They can't wait to spoil her rotten. You really should stay away for the next few days and let them indulge themselves." I smile as I affectionately think of my parents and my daughter. Isabella adores her 'Nonna' and Grandpa. Mamma chooses to be called 'Nonna', the Italian version of Nanna. I couldn't curb my baby's excitement at seeing her grandparents. The train journey here couldn't be over quick enough for her.

"Well I can't see me spending much time at Mamma and Dad's, can you. They're taking Bella out to the zoo tomorrow after breakfast, she's fine by the way, so I'll be bugging you most of the day, I think, and then it's Ben's party tomorrow night and I bet we won't see the light of day much before lunch on Sunday, will we?"

"Hey, I don't mind you hanging around here. You can help out in the gallery, it'll give me more time for painting. How is life at a busy magazine anyway, city girl?" I moved away from home when I went to university and never came back. Bella, my three-year-old and I live in London where I work as a project manager for a fashion magazine. I started as an intern and worked my way up. My job is busy and demanding but most of all, I love it. Bella goes to nursery, which costs a fortune, and I couldn't possibly afford it if it weren't for my wonderful parents.

I'm a single mum who would like to think she's bringing her daughter up independently but the truth is, I couldn't do my job and live my life if it weren't for the financial support I get from my parents. Bella's dad doesn't even know she exists so when I told my parents I wanted to stay in London after Bella was born, they insisted on sending me monthly payments to help us survive.

My parents run a caravan/camping park not far from the beach in Layton on Sea. The main house is also used as a guesthouse so they are always busy through the summer. Dad is also a taxi driver, bringing in extra money, which always helped us through the winter months in a ghostly seaside town when Em and I were growing up. Dad uses that money to help Bella and I survive, and I am eternally grateful.

I follow Em into the kitchen, chatting as she makes us a cup of coffee. "Work's good. We're busy and I love that. I've arranged with Mamma and Dad that Bella is going to stay up here for most of the summer. I'll miss her but it will make life so much easier.

Mamma's happy to have her and it means I don't have to balance my time between work and my baby. I'll visit at weekends and Bella will get to spend time at the seaside with you lot."

"Oh, Luce, that sounds good. I can't wait to spend some time with Bell. We can go to the beach and have picnics, oohhh!" I watch the grin spread on my older sister's face at the thought of sharing with Bella all the things she used to do with me. We're only a year apart and very close. When we were little girls, we went everywhere together on adventures. I feel a slight pang of jealousy that I won't be joining my sister and daughter in their summer fun.

"So, have you spoken to Sarah recently, Luce? This party sounds like quite a big affair, you know." Sarah is my best friend from school and her husband, Ben, is holding his thirtieth birthday party this weekend, hence my visit home.

"I spoke to her earlier in the week and she still didn't know if Declan is coming or not. You know, I bet he is and she just doesn't want to tell me." Em rubs my arm and gives me a sympathetic look.

Declan was my childhood sweetheart. We started dating when I was fifteen years old and he was seventeen. We finished a few months after Declan went off to university. I should have been broken-hearted but I actually enjoyed being single for a while until I went off to university and never looked back. I bumped into Declan a few years ago at a works party in London. That was awkward. Declan was with his fiancée, Becky, who seemed to know all about me. I, on the other hand, knew nothing of her except that she was obviously a little insecure. Her shows of affection in front of me were embarrassing.

"Is he still with his fiancée, Luce?" I shrug my shoulders in answer. I haven't had contact with Declan since that time in London. I have no idea what's happening in his life and I'd like to keep it that way.

"You never really told me what happened that week when you saw him in London, did you?" Em looks at me, eyebrow raised in question. I feel a slight blush on my face but try to remain impassive as I respond to my sister's question.

"That's because there's nothing much to tell, Em. I saw him. His girlfriend was completely over the top and that was it really. You know, I realized years before, that he was never the one for me. Declan and I just drifted along together as boyfriend and girlfriend. I never got those goose bumps you should get, or my heart beating faster. You know what I mean?" Em looks at me with sad eyes and I feel a familiar shiver run through me.

My beautiful, talented sister was engaged to the love of her life, Jamie, and was all set to walk down the aisle two years ago. Jamie was in a road traffic accident, colliding with an HGV three months before the wedding. He only had a small car and didn't stand a chance. I know from the look in her eyes that she knows exactly what I'm talking about and I suspect she will never find anyone like Jamie. I touch her hand but she pulls away.

"Don't, Lucy. I'm fine. I just know those feelings and now when I think about how he made me feel, I realize that I may never feel that again and it's sad, right? I'm twenty-nine years old with no prospects what so ever."

"Hey, don't write yourself off just yet, Emilia Meyer. You never know what the future holds, girlie." She passes me my coffee, shrugging her shoulders as she walks past me to the living room.

"I never like to think too far ahead any more, Luce." Em takes a seat on her two-seater sofa and I plonk myself on the floor in front of her.

"OK, let's not get too maudlin, Em. Tell me what you're wearing for the party tomorrow night?" This brings her back to the here and now and she smiles. My sister loves fashion nearly as much as me, so talking about party clothes cheers her up immediately, even if it is just a momentary thing.

"Well I have a choice of three dresses and I need your expert advice, Luce." I watch as my sister disappears into her bedroom, her voice fading as she goes.

"What do you think?" She stands before me, holding up the three very different dresses. One long, one mid length and the other short. I touch each one, feeling the fabric and imagining Emilia in the garment.

I choose the long black maxi dress with the draped waist that I know will define my sister's perfect figure. We're both of the same build, about five foot seven and quite thin. I have a larger bottom than Em who always complains about this. I struggle to see why as I hate my fat backside! The dress has no sleeves with a high neck but a low 'v' back.

"Oh, this one, definitely this one, Em. With the right jewellery, we can make this look so glamorous. I've bought a bag of sample jewellery with me, we can look through that." Em almost skips back to her room. See, just what she needed... a fashion distraction!

I follow Em through to her room, bags in hand. I will be sharing Em's double bed as she only has one bedroom. I place my bags on the floor and take a seat on the bed as I watch my sister hang the chosen dress on the wardrobe door.

"Thanks, Luce, I knew you'd pick the right one. I did choose that one myself but I just couldn't make a final choice. How about we go out for a walk?" I grin at her words. The thought of a stroll down to the seafront and along the pier is just what I need. That's a real welcome home.

Em's gallery is just across the road from the beach so it's only a short walk. The familiar chime of the bell sounding as she opens and closes the gallery door has a place in my heart. That sound always makes me think of my beautiful, talented sister. No matter where I am or what shop, the sound of the bell transports me right back here. We head out into the late afternoon sunshine and I already feel comfort from the sound of the sea.

We march along, a comfortable silence between us as we head straight for the pier. We don't discuss where we're going, we just know. Once there, I stop and hold onto the rail as I take in the sea air and the sound of the gulls. There are many people out this afternoon. It's not yet prime season but people seem to be coming here earlier and earlier. The main months used to be July and August but that has changed and although it's only the end of May, there are plenty of holidaymakers about.

Em and I take a seat outside a little bar called Tofu. This is new, well, new to me. It certainly wasn't here when I was around Layton. There were never bars or bistros and there are plenty to choose from now. The outside tables all seem to be positioned perfectly so that you have a lovely view of the sea and the beach behind us. I take a seat and Em heads off inside to get us a drink. I can't help taking a trip down memory lane as I sit here.

Our summers were special living here. I don't know if it's my imagination or if the summers were actually longer and warmer when we were younger. Em and I used to race home to get our homework done so that we could meet our friends down at the pier. Dad was really strict about us getting homework done on the day we received it and then we had chores to do, helping out around the campsite. Em and I would rush, rush, rush, so that we could see our friends.

When I started going out with Declan, I had all the more reason to rush out in the evening. Em was seeing a lad called Joseph and she was as eager as me. There was quite a big group of us who hung around together. Sarah, my best friend, was already seeing Ben. I can't believe she ended up marrying him. It's Ben's birthday party that I'm here for this weekend. They were off and on so many times through the last few years of school. We were the three steady couples, and there was Oliver Ashcroft, Declan's best mate. Oliver had three girls who he sort-of went out with in turn, almost cyclical. They were Rachel, Alison and Debbie. We never really knew which one of the three he'd show up with and perfected the art of not looking surprised, so as not to offend the preferred choice of girl on that particular day. The rest of the gang was singletons. Altogether there were about fifteen of us who hung around together at the pier.

"Hey, you look lost in thought." I look up and smile at Emilia.

"I was just thinking about the gang and when we used to all hang about here after school."

"Oh, they were fun times, weren't they, Luce?" We both look over towards Emilia's shop. There are some tourists looking through the window.

"I'll go and see if they want to have a look around, Luce, will you be OK?"

"Yes, fine, you go. You might miss a sale otherwise. I'll just wait here for you." She quickly makes her way back along the pier calling out to the tourists to wait for her. I watch as she falls into a jog, eager to open her gallery and possibly sell one of her beautiful paintings. Most of Em's work is of the local area. There are many sea views but also some of the other quaint sites that can be seen in Layton. Tourists like to buy them as mementos of their time here.

I close my eyes and enjoy the warmth of the sun on my face. This feels so good. My thoughts drift to my gorgeous daughter. Oh, I hope Isabella is being good for Nonna and Granddad.

"Lucia... hi?" Just referring to me as Lucia, I know who this is and I freeze. It's Oliver Ashcroft, the only person apart from my family who refers to me as Lucia, my proper name. I open my eyes, wishing I could just disappear right now.

"Hi, Oliver, I take it you're here for Ben's party too?" He nods his head in reply before pulling up a chair and taking a seat opposite me.

I don't speak. I don't know what to say. When we were young, Oliver treated me with contempt most of the time. If he wasn't being horrible, he was making fun of me. He was, *is*, Declan's best friend, yet the feeling of hatred I felt from him toward me broke my heart.

"So how are you, Lucy?" I look up and try to remain calm. His vivid blue eyes are mesmerizing and I can't let him see any emotion.

"I'm fine thanks, Oliver, what about you?" If I keep it polite, he might just go.

"Not so bad." I continue to look out to the beach. I'm trying so hard not to look at his face. Oliver Ashcroft is the best looking male

15

I have ever come across. I had a long-standing crush on him long before I started dating Declan. He has dark blonde, almost brown hair, and the bluest, blue eyes I've ever looked into. His hair is longer than when I last saw him, it suits him. It's floppy and messy and… sexy. Shit, did I just think of him as sexy!

"Lucy?" I have to look up, it would be rude not to.

"Oliver?" He smiles, a small apprehensive smile. I catch my breath. He's beautiful when he smiles. I quickly close my eyes. I cannot look at him. I cannot have feelings for him, not again.

"How's Declan?"

My eyes shoot open. Why is he asking me?

"What?" I'm glaring now. He looks uncomfortable.

"I just wondered how Declan is. I haven't seen or spoke with him, you know, since that week in London." My mouth has gone dry as I take in what I'm hearing. He hasn't had any form of contact with Declan.

"Well I have no idea, Oliver. I haven't seen or spoken to him since then either." He frowns at my words and scratches his head, messing his floppy hair. I watch his actions like someone under hypnosis.

"Oh, right. Is he going to Ben's party?" Why the need to ask me?

"I have no idea, Oliver. Why don't you give him a call and ask him yourself?" He takes his phone out of his pocket, pressing buttons as I try not to stare.

"Declan, its Oliver. I know, long time mate. I was just wondering if you're coming to Ben's thirtieth tomorrow night? I'm in Layton now. Yes, yes, great. OK, I'll see you at the White Hart, yep, eight sounds good. See ya mate." I try not to look as I eavesdrop on this conversation. I really didn't expect him to phone right now. I guess from what I've heard, Declan will be there tomorrow night. That should be… interesting. I wonder if he's got a girlfriend or married even?

"So, how've you been, Lucy?" He asked me like he didn't just interrupt our conversation to call Declan, like we're old acquaintances that need to catch up. I want to be honest and tell him about the last few years but I don't.

"Fine, thank you." My voice is sarcastic, I can't help it. Oliver being nice to me is not something that happens often.

"So… you didn't get back with Declan, then?" I shake my head, laughing sarcastically.

"No, did you think I would?" He smiles, a sad smile.

"You were the love of his life. I just thought…" He doesn't finish and I don't want to continue this conversation. I stand and look over to Emilia's gallery. There's no sign of her so I'll just head back.

"I'm going now, Ollie. I'll no doubt see you tomorrow." I smile but it's not genuine and he knows it. He coughs uncomfortably. My heart is pounding. I just want to get away from him now. Too many bad memories! I turn to walk away, taking a deep breath in the hope that I'll feel better.

"Lucy?" Oh God!

"Have you really been OK?" I swallow hard. I need to put on a brave face now, really, I do. I grin, hoping I look more realistic than I feel.

"Yes, Ollie, I've been absolutely fine, really." He reaches out and touches my hand, taking a hold of it. I freeze. I can't walk, I can't breathe actually. Our eyes meet and I swallow hard again. I can do this, I can deal with Oliver Ashcroft, I've had years of practice.

"Well if it isn't Ollie Ashcroft!" Oh, shit, it's Em. She just loves Ollie. Shit, shit, shit! I look at his hand, still holding mine and I pull away, fast. Oliver stands and takes Emilia in his arms, kissing the side of her head. There was a time when I was envious of his affection for my older sister.

"Emilia Meyer, my favourite Italian beauty. How are you, gorgeous? I'm sorry to hear about Jamie, Em, really I am. Such a tragedy." His voice is so gentle when he speaks to Em. I watch my sister's eyes glaze over and feel her pain. Every time someone mentions Jamie, she seems to switch off. Ollie kisses her again and it seems to bring her back.

"I'm OK, thanks, Ollie. How are you? Lucy said she saw you a few years ago in London. What have you been doing with yourself? You certainly haven't been around these parts." Ollie looks over at me when Em mentions London. Our eyes meet and I smile, trying to look like this is normal. He frowns and looks lost for a second, lost in thought, before he comes back to us and answers Em.

"Well I've been all over the Middle East with the bank but that finished about two months ago. I've resigned from banking, finally. I got away from doing what my father insisted I do and now I'm into property development. I've some work planned with Ben so you might be seeing a bit more of me round these parts, Em. We can spend some time together if you like, you know, like old times." His smile is so genuine when he speaks to Em, I'm almost jealous. I look away feeling a little sorry for myself.

"You'll be at the party then, tomorrow?" He nods in response. Em giggles in delight.

"Declan's coming too." They both look at me, I can see them from the corner of my eye; I don't look back.

"You know, I think most of the old gang will be there. It's going to be fun." Emilia sounds thrilled. I need to get away from this. I have to prepare myself mentally for tomorrow night. I need to perfect my fake smile. I start to walk away. I can't look back. I can't look at his beautiful face again, not today. Not until I've perfected that smile.

"Lucy, wait for me?" Em finally catches me as I walk along the beach. I need to walk and get all those memories out of my head. Em grabs my arms and pulls me to stop.

"What's wrong, Luce? Talk to me please? You're not still holding a grudge with Oliver about the way he used to tease you, are you?" I look at my sister, I want to talk to her but I can't. I can't talk to anyone, not one single person… about Oliver Ashcroft, my first real crush.

Chapter 2

I've always been an early bird. When we were kids I used to jump
on Emilia, trying to wake her, something she claimed was unnatural,
waking so early, and she hated me for her dawn calls. Emilia loves
her bed, the one thing we really don't share. I love to be up as early
as possible, wasting the day in bed is really not my thing. I will try
my best this morning not to wake sleeping beauty, who is currently
cuddled up to me. I remember some of the harsh words she used to
growl at me, awful. Actually, I would really like to go for an early
morning walk alone. When I get the chance, I go for a jog in the
morning. It's not that often, having a three-year-old seems to stop
me doing anything for myself. I wouldn't change having Isabella
for anything but sometimes, I wish I was nearer my family, their
support means everything. I should really jog this morning but I'd
rather go and have a stroll around and remember everything I love
about this beautiful seaside town.

Emerging into the early morning sunshine, I take in a deep
breath of sea air. Oh, it feels good. The grin on my face as I head
off towards the beach shows just how happy this place makes me
feel. Em's gallery is planted right in the middle of a row of shops.
The shops are on the main road adjacent to the sea front. It's a
typical seaside town view, although the type of shops that used to
be here are gone. I realize as I walk that not one of them is the same
as when I lived here, oh, apart from Em's place. Em's gallery has
always been just that, but when we were kids, an eccentric older
man called Giles owned it. He wore a traditional painters smock and
smoked roll ups. We all thought he was a bit weird but in reality, he
was just different. Em bought the gallery when he passed away. She
got it for a good price, all equipment included. Giles' family were

pleased they didn't have to bother clearing out. I think it was his niece and nephew who inherited the shop and flat. They did clear the flat and then James and Em cleared anything she couldn't use from the gallery. It looks really different now. She repainted the walls and installed new lighting, changing the layout to a more modern, open plan space. Obviously, she now displays her work to sell. She has a workshop out the back, the same as Giles, and there are still some of his old easels mixed in with Em's.

There aren't many people about just yet and I savour my time alone. I look at the shops as I walk. A hairdresser's has replaced the old sweet shop where we were daily visitors once upon a time. The shop on the corner that was the newsagents is now a café. It's open and serving breakfast. I think about stopping for a full English but change my mind. I don't like going into pubs and restaurants alone, never mind taking a seat and eating. Instead, I cross the road and head for the pier. Some of the cafes I saw yesterday are just opening up. I might get a coffee and sit outside for a while, that I can do without feeling self-conscious.

I take my seat after ordering my coffee inside. I remove the casing of my breakfast muffin, my mouth watering at the aroma of the buttery cake. I break a piece off and enjoy the sweet treat as I watch the waves breaking on the beach.

Maybe I should move back here with Isabella. It's a perfect place for a child to grow up and she'd have all my family around. I know she'd thrive but what would I do for money? I've only ever worked at the magazine since uni and to be honest, I love it. There's nothing around these parts that even resembles the sort of place that I could work. Maybe I need to retrain in something else. The waitress brings my coffee as I ponder over what other career I could choose. I sigh at the realisation that there is nothing else I would like to do. I decide that I will make an effort to listen hard when I meet old friends tonight at Ben's birthday party. Maybe one of them can inspire me with a new career choice.

Once I've finished my coffee and muffin, I make my way along the pier to the beach. I shudder as a cloud passes over the sun. It's warm this morning, until a reminder that we're only just stepping into the summer months floats by. I stop and look up to check just how many clouds there are, trying to judge if I will stay warm for my walk. I'm wearing my joggers and hoody, I didn't think a coat was necessary. I smile when I see there aren't really many clouds in the blue, blue sky.

"Morning, Lucia." I'm sure my heart stops when I hear his voice. I peek over my shoulder as he walks up behind me, blue jeans rolled up to his ankles, his shoes in his hand. I try not to check him out but I have no will power whatsoever. He's wearing a light grey hoody and as he stands before me, I realise we're matching. He glances down, then back at me, chuckling.

"Snap, matching hoodies today." I let out a small laugh.

"Mmm, morning, Ollie." I scuff at the sand with my bare feet, trainers in hand. Concentrating on the sand moving between my toes helps me to control the blush that I know is taking over my face and neck.

"I went out for a drink with Declan last night, Luce." I look up at this comment, trying to gauge the look on his face. His icy blue eyes are fixed on mine as he waits for my response.

"Is he OK? What's he up to these days?" Our eyes are transfixed as he answers.

"He's good, really good. He's been living in Australia for the past six months. You know he has family over there. Well he's been bumming around doing bar work and stuff, enjoying the Aussie life." I smile. I'm glad he's happy. Declan's a good guy, he just wasn't the one, you know, the one for me.

"Well I'm glad he's happy, Ollie. Is he going back to Australia, or is he back for good?"

"He's only here for a few weeks… ummm," now Ollie is shuffling sand around. He looks like he has more to say but doesn't know how.

"What, Ollie?" Our eyes meet again and I ignore the thumping of my heart. If I'm honest. I'm shocked that he still has this effect on me. You'd think it would have worn off by now. I'm suddenly transported back to the days when I used to watch for him as he walked past my classroom. I used to try and tell him telepathically to look at me but he never did. I watch as he lifts his hand and runs it through his floppy hair. I swallow hard. He hypnotizes me so damn easily. I look out to sea, trying to focus on our conversation. He probably thinks I'm uncomfortable talking about Declan. That's just not the reason. To distract my over active romantic thoughts. I remember the times he was so horrid to me that he made me cry. The last time comes to mind and I feel the tears in my eyes.

"Lucy, are you OK?" He touches my arm and I jump. He may as well have touched me with a burning flame. I take a deep breath and look at him.

"Yes. I'm fine. So. what's the rest of Declan's news then?" I smile to reassure him so that he tells me the gossip.

"He has a new girlfriend, Summer, she's here with him, Luce." I grin.

"An Australian girl?" He nods. This time I touch his arm and I swear he flinches. God, do I repulse him that much? I swallow the sob that would love to make an appearance and smile instead.

"It's OK, Ollie, I'm happy Declan's found someone. Is she 'the one'?" I make quote marks with my fingers and Ollie laughs.

"You know, I think maybe she is. I haven't seen him so happy, Luce, not since... well, never actually. I don't think he even looked that happy when he was with you." This time I hit Ollie's arm, mocking offence at his harsh, but honest words.

"Well you'll get to meet her tonight; he's bringing her to Ben's party."

I smile, wanting to leave. I need to get away now. "Right, well I'll see you later then."

He frowns.

"I'm walking too, Lucy, can I join you or am I really that bad to be seen with?" His head is tilted as he waits for my reply. How can I say no? I want to. I want to beat his chest and cry and tell him he's hurt me so bad, but I don't. I just nod my head and we fall into step alongside each other... silently.

We walk along the beach and turn off to the main road, stopping to put on our shoes before crossing over to what we used to call 'the green'. We walk across the lawned area and head for the park. Neither of us discusses our intended destination, it just happens. We walk through the archway that is the entrance into the flower gardens of the local park as Ollie looks over to me whilst heading towards a bench. I follow. I can't tell you how many times we've all sat on a bench in this same spot at one time or another in the past. We take a seat, side by side and again, share silence. This time though, it is killing me. I want to get up and walk off but something is pulling me here, namely Oliver Ashcroft. I want to talk, to ask him why? Can I? Should I? The silence is broken.

"Lucy, I'm sorry." He turns to me as he speaks and I feel my cheeks redden instantly. He takes my hand and I hold my breath. I shake my head. I want him to stop now. I can't do this. I can't open up these healed wounds. I thought I'd finally moved on – I was wrong.

"Lucy... in London. I'm sorry. I never meant to hurt you. I thought—" I hold my hands up to stop him. I really can't do this. Just the memory of his harsh words that day, the harshest words he's ever used, still hurt. He was there that time in London, the time I saw Declan. He was there and, by God, did he hurt me bad. His hands are now on my shoulders, his eyes fixed on mine. I turn to look away but he pulls my face back, his fingers under my chin.

"Can we start over, Lucy? Can we be friends and see how it goes. Maybe if we start anew, you'll one day let me explain? I never, ever meant to hurt you, ever." I raise my eyes and force myself to hold it together. My words are mumbled.

"I'm not sure Ollie. Maybe… one day." His smile is slight. God, a few years ago I would have loved to be right here, this close to him. I would have been willing him to kiss me. I force myself not to now. I close my eyes. Too late. His lips brush mine, very softly and very quickly. My eyes flick open as he touches my bottom lip with his thumb. My body has turned to mush, jellylike mush.

"Lucy Meyer, you have no idea." It's a statement that I don't understand or choose to ignore. We do need to talk one day, though. I need to speak to someone else first but who? I've never talked to anyone about Ollie and I really don't know who I could trust.

I made my excuses about needing to get to Mamma and Dad's before they went out and left the park bench as quick as a flash. My emotions are a real mixed bag after that little chat. I want to be angry with Ollie, to blurt out everything, but he always seems to have an effect on me that basically turns me into a dreamlike teenager all over again.

As I walk into the kitchen at Mamma and Dad's, all thoughts of Oliver Ashcroft are pushed to the back of my mind as I hear that little voice chattering away to her nonna. The delicious aroma of eggs and bacon hits my nostrils as I catch sight of Mamma who is busy preparing breakfasts for the guests in the main house as Isabella sits patiently at the large, worn kitchen table, munching her cereal between sentences. The look of delight on her face when she sees me makes my heart stop, just like it does every single day. I love my daughter more than life itself. She is the reason I get up in the morning feeling happy and contented.

"Mummy!" I laugh as she spits milk everywhere when she calls my name. Mamma turns swiftly from the cooker, a similar smile to my daughter's spread across her face.

"Lucia, baby, good morning. Why are you here so early? I thought you'd make the most of an undisturbed morning with madam staying here." She nods her head in Bella's direction, the look of love for her only grandchild so obvious as those shiny dark eyes glisten. I take a seat opposite Bella and pull out my tongue. She follows suit and I gasp in mock horror.

"Lucia, don't teach the baby such bad things." Bella giggles as Mamma tells me off. I give her a conspiratorial wink before apologizing.

"Sorry, Mamma." Em and me have always been expected to call Mum 'Mamma'. It's something we never even realized was different until our school friends started to come round to play and pointed out that we were 'foreign'.

Mamma passes me a mug of steaming coffee and I smile at her beautiful face as she finds a seat and assesses me in that way that mother's do. She's frowning so I smile, trying to ward off any suspicions she may have.

"I thought you were helping Emilia in the gallery today?" Her head is tilted as she questions me.

"I am, Mamma. Don't worry, she was still sound asleep when I left for a walk. I just thought I'd call and see my favourite girl before you whisk her off to the zoo." I'm not sure she believes that's my only reason but she nods anyway and stands up to return to her cooking. Dad wanders in from the dining room with more breakfast orders. He stops, gives me the once over, then bends to kiss the top of my head.

"You OK, Princess? What are you doing here this early?" I tut at yet another set of questions as I notice my parents share a concerned look.

"I just told Mamma, I came to see Bella before you head off out later." I watch as Dad heads back to the dining room with more breakfasts. Mamma finishes off the orders then wipes her hands on the front of her apron before taking a mug of coffee for herself and sitting down next to me.

"Bella, sweetheart, why don't you go and wash your face and find me some hairbands to tie back your hair?" I watch as my daughter obediently takes her empty dish to the dishwasher then heads out of the room in search of hairbands and a clean face. Mum nudges my shoulder with hers.

"Have you bumped into any old friends yet, sweetheart?" I smile, knowing that my mamma is dying to know what's wrong. I look at her and she nods, giving me the chance to speak.

"I saw Oliver." She chuckles.

"Oh, that handsome boy, Oliver. The one you had that crush on for years. I always liked him, you know? Those blue eyes of his are something else, aren't they? He was Declan's best friend, wasn't he? What about Declan, is he here for the party too?" I nod my head before answering.

"Yes, Mamma. Oliver saw him last night. Declan's been living in Australia and has a new girlfriend who's here with him." Mamma takes hold of my hand.

"Does that bother you, sweetheart?"

I shake my head, sighing deeply.

"So what's bothering you, baby girl?" I try to find a way to start talking about this. I can't find the words.

"Look, I know this is a taboo subject but does this have anything to do with Bella?"

I nod my head. The first time I have ever, and I mean ever, come close to discussing Bella's unknown father with either of my parents. Mamma takes a large swig of coffee like its brandy and it will help with what's coming next.

"He's here in Layton, Mamma, and I don't know whether I should or shouldn't tell him about Bella." I look into her beautiful, deep brown eyes, praying that she has all the answers.

"Are you going to tell me who he is?"

I shake my head. "Not yet. I can't. You know I always wanted to tell him first. I don't want him to think that everyone knew he was a daddy and he didn't."

"And what do you think his reaction will be, Lucia?" Mamma sounds stern, angry almost. I don't blame her. I know my parents found it hard to deal with the fact that I wouldn't reveal who Bella's daddy is.

"I have no idea, Mamma, and that scares me. I want him to love Bella like I do, but what if he rejects her?"

Mamma sighs. This time, she sounds sad. She pats my hand before pulling it to her mouth and kissing my palm.

"You know, I can't imagine any man rejecting that beautiful little girl. If whoever he is does reject her... well, sweetheart, he's not worth being in her life then, is he?" Mamma's arm is around my shoulders as Dad walks in, carrying a tray full of dirty dishes.

"You girls OK? Where's my favourite girl?"

"I'm here, Granddad, look I washed my face, and Nonna, I have the bands for my hair." I look to my parents, who are smiling adoringly at my daughter.

Bella is tiny and petite like a little doll. She has long, dark hair that curls perfectly. Her eyes are as dark as mine and Mamma's and Emilia's. When she smiles my princess has the cutest dimple on her left cheek. She smiles a lot, my Bella. Sometimes I look at her happy face and imagine telling her that her daddy doesn't even know she exists. I feel cruel and evil. I know I have to make this right... somehow.

Chapter 3

No more words of Bella's dad were mentioned as I watched my parents and my adorable daughter get ready for their afternoon at the zoo. It was like watching three small children as they excitedly made a picnic before heading off together. I almost went with them, the need to be with Bella was overpowering after speaking to Mamma.

As I walk into the gallery and here the ding of the doorbell, Emilia peeks her head around from her workshop out back.

"Oh, here you are. I was about to send out a search party. I take it you've been for a trip down memory lane, have you?" I smile at Em, sighing as I walk over to the kettle and begin to make coffee.

"Hey, Luce, what's up?" I switch on the kettle and prepare two cups before I turn to my concerned sister.

"Nothing, Em, I'm fine. Well, sort of. Well, actually, I'm not." She's frowning at my mixed-up answer to her question.

"Shall we start again? Are you OK?" I shake my head.

"Not really, Em. You see I just spoke with Mamma…" She places her paintbrush down carefully, her eyes fixed on me. I watch as she rubs her hands down the front of Dad's old white shirt that she wears for painting. Em lets out a deep breath then speaks in a whisper.

"Is this about Bella?" I nod my head and frown. How did she guess?

"How, Em?" She smiles and touches my arm.

"Well I guessed that sooner or later, you'd confide. Bella needs a daddy in her life and if it's the real macoy, that's even better. I just knew, Luce, I don't know why or how, I just did." I continue to make coffee as Em talks. She makes her way to the front of the shop and flips the old metal sign to 'closed'.

"Come on, let's go upstairs, Luce, and chat shall we?" I follow my big sister upstairs and prepare to offload the secret I've been carrying around for over three years.

My heart is beating ten to the dozen as Emilia and I take our seats. I want to get this over and done with now. I want Em to know so that she can help me sort out what to do next.

"So, what did Mamma say when you told her?"

"Oh, Em, I haven't told her who, not yet. I want to tell him before I share this with too many people. When he does find out, I don't want him to think that everyone knew except him." Emilia's mouth is open, her face pale.

"So, no one knows, Luce, no one?" She sounds shocked.

"Nope, oh unless you count the lady at the register office who recorded Bella's birth." I smile at Em who nods her head.

****

As I tell the tale of my daughter's conception, I'm transported back nearly four years ago. Work was so busy, I loved it at the magazine. I'd not long been promoted to project manager and I was determined to make a name for myself. I had no time for a social life and that suited me back then. I'd been working for a new client with Lisa, my old mate from uni who also began as an intern. Lisa is what I consider the perfect woman. She's petite, with pretty long, straight, blonde hair, hazel eyes and she has curves in all the right places. We were both promoted together and Will, our boss, thought it would be good to take on our first assignment together. The project went really well and we had, what we thought, the best launch party ever planned. The client was really pleased with the project and the excitement about showing the ads was at fever pitch in our office.

Nearly four years earlier

I can't believe my eyes as I walk into the main gallery. It looks terrific. I hold my hand to my mouth and look sideways at Lisa. She's mirroring my actions. As we take in each other's reaction, we begin to giggle.

"It looks amazing in here, doesn't it, Luce?" I nod my head, spinning around and taking in the room. We chose an art gallery and the black and white pictures displayed on the bare brick walls set the scene perfectly for the client's launch of their new winter coat range. The artwork is all set in and around London and New York, and the monotone colour just adds to the chicness.

We've arranged for champagne to be served to guests on arrival and canapés to be handed out by the rather gorgeous waiters who are passing us by right now. I raise an eyebrow at Lisa as we both take in the sight of the lovely looking man who just offered us a glass of bubbly. We both declined, too eager to get this night under way to even think about having a drink. Passing through from the main gallery, we enter the room where the magazine stills are displayed. The pictures are also black and white but every other one has one primary colour added somewhere. The entrance from the main gallery is almost like an introduction to what comes next – colour. It works so well and I take in a deep breath, proud that we found this place and that it has all worked out so well.

"Lucy, Lisa, over here girls?"

Our boss, Will, is waving us over with a huge grin on his face. I can only assume from his smile that he's happy so far. As we walk over, he hastily grabs each of us in turn and hugs us both.

"This setting is perfect. Well done, you two. Are you all ready then?" We answer in unison, my partner in crime and I.

****

The show went perfectly and Lisa and I haven't stopped all night. Talking to the clients and explaining our thought process was so exciting. I'm beginning to feel a little tired as I head out of the main show room to the back in search of water. I'm thirsty, all this talking is hard work. I spot Lisa and point towards the door so that she knows where I'm heading. We divided ourselves between rooms, Lisa working her way around the main gallery and me around the smaller room. The plan is to swap halfway through the night. I grab some water and greedily empty my glass before heading back out.

"You ready to swap rooms now, Luce?" Lisa seems much more relaxed than me.

"Yes, Lisa. How come you're so damn relaxed? My head's pounding. You look absolutely fine." Lisa chuckles and points to the tray in the hands of one of the waiters.

"I may have had just one glass of champers to give me extra courage." I tut before laughing at my friend. I lean in to whisper.

"Cover me then while I have a crafty glass, will you?" She does just that as I swiftly take a glass from the tray, down the luscious fizzy liquid and replace it, all under the watchful eye of the waiter who seems most amused. Lisa pats me on the back.

"There you go. You'll feel much better now." I grin as I watch her disappear into the other room with a wave in the air.

****

I've been meandering around for a while now, chatting to guests and answering any queries they have. As I hear my name called, I turn, expecting to see one of my work colleagues. I'm shocked to see Declan standing before me. His grin tells me he's pleased to see me. I'm sure my mouth is on the floor. What is he doing here?

"Declan, hi! I must admit I wasn't expecting to bump into you tonight." His eyes are fixed on my face. I feel a slight blush as I wait for his response.

31

"Actually, Luce, I'm here with my fiancée, Becky. I'm her plus one." I swallow hard. He has a fiancée, wow!

Declan and I just sort of drifted apart when he went off to university. We never actually finished our relationship, but then I wasn't really that bothered in the end. Declan and I drifted through most parts of our relationship, if I'm honest. As I look at him, I can honestly say that there's no pang of feeling, you know, like I expected. I thought that one day I'd regret not being with him, but I don't. The news that he's moved on has sort of cheered me up.

"Declan, there you are, honey." I assume the petite blonde linking her arm in Declan's is Becky, his fiancée. I smile and hold out my hand to greet her.

"You must be Becky. Declan was just telling me about you. Hi, I'm Lucy, an old friend of Declan's." Becky looks from Declan to me, her face reddening slightly. She looks directly at Declan as she speaks.

"Lucy, as in THE Lucy?" Declan looks to me, an apologetic smile on his face.

"Yes, Becky, THE Lucy." I'm a little stunned. They keep referring to me as THE Lucy, emphasizing the word THE as if I'm someone to avoid or something. I smile awkwardly, trying to think of an excuse to just leave. Becky directs her next words at me and I almost feel sorry for her obvious insecurity.

"So, you're the girl who broke Declan's heart. The girl who never loved him back. Well, don't worry, Lucy, he has me now. I love him so much, I'm definitely making up for you." Now I'm stunned! Declan clears his throat ready to speak. I look directly at him, waiting for his explanation.

"So, how's work, Lucy? I take it you've fulfilled your dream and that you're working for the magazine?" Can these two people stun me any more. I can't believe he's completely ignored what was just said and moved on. Did I just imagine that little speech from Becky? I frown, rubbing my hand across my head as I try to think of an answer.

"Yes." Is all I can manage. I look at the 'happy' couple and I'm lost for words. Becky leans in and kisses Declan full on the mouth.

"Shall we go and see Mummy and Daddy now, honey?" Declan follows her, waving goodbye as he's led across the room like a puppy. I turn around only to be sent into shock for the second time this evening.

"Hi, Lucia, what are you doing here?"

Now I know my face is beetroot red. It's Oliver Ashcroft. His smile seems genuine but I would never trust Ollie. Usually a smile from him indicates I'm about to be pulled apart in the most embarrassing way possible. Oliver has never liked me, even though he is Declan's best friend. I used to think that he'd at least make an effort for his friend's sake, but I was so, so wrong.

"Hi, Ollie, I'm working. I'm the project manager for the designer. How about you? Ladies' coats don't seem your thing."

He tilts his head smiling at me. For a second, I get lost in those beautiful ice blue eyes of his. You know, I don't think my crush from school has died at all for this man.

"I'm in London for a few weeks and I dropped in to see Declan. He was coming tonight so invited me along. His fiancée, oh, have you met Becky?" I nod in response, he continues to talk. "Well Becky's mum is connected to your magazine somehow, she works in law, I don't know how, but anyway, Becky's parents are here and it's a family do, so I came along." I smile as he tells me his tale. I would love to wrap my arms around his neck and kiss him. He's gorgeous, always has been and… he just gets better with age.

"Lucy?" Oh God I must have drifted into my teenage crush world. Oliver is frowning at me as he watches. "Are you OK?"

"Yes, yes, I'm fine. Sorry, I was just thinking about work, sorry. You know what it's like when you try and socialize and work at the same time. My minds all over the place." He touches my arm and I wince. He's never nice to me. It's my turn to frown.

"What?" He's smiling as he asks, his hand still on my arm.

"You're never nice to me, Oliver Ashcroft, not unless you're about to make a fool of me. Please tell me you're not going to show me up here? I'm working, Ollie, please don't." I can feel panic rising through my body. Oh, please let him just go away, please? His hand now takes grip of my arm and he pulls me to a door at the back of the room. He pushes the metal bar and the exit door opens. Pulling me outside, he pushes me against the wall. His face is close to mine, his hands on either side of my face as he leans in to me.

"Lucia Meyer, I'm sorry. God, Luce, I never knew I made you feel like that. Why didn't you just take me to one side and tell me to back off?" I look down. I'm not used to kind words from Ollie. He just apologized. I'm shocked.

"How do you know my full name, Ollie? And why do you use it?" I need to change the subject. I can't go down that route with him. I need to just focus. I have to go back in and work. He laughs.

"Em told me. I asked her once why she had a fancy Italian name like Emilia and you were Lucy. You know, I think maybe once upon a time your sister had a crush on me, Luce?"

I can't hold in the laugh. If only he knew! He has the wrong sister.

"Why are you laughing?"

He looks hurt. I feel bad. No hang on, maybe this is payback for all the times he made me feel small. I grin at him before I answer.

"Payback."

"What?"

"You look hurt that I'm laughing at your crazy idea. Well, that's payback for all the times you hurt me." He runs his hand through his hair.

"Was it that bad?" I nod in response.

"You even made me cry a few times." I look up and his eyes are boring into mine.

"Fuck! Really?" I nod my head again.

"Look, I have to get back inside, I'm working, Ollie."

"I need to make it up to you, Lucy."

I shake my head.

"No, you don't. We were kids, I've forgiven you, Ollie. Please, let me get back to work?"

He moves back so that I can step aside from him. I walk towards the door and look back. He's deep in thought as he kicks stones around the floor, his head low.

"Ollie?" He looks up, his handsome face full of concern.

"Yes, Lucy?" he sounds sad. I smile.

"You got the wrong sister." I hear him gasp as I quickly make my way back in the room and get lost in the sea of people.

The evening is coming to a close. Will is gushing with praise for Lisa and I. We stand proud as his two protégés and accept his wise words eagerly. There are only a few people milling around now so we all take a glass of champagne and toast the evening.

"There's a few of us going on to a wine bar after. I'd love it if you two could come?" Lisa and I grin at each other as Will waits for a response.

"I'm up for a few drinks, what about you, Lucy?" Lisa nudges me and I nod my head.

"I'd love to, Will. Why don't we just finish off here and we'll meet you there?'

"Good idea, girls. It's the bar across the street, inside the hotel."

"OK, we'll be with you in about half an hour, OK?" Will nods as he heads off to find his party who all seem to have drifted towards the main entrance.

****

Lisa and I take five minutes to catch up and have another glass of champagne before finishing up and leaving to join the others.

Well, this is uncomfortable! The party at the wine bar includes Declan and fiancée, Becky, her parents, oh, and Oliver for good measure! There are a few others, including Will's wife, Marianne, who I love, so I try my best to avoid my old school friends by chatting with them. I managed to tell Lisa who everyone was on a trip to the loo. She just keeps grinning at my discomfort – thanks, friend! All is going as well as can be expected when Becky decides to announce to the room about Declan and I.

"Mummy, I haven't introduced you to Lucy, Declan's old girlfriend. You know, the one he loved who never loved him back." All eyes are on me. The heat radiating from my blushing face could burn my spectators. Declan whispers in Becky's ear but it's too late. She's said enough. Will hurriedly tries to avoid a confrontation by standing in front of me as he fills up glasses with wine. Lisa puts a hand on my knee. I look up at her, my eyes awash with tears. I look down again to hide my watery eyes. I feel hands on my shoulders and catch my breath when Ollie whispers in my ear.

"Hey, Luce, do you want to leave?" Oh God, yes, I want to find somewhere to hide and quick. I have never been so embarrassed in my fucking life.

I turn and whisper to Ollie. "She even beat you, Ollie. That was harsh." He holds out a hand for me to take as I stand. I turn to Becky's mother, then the rest of the party, smiling as best I can.

"On that note, I think I'll leave. I'm glad this evening went so well. Goodnight." I can hear the murmuring as Ollie and I walk away. Declan calls out after us.

"Lucy, Ollie, wait." We stop in the hotel foyer as he walks towards us, a look of complete embarrassment on his face.

"Lucy, I'm so sorry." He raises his hands in the air as if defeated.

"Hmm, there seems a lot of that tonight." I look at Ollie, who grins at me.

"Go back to your fiancée, Declan. Goodnight." With that, I head for the door, Ollie at my side. As we exit into the darkness of the night, he turns to me.

"Can I take you home?" I nod my head, looking forward to getting home more than anything. As far away from Declan and his stupid fiancée as possible.

Chapter 4

"Would you like to come in, Ollie? I do have coffee if you'd like but if I'm honest, I need another drink after that little fiasco back there." He chuckles before answering.

"Are you sure, Luce? I thought maybe you'd had enough of the past for one evening." I frown thinking about the past, he's right.

"You're right. Let's leave it, shall we?" I open the cab door and lean back into the car once outside.

"Thanks for the lift, Ollie. Oh, and the apology earlier. Maybe next time we meet up it will be more... normal." I close the cab door and head into my building, not waiting to hear his response.

Well, what an end to a night. I hope to God that Will isn't upset by Becky's little outburst. Her parents didn't look too pleased. I know I'm biased but she really doesn't seem like Declan's type at all.

I have a small, one bedroomed flat, which I'm sure would fit inside my parents lounge back in Layton on Sea, so it doesn't take long for me to find a glass of brandy from the kitchen and take a comfy seat on the sofa. I sit, my eyes closed, and think over the evening. I smile at the thought of Ollie. Even though he made me cry in the past, I still find him incredibly attractive. His face, that close to mine, gave me goose bumps all over, earlier tonight. I frown when I hear the intercom buzz. I've been home about twenty minutes and I'm not expecting anyone. I wonder if it's Lisa? Placing my glass on the side table, I head to the door.

"Hello?" I talk quietly, curious about my visitor at this time of night. It could be a drunken person, you know, wrong flat. It happens quite a lot.

"Lucy, it's Ollie I changed my mind. Can we talk?"

OH MY GOD! I look at the intercom and debate what to do. Should I? Shouldn't I? I press the button to let him in, saying nothing. He buzzes again.

"Yes?"

"What floor are you on?" I smile.

"Third." I stand by the door and wait. My mouth is dry and I'm nervous and curious all rolled into one.

As he walks through the door into my tiny flat, I get those familiar butterflies in my tummy as if I were fifteen-years-old and he'd just said, 'Hi' as he walked past me at school. He turns to look at me as we reach the living room and I know he can see my blush. He tilts his head, smiling. He goes to talk but then seems to change his mind. I frown. Oliver Ashcroft looks adorable. He always did and I can't help but take him in, all of him. He's wearing fitted black trousers and a white shirt, the neck open. His floppy, dark blonde hair is perfect, just as perfect as his blue eyes. I have to force myself back to the here and now. No more dreaming, Lucy!

"Why the need to talk, Ollie? What do you need to say that's made you turn up here so late?" I'm actually full of nerves as I ask. I'm not sure what I'm expecting to hear and that makes me wary.

Ollie looks around the room, taking in his surroundings before clocking the brandy on the table. He nods to the glass when he speaks.

"Can I have one of those, Luce?" I walk to the kitchen and pour him a glass. All the while, I'm wondering why he's here and what we need to talk about. I like that he's here, my heart is thumping in my chest with anticipation. I hope this isn't anything awkward and that he wants to be friends in some sort of way because I'm not interested in the old relationship we had. He made me feel insecure and I don't need that in my life.

"Lucy?" I turn quickly and find him watching me from the doorway. I snatch up the glass of brandy and offer it to him. As he takes it, I watch his hands. I remember how I used to look at those hands when I watched him smoke. If he brought one of his regular girls on our nights out at the pier, I would watch in envy as he held their hand or touched their face. The fact that I was with Declan never seemed to stop my dreams. Neither of us has moved and the silence is heavy in the air. I'm lost between the 'then and now'. I want to dislike him, my life would be so much easier, but I don't. I decide to speak.

"You know, Oliver, I want more than anything to dislike you. I want to hate you for all the times you made me feel small and insecure, but I don't, I can't." I watch as he takes a large swig of brandy. He swirls the amber liquid in the glass, focusing on that, rather than looking at me. I get it. I get that he feels guilty, that's why I can't hate him. He has a conscience.

"Would you like to go and sit down?" He glances at me and I can't help but smile. For once, I appear to have the upper hand. I move towards him, waving my hand so that he moves away from the door. I push past him and stop momentarily, allowing myself to take in his face at such close range. He's focusing on his feet so I take a good look. Yes, he is definitely more handsome now, oh and he smells divine, God dammit!

I pull on his arm as I move away so that he follows me. Touching him evokes so many feelings within. I still have that crush, for God's sake, I'm twenty-four years old and I still have a girlie crush.

The moment our eyes meet, I feel my temporary serge of self-confidence disappear. I can't fathom out what emotion I see in his beautiful eyes and it's killing me, waiting and wondering what he wants with me. I look down at my hands, I have no idea what to do or say.

"Lucy, when we were at school, you know all the teasing…" I nod my head, trying not to go back there. "Well, I never meant anything by it. You know, I really liked you." My head shoots up involuntarily. I'm shocked. He liked me, really liked me!

"Well, excuse me, but am I stupid or WAS I stupid? I thought if you liked someone, or REALLY liked someone, you treated them with kindness and respect. Most of the time when we were growing up, Oliver, you treated me like a rabid dog." My face is blushed, this time it's because I'm angry. I'd like to shout at him but it's not my style. I think the words and never have the nerve to actually say them. I'm always the one who thinks about what I could have said… after the argument.

"Lucy, I want to explain. It will sound silly and immature but I need to tell you." I hold my hands in the air.

"Well, go ahead, Oliver, explain." I'm not sure I want to hear this but I guess it's about time we sorted things. I'm staring at him, my eyes boring right through his head. As he looks at me, the look in his eyes is one of affection and it throws me, completely and utterly throws me.

"You know, Lucia Meyer, I remember the first time I saw you, in school. It was your first week at Layton Comprehensive and I saw you walk over to meet Emilia at lunchtime. I watched and stared, Luce. I'd never really been that interested in girls until I saw you. I really liked you. You blew me away. I knew I couldn't go near you. You were two years younger than me and that was just not the done thing… so, I spent weeks watching you from afar. I found out your name pretty quickly, actually, I knew Emilia so it was easy. She warned me off you, so that was it, I knew I couldn't go near. Emilia was my friend and anyway, you were a first year – out of bounds." I'm hearing his words but I can't quite believe what he's saying. He liked me. I want to cry. Years of loving him from afar and now he tells me he liked me. I know his boyhood crush has probably gone but I'm gutted. Really gutted. I used to lie awake at night, dreaming about what it would be like to be kissed by Oliver Ashcroft. In fact, if I'm honest with myself, those dreams have never really stopped. I can't look at him. I want to jump on him and kiss his face off. I want to tell him about my crush, about my dreams of marrying him one day, about the times I'd watch in hope that he'd look at me, that he'd smile at me. Instead, I focus on my hands. I pick at my nail polish, flakes of red falling onto my skirt.

"Lucy, please look at me?" I take a deep breath and glance at him, trying hard not to look into those ice blue eyes that captivate me. "I was devastated when you started going out with Declan. He knew I wanted to ask you out and yet, he still went ahead and got in first. You know, I hated him for a while. I didn't speak to him for weeks. He was my best friend, Luce, he knew I liked you so damn much, yet he went and asked you out." I can't take my eyes off him now. My heart is being ripped right out of me, I'm sure. The news that he liked me and wanted to ask me out is like a dagger running through me. I'm shaking my head.

"Declan wouldn't do that…" I look at him, he's nodding his head, his face solemn as he tells me this news. News that the boyfriend I had for most of my teenage years was a scoundrel who hurt his best friend over ME!

"Lucy, I'm sorry I teased and bullied you. It was my way of coping. In a sick kind of way, I could get back at Declan by being horrid to you. He never stuck up for you, did he?" I shake my head, thinking back to the pier and our nights together. "You see, if he stuck up for you, then I'd have told you and he was scared that you'd finish with him." I pull my hand to my mouth, shocked beyond belief.

I close my eyes and try to focus on the here and now. We're older, we've all moved on. There is no point in raking over this. We need to move on. I need to pull myself together and grow up. I need to stop with the silly, girlish dreams and make peace with Ollie. I feel him take hold of my hand, my skin burning at his touch.

"Ollie, can we just forget all this now and move on, please?" His thumb is rubbing my hand, I glance down and suppress the urge to tell him I love him. God knows where that's coming from. I want to tell him, desperately… but I don't. I take a peek at him, he's watching me intently. He sighs deeply.

"Lucy, I'll do whatever you want. I just want you to forgive me, to accept my apology. I know it was a long time ago but I hate the thought that I hurt you."

I smile at him. The smile is real. The affection I feel for him runs so deep. He doesn't need to know that. We can be friends

41

though, we can make up and never talk about this again. I take both of his hands, he smiles.

"Oliver Ashcroft, let's be friends. Let's never talk about Declan or this again. I spent far too many sleepless nights mulling over you, Declan and me. I don't want to start that again." His head is tilted when he answers, his voice full of emotion.

"OK, beautiful girl, whatever you want." We sit and stare for what seems like minutes but is actually just seconds. He pulls me to him and I close my eyes, taking in his feel and smell. He really is perfect and I don't know how I'm possibly going to be friends with him but I'll try. When I feel his lips kiss the side of my head, I gasp. This is pure torture. I think maybe him being horrible to me is the better option. Oliver pulls away, holding my shoulders.

"Let me take you out, Lucy? I want to go out with you and have a good time. I want to talk about things you like, things that make you laugh, things that make you cry. I want to be your friend, Lucy." I swallow the tears that are threatening to erupt. I want more, but I will not make a fool of myself. I'm too scared to be honest to tell him how I really feel. I nod my head in agreement.

"OK. So, I'll come over tomorrow and take you out, is that a date?" I frown, he laughs. "OK, not a date-date, but can I come over and take you out?" I nod my head.

****

I didn't sleep well. The thought of actually going anywhere with Oliver Ashcroft is a dream come true. Ollie went home promising to return and take me out for the day. There was no way on earth I'd refuse. I knew it would be painful, heartbreakingly painful, but I want to be near him in whatever form that takes. A friend is OK, it isn't perfect but it's something!

He's coming to meet me at eleven and I've been ready now for half an hour. He won't be here for another half an hour, what the hell can I do to fill the time? I run to the bathroom for the tenth time and check my reflection. I'm wearing my black jeans and a red fitted sweater. I've pulled my hair up in a ponytail, tying it back as the weather is so windy today. My make-up is simple. Eyeliner, mascara, a hint of blusher and red lippy. I love jewellery and spent ages deciding which earrings to wear. I chose some large gold studs and a matching gold necklace.

I look at my hands – I've even re-done my nail polish after the mess I nervously made of them last night. A ring! I curse as I head to the bedroom, realizing I've left my ring off. I rummage in my jewellery box and find the plain gold band that my grandmother left me. It's so unusual and I love it. Wedding rings these days are usually thin, narrow and pale in colour. The one my grandmother left me is over half an inch thick and a much brighter colour than anything I've ever seen. I never knew my grandmother, she passed away when Emilia and I were very young. I smile as I think of my dad and then gasp as I hear the buzzer. He's here! So off I go for a day out with my 'friend'.

He whistles when I open the door, my blush instantly appearing at the sound of his affection.

"You look beautiful, Lucia." I love the way he says my name, pronouncing it as perfectly as my mother in her native tongue.

"Well, thank you. You don't look so bad yourself." Honestly! He looks amazing. Simple blue jeans, a black jumper covered by a warm black jacket that I'd just love to get inside and finished off with black ankle boots – perfect! I take in his delicious smell as he reaches round my shoulders with his arm while we wait for the lift. I'm conscious that this is too much but I can't tell him not to touch me. I love it when he touches me. I love him full stop, if I'm honest. Maybe spending some time with him will put me off this perfect image I have of him. After all, most of my love is built on dreams rather than fact. Maybe I'll find out he has some terrible bad habits that I hate and in turn put me off him – oh, please, let that happen?

We step out into the late morning sunshine and I can't help the overwhelming feeling of contentment I get now that he's here – with me!

"Where are we going, Ollie?" He grabs my hand and I gasp inwardly at the feel of his skin. He pulls me close to him as we head to the tube station. It feels natural and I have to admit, I love him holding me. I feel precious for the first time ever. I have never been on a real date and felt this precious.

"Camden Lock. Is that OK with you?"

"Umm, yes, fine. Do you like it there?" He turns to me smiling.

"Yes, beautiful, I do and I want to share lunch with you while we watch the world go by." This is feeling more like a real date with each second that passes.

He holds me close as we wander around the market stalls, giggling as we barter with stallholders for things that we have no intention of buying. I buy a hat, I love hats. Ollie oos and ahhs over each one that I try on. When we find a seat on the old Lambrettas made into seats that overlook the canal, I turn and he's watching me.

"What?" He grins at my question.

"I used to dream about taking you out to eat. I can't wait to watch you eat." I feel my face burning. How can I possibly eat in front of him now, knowing he's watching me? Wild, mad, enormous butterflies with clogs on, are dancing around in my belly right now. I look at the noodles I foolishly picked, I look at Ollie, his grin spread across his face.

"Umm, yes, Luce, noodles. This will be fun." I hit his arm and he pulls me to him. Before I can even think, he kisses me. Ever so lightly and ever so perfectly… he kisses me. I keep my eyes closed. I don't want to interrupt this perfect moment with reality.

"Lucy." I slowly open one eye. He's frowning. "I'm sorry, I didn't mean to do that, it just happened." So how do I take that? Does he mean he's sorry he kissed me? My heart hurts. I love him, I can't help how I feel. I love him. I love it when he says my name, when he smiles at me with his head tilted, when he calls me beautiful. I love his smell, his face, his everything! Oh God, I groan inwardly. I look at my noodles, all appetite lost to love, mind blowingly, unrequited love!

I gaze out at the canal, trying to focus on the people around me rather than the person at my side. Everywhere I look, there are couples who appear madly in love. What did I do wrong? Why can't I find happiness? Why can't he love me? I risk a glance and find him watching me. He frowns when I look and my heart hurts a little. I love his smile, not his frown!

"Ollie?"

"Luce?" I watch as he munches on a dumpling. I lean over and rub some grease from his chin with my thumb. He grabs my hand and kisses my fingers. My whole body seems to turn to mush right then and I can't help my reaction.

"I love you, I've always loved you. I…" I cover my eyes with my hands. What am I doing? I feel him come closer, pulling my hands away.

"Lucy, look at me?" I can't breathe. I'm so scared. I look at him, he's grinning.

"God, I love you too, beautiful, I love you so much it hurts. I've always loved you. I dream about you constantly. I've spent years wondering what you're doing, if you're happy, if you're in love." As he takes me in his arms, I feel warm tears of joy trickle down my cheeks. Is this really happening? Oliver Ashcroft, the person I've loved forever, loves me back!

The trip home passed in a blur. My mind is completely fucked! I love him, he loves me! Wow, fucking wow!

As we stumble through my front door, I have never felt my inhibitions melt away like they just did. I want so desperately to show this man how much I love him. I want to taste every inch of him. To kiss him, to lick him, to be kissed by him, to be licked by him, oh wow, this is mind blowing.

"Oh God, Lucy, this is too much, baby. This is all my dreams come true, sweet, beautiful Lucia. You are my dreams." He picks me up and carries me across the hall to my bedroom. My heart is beating out of my chest and I can honestly say, I have never, ever, been so happy in my life.

His kisses are just perfect. I feel my body melting as our tongues explore and dance. I moan as he pulls my top over my head, kissing every inch of skin as he does. I groan, loving his touch, his kiss. I love him, this is perfect. I lay on my bed as he undresses me, his face full of love as he takes in my body. This would normally make me uneasy but I feel precious, yes precious, as he looks at me lovingly and kisses each part of me while he undresses me.

"You know, you are perfect, Lucy. So much better than I ever dreamed, baby." As our lips meet, I feel the pulses run through my body to my groin. I have never wanted anything so much in my life. My dreams are nothing in comparison to the reality. This man means everything to me, I love him with all my heart.

I arch my back as he licks from my neck down to my nipple. I'm lost in a world of wonderful sensations. I want to touch him, to feel his body.

"Oliver, I need to take your clothes off." We stop and he looks at me, his eyes full of lust. He pulls his sweater over his head and I gasp at the sight of his perfect body. I reach up and touch his taught skin. Oh my! He really is a dream! I kiss his shoulder and feel him shudder.

"Lucy, you drive me wild, baby."

"I love you, Ollie, I've loved you forever." I watch as he loosens his belt and pulls his jeans down. I'm overwhelmed right now. This is just, too much! I can't take my eyes off his naked body. As he leans over me, I use all my strength and push him over. I straddle him, pulling back to look at him. He's perfect, I'm honoured.

"You know this is my dream come true, Oliver Ashcroft. I dreamed of loving you and marrying you and living happily ever after with you. You are my everything" I lean down as our lips meet and I feel the pulses run through me. He pushes me over, his arms either side of me as he leans over me. The feel of his kisses running down my body fill me with pure want. This is everything I ever dreamed of and more.

46

I arch my back as his kisses trail down my stomach. His tender kisses fill me with a desire I never knew I had.

The fire in me burns bright as his lips follow a trail down from my belly button. I run my fingers through his lovely, soft hair, tugging gently with each of his kisses.

"Lucy, I love you." My dreams are finally reality.

"I love you too, more than you'll ever know."

Making love with Oliver is perfect, just perfect. I love every tiny movement we make together. His kisses fill me with electricity, making my heart lurch. I'm completely lost in this perfect, passionate moment, with the love of my life. As we move together, I memorize every feeling of being as close as possible to the man of my dreams – nothing will ever beat this!

The feeling of his kisses on my neck as he whispers my name melt my heart, completely. I have never felt beautiful, ever, in my life, until now.

We lie together, fulfilled and complete in our newfound love that's been alive and unspoken for nearly a decade. I run my fingers across his chest, tickling through his chest hair. I'm lost in sheer wonder at our unity. We could have gone on forever, not knowing how the other felt. I look up at his beautiful face. He kisses the end of my nose and I breathe a deep sigh of contentment.

"You really are perfect, Lucia. You are all my dreams come true. Thank you."

"Please don't thank me, Ollie, that sounds almost formal."

"I have never felt so much as I do with you, baby. You really are… IT!" He leans in and kisses me and I have never felt so loved.

"Lying next to you is perfect, Ollie. I adore you, forever."

****

Chapter 5

I look up at the smiling face of my sister, Emilia, feeling the huge weight lifted from my shoulders now I'm sharing this story.

"I'm actually lost for words, Luce. You and Ollie, oh my God! How did I never notice that you liked him, or him you for that matter? I thought you hated each other, if I'm honest."

"Hmm, well I thought he hated me too, Em." I sigh as I remember that perfect night with the man of my dreams. It sounds so corny and pretentious that we found each other and declared our feelings and were actually… in love. I look around the room, trying to find the words to carry on this romantic tale that didn't end the way I wanted it to.

"So, tell me more. Is he Bella's dad? Why aren't you together? What happened? God, Lucy, this is so lovely. I get shivers knowing you're going to ruin the dream now, aren't you?"

I look up at my beautiful, insightful sister, nodding my head.

****

"Lucy, wake up, beautiful." His kisses on my cheek and across my chin make my heart race. I groan.

"Oh, my God, this wasn't a dream, then? I did just spend the night with you and make mad, passionate love all night until I was so exhausted, I had to sleep." He grins, nodding his head.

"Best night of my life, Miss Meyer. You are incredible and I love you." I'm sure he can hear my thumping heart. I would love to jump up and do cartwheels right now but I just grin instead. I jump up and out of my bed and head to the bathroom.

"I need to brush my teeth, Ollie. I need more kisses, but not with morning breath." I hear his chuckle as he follows me.

"I'd kiss you anyway, for the record, but if you're brushing, then so am I." We stand side by side at the sink. I brush and rinse, passing him my toothbrush, watching as he follows my routine. When he's finished, I dab at his mouth with the towel before kissing him lightly on his perfect lips.

I turn to leave the bathroom but I'm pulled back as I try to exit. I look over my shoulder as Ollie grins.

"Take a shower with me, Lucy?"

Just the thought has pulses firing everywhere.

"That sounds wonderful." I nod my head, brushing past him to turn on the water. I stand with my back to him as I test the water temperature. I feel his hand across my belly, I gasp. He pulls me close to him as I close my eyes and luxuriate in the feel of being in his arms. His kisses on the back of my neck and my shoulders make me moan. I feel his smile at my enjoyment. I step away from him into the shower turning to face him as he follows me. He pulls me close, his hands linked at the back of my neck. I run my hands up and down his broad back as we both stand and enjoy the river of hot water cascading down our bodies. We don't speak, there is no need for words right now, just pleasure.

I take the shower gel applying some onto the sponge. Ollie leans against the shower wall as I begin to wash his wet body. I kiss and wash, enjoying my exploration of him. His little gasps as I follow the sponge with my fingers fill me with lust. Once I've finished his front, I turn him around and begin the same routine, first the sponge, then my fingers.

"Lucy, this is torture, baby. I'm going to have to take you soon, you're killing me."

"Oh no, you have to pay me back now. I need washing, Ollie" I hand him the sponge as he turns. I kiss his mouth. He pulls my head to him but I back off.

"No, wash first, please." His groan amuses me but he follows my instructions and begins to sponge me down. It doesn't take long for me to realize just how he was feeling. I'm on fire and I need him. Before he turns me around, I stand on tiptoe and kiss him hard on the mouth. He shakes his head.

"Nope, not happening. You're feeling the torture too. It's only fair."

We're standing, face to face, completely washed and clean, our eyes fixed. The sensations running through my body right now are killing me but at the same time I'm filled with excitement. As I see his hand reach up to touch me, I gasp, the anticipation driving me wild. I tilt my head into his hand as he touches my face.

"You're beautiful, Lucy, truly beautiful." I open my mouth as I feel his lips on mine. I want to be lost in him all over again.

Once we step out of the shower, I get the urge to just pull him right back in again. I don't want this to end, ever.

"Come on I'm taking you out for lunch today. This time, though, it's a date, OK?"

I nod, a silly grin spread right across my face as I follow him into my bedroom.

****

I turn and smile as he enters my tiny kitchen. He looks delicious even if he is wearing the same clothes as yesterday. I pass him a mug of coffee and we leave and take a seat in the living room. I place my mug on the table as I take my seat on the floor in front of him.

"So where are we going today?"

He touches my cheek as he answers. "You choose. Where would you like to go?"

I rub my hands together, smiling excitedly. "That's easy then, my favourite place to hang out on a Sunday is Covent Garden."

He doesn't look impressed. "Really?"

I nod my head in answer.

He scratches his head. "With all the tourists, really?"

I nod again, laughing. "Most definitely my favourite place, even with all the tourists."

He shrugs, looking bemused at my choice. "Covent Garden it is then, beautiful."

****

I made him stand and watch a juggler, then we watched the crowd as they watched a man dressed as a gold statue. I never tire of seeing the audience and their fascination with this art.

We're seated outside at one of the restaurants in Covent Garden and I couldn't be happier. I order pizza and smile when Ollie takes a slice to try. He ordered pasta, which I've already tried more than once.

"This is actually better than I thought, Luce." He waves his hand, indicating the place. I feel happiness run through me that he likes it here.

"See, you don't even notice the tourists, do you? And if you like people watching, this is the perfect place, right?" He nods his head and leans across the table to me. He touches my face as he speaks.

"I always knew that if I got to spend time with you, I'd love it, Lucy. I just knew you'd be perfect." I want to cry tears of happiness, but I don't. I just smile and kiss his hand as it sweeps across my mouth.

It's late evening and we're wandering back to my place. I feel all warm and fuzzy as we walk along, his arm firmly around my waist.

"So how long are you in London for, Ollie?" He sighs before answering.

"One more week then I'm off to Dubai for two months. Then I'll be back for two months before heading out to Hong Kong.

There's no time limit on Hong Kong, it all depends. I could be there for a few weeks or a year, I won't really know until I get there." The lump in my throat is the size of a tennis ball. He's going away. I've finally found him and told him how I feel and he's leaving... in a week. I stop walking. He touches my face.

"So, this is just like a holiday romance for you, really?" my world is crumbling as I speak. He's shaking his head furiously.

"It isn't, Lucy. The way I feel about you is real. I want to be with you. I will sort it, I will do whatever I have to if you want us to be together." I feel slight relief at his words but the enormity of our situation lays heavy on my heart.

He leaves for Dubai in two days' time. We've been almost inseparable this week. I managed to convince Will that I should have a few days off which made it much easier. As each day has passed, my heart has got heavier and heavier. I can't honestly see how this relationship is going to work. I'd like to jump on the plane with him and never leave his side but I've just got promoted and I love my job. I'm torn, completely torn and to make it worse, Ollie hasn't mentioned leaving once since he first told me. When I've tried to talk to him about it, he shushes me, claiming he doesn't want to think about it. Ollie's working today, planning his trip so I'm at the office too. I feel sad and loneliness is creeping in too. I don't want him to leave. That wasn't in my 'happy ever after' dream. I frown as I pick up the phone on my desk. I'm not in the mood for work and that isn't like me.

"Good morning, Lucia Meyer speaking."

"Lucy, hi, it's Declan, how are you? I'm so sorry about what happened last week. I had no idea Becky could be so horrid." I'm flipping a pencil between my fingers as I listen to him speak. I'd like to be angry with him or at least feel some emotion but I don't, nothing!

"Listen, Declan, don't give it another thought. I'm fine and what Becky said didn't bother me, really."

"Oh." He sounds disappointed. Should I feel bad? I don't.

"Well I was wondering if I could take you out, maybe for dinner, just to make things right between us." I scratch my head with my pencil, frowning. I don't want to go out for dinner with Declan, I want to be with Ollie.

"I don't think that's necessary, Declan. Really, there's nothing to make right." He laughs.

"OK, how about lunch?" Shit! He's not giving up.

"OK then, we'll meet for lunch. Do you mean today?"

"Yes, what time?"

"About twelve thirty, is that OK?"

"Fine, should I meet you at your office?" I go to say yes, then a vision of Becky and her mother come to mind. The last thing I want is another scene at work!

"No, I'll meet you at Green Park. It's not too far for either of us, is it? Next to the ice cream place." He knows exactly where I mean. We met there a few times after I came to London. Nothing in it, just for coffee, as friends.

"OK, I'll be waiting."

Once I've said my goodbyes, I sit and contemplate lunch with Declan.

The morning has flown by. I'm not that pleased, if I'm honest. I really don't want to go for lunch with Declan. I do know, however, that I'm going to tell him about Ollie. I'm not nervous. I'm anxious to see his reaction when I tell him how I know about him asking me out when he knew Ollie liked me. When I think back, there was never a time that Declan tried to force Ollie and me together. You know, if your best friend and your girlfriend didn't get on, you'd try everything, surely. Now I see why he didn't.

Lisa stops by at my desk for a chat as I'm getting ready to leave for lunch.

"Meeting anyone nice today, Luce? No, you can't be, you look too anxious."

"Am I that transparent? I'm meeting Declan. He wants to make things right between us, you know, since last week with his girlfriend and her little show." Lisa whistles.

"I thought you'd steer clear of him for good now. By the way, who was the guy you left with? He's an absolute dream." I smile at my friend's comments about Ollie. I'm not ready to tell anyone about us finding each other though, especially now he's going away.

"Oh, that's Oliver, a friend of mine and Declan's from school. He's off back to Dubai day after tomorrow." Lisa sighs.

"Shame, I would have liked a proper introduction to him. Lovely boy." I can't stop the frown on my face. It's OK for her to be nice about him, but I don't want her having ideas that he's available. Lisa notices my reaction.

"Hey, are you two, you know, an item?" I smile, I can't help it. Just thinking about him and the last week I've spent with him gives me goose bumps.

"Well it's complicated but sort of. Please don't tell anyone though, Lise, it's early days and he's off to Dubai for two months so you never know, do you?"

"Well, I'm jealous, Lucy Meyer. He's just gorgeous. Definitely a keeper." I try to focus, I need to go and meet Declan.

"Right, I need to go. Wish me luck. I'm really not looking forward to this, Lisa." She pulls me to her, hugging me tight.

"You'll be fine. Just don't give in, he should damn well apologize for his girlfriend's comments. Anyway, what was that about? Telling the world that you never loved him back? Kind of weird, don't you think?"

I'm lost in thought, going over Lisa's words as I walk to meet Declan. She's right. That was kind of weird. I can't say Declan was the love of my life but I did love him in a way. It's a little weird that he's told people I never loved him back. I think back and scrutinize my behavior when we were together. Did I give anything away about how I felt about Oliver? Maybe I did!

As I approach the ice cream stall, I spot him. He looks well. Declan is good looking, he just never really gave me goose bumps or made my heart race. When I was with him, I thought maybe that was just stuff you read in books and magazines and that reality was what I had! Declan is about six feet tall with dark hair and hazel eyes. He has a square jaw which Sarah used to say was sexy. He's very muscular and used to make me feel really protected.

Thinking back, Sarah, my best friend at school, really pushed me to go out with Declan. When she found out from Ben, her boyfriend, that Declan was going to ask me out she went on and on until I said yes.

"Hi, Lucy, you look well." He pulls me in for a hug. I can't not hug back, although I really don't want to be this close to him. I force a smile on my face.

"Thanks, Dec, you look good yourself." We turn and walk, side by side. I know where we're heading. It's the only place I think I've been with Declan since I moved to London. The little sandwich shop about five minutes' walk from here.

We take a seat and place our orders. In that respect, nothing has changed. We both order BLT, our favourite, with salted crisps. Declan smiles and I smile back, this time its genuine. Nostalgia creeps into everyone's world every now and again, doesn't it? He raises an eyebrow when I order an espresso coffee. I feel the need to explain.

"My friend Lisa introduced me to them and now it's the only coffee I like. Everything else seems tasteless now." He smiles a woeful smile.

"See you moved on and I don't know Lucy any more. The old Lucy has changed." Now it's my turn to frown.

"We all change, Declan, as we go through life. I'm sure there are things about you that I have no clue about either. Our relationship was in the past, when we were younger and... God, I'd worry if I hadn't changed since then, if I'm honest."

I watch as he fidgets in his seat. I don't want to talk about last week but I guess that's what we're here for so I wait for him to commence.

"I saw Ollie last night." I wasn't expecting that and my heart misses a beat. Did Ollie tell him about us? I try and appear calm even though my heart is beating out of my chest.

"Right, everything OK?" he smiles, and I guess that he knows nothing of mine and Ollie's last week together.

"Yes, I wanted his advice. To be honest, he didn't really say much. He's having a real hard time from his dad though, which probably had something to do with it. Do you remember the pressure he used to get from his dad, well it sounds like that's still going on. Anyway, I think just talking to him and voicing my thoughts out loud made me understand what I needed to do." I'm frowning now. I'm worried about Ollie and his dad and what is Declan talking about, advice?

"I'm not really following you, Dec. What did you need advice about?" Declan reaches across the table to take my hand. Just then the waitress brings our food. I sigh with relief. I don't want him to touch me. I certainly don't want to hold hands with him.

I start to munch on my sandwich, praying that there's nothing much to this conversation. I look up and realize that Dec isn't eating.

"Why aren't you eating, Dec? It's your favourite." He grins.

"Lucy, I split up with Becky." I drop my sandwich back on the plate and wipe at my mouth with my napkin.

"Oh, I'm sorry."

"Don't' be sorry, she wasn't right for me and she damn well proved it last week with that little performance in front of you. I'm so sorry, Luce." I nod my head in response.

"It's fine, Dec, really. Please tell me you didn't finish with her over that. I'd hate to think that I caused your split." He grins again and I begin to feel uncomfortable.

"No, Lucy, it wasn't because of that. You see, I'd not been with her that long, it was just well…" I watch and wait. Gosh, I want to be anywhere but here right now!

"Lucy, I still love you. I never stopped loving you. Drifting apart when I went to uni was stupid. I should have come home more often. I miss you, Lucy, I love you." I feel sick right now. What the hell do I say to that? I push my plate away, knowing that I will never, ever eat another BLT sandwich as long as I live.

"Declan, we've been apart for a long time now. We've both moved on. I think you're mistaken." He's shaking his head.

"No, I know. I've known for a long time. Seeing you last week made me realize that I needed to do something about it before it's too late." I sigh, here goes!

"It's already too late, Dec. I've moved on. I'm different. I want different things in life now." The look on his face would break my heart if I cared just a tiny bit. That only confirms my thoughts. I don't care about him at all now. Not one bit!

"Declan, why did Becky refer to me as the girl who never loved you back? Where did she get that from?" He fidgets again.

"I told her that's how I felt. It was never said the way she described, Lucy. You know, back when we were at school, I used to watch you… watching Ollie and I kind of knew you had feelings for him. I just kept telling myself it was all in my head." My heart is in my mouth right now. He knew! Oh, my God! Did he tell Ollie this last night? I move around in my seat, bracing myself for my next sentence. I have to tell him the truth.

"You're right, I did have feelings for Ollie. I'm sorry. I never did anything about it. He hated me anyway, Dec. Well I thought he did. It was just… well, circumstances were that you and I got together, and bit by bit, I knew it wasn't right. I was mad about Ollie for a long time." I watch and take in his reaction, shocked. He smiles.

"I know, Lucy. I know you had a mad crush on him. I know if he asked, you'd have broken up with me in a flash. I just kept hoping that your love for me would grow, but it didn't, did it?" I shake my head, ashamed to admit how I felt.

"I've always loved him, Dec. I always will. He was my dream, is my dream."

Declan takes my hand, a smile on his face that shows defeat.

"I get it, Lucy, really I do. I just needed one last chance to see if you'd love me back. I think I knew deep down it was never going to happen." Now I feel bad.

"I'm sorry, Declan, really sorry." He pushes his chair back.

"Hey, it's time to move on, right?" I nod my head feeling very heavy-hearted right now.

I don't go straight back to work. Instead I walk through the park, thinking over the conversation of the last hour. I still can't get my head around why Dec kept going out with me if he knew I liked Ollie. I need to speak to Ollie now. I pull my phone out of my pocket and dial his number. My heart is beating fast just listening to the connection of our phones. It goes straight to voicemail so I leave him a message.

"Hi, handsome man of my dreams. Just wanted to check that you still love me. Speak to you later. Love you."

****

"I don't understand Lucy. Why, if you loved Ollie and he loved you, and Declan knew… why aren't you together?" Em waits for my response, her face etched with concern.

I hold back the tears. I've cried so many nights and days, thinking over and over. Calling him, leaving voicemails, texting. The silence at his end just about killed me. The only reason I kept going was because of Bella.

****

When Ollie's number appears on my phone, I can't help the grin that spreads across my face. I take a quick glance around the office to check who's in earshot then click to answer.

"Hi, Ollie, you OK?"

"Yes, I'm OK, thanks, Lucy. I need to see you. Can you meet me later?" I move uncomfortably in my seat. This doesn't sound like the Ollie I've spent time with the last week. He sounds distant with me, almost stand offish.

"Yes, that's fine. I thought we were meeting up anyway."

"Right, can you come and meet me at the office later, about sevenish, I should have finished by then?" I frown. His office? Why does he sound so off?

"Mmm, yes, if that's what you want. I'll see you then. Ollie?"

"Yes?" He doesn't want to speak, maybe there's someone with him and he can't.

"Can't you speak right now?" I hear a nervous cough.

"Not really, see you at seven, OK?"

"Ollie?"

"Yes?" He sounds aggravated. My heart is thumping.

"I love you."

"See you later." He hung up without even acknowledging what I just said. I drop my phone on the desk and flop back in my seat. Shit! A cloud of doom descends over me and I know this isn't good. I sense that tonight's meeting is bad news.

****

I've whiled away most of the afternoon just browsing through magazine spreads whilst going over every conversation in my head that Ollie and I had over the last few days. I can't remember anything I've said that could have upset him. I wonder if there's more to that meeting he had with Declan last night than Declan actually told me.

I leave work at six and head to the coffee shop around the corner from Ollie's office. I don't want to go home. I need to be surrounded by noise just now and here seems just right. I can get lost in the crowd and wallow in the sorrow that has crept up on me as the afternoon went on. I'm expecting the worst. He's going away and doesn't want to commit to anything. That's the line I'm expecting anyway. I'm a little confused though as he said he loved me. I love him and always have. He is my dream come true and I would do anything to be with him. I'll leave my job if I have to, if that's what he wants. I swirl the cold coffee around my cup as I decide whether to beg or just take the rejection and leave.

I feel sick as I approach the reception of Ollie's building. I give the security man my name and he checks before nodding and letting me through the barrier. I look back as he tells me which floor to find Ollie. I feel like crying but smile my thanks and walk to the lift. My legs feel heavy. Maybe I should just phone him and tell him I know why he wants to see me and get this over and done with quickly. That would be the easy way but I know that if this isn't going to be, that I have to see his face. I have to know that he doesn't want me so that I can move on. I'm twenty-four years old and if I need to let my dream go, I will. It will break my heart but I don't have a choice... Ollie holds all the cards here. I'm his if he wants me, but if he rejects me now, I have to accept this was never meant to be.

As I exit the lift, his secretary looks up with a fake smile. I give her my name and she asks me to take a seat while she calls through to Ollie. This feels strange. I feel strange. I don't want to end my new relationship with Ollie and I certainly don't want to discuss it in his office of all places. I decide I'm going. I'm not doing this here. I stand up and straighten my skirt. As I throw my bag over my shoulder, the secretary calls to tell me I can go through to Ollie's office now. I freeze. Do I stay or do I make my excuses and run? Two older men walk past me as the secretary speaks and one looks over his shoulder when she uses my name. He stops for a second and gives me the once over before proceeding with his colleague.

He looks familiar but I can't place him. I'm standing stock still, not wanting to move. I can't go in, I'm too afraid.

Ollie calls my name and I feel the blood drain from my face. I look up and he's there in front of me. I'm transported back to being fifteen again. Ollie may as well have Rachel or Debbie or Alison hanging off his arm because the look he's giving me is the one I'm most familiar with from my time as Declan's girlfriend. He turns to walk back, guiding me as he holds my elbow. I look at his hand and I feel like screaming NO! Instead, I follow him like a puppy dog and wait to be tossed aside like a dirty mongrel. He closes the door and I spin on my heel. I need to go as soon as he says his piece. I can't linger with this.

I'm facing the door, ready to go. I don't need to watch his lips as he tells me this is a huge mistake and he doesn't love me.

"Lucy." I don't look, I can't.

"Please, look at me." I shake my head. The tears are already free falling.

"Just get this over with, Ollie. I'm not stupid. I know why I'm here. I don't understand it but I know why." He coughs and I know this is it.

"Lucy, I'm leaving the day after tomorrow and I won't be back for a while, you know that." The silence in the room is killing me. I turn around just to see his beautiful face one last time.

"You said you love me, Ollie." My voice is all high pitched and whiney. If he's not careful, I'll be on my knees begging him to love me.

"Yes, well, I was foolish. We live in different worlds. I can't go away and leave you hanging, it's not fair. I can't promise you anything, Lucy, I'm sorry." I look at those ice blue eyes and I swear there are tears waiting to fall. He looks so formal though, like I'm a client he's discussing business with.

"You said you'd sort it, that we'd be together. Ollie, I will do anything for you. I'll give up my job and follow you anywhere if that's what you want. Please don't break the dream." I know I'm starting to beg but I love him, he loves me? I watch as he runs his hands through his floppy hair. He closes his eyes and takes a deep breath before looking directly at me, not an ounce of emotion showing as he speaks.

"I don't love you, Lucy. I got carried away with the moment, with your romantic fantasies. I'm sorry. Look, I don't want to see you again, OK?" I gasp at his harsh words. My heart is shattered. I can feel the tiny shards falling, cutting through my body like ice. I look at his face for any sign that I'm imagining this, hoping he'll sweep me off my feet and tell me he loves me. He doesn't speak, he just looks away. The feeling of sickness overwhelms me. I walk to the door and leave as quickly as I can. I don't look back. I just go, my broken heart left behind in a shattered pile on his office floor.

****

Chapter 6

It takes a while for Emilia and I to stop crying. I thought once I told my story I'd feel healed but I don't. The heartbreak never went away, I just buried it. I don't like the sympathetic look on my sister's face though. I don't want sympathy. Em shakes her head as she wipes at her face with a tissue.

"Well if I'd known all this I would never have been hugging him and kissing him yesterday, Luce. I can't believe you've carried this heartbreak around with you for over three years. Haven't you told anyone?" I shake my head.

"Not really. Lisa helped me through the first few days. She knew there was something between Ollie and me but she didn't know our history. She's a good enough friend that she never questioned me, she just helped me. You know, when I found out I was pregnant, I expected her to ask me then but she never did. She respected my wishes and never mentioned the daddy word."

"So, what now, Luce? He's bound to find out about Bella. He's not stupid. He'll do the math and realize something, that's for sure." I smile at my sister. I know she's right and I just need to find out a way to tell him. I just haven't got that far yet.

"Hmm, that's the reason I'm telling you all this, Em. I need help. I have no idea how to approach this. I need your advice and support, big sister." Emilia sighs and I know why. This is a huge problem and if I have no clue how to deal with it, she can't possibly, after only just finding out.

"You know, we really need to start getting ready for the party later. I will help you, Lucy, in any way I can, but I need to digest what you just told me. I need to work through this story and see how

I can help you tell Ollie about Bella." I feel sick when I hear my sister's words. Reality spoken aloud is really scary.

"Lucy, does he even know you have a child?" I frown as I pull myself up from the floor.

"I don't think so, Em. Why would he? He's never been here in Layton when I have with Bella. Unless Ben's said something, or Sarah. I don't know how much contact Sarah's had with him. She never mentioned anything so I don't know.

My thoughts are all over the place as I get ready for the party tonight. If I'm honest, the thought of my best friend's husband's thirtieth birthday party doesn't sound all that appealing any more. Before I arrived here this weekend, I was really looking forward to seeing my old school friends again. Now all I can think about is Oliver Ashcroft. You know, I don't think there's ever been a day, not since primary school, when I haven't thought of him. The man owns my heart without a doubt and he well and truly trampled on it in London so why, oh why, do I still feel like I belong with him?

I'm playing around with Emilia's hair as we chatter about nothing in particular. Every now and then, she gives me a look, the look that tells me she knows I'm not listening to a word she says.

"Are you going to be all right tonight, Lucy? He'll be there and you'll have to talk to him." I look at my sister's beautiful reflection in her bedroom mirror.

"I'll be fine. I've seen him this morning and it was—" she frowns.

"What, Lucy?"

"It was awkward but OK. He wants to talk, but it has to be the right time and place. He wants to talk about us finishing. I, on the other hand, have to tell him he's a daddy." Emilia winces at my words. I laugh at the scariness of what I've got to do.

"Hmmm. Lucy, I'm so sorry. I'm sorry he doesn't love you. I can tell by your eyes that you still love him, sweetheart." Her soft words have me falling to my knees. I'm leaning my forehead on her shoulder from behind. My heart is thudding and I feel sick.

"I know it's not the same, Lucy, but I kind of know how you feel. I still love James with all my heart and I don't think I'll ever stop. It hurts, doesn't it?" I'm watching her reflection and nodding my head. Loving someone who can't or won't love you back is pretty shit. I sigh and lean in to kiss my beautiful sister. No one would have guessed that we'd end up like this. Two girls, broken-hearted and unable to move on and love again.

Emilia looks absolutely gorgeous by the time we've finished her hair and accessorized her beautiful but plain black dress. For a second, I think of James and how he'd whistle and make a fuss. I quickly move the thought aside, knowing she can read my mind.

"Stop thinking, Lucy, and let's get you ready." I smile when she slaps my bottom as I walk past to retrieve my dress from her wardrobe.

I have to admit, I'm kind of excited about my outfit for tonight. Working for a fashion magazine has to have some perks and tonight I'm wearing plenty of them!

I pull my dress out of its protective cover and wait for my sister's reaction. I'm not disappointed at her oohs and ahhs. My dress is also black but nothing like Em's. I have the luxury of going to tonight's party in a Stella McCartney gown and I'm very proud of that!

This beautiful piece of couture is described as an 'asymmetric ruffled hem gown' which basically means it is a short bustier dress with a sleeveless fitted bodice with a ruffled hem and a long rear train. Em hasn't said a word as I walk towards her offering her the gown so that she can help me step into it. I'm just grinning like a child on Christmas morning. I had to do a lot of grovelling at work to get my hands on this baby and I'm going to enjoy every moment I'm wearing it.

"Fucking hell, Lucy, that's just... beautiful, you're just beautiful." Em bends forward as I step into the beautiful dress, my heart beating fast with excitement. I turn and let her fasten the zip before spinning around. I can't help myself. I feel like a princess.

This is by far, the most expensive dress I have ever worn and it is definitely making me feel better after my heart to heart with Em today. I take a seat as Em fiddles with my hair putting it up on top of my head. I place silver droplets in my ears and grin back at my ecstatic looking sister.

"Hey, this is just what we needed, baby sister. I can't wait to walk in that room with you tonight. They won't be able to keep their eyes off you, Luce."

"What about you? You look divine. If ever we were to find you a man to raise your spirits, it's definitely in that dress, beautiful." Em looks a little awkward hearing my words. I touch her arm and she smiles.

"Why don't we just go and have a good time, just the two of us, Luce?" I look into her sad, dark eyes, recognizing that she still isn't ready to move on. Hell, why should she? I'm certainly not!

"That's a deal. The two Meyer sisters, like old times, hey?"

I stand up and tiptoe to the wardrobe, careful not to step on the train of my very expensive, borrowed dress. I find my borrowed shoes and feel, just for a nano-second like I imagine Cinderella did when she was visited by her fairy godmother. I pull on my black suede Dolly Court shoes with their crystal-embellished platforms and grin as I turn to Emilia.

"Tada!"

She laughs, excitedly.

"Perfect, Luce, just perfect!" We giggle as we make our way to the living room to enjoy a glass of Prosecco.

The taxi driver beeps his horn outside on the street. We look at each other, excited and nervous at the same time. It's a long, long time since we've been together with all our old school friends and to top that, there's the Ollie thing going on. This night could go either way really. It could be fantastic, catching up and sharing our lives, or it could be a total disaster – I really hope it's the first option.

Ben's family has money. His dad was in property development before it became fashionable and has made an absolute fortune. Ben works for the family business, training in each aspect of the building trade over the years. He's now partner with his dad and his older brother, Kyle, his dad taking a back seat and letting the boys basically run the business. Sarah has two very beautiful little girls: Rhianna, aged four years, and Georgia, aged two. Sarah is a stay-at-home mum who enjoys the delights of coffee mornings and play dates with the other mums in and around Layton. She's always full of interesting stories about others and their lives.

Ben's party is at the local golf club about a mile out of the town. It's actually a spa resort and is somewhere we used to dream of visiting when we were younger.

As the taxi pulls up at the front of the building, I feel my nerves on end. I want to see Oliver. I'd love to tell him I don't care anymore and I've moved on, but the truth is, I dream that one day he'll tell me he still loves me and we'll live happily ever after. I'm a fool, I know, but I can't control my dreams, I've tried.

I follow Emilia into the foyer and stand behind her as she gives our names. I feel like the little sister when I first started secondary school and Em showed me around the dinner hall. I follow Em, looking straight down at my feet as she leads the way to the party. My heart is in my mouth when I hear the first voice call out my sister's name. Here goes! It's party or bust!

Fortunately, the first voice I hear is Sarah's. I sigh with relief. I look up for the first time and admire the beautiful setting. The room is large with a tropical oasis on one corner. There are two bars, one at each end of the room. The dance floor is large and surrounded by large, round tables, most of which are taken. There is a DJ in the opposite corner to the oasis who already looks in a world of his own as he reels out the usual wedding/party songs.

"Lucy, Em, I'm so glad you're here. Come here." In turn, she pulls us both in for a hug. I feel pleased to be here now that I see the look of delight on my old friend's face. I peek over her shoulder and spot Ben, headed our way. I can't help but grin.

"Happy birthday, handsome!" I pull him to me and hug him tight. Ben is just the loveliest man. He treats Sarah like a queen and his girls just worship him. I look as the two of them give each other a wink and feel a tiny pang of jealousy.

Sarah is my complete opposite. Short, cropped, blonde hair with big, baby blue eyes. She's tiny, almost doll-like and has never worn anything above a size six. Ben has been known to pick her up and throw her around like his very own doll. He's a good foot taller than her, skinny, with scruffy blonde hair that constantly has that just jumped out of bed look. The two together look like they're from Scandinavia.

Tonight, Sarah looks beautiful in a short navy sequined fitted dress with high heels that still only make her shoulder height on Em and me. When we were younger I used to feel like big bird next to my pint-sized friend.

"Lucy, you look stunning. Let me guess? That has got to be a designer dress?" I nod at my friend, giggling.

"It's only borrowed, Sarah, but don't tell everyone that." She gives me a wink and looks over her shoulder. She calls over a waiter who brings us champagne. This is the sort of life I'm used to with work in London. Not here, in Layton, at my best friend's husband's thirtieth birthday party.

No sooner have we had a catch up with Sarah and Ben, than I hear familiar voices calling my name. Jordan, Mark, David and Anna are ambling their way over to us, looking very pleased to see Em and me.

Rachel and her husband, Owen, soon join us. I haven't met Owen before. Rachel got married the same year Em and James should have. I feel the hurt inside when they gush about their happy day to everyone. I discreetly touch my sister's arm to let her know I feel her pain. When I take a look at her, she's trying hard to focus on anything but what Rachel is actually saying. I take this as my cue to save my sister. I cough lightly and excuse us as I drag Emilia off to the bar. No one seemed to notice, and so what if they did –

my sister was drowning in sorrow right then and I needed to save her.

I order two double gin and tonics, giving my sister a dig in the ribs as the barman eyes her up. I lean in to whisper to Em.

"I think you've pulled, Em." She takes a look and cackles loudly.

"Lucy, he looks about twelve years old."

"Actually, he's twenty and he's my cousin, Adam. I can introduce you if you like, Em?" My mouth goes dry and I feel my heart almost beat out of my chest. Should I just pretend I haven't heard his voice or would that be obvious?

Come on, Lucy, you can do it! Look at him and smile like you don't care.

As I look up, a false smile plastered on my face, I feel myself dying all over again. There he is, Oliver Ashcroft, with a girl. He has his arm around her waist and she looks mighty pleased to have him as her partner. I quickly take all of her in. Every beautiful inch of her, and feel my heart splintering. She is smiling the most dazzling, white smile, her green eyes sparkling as she watches Ollie speak. His new beauty has long, auburn hair that falls onto her shoulders like a stole. I look at Em, desperate for some guidance. She looks as shocked as me. I vaguely acknowledge Ollie speaking. He's introducing us to the beauty at his side. I continue to smile, knowing that my face is giving everything away.

"Lucy, Emilia, this is Abbie. Abbie, Lucy and Em are old friends from school." Our eyes meet as he utters those words. My mouth is dry and I want to run, fast.

Beautiful Abbie holds out a perfectly manicured hand and I find myself shaking it. Her hand feels icy cold. I remember my mum always saying 'cold hands mean warm heart'. I inwardly scoff. I don't want her to be nice. I want to hate her.

"Ollie's told me so much about you." Her eyes are on me as I blush. Why? Why would he tell her about me? I look at him and his eyes are glued to me. I want to kiss him. Fuck! Why, whenever I see him, do I lose all sense of logic? I look away, trying to compose myself. Em senses my discomfort and takes over socializing for me. I stand like a statue as the two girls chatter about nonsense while Ollie just looks at me. I widen my eyes, you know, in that way that asks 'WHAT?'

Ollie moves towards me and I freeze. I don't want to feel him near me again. It's more than I can stand.

"Lucy, I need to talk to you." I glance around me. No one seems bothered that he's speaking to me. No one seems to be wondering why he's talking to me when he has the most beautiful girl in the room with him. He leans over me and interrupts Em and Abbie, who seem to be getting on far too well for my liking.

"Do you mind if I just borrow Lucy for a few minutes?" Abbie gives me a genuine smile and Em looks at me as if to say it's OK. I frown as I'm gently pulled away from them and guided from the room. The electricity racing through my body from his touch overwhelms me as I let him lead me away from my sister and Abbie.

I look up as he leads me through a large wooden door with a sign above reading 'members only'. He holds the door and I walk past him, inhaling his delicious scent. I inwardly kick myself for even acknowledging how wonderful he looks. I've taken in every inch of him. I can't help it. It's an involuntary action, something that happens far too often when I'm around him. I remember the time I blurted out that I love him. Now, that wasn't planned – at all! He leads the way to a table, hidden in a wooden style booth. He offers me a seat and I take it without question. I admire him as he takes the seat opposite me. He's wearing a dark grey suit and a black shirt, no tie. I focus on the buttons of his shirt, trying not to think of his perfect body underneath. I can feel my heart starting to ache.

"Lucy, I need to talk to you and I can't stay in that room all night when I need to tell you…" I don't look at his face, I can't. I wait for him to continue, trying to take in his words and not think about what I need to say.

When he doesn't speak, I look over the table and take in the sight of him. His elbows are resting on the table, his chin in his hands. He's watching me, just watching. My heart flips as he smiles. His eyes are as beautiful as ever, completely holding my attention. I shuffle in my seat, trying to gain a bit of self-control, which is near on impossible with this man. I need to take control before he stamps on my heart again like I fear.

"Ollie, you have nothing to say that we haven't already discussed. You asked if we could be friends and I said maybe one day. I'm not ready to…" I'm not ready to be friends at all. My heart hasn't recovered yet from losing his love, so being friends isn't something I want, if I'm honest.

"Not ready to what, Lucy?" His fingers gently touch my hand as I swallow hard. I sigh deeply.

"Not ready for friendship, Ollie. I can be civil. I'll always speak to you but…" oh, this is hard. I look at his puzzled face and smile in spite of myself. I love him, that I know for sure. Em's words come back to haunt me and I force back the tears that want to fall. 'I'm sorry he doesn't love you, Lucy.' Yes, that's right, he doesn't love me, he told me all that time ago, in his office. The day he shattered my heart and soul.

"Lucy, I need to tell you about me, about my life. It's changed, Luce. I want to tell you. Please, let me explain?" His voice is almost pleading and I almost give in. I need to tell him about the changes in mine though and I think my news will have far more impact than him telling me about his plans to stay in Layton. Oh, but what about beautiful Abbie? Maybe she's what he wants to talk about. I feel my heart plummet again at the thought of his beautiful lady friend. The thought that he's married crosses my mind but I think back. He would have introduced her as his wife, surely?

"Is this about Abbie, Oliver? I don't need to know really. I can see you've moved on. I don't need to hear details, thank you." His laugh hurts. I wasn't expecting him to laugh. Did he not care for me at all?

"What do you mean, Abbie?"

"Well I guess she's your partner, or is she your wife? Whichever she is, Ollie, I can see with my own eyes. I don't want or need details, thank you." I feel stronger than I thought. I take a look at him, wanting to stop loving him. Nope! It's still there, as powerful as ever. Damn you heart, stop needing him… please?

"Abbie is Catherine's partner, Lucy. You know, my sister, Catherine? They live together. Catherine should have been here tonight but she had to work. She's a surgeon and was called to the hospital on an emergency so I dragged Abbie along with me." I'm not sure how I feel. I know my blush is bright.

"Sweetheart, I want to talk, really talk. I need to tell you about London." I can feel my heart in my mouth. He called me sweetheart… why? I take a deep breath and decide to talk about it. I have to.

"Ollie, I don't need to hear any more. You broke my heart that day. You shattered it, actually. I tried so many times to speak to you. I needed to speak to you and you just ignored me like I never existed. I have never felt so broken in my life." I look into his face, wanting to see some kind of remorse. It's there, at least. The sorrow is etched on his face. I'm kind of relieved that he cared in some way. There were days when I thought I'd imagined the whole week we shared, that it was just one of my many dreams about Oliver.

"Lucy, I was forced to choose. I was pushed into a corner and I'm sorry. I never meant to hurt you and I've regretted it every day since."

"What do you mean, forced to choose. Choose what?" He looks disgusted, like he's ashamed to tell me.

"You know my dad got me that job at the bank? It was all he ever wanted. He lived his ambitious dreams through me. I told him about you and how I wanted to be with you. I wanted to find a way for us to be together and I foolishly thought if I went to my dad, he would help. But looking back, Lucy, he was never around when I grew up. He was never there for my mum so why would he understand that you were, are, the love of my life? Telling him about you

72

threatened his dreams, I should have realized, but I didn't, not then."
My life has come to a standstill. This man, the man I love with every part of my being, just told me he loves me. That his dad forced him to choose his job over me. I look into his eyes and watch as a solitary tear slides down his cheek.

"I will never be able to make it up to you, Lucy, but I want you to know that I'm so damn sorry. That I have regretted that day every day since and I will regret those harsh words I said to you for the rest of my life. I didn't mean them. I said them so that you'd go, because if I didn't, I would have caved and my dad would have cut me off completely. I couldn't see a way out. He threatened to make sure I never worked again if I didn't do as he asked. Lucy... I'm sorry."

I don't say a word. Not a single word. Nothing seems appropriate right now. I need to tell him about Bella but I don't want to tell him on the back of what he's just said. It wouldn't be right. But hold on...

"Well we only met here, this weekend, because we're here for Ben's party so I'm guessing that if you hadn't bumped into me, you wouldn't be telling me this." I tilt my head, staring him straight in the face. Get out of that one, Ashcroft!

"Hmm, I can see how it looks. Honestly... I have been spending time here trying to build my own career away from banking. Once I was up and running, I was going to come and find you... once I found out if you were still single, of course. Are you?"

My breaths are deep as I take in what he's told me.

"Yes, Ollie, I am." My heart melts at the sight of his grin. Anger is still bubbling under the surface, though. He broke my heart and I'm not forgiving him just yet.

"Ollie, we need to talk and here isn't the place. Can we meet up, tomorrow maybe?" He looks optimistic; I feel dreadful. How will he react to my news? I really have no idea.

"Of course, we can. When?" I think. I need to go and spend some time with my family, tell my parents about Ollie, before we head back to London on Tuesday. Maybe the evening is better. I can get Bella to bed then we can go out for a walk or something and I can tell him.

"Why don't we meet at the pier tomorrow night? There's things we need to clear up and it will be more private there." He's frowning. I think he thought I meant a date.

"The pier, are you sure?" I nod my head and he shrugs his shoulders.

"OK then, the pier it is, Lucia." Goosebumps rise all over me when he uses my full name. I love the way he says it. I close my eyes for a second, just to block out everything and enjoy a solitary moment of loving Oliver Ashcroft all over again.

"You OK, Lucy?" I open my eyes and find him staring at me. I nod my head in reply.

"Oliver, Lucy, how lovely to see you both here. I take it you're here for the party next door, looking so dressed up?" We both turn quickly at the sound of my dad's close friend, Bob Benson's voice.

"Hi," is all we answer in unison. He's grinning as he leans down to peck my cheek.

"You do look absolutely divine, Lucy, doesn't she, Oliver?" I glance at Ollie who is watching me.

"She looks perfect, Bob, a dream come true." I blush at his words, loving that I'm a dream, his dream.

"So, Miss Lucy, how's little Isabella? Is she with your parents tonight? "I freeze. I don't look at Ollie, I can't. I put on a fake smile and nod my head at Bob. Fuck, fuck, fuck. Please let him just go away now and not say any more…please?!

"I bet she's being spoiled rotten by her doting grandparents, isn't she?" I peek at Ollie who is watching me closely. I can't ignore Bob's question.

"Hmm, yes. They all went to the zoo today and I bet Mamma and Dad enjoyed it more than she did." Ollie coughs loudly and I swallow hard.

74

"I bet they did. Anyway, I'll leave you two in peace. Say hi to your parents, Lucy, and I'll see you here at the club I've no doubt, Oliver." We watch in silence as he walks towards the bar, completely oblivious to the can of worms he's just opened.

"Who's Isabella, Lucy?" I suddenly feel chilled to the bone. What should I say? This isn't the time or the place to tell him about being a daddy.

"She's my daughter, Ollie. I have a daughter." I look at him, waiting for a reaction. He doesn't move, or speak. I watch as he closes his eyes, holding one thumb and forefinger over each. He continues to sit like this as he speaks, quietly.

"So, you moved on then?" I'm not sure how to answer that.

"Ollie, we need to have a real talk and here isn't the place. Will you still meet me tomorrow and we can talk properly?" He moves his hand away from his face and stares at me. He looks hurt. I don't know how I'm going to get through this evening.

"OK, Lucy. I'll meet you tomorrow." Before he can say any more, I quickly stand and make my way to the large wooden door that leads back out to where the party is.

My heart is racing as I frantically look around the room for Emilia. I spot her as she waves. I make my way through the many people standing around the edge of the dance floor, desperate to gain as much space between Ollie and I as possible. The quizzical look on my sister's face tells me I'm not looking as normal as I'd hoped. I pull Em to one side and whisper in her ear.

"Bloody Bob Benson came over while I was talking to Ollie and asked how Bella is." Em gasps as I look over my shoulder, checking if he's returned to the party. I instantly meet his gaze and freeze. The look in his eyes tells me he's thinking and wondering. He tilts his head at me but gets pulled into a hug by an old friend and has to look away. I breathe a sigh of relief. I don't want him to think and come to the wrong conclusions.

"So, what did you say, have you told him?" I shake my head at my sister who is also looking around, I guess for Ollie.

"I told him I have a daughter but that's it. I made a hasty retreat after arranging to meet him tomorrow. I need to tell him Em but not here. It's just not right, is it?" She smiles sympathetically.

"When will it be right, Luce? You just need to do it really. What if he asks someone about Bella, like Sarah or Ben? They can hardly lie, can they? Once he knows how old she is, I'm sure he's clever enough to come to his own conclusions."

"Right, I'll go and speak to Sarah and ask her not to mention Bella's age to anyone." Emilia grabs my arm as I turn to leave.

"Lucy, you can't do that. You'll have to give Sarah an explanation if you want her to lie for you, or withhold the truth. You haven't told Mamma and Dad about Bella, and Ollie deserves to know before the rest of Layton, doesn't he?" I rub my temples with my forefingers. I don't know what to do. I look up as Declan and a pretty blonde girl walk towards me. His smile is wary. Oh, this is all I need. After the last introduction to one of his girlfriends, I'm not feeling very friendly.

"Lucy, Emilia, how are you both?" Em steps forward and hugs Declan. I watch him, watching me, as he hugs my sister. I smile, a weak smile. Quite frankly, it's all I can manage right now. I just want to get out of here.

"Declan, you look well." He leans in and kisses my cheek. I take a look at the petite girl at his side who is smiling. A sincere, very sweet smile. I hold out my hand to her. "Hi, I'm Lucy." I take in her tiny frame next to Declan, thinking that she reminds me of Tinkerbell, with long curly hair.

"I'm Summer. It's lovely to meet you. Declan has told me all about you. What's it like to be back in your hometown with all your old school friends? It must be quite strange." I smile at Summer. She seems really nice.

"It is strange, actually. Although I can recognize all of them, I don't feel like I really know any of my old friends any more. Oh, apart from Sarah and Ben." Declan gives me a sad look. I look away, not really wanting eye contact with him, only to find Ollie staring at me again. He's standing at the bar with Jordan, Mark and David. David turns to see what he's looking at and gives him a dig in the ribs before whispering to him. The others laugh, I turn away.

"How long are you here for then, Declan? Ollie told me you've moved to Australia."

"Back for another three weeks then we're off, aren't we, Sum?" He turns to the pretty girl, who gives him such a loving smile. I'm envious. Not of their relationship, just the love they share. I wish I could get over Oliver and move on. I want to find some kind of happiness.

****

The night actually went quite quickly. I spent some time with the old gang and it was surprisingly jolly. When Oliver was there and I just did the avoidance thing. If he moved near me, I either moved a step away or went to the loo. I have never been to the loo so many times in one night. I even danced to avoid him at one point. When the DJ slowed things down, I made a hasty retreat outside for fresh air. Sarah caught up with me, asking if I'd go back to hers for a few more drinks. How could I say no to my best friend from school?

So here I am, me, Em and the rest of the gang, oh and Ben and Sarah's families, all enjoying more drinks in Ben and Sarah's back garden. The night is surprisingly warm but just in case, Ben has powered up two patio heaters. I watch as Emilia stands, laughing with Ben's older brother, Kyle. I know she said she doesn't think she'll ever love anyone like she loved James but that doesn't mean she can't be attracted to someone. I like the idea that my sister might fancy someone. Kyle is gorgeous. He's over six feet tall with short, dark hair and dark eyes, I'm guessing brown. Kyle and Ben are like chalk and cheese, completely contrasting in looks and colouring. Em seems to like him and that makes my heart feel happy for the first time tonight, well since my chat with Oliver.

"It's nice to see her smile, isn't it?" Instant goose bumps rise all over me when he speaks. I look at him as he takes a seat next to me at the table. I can't just get up and walk away, it would be too obvious. His hand is on my arm as he speaks.

"Please don't leave, Lucy?" That's all he says as he sits and watches me. I can hear my heart beating in my ears, loud and clear. I look around the garden, watching as everyone else seems to be full of joy and happiness. There's laughter in every corner of the garden. I feel sad. I look at him and I want to just sit in his lap and let him hold me. Would that be wrong? He takes my hand and I close my eyes, enjoying his touch. I want to make this right between us. About Bella. I want him to know, desperately.

"Oliver I…" He reaches up and pushes a stray hair from my face. I lean in to his hand, closing my eyes. A soft moan escapes me. I flick my eyes open, hoping he didn't hear. He's moving forward in his chair. He's facing me, our faces so close they are very nearly touching.

"Lucy, Lucia Meyer, I love you. I need you to know that I have never stopped loving you." I don't notice the tear that escaped my eye until he wipes it away with his thumb.

"I don't care that you have a child with someone else. I never expected you to stay single. You had no idea that I didn't mean what I said. You said you're single now, though?" He tilts his head and I nod in reply.

"So, let me meet your daughter. Let us be friends, me, you and Isabella, that's her name, isn't it?" I nod my head as my heart twists tightly. I gulp in a sob. He touches my face. I love the way he says her name. Our daughter, Isabella!

"I can't be friends, Ollie." He frowns.

"Why? I promise I will try my best to make up to you for all the hurt I caused. Please let me try?"

"Ollie, friends isn't enough. I never stopped loving you either, I never will. I am trying to live with it. If we try and be friends, I

78

know I will just end up with a constant broken heart." He laughs, rubbing his thumb across my cheek.

"So, let me love you then. I do anyway, let me show you just how much. Let me spend the rest of my life making up to you and showing you just how much you mean to me, please?"

"We need to talk some more, Ollie. Not here though."

"Come home with me now, then. We can talk all night if that's what you want."

"I can't." He smiles.

"Oh, right, your daughter?" I shake my head.

"She's with my parents. I need to share some things first though, with my parents, then I'll meet you tomorrow, like we planned. I promise, Ollie, that I'll tell you everything then." He's frowning.

"Everything? What do you mean?"

"Ollie, all I'm asking is for you to wait one day, please?" He sighs, a look of anger in his eyes.

"Lucia, I've spent too much time away from you, I can't do this anymore." I hold my breath, hoping he'll wait just a little longer. I watch him agonize over my request, running his hands through his hair in agitation "This is killing me. I want to be with you but if I have to wait one more day, I will because I love you." With that, he stands and walks to Ben. He says his goodbyes then calls to Abbie who follows him. I watch as he walks across the garden, head low. He turns and gives me one last tiny smile then leaves. My heart has stopped. I want to run after him and shout to him that he's Bella's daddy and that I love him so much it hurts, and then I want him to take me in his arms and tell me everything will be OK now.

Chapter 7

It's only seven thirty and I'm wide awake. I know Mamma and Dad will be up. Mamma will be cooking and Dad will be serving breakfasts at the B & B. I know they're fully booked because half the party from last night were staying there.

I need to go and tell them about Ollie, so that I can tell him about Bella.

I head for the kitchen to make myself a strong coffee. My head hurts from lack of sleep. I've been awake most of the night, willing today to come sooner. I want this all out in the open now. The only way I can move on either with or without Ollie is if I tell him and my parents. I'm guessing he'll be angry when I tell him and most likely won't want anything to do with me. He needs to have the choice though, about being Bella's daddy.

"Pour me one will you, Luce?" I spin around, shocked that Em is up at this hour.

"Of course. Why are you up this early on a Sunday, Em? You're not opening the shop this early, surely?"

She smiles as she takes her mug of steaming coffee. I watch as she sniffs the alluring aroma before sipping her drink.

"I thought I'd come with you. You are going to see Mamma and Dad, right?'

I nod my head.

"So, I thought you might need some moral support. Oh, and I can entertain Bella while you tell them." I pull her into a hug, nearly splashing coffee everywhere as I do.

"Thank you, Em, that means a lot you know."

"Right, so you shower first, then me. If we get there early enough, we can help with breakfast then you can tell them." I blow my big sister a kiss as I head to the bathroom. She really has no idea how much better I feel knowing she's coming with me.

Our feet crunch on the gravel of the driveway approaching our parents' house as I take a glance sideways and catch my sisters eye. She pulls me tight, her arm firmly around me.

"It'll be OK, Luce. This isn't half as bad as when you told them you were pregnant, is it? Remember Dad's face when you refused to tell them who the father was?" I nod my head, grimacing at the memory. Dad is a man of few words but his facial expressions have always been a giveaway about how he's feeling. That particular day he got up and left the room. He went out and didn't return for about four hours. Me, Em, James and Mamma just sat and waited. None of us really spoke. Every now and again, Mamma would give me a look that told me she was sorry. I guessed she was sorry for the mess I'd got myself in and sorry for my baby who would grow up without their daddy. When Dad did return, he was full of practical plans. It was as if he'd gone away, had a think and now needed to get back into being my ever-loving dad. He did take me to one side and tell me that no matter what me and Em threw at him, he would always be there for us and he has been true to his word ever since.

His smile is broad at the sight of Em and me when we enter the kitchen.

"Good morning, beautiful girls. Are you a sight for sore eyes. Mamma is not in the best of moods this morning, is she, Bella?"

"Muuummmmy." Bella's greeting melts my heart as I take my beautiful girl in my arms and smother her chubby cheeks with kisses, the dimple on her right cheek showing as she giggles from my kisses. That dimple is the only thing she has that is not from me. When Ollie smiles, he has the exact same dimple. On him, it's sexy; on Bella, it's cute.

"So, Mamma's grumpy, hey, Dad?" He laughs as he leaves the kitchen armed full of breakfasts. Mamma throws a tea towel at him, a smile just cracking her face.

"Morning, girls, take a seat, I'll get you something to eat." I glance at Em who shrugs as if to say 'why not'. I can't help but grin.

"Two full English then please, Mamma?" She turns and smiles as she takes another egg from her basket on the kitchen counter.

"Bella, tell your Mamma what we saw yesterday, sweetheart." I look at that dimpled cheek and get lost in thought as my daughter lists off every animal she saw at the zoo yesterday. Em makes all the animal noises as Bella giggles, I just watch and hope that everything works out in the end.

We finish our breakfast and busy ourselves helping Mamma clear the mess in the kitchen.

"So why are you two really here at this hour of the day? It certainly wasn't for breakfast." I blush and Em digs me in the ribs.

"I'll take Bella out to the play area, Luce. Mamma, Lucy needs to talk to you and Dad." Mamma doesn't say anything, she just dries her hands on the dishtowel and calls my dad. He gives me a look as he enters the kitchen. A look that asks 'you need help?' I shake my head but point to the kitchen table.

"Dad, please sit down? I need to talk to you and Mamma. It's nothing to worry about." I watch as my Dad warily takes a seat. He doesn't believe me when I say don't worry. What parent does?

Mamma pours us all a cup of tea. I cough to clear my throat and look at each of my parents in turn.

"Thank you from the bottom of my heart for all the help and support you give me with Bella. I don't know what I'd do without you." Mamma wipes a tear with her dishtowel while Dad pats her hand.

"So, are you finally going to tell us who her daddy is, sweetheart?" Mamma looks directly at me and I blush again, nodding my head. Dad takes my hand now and gives me a reassuring smile.

"I may as well just come out with it. You don't need to know the where and how, do you?" They both shake their heads, eager to know his name. I take a deep breath and tell them.

"It's Oliver. Oliver Ashcroft. He has no idea but I need to tell him. I wanted to tell you before I tell him. I'm seeing him tonight. I have no idea how he'll react."

I take a look at my parents who are looking at each other. Mamma speaks first.

"Did you love him, sweetheart?" I nod my head and can't stop the tears. It's Mamma asking me, how can I not cry?!

"He broke my heart, Mamma. You know I always secretly loved him, since, well since forever." Mamma nods her head, she knew! "He never gave me a chance to tell him about Bella. It all started and ended very quickly, but now, this weekend he told me why. He's sorry and wants to make things work. So I have to tell him, don't I?" My parents are both nodding their heads. Dad says nothing as usual but his eyes are full of pain. Mamma pulls me to her, kissing the top of my head as I cry.

"What if he breaks your heart again, Lucia?" My dad is frowning when he asks. I sigh. They need to know more.

"It was his dad. He made him choose. He threatened him, that he'd lose his job if he carried on seeing me. You see, Oliver wanted us to be together but his dad had other plans. He's left the bank now and is working on his own away from his father. I don't know what will happen between us but that's a separate issue from Bella." Dad nods but still looks skeptical.

"Nonna, look we found daisies." Our conversation is over. We all look up as Bella skips across the kitchen, her innocence making my heart bleed.

"You all OK?" Em looks at each of us in turn and we each nod our heads. She grins.

"Only one more hurdle then, Lucy, and you're on the home straight."

"Yes, but this hurdle's by far the highest, Em." I feel her hands on my shoulders as she stands behind me.

"You'll be fine. We'll go back to mine now and rehearse what you're going to say if you like." I look at Mamma and she nods in agreement.

"I need to spend more time with my baby girl, Lucy. You can't have her back yet." Mamma pulls Bella onto her lap and the two hug. I watch as my daughter kisses my mother's cheek. So cute!

We've decided to have a walk along the beach on the way back. I'm a little apprehensive in case we bump into Ollie again like I did yesterday. Emilia is chatting away and once again, I'm in my own little world.

"Lucy!" I look up as Em frowns at me. She nods her head so I look. Declan and Summer are walking towards us. I paste on my best smile.

"Good morning, you two. Making the most of the good weather? It's not always like this, Summer." She grins.

"Morning, Lucy, Emilia. This beach is just lovely. If we could have this weather all the time I'd insist that Dec brings me back here to live." Declan looks on lovingly at Summer. I can see he is truly happy and I'm pleased for him.

"When are you going back to London, Lucy?" His smile when he addresses me is different now. It's just friendly and I like that.

"Day after tomorrow. You know this is the first time I'm not looking forward to it either." I'm speaking to all of them when I say that.

"I get that, I really do. Why waste time in the big city when you can have this?" Summer waves her arm around us and I sigh.

"I work for a fashion magazine though, Summer, not much call for that around these parts."

"You need to turn your talents to something new then. Think outside the box, Lucy. I bet there's something around here just calling out for the Lucy touch." I can't help but smile at her enthusiasm.

"Will we see you before you go?" Declan tilts his head in question.

"I hope so. I'm not sure what we have planned. Are you staying at your parents?"

He nods.

"Shall I give you a call later then? Maybe we could meet for a drink or something?"

"That would be nice, Luce, and you Em of course. We say our goodbyes and I feel glad now that I saw Declan this morning."

"It would be nice if you two could be friends, Lucy." I nod at my sister as we continue our beach walk.

****

Getting ready this evening is the hardest thing I think I've ever had to do. It's not a date but I still want to look good for him. I always will. There is nothing like the feeling I get when Ollie looks at me with love in his eyes. I stand in front of my sister's bedroom mirror and assess my look. I'm wearing tight, black capri jeans and a pale pink three quarter sleeve t-shirt. I've pulled my hair up into a ponytail. My only jewellery is hooped earrings. I check my face and decide on a little more bronzer. I need some sun, maybe a day at the beach tomorrow? My colour is so winter white right now.

I pull on my converses and stand in front of Emilia. She smiles.

"You gonna be OK, Luce?"

I rub my forehead. "Probably not, but I have to do this and I can't put it off any longer. Do I look OK?"

"You look beautiful as ever. He won't care about that anyway. He's desperate to see you, oh and Luce?"

"Yes?"

"You know how we talked about him not loving you, well after seeing him last night, I think that's completely wrong sweetie. The look of love on his face when he saw you was magical. I really hope this all works out for you, Luce, I really do." Em jumps up from her seat and gives me a hug. Swallowing a big fat sob at hearing my sister's words I check the time and realize that I'm going to be late if I don't get a move on.

"I'm going. Will you be in all night?"

Em shakes her head. "No, I'm off round to Sarah and Ben's. You know, they're having a barbecue."

"Oh, right, yeah, I forgot. Well have a good time and tell them I'm sorry I couldn't make it." I run down the stairs and out of the side door at the back of Em's shop.

As I head along the pier I can see him waiting for me. My heart is in my mouth. He looks gorgeous, absolutely perfect! He's wearing worn blue jeans and a plain white t-shirt with black converses. He doesn't need anything more, he's perfect. I feel my face blush as I reach him. His smile shows me how much he wants to see me. I feel like a fraud. He has no idea why I'm here.

"Lucy, hi!" He pulls me to him and kisses my cheeks, gently and slowly. As he pulls away our eyes meet and I sigh.

"Hi." He just stands… and stares. I want to kiss him so bad. I stare back. I want just a few minutes more of his love before I break his heart. I know I'm going to hurt him.

"You look beautiful. So, what would you like to do? Have you something in mind?" I decide to move this forward and quick. I take his hand and we walk. The feel of his thumb rubbing my hand makes my body burn. I look sideways at him and realise he's watching me.

"We need to talk so I thought we'd find somewhere quiet." He nods and smiles.

We take our seats outside one of the wine bars, overlooking the sea. I offer to go and order drinks. I can't sit alone and wait, not now. Ollie raises an eyebrow at my offer but takes it in good stead.

"I'll have a pint please, Luce." I smile and head to the bar quickly. I place our orders and head back to the table.

"The barman will bring them out." Ollie nods his head, swinging one foot up onto the opposite knee.

"So, Lucia Meyer, is there something special you want to talk about or just what I said yesterday?" He's watching me closely, I swallow hard. The barman coughs to interrupt us as he places our drinks on the table. I mumble thank you, lost in my thoughts. I wait for him to leave then look into those ice blue eyes that I love and adore.

"This is about something special, Ollie." He tilts his head not taking his eyes off me. I pause, take a deep breath then start…

"You know when you left me, in London?" He nods and fleetingly looks away.

"Well I tried so many times to get in touch with you, Ollie. I phoned, I texted, left voicemails but you never got back to me. I wasn't just trying to be a nuisance, Ollie." He holds up his hand to stop me.

"Lucy, you were never that. Every time I heard from you, I picked up the phone to call, but it would have just made things worse. I thought if I didn't contact you, you'd get over it quicker and move on." I shake my head, laughing quietly.

"Ollie, I needed to talk to you, NEEDED." He frowns. This time I hold up my hands, I need to tell him.

"You see, I found out I was… pregnant… I needed to tell you." I watch and wait. I know it will take a few seconds to register. So, I wait. I look into his beautiful eyes, hoping that he doesn't instantly hate me.

"Isabella?" He waits, I nod.

"She's mine?" I nod again. I lean over to take his hand, he pulls away. I close my eyes to regain some composure. When I look again he's just watching me. When he speaks it's just a mumble.

"You had my baby." He's not waiting for an answer.

"Why didn't you keep trying, Lucy? Why didn't you just tell me on the fucking voicemail?" His eyes are on me, not only ice in colour but ice cold with emotion now too.

"You finished with me, telling me you didn't love me and that you just got carried away in my foolish dreams. I didn't expect you'd want a baby with me, Ollie. When you didn't respond, I just thought you'd deliberately erased me from memory. I didn't know what to do."

"So, you did nothing." His face is hard. I look away, focus on the sea, the waves crashing on the beach. I jump as he bangs his hand on the table.

"For fuck's sake, look at me, Lucy." I turn and look, feeling scared.

"I'm sorry I didn't try harder, Ollie." I watch the tears trickling down his cheeks. I feel my heart breaking as I lean over and touch his face, gently wiping at his watery cheeks. I want nothing more than to kiss away his pain. I stand and move around the table. He watches silently. I bend in front of him, pulling his face into my hands.

"I'm so sorry, Oliver. Please forgive me? Let's start again." He's shaking his head. I don't let go, scared if I do that he'll get up and walk away.

"Tell me about her. How old is she? When is her birthday? What did she look like when she was born? What does she look like now?" His voice breaks as he pulls away from my touch, leaning forward to bury his face in his hands. I wait silently, running my hands through his hair. He looks up wiping at his face with the back of his hand.

"You know right now I'd love to slap you, Lucy. I can't believe you just told me that I have a daughter who is what, three years old?" I nod my head. "And you have the audacity to ask me if we can start again. This is one fucking bombshell you just dropped, Lucy. I can't think about anything right now, other than I want to see my daughter." I nod my head, trying to make it better.

"You can meet her, of course you can. I didn't know if that's what you'd want, Ollie. I didn't know if you'd even want to acknowledge her." He leans forward, our faces just millimeters apart.

"I really fucked up when I said those things to you, didn't I?"

"Just a little." I kiss his cheek. It's not a sexual kiss, more a comfort kiss. He pulls away so I stand in front of him. I don't know what to do now, what to say. I leave him for several silent seconds.

"Would you like to walk? I can answer all your questions while we walk if you like?" He stands and we walk away, our drinks untouched.

"I don't know where to start, Ollie." I take a look at him as we walk, side by side, not touching. The evening is warm as we make our way back along the pier. He doesn't speak for a few seconds, lost in his own thoughts. I listen to the familiar sound of the waves and remember a time in years gone by when I used to wish more than anything, he'd look at me when we walked along this same route. The sound of the sea always makes me think of home and whenever I think of home, Oliver Ashcroft appears in my thoughts at some point.

"I'd like to know everything. You know right from when you first found out you were pregnant and every single day since then." He looks at me, the hint of a smile on his face. "I know that's not possible Luce but I'd love to know as much as you can tell me. I've lost her first three years and I feel robbed."

"You know, Ollie, this is going to be difficult. I'm not solely responsible for the fact that you only just found out about Isabella. I tried. I tried for weeks to get in touch with you. When I first found out I was pregnant, to be honest I didn't know what to do. The thought of an abortion horrified me but I did think about it. When you didn't respond to me, it seemed like the easy option. Do you have any idea how scary it was, thinking about a future as a single parent?"

As we stroll, we're both trying to come to terms with what's happening. I'm so used to Bella being just mine and I'm not sure if I want to share her, or how to if I'm honest. Ollie's just found out he's a daddy, how must that feel?

"We have a lot to sort through, Ollie. I know you want to know all about Bella and I'm happy to tell you, but there's also the practical side of things." His frown is deep as he steps down onto the beach. He takes my hand, helping me off the wall as I jump. I miss my footing and he catches me. I grab his upper arms as he holds me tight around the waist. Our eyes meet and the memories of that week so long ago come flooding back. The week when our beautiful baby was conceived. I was so in love. We stand and stare, neither moving nor speaking. I look down, listening to the waves crash onto the beach. I can feel his breath on my face. When he says my name, I flinch. The sadness running through me right now is so damned painful.

"What do you mean, Lucy, practical side of things?"

"Well, do you want to be part of Bella's life? If you do, then there's lots to sort. We live in London, Ollie. You haven't even met her yet." I feel like I'm drowning as I'm speaking. This is so difficult. He takes my cheeks in his hands, staring into my eyes with his ice blues.

"Yes, I want to be part of her life. I want to meet her, and love her, and make up to her for the three years I've not been around for either of you." He pulls away and sits down in the sand, his back to the wall. I watch him as he focuses out to sea. I take my seat next to him, our shoulders touching then I begin my story.

"It was about a month after you left that I realized my period was late. I was so wrapped up in self-pity before that and hadn't given it much thought. It was only when I was at work one morning and Lisa my friend was moaning about cramps that I thought back and began to count the weeks. Lisa was really good. She was so supportive. We went out at lunchtime and I bought a box of two pregnancy tests. Lisa stood guard in the work loo while I peed on a stick. We waited silently and when the two lines appeared, I went back in the cubicle and peed on another. You know I can't tell you how it felt. I loved you so much and the thought of your baby growing inside me almost tipped me over the edge. I was only just managing to function since you left. I know it sounds silly, we were only together for such a short time, but for me, Ollie, you were the one. When you told me you didn't love me, I had to pick myself up and try to get used to the idea that you and me, my dream, was never going to happen. So, when I found out about Bella, I was so confused. Lisa was great, helping me to decide what to do. She was practical and I needed that. She got details about abortion, just in case." I look at him, expecting him to speak but he's just staring, his eyes awash with unshed tears.

"I did think about an abortion, never telling you about the pregnancy and just getting on with things, but I couldn't. The baby was a part of you and if I couldn't have you, well I could love your baby. Probably not the best reason to become a single mother but there was always a guarantee that she'd be loved. So I came home for a weekend and told Emilia and James. They came with me to tell Mamma and Dad. Mamma cried lots, Dad disappeared for a while, to think. When he came back, he was full of practical ideas. How he was going help me, to make sure me and the baby never went without."

"You see, Lucy, that should have been me, providing for you both, making sure you were looked after."

"Well I told my family, then I went back to London and decided to try and contact you. You deserved to know that I was pregnant. I wasn't going to force you into anything but I thought you should know. I tried so many times, Ollie. I think after about two weeks, I resigned myself to the fact that you didn't want to know me at all and so I sort of second guessed that you wouldn't want a baby with me either."

"But you could have tried to contact me through my parents, Lucy. You came back here, didn't you? Why didn't you go and see my mum?"

"That's not really how it works is it, Ollie? You don't turn up at someone's parents' house announcing that they're going to be grandparents when their son has made his choice clear. To me, you ignoring me showed just how much you regretted that week so you see—"

"But three years, Lucy. How have you kept her a secret from me? I can't believe you didn't see my family when you were here. They would have told me."

"She isn't a secret, Oliver. I am very proud of my daughter and would never keep her a secret. I have seen your family on several occasions and Bella was with me. Do they all know about me and you?" His face tells me he's thinking.

"Who did you see? Mum, Dad, Catherine, who?"

"Your mum and dad, oh and Catherine. I saw Catherine a few times in the supermarket. She even spoke to Bella. Why?"

"Well I only told Dad about us. I was too ashamed to tell my mum and my sister that I'd let him force me into giving up on you. So what was Dad's reaction when he saw you?" I think back, trying to remember.

"I never really knew your dad, Ollie. He was never here much when we were kids, was he? I spoke to your mum really. Your dad did look uncomfortable though. He walked off when your mum fussed over Bella. Maybe he guessed or maybe I'm over thinking things. He didn't know how old she was or anything."

I open my bag and start looking through. I pull out the envelope I carefully put in there earlier tonight. I hand it to Ollie and prepare to leave. I stand up, brushing the sand off my jeans.

"There's a selection of photos in there, Ollie. I had to take them from Emilia so she would like them back at some point. I'll sort you some of mine once I'm back in London, I have plenty at home." His hand is shaking as he takes the envelope, our eyes fixed.

"Don't go, Lucy, please? I want you to tell me about her while I look at her, please?" A tear escapes, I wipe it away quickly. I shake my head.

"I don't know if I can, Ollie. Em's written on the back of each one so you can see her age and stuff. I need to go now."

"You can't. I want to see her, Lucy. When can I see her?" This is hard, really hard. My heart is broken, irreparable. The thought of sharing my Bella with him is just... overwhelming. I hold my hands up and shrug my shoulders.

"Give me your phone number, I'll call you tomorrow. Can I come and see her tomorrow?"

"Look, Ollie, she has no idea who you are. She's never had a daddy and is only three years old. You will have to take things slowly with her."

He frowns. "Why, Lucy? I don't want her to go for one more day not knowing me. She's my daughter and I want her to know me."

"OK, call me tomorrow and we'll make arrangements." I type my number into his phone before turning to walk away. A sea of thoughts are rushing through my head. Oh my God, he'll want her for the weekend and holidays. How will I cope without my angel? What if she loves him more than me? I can't stop the tears as I make my way back to the gallery. I hear him call my name but I don't look back. I'm hurting so bad right now and I feel so selfish. My baby needs her daddy in her life. What if I get jealous of Bella? After all, he will love her more than life itself, I know that. What if I get jealous that he loves her and not me?

As I let myself into Emilia's flat, I realize the enormity of what's about to happen. My life will never be the same again. I dreamed so many dreams about having Oliver Ashcroft in my life but I never thought it would be indirectly through our child.

I pick up the photo albums left strewn on the table from earlier when Em and me were sorting pictures for Ollie. I take a seat on the sofa and look at my daughter's life in pictures. I can't help but giggle and smile. Looking through Em's eyes is a totally different experience, it's touching. The first photo is of me the week before I gave birth. I look huge. Em is standing behind me, her arms wrapped around me. Her hands wouldn't touch. We're laughing as she's trying to touch her fingers. Jamie took the picture. I feel my heart lurch when I think of Jamie. I turn the page and there are the pictures from the day Bella was born. I look so tired but so happy.

There's Mamma and Daddy each taking a hold of their first grandchild. There's Jamie holding her tiny face up to his. I look into his happy eyes and feel a tear escape. He was so in love with Bella. Emilia and Jamie came to stay with me for the first two weeks after I left the hospital. Jamie even took turns getting up in the night for feeds. I skip through the pages looking at trips to the park, the beach, the zoo. Bella's first Christmas when we dressed her in a reindeer costume. Her first teeth, her first haircut, her first shoes. Em has everything here. It's wonderful to look at. I feel a pain in my heart, thinking about just how much Oliver has actually missed. These photographs are just a snapshot of Bella's short life but my God there's a lot packed in. My mobile rings, bringing me back to here and now. The caller's ID is unknown. I frown, guessing this could be Ollie.

"Hello?"

"Lucy, its Ollie. I… Lucy…" His voice is broken. I can hear pain and emotion. My guilt is growing by the second here.

"She's beautiful, Lucy, adorable. So like you. So damn cute. Lucy…"

I swallow back the tears. "Yes, she is, isn't she?"

"Lucy?"

"Yes?"

"Thank you… thank you for keeping our baby. Thank you for telling me. Lucy…" I can't speak. The tears are flowing. I sniffle loudly and swallow a sob. I'm a mess. My nose is running all over my face as I wipe and wipe with my hand. The tears just keep damn well flowing!

"Please don't cry, Lucy."

I rub at my face again, feeling the soreness of my salty tears on my skin.

"Can we meet tomorrow Lucy?"

I nod my head, still unable to speak.

"Lucy?"

"Sorry… yes, fine. Shall we meet at the beach? Same place as we were at tonight. About eleven. Bella loves the beach. You can play." I hear the tears in his voice when he responds.

"I won't be able to sleep tonight, Lucy. Thank you, sweetheart. Thank you."

Chapter 8

Not surprisingly, I haven't slept well. I've tossed and turned the night away going over and over how I will tell Bella. Imagining how she'll react. I've imagined every possible scenario. Bella loves him, Bella hates him, Bella plays up, Bella won't speak to him, Bella won't speak to me. The worst is that Bella hates me. I know she's only three years old but what if she senses things and hates me? I pour my second cup of coffee of the morning even though its only seven o'clock. I wander over to the lounge window and look out onto the empty street. The sun is shining, which would normally make me smile. I've lost the ability to smile right now. The only emotion I have is angst mixed with a heap load of guilt. I feel like this whole mess is my fault. Maybe Ollie's right. I should have spoken to his parents. I shudder at the thought of what Mr Ashcroft would have done if I'd told him I was pregnant. He would have found a way to force me to have an abortion I'm sure. My phone bleeps a text. I reach and grab it from the table. It's Ollie.

"Hi, Lucy, are you OK?" Hmm, I'm not surprised he's up this early.

"Yes, thank you. I'm wide awake though, didn't sleep much. What about you?"

"Same here. Would you like to meet for coffee? I'd like to see you alone before I meet Bella." I wonder what he wants to see me about? My mind is racing. This is hopeless. I should just go and see him.

"OK, I'll meet you at the pier in fifteen minutes." I don't wait for a reply. I rush to the shower.

I'm dressed in my old jeans and a white t-shirt, my damp hair pulled back in a ponytail. I slip my feet into some flip-flops and quickly scribble a note for Em telling her where I'm going. I check my reflection in my compact mirror, tutting loudly at the dark rings under my eyes. Oh well, it's not me he's interested in right now, is it? I grab Em's hoodie from the arm of the sofa and head out to meet Ollie.

He's already there when I get to the pier. His face is a mixture of emotion. I guess he's as confused about this as me. As I get closer, I take him in. He's beautiful. Even at this early hour, he looks divine. He's wearing faded jeans and a dark t-shirt. His hair, like mine, is still damp. As I reach him, he pulls me close and hugs me tight. I'm lost right now. I don't know how to react. I let him hug me for a few seconds then decide 'what the heck' and hug him back. It feels so good. Being in his arms is perfect. It always will be. I come to my senses and pull back. Our eyes are fixed as he continues to hold onto me.

"Thanks for coming, Luce." I smile, a small, wary smile.

"Shall we grab a coffee?" He nods in reply, turning to walk to the coffee bar. He's holding my hand, I don't let go. I get the feeling this will be the last time we'll see each other, just the two of us. Once he's met Bella, this will be all about her, which I'm happy with. I know this, this thing between us is all in my head, my dream. I need to let the dream go now and think about practical reality – my daughter.

We take our seats and order coffees when the waitress arrives. We haven't spoken, we just stare. It's comfortable but unnerving all at the same time. Being with Ollie always seems 'just so' to me, the right thing. He says my name and I snap out of my thoughts.

"Lucy, you know I can't wait to meet Bella, don't you?"

I nod my head, grinning at the mention of her name. "She's perfect and I know you'll fall in love with her instantly."

He takes my hand. I let him. "Lucy—"

"Ollie, what's wrong. You're not having second thoughts about today, are you? If this is too soon and you want more time, just say."

He shakes his head frowning. "No, I just told you, I can't wait to meet her. I haven't slept at all. I've been going over and over in my head how this will work out."

I smile. "Me too. I've gone over every eventuality until I'm lost in it all."

He smiles and tilts his head. We sit silently for a while, sipping our coffee.

"Lucy, I love you."

I let go of his hand. I can feel the lump in my throat, my heart is pounding. "Ollie this isn't about us right now. It's about Bella."

He shakes his head. "No, it's not. It's about me and you, loving each other. Me and you, who have a little girl, together. Please let's try again? I promise I will do everything I can to make your life perfect. I want to love you both, look after you both. Wake up every morning to both of you. Please Lucy, at least think about it?"

I look out of the window across the sea. The sun is glistening across the water. It's beautiful. I look back and he's watching me, waiting. "Ollie, I can't. What if you break up with me again, your dad won't want you to take on Bella and me. I can't bear to go through that and put Bella through that. If we just keep this to you and Bella, then she'll never get hurt, will she?"

He's shaking his head. I have to look away. The tears are forcing their way out. "Lucy, listen to me? I've cut ties with my dad, I told you. He will never, ever come between you and me again. I want to make it up to you, please let me? I promise I'll never knowingly hurt you. I have no intention of ever breaking up with you. If you take me back, then I promise I'll make you happy, you and Bella."

"This isn't just going to happen overnight, Ollie. Bella and I have a life in London. I had to move on and make a life for my daughter. We'll be practical. You can see her as often as we can arrange it. But that's it." My heart has taken just about as much as it can. I would love, yes love, more than anything to say yes to him. To let him love me like I love him. To live happily ever after but that's the dreams again. Me and Ollie, that's all we've ever been really… a dream. The reality is Bella. I need to protect my girl. I know he'll always love her and I'll make sure he never hurts her. That's all I have the energy for with Ollie. I'm too afraid of anything else.

He lets go of my hand and sits back in his seat. "I'm not giving up on you, Lucia Meyer. If it takes a lifetime, I'll prove to you how much I love you."

I look away. His words wrap around my heart and pull so tight I can't breathe. I watch the shards of light across the water and wait. I wait for my breathing to calm, for my heart to slow down, then I take a look at him. His ice blues are dancing. He's smiling and I can't help but smile back.

"I love you Lucia, mother of my beautiful daughter. I'll prove it to you until you can't resist me anymore. And when you give in, I will marry you and show you just how perfect life can be."

I laugh. He frowns.

"You know I never realised until just now, Ollie. You're just as much a dreamer as me." He gives me a wink and I feel my body heat up. This is going to be damned hard.

****

Em is walking with me to fetch Bella. My nerves are in tatters. She's chattering away and I'm not listening. This seems to be the norm for us right now. I'm lost in thought until I hear the name Kyle. I shoot my head round and look at my sister.

"Sorry, Em, I was miles away. What did you just say?" She giggles.

"Nothing, it doesn't matter. Are you sure you'll be all right going on your own with Bella, because I can come along too if it will help?" I shake my head.

"I'll be fine. Please tell me what you were saying. You mentioned Kyle." She grins and I watch as the blush rises from her neck to her face.

"Well, I saw him at Sarah and Ben's last night. He, well, he…"

"What, Emilia, what did he do?" My heart is racing. Has my sister finally found someone? Someone who she likes, who is actually a complete hottie!

"Well he asked me out, nothing too formal or anything. We're going to a gig together. You see, we like the same music, and he got some free tickets from a friend and, well he asked me to go with him." I'm jumping up and down. The joy of hearing this news could not have come at a better time. I pull Emilia in for a hug.

"Oh, Em, I'm so happy for you. He is so sexy!" She hits my arm.

"You can't say that, Lucy. Firstly, it's just a gig we're going to, and secondly, he's asked me out so you can't fancy him." I laugh out loud.

"So, you fancy him then?" Em laughs.

"It would be difficult not to wouldn't it. He is flipping gorgeous." I decide not to push this too far with Em. I know how difficult she's found it to even look at anyone since Jamie so this is big, real big news. I put my arm through hers and we walk in silence the rest of the way.

****

We're settled on the beach. Bella and I sit in our spot, on our favourite rug with a few other bits and bobs, just like any other visit to this beach. Only this isn't just any other visit, it's the day my baby meets her daddy for the first time, and I feel sick. I'm trying so hard to act normal. I thought maybe I should tell her but I'm lost for the words that explain. Should I just tell her Daddy's coming to meet us and see what she says or should I wait until he gets here and introduce him as Oliver?

"Muuummmmyyy, come on, let's get water for a sand castle?"

"Sorry, sweetheart, come on, let's go." I grab a bucket and we head off down to the water's edge.

I watch the delight on Bella's face as the tiny waves break and splash her legs. She bobs around grinning at me and I feel sad. Just a little bit sad, that I have to share her. She's always been mine, just mine and I love her so much. I can't imagine anyone else loving her like I do. I hope Ollie tries. As we turn to head back up the beach, I spot him, standing by our things, his hands deep in his pockets as he watches. My heart is in my mouth as we walk the short walk back up the beach. I take a deep breath as we approach and glance at my baby. She's looking, trying to fathom out why that man is standing by our things.

I feel my heart miss a beat as we reach Ollie. Bella looks straight at him and grins. It's as if she knows him already.

"Hello." It's all she says but I know it's had a huge effect on Ollie. I watch as his eyes fill with tears. He briefly looks away, I think to compose himself. When he looks back at Bella, he's smiling.

"Hello, little girl." I watch him bend before our daughter and swallow the sob that's begging to escape.

"Bella, sweetheart, this is Daddy." Ollie and I briefly look at each other and then I have no choice but to pull my hand to my mouth to cover my sob. Bella reaches forward and hugs his legs.

"Daddy." Her voice is a whisper. I'm so moved, I'm speechless. Hearing her call him daddy and seeing the look on his face is enough to bring a grown man to tears. I drop down and take a seat on the rug. Bella lets go of Ollie's legs and takes his giant hand in her tiny one.

"Have you come to build sandcastles with us, Daddy?" I quickly wipe away my tears so that Bella doesn't see them and try my best to smile brightly when she looks at me. Ollie still hasn't spoken.

"Look, Mummy and I got water." She points to the bucket as Ollie falls to his knees beside her.

"OK, Princess, let's build sandcastles." I watch in silence as Bella instructs Ollie in her usual bossy manner. Every now and again he looks at me and my heart leaps in my chest. Bella tells him all about her visit to the zoo with Nonna and Granddad. I watch as he listens intently, taking in everything about our beautiful baby girl. As she passes him the spade, he gently touches her fingers, Bella grins and takes his hand. I look at her face, comparing the dimple with that of her Daddy. I reach forward and kiss her cheek.

"I love you, Mummy." I take a shaky breath.

"I love you too, sweetheart." When I look at Ollie, his face is turned away. I touch his hand.

"Are you OK?" He nods without turning.

"Bella sweetie, why don't you go get some more water? Mummy will watch you" She grabs the bucket and heads off to the water.

"Ollie, look at me." He turns. I reach up and wipe away his tears.

"Are you OK with this?"

He nods. "Yes, Lucy I'm fine. I'm just a little overwhelmed with how perfect she is. Thank you, sweetheart, for letting me see her."

I push up onto my knees, quickly check that Bella is OK and swiftly kiss his cheek.

"She likes you, actually I think it's more than like. It's like instant love and I'm a little overwhelmed myself, Ollie." Bella sploshes water on his jeans and I watch as he smiles lovingly at her.

"Would you like an ice cream, Bella?" Bella looks to me first before answering. I nod my head and she grins her dimple grin at her Daddy.

"Yes, please?"

Ollie tilts his head then looks to me. "Can we go and get an ice cream?"

I nod my head, ignoring the anxiety that's fighting to get out. Ollie smiles.

"Hey, why don't we all go? We can sit and have one at the pier." Bella is jumping up and down. I smile at my baby and curse the fact that I will only allow myself to be friends with this man who already broke my heart.

We're seated outside the ice cream parlor on the pier, surrounded by our bags, and I watch my daughter as she takes tiny licks of her ice cream. I check Ollie and find him watching Bella. His face shows complete fascination and it's truly heart-warming. I can't imagine how it must feel to only meet her now. He's missed so much in Bella's three short years and I'm sorry for that. I giggle as I watch the creamy trail of ice cream drip down his cornet and onto his hand. Ollie doesn't appear to notice. Bella looks to see why I'm giggling and frowns.

"Daaaddddyyy, you're dripping your ice cream." Ollie quickly licks away the cream and touches Bella's cheek. I watch as she leans into his hand, which looks like a giant's compared to her tiny face.

"Thank you, sweetheart. I nearly had messy trousers, didn't I?" She nods her head and for a second, I feel completely isolated from their conversation. I wonder what it will be like when he wants to see her without me. What will I do? Just the thought sends shivers through me.

"Are you OK?" Ollie touches my hand, bringing me back to reality with a sharp shock.

I nod, smiling in case Bella is watching.

"You sure?" I take a sip of my coffee, watching him over the top of my cup. He glances from me to Bella, then back at me, frowning. He leans over, whispering so that Bella can't hear.

"Thank you, Lucy, I know this can't be easy."

I swallow my coffee and place my cup down. I reply in a quiet voice. "It just feels so weird, that's all. I'm happy that you get along, it will just take a little getting used to, you know, having you around for Bella."

He sighs. "I want to be around as much as you'll let me, Luce. I don't want to miss anything else in this little lady's life." He touches Bella's cheek then looks to me. The emotion in his ice-blues knocks me for six.

"I know you do and we'll try and sort it so you can. It's not going to be easy, us living in London and you here in Layton." Bella is fully occupied eating her ice cream and we need to talk so this is good.

"Well I can come down to London. I'm free most weekends so maybe that could be a start. When do you go back?"

"Tomorrow afternoon." He looks crestfallen and the guilt swipes through me again. Am I just going to spend the rest of my days feeling guilty about Bella and Ollie?

"Right, so soon. Well, can I come and see you at the weekend then, Luce?"

I frown. "Oliver, this is about you and Bella. Yes, you can come and see Bella. What will you do, take her out?"

Now he's frowning. "Well I just thought maybe that as she's only just met me, you'd like to be with us. Sorry if I got it wrong." His voice cuts through me. He's right, I should be there with them both. I need to stop thinking about my feelings in this.

"You're right, sorry. We can all go out if you like. Which is best for you, Saturday or Sunday?"

He shrugs in response. "It won't matter. I'll come down on Friday night and leave on Sunday evening so I'll be free both days."

I have no plans for the weekend but I don't know if my heart can take two days of Ollie in a row. I breathe deeply and mentally scold myself for thinking of me, yet again. I need to think of Bella!

"OK, so if you're there all weekend we can do something both days if you like." His grin tells me all I need to know. I look at Bella who is now covered in melted ice cream. She deserves this so much. How can I deprive her of her beautiful daddy?

"Thanks, Luce. I promise I'll make it OK for you."

I smile back, knowing that it won't be that easy. I love him. Always have, always will. Being with him just takes pieces out of my heart. I won't give in though, I need to protect myself. There is no way on this earth I want to go through the heartbreak I went through before. I need to look after me.

****

I hate saying goodbye to my family. This weekend has gone far too quickly and I haven't spent nearly enough time with my parents. Dad is giving us a lift to the station and is busy packing our luggage into the car. Mamma has made up a bag of goodies to keep us going on the journey, which Bella is now busy sorting through with a look of joy on her face with every item she encounters. I look at Mamma and Em who are both watching me intently. We had dinner together last night, a proper family dinner and I talked them all through how Bella and Ollie's first meeting went. Bella was very helpful with her animated description of seeing Daddy. Mamma cried quietly and even Dad had a tear in his eye when they heard Bella say Daddy. Em was my support as usual, going over practicalities with me. I've made plans for Bella to come and stay in Layton for a few weeks over the summer so Em is going to plan with Ollie to see her then. I'm not sure how I feel about that but at least if Em is there, I know Bella will be secure. Ollie texted me this morning wishing us a safe journey and telling me thank you for what seems like the hundredth time. I call Bella and tell her she needs to visit the toilet before we set off. Mamma grabs her hand and they head off back into the house giggling.

"Lucia." I look up as Dad calls me. He nods his head in the direction of the driveway. Em and I look and share a gasp. Ollie is walking up the driveway, hands deep in his pockets, his head low. My heart is thumping as Dad walks towards me and Em rubs my arm.

"Do you want me to ask him to leave, sweetheart?" Dad is frowning, his discomfort obvious. I shake my head.

"He's Bella's daddy. If he wants to see her, then that's OK with me. Is it OK with you, Dad?" He pulls me into a hug, talking quietly in my ear.

"Whatever you're comfortable with, Lucy. I'm here for you, OK?" he pulls away, brushing some stray hair out of my face. I hear Ollie cough awkwardly. Dad lets go of me and steps aside, nodding at Ollie in greeting.

"Lucy, I just wanted to see you both before you leave. Is that OK?" I nod my head although I'm not feeling so sure inside. I get that he wants to see Bella but he has to stop referring to me as well. It's too much for my heart! I need him to pull back and let me just be Bella's mummy. I hope he can or this is going to be upsetting.

"Why don't you go inside, Ollie, she's at the loo with Mamma. Come on, I'll take you." Em gives me a wink as she shows Ollie into the house. I give Dad a big hug, then jump in the car. I'll stay here, it's safer that way. I don't want to say goodbye to him and I certainly don't want to watch him with Bella. Insecurity is seeping through me right now. I don't think I'm strong enough to do this.

Bella jumps into the car with me, her dimpled grin pulling at my heart.

"Daddy came to say bye-bye, Mummy. Look, he gave me this." She holds out a small, pink, silk purse that's tied at the top with ribbon. Bella opens it and shows me a tiny gold St Christopher pendant on a delicate gold chain. I look out of the window and catch his eyes. He blows a kiss to Bella and I feel that familiar pull at my heart. I look at Mamma who has watched all of this. She pulls her hands to her heart and mouths "I love you" to me as we pull away. I quickly wipe away the solitary tear as I catch Dad watching me through the rearview mirror. I hear his sigh and doubt that this will all end happily.

****

I watch the landscape pass us by as the train speeds its way back to London. Bella is draped across my knee, sleeping in such a cute way. The older lady opposite us smiles as she looks at my princess. I run my fingers through my daughter's hair and wonder how it feels for her, now that she has a daddy in her life. I suppose Ollie's just another person to Bella. She has no idea how important Ollie is or just how much she's going to need him as she grows up. My phone ringing breaks my thoughts. It's Ollie.

"Hello?"

"Lucy, you didn't mind me showing up today, did you?"

"No, Ollie, its fine. Oh, and thanks for getting Bella the necklace."

"Please don't thank me, Luce. It was nothing. I owe her everything, please don't thank me." I sigh. This is new. How should I behave? What should I say? I have no flipping idea and I'm scared.

"Lucy?"

"Yes?"

"Will you be OK if I phone Bella later to say goodnight?"

"I'll be fine. If you call at seven, I'll make sure she answers, OK?"

I hear his sigh. "Not really, but if that's how you want to be, Luce, then OK." I sigh now.

"Lucy?"

"Yes?"

"I love you, more than ever now, baby. Please re-think this. Please let me make it right with you." I swallow the sobs that are eager to fill this train, shaking my head. He's just overcome by emotion right now. Bella has that effect on people. He needs to take some time to adjust to our new situation too.

"Ollie, you're just dreaming again. Please let's just be Bella's parents right now." His voice sounds broken when he speaks again.

"I'll call later then. Lucy, take care, sweetheart."

As I click the button on my phone, I bury my head in my hands and silently sob. I feel a nudge and look up as the lady opposite hands me a tissue. I take it mouthing thank you as she looks on sorrowfully.

****

So much has changed in my life this weekend and walking into our apartment feels strange. I watch as Bella heads for her bedroom without a care in the world and realize that for the first time since I came to London many years ago that I'm not happy to be home. I feel homesick for Layton on Sea, for my mamma, my dad, Emilia and yes, I admit to myself, Ollie. I dump our bags in my bedroom, head straight for the kitchen and switch on the kettle. My phone rings and I smile when I see Lisa's name appear on the screen. That's what I need, some reality chatter with my best friend in London town.

"Lisa, how's things, sweetie?"

"All good. We missed you today at the team meeting but I'll fill you in tomorrow in work time. How did your weekend go, Luce?" I sigh and get ready to tell my friend the long story about Bella and Ollie.

"Wow, Luce. I kind of guessed it was him, but you never talked so I never asked. You OK?" I shake my head as I answer.

"No, Lisa, I'm not. I have no idea how to handle this. I'm scared to death if I'm honest."

"Why don't I come over with a bottle of wine and we can hash it out whilst baby Bella's in bed?" I smile and relief washes over me. Lisa's helped me through so much as a single parent. Sometimes she doesn't even offer advice she just listens while I talk things through out loud. Lisa is definitely what I need right now.

"Oh, Lise, you're a star. That sounds perfect."

"Have you eaten?"

"No"

"Right, I'll call and get food on the way too. Any preference?" I laugh as I answer.

"Just get yourself here. I'll order take out, OK?"

"Right, so make sure it's our favourite chinese then, please? See you in about an hour, OK?"

"OK, Lisa. Bye."

I've just finished drying Bella's hair after her bath when the door buzzer sounds. Bella runs to answer the intercom. I smile as I watch her. She's so grown up.

"Hello, beautiful, it's Auntie Lisa, you gonna let me in?" Bella nods before answering.

"OK, Auntie Lisa, come on in."

Bella's jumping up and down with excitement as we wait at the open front door for Lisa to appear. Bella jumps into Lisa's arms as she passes me the bag of goodies she brought with her. I watch as the two spin around and around in the hallway until Bella screams out in delight. Lisa nuzzles her neck before letting my giddy daughter down. They follow me to the living room as Bella jumps up and down telling Lisa everything about the weekend. She doesn't mention Ollie and I kind of feel worried. Bella talks about Nonna and Granddad, Emilia, oh and the zoo but then she disappears off to her bedroom. Lisa gives me a look as we watch Bella depart and I frown, scratching my head in wonderment.

"Doesn't seem to have affected the little one, Lucy." I pull my legs under me as I relax on the sofa.

"No, she's fine with everything. It's me that's a nervous wreck, Lisa." Bella reappears with her hands behind her back. She's looking at Lisa as she walks across the room. Lisa watches, smiling at Bella.

"What are you up to, little Miss?"

"Guess what I've got, Auntie Lisa?" Lisa plays the game as Bella giggles.

"I don't know, sweetheart, what have you got?"

"Tada!" Bella holds up the pink purse and Lisa looks over at me. I smile, weakly.

"A purse?" Bella shakes her head laughing.

"No silly, look." With her tiny fingers, we both watch, as it takes an age for Bella to untie the ribbon and reveal her hidden treasure.

"Look, Daddy bought this for me. It's to keep me safe Auntie Lisa." We share a look and I feel my heart in my mouth. See, she hasn't even mentioned that she only just met her daddy. It's like he's been in her life forever. I know that's a positive thing but it's still a shock to me.

Chapter 9

This feels strange! Ollie has called Bella every night, which she loved. I have a work party to attend tonight, and because he's coming to London, Oliver offered to babysit. I'm getting ready and my heart is well and truly in my mouth. I'm taking extra time over my appearance as if I'm off out on a hot date. It's hard to acknowledge that the only reason is because Ollie will see me before I go out. Bella is excited that Daddy is coming over and I promised Ollie that I'd keep her up for him. There are so many firsts he needs to experience and putting our baby girl to bed is most definitely one of the top ten.

Most of the week at work has been taken up with a photo shoot and Will insisted we take everyone out as a bit of a wrap party. I usually look forward to evenings like this but knowing that Ollie will be here in my apartment, putting our daughter to bed, is somewhat of a distraction.

I check my appearance and frown. I look tired, again! I haven't slept well all week. When I have managed to grab a few hours, I've dreamed about Oliver Ashcroft. I have given Lisa the task of trying to occupy my time and distract me from all thoughts Ollie, but even she can't control who I damn well dream about. I brush on an extra coat of blusher to try and brighten up my drab face. There, that will have to do. I'm wearing a dark red, above the knee, fitted dress that has three quarter sleeves. My hair is pulled up in a messy bun with dangly gold earrings draping my neck. I pull on my high red shoes and sigh. 'You'll just have to do, Lucia Meyer' I tell myself as I head to the living room in search of my daughter.

Bella is ready for bed in her cute pink pj's and is now snuggled up on the sofa with her cuddly mouse and a cup of milk while she watches *The Little Mermaid*. When I hear the buzzer sound, I know she won't run to answer because nothing, I mean nothing, will pull her away from Ariel. I want her to answer because I'm too scared but I can't be that cruel. I sigh, take in a deep breath and head to the door. I breathe in sharply when I hear his voice. My heart has stopped. Damn him. He actually stops my world from turning at just the sound of his voice. I press the switch to open the door for him and wait by my front door for Ollie to appear. I close my eyes and count to ten, telling myself this is nothing out of the ordinary and I need to calm down. I have to get used to seeing him – a lot – so I need to deal with it, right!

Wrong! I will never get used to the feeling of breathlessness whenever I see Oliver Ashcroft. He looks fucking gorgeous and I want to cry. We check each other out as he approaches the front door and I feel very inferior. He has just travelled a couple of hours from Layton and still manages to look edible in his scruffy jeans, a pale blue t-shirt and tatty old converses. I open the door wider to welcome him as he grins. I check out the dimple, feeling the pounding of my heart as our eyes meet.

"Hi, Lucy. You look gorgeous." I scoff at his words. Oh no, I don't!

"Bella, look who's here, sweetheart." My heart pounds harder as I watch their greeting unfold in front of me like a romantic film.

"Daaaadddddyyyyy!" She runs to him, her arms wide and Ollie bends to pick Bella up. He spins her around kissing her face as Bella giggles. I somehow feel like an intruder in my own home right now.

I watch as Bella parades Ollie around the apartment, showing him the rooms like an estate agent. Ollie makes all the right noises and fusses most over Bella's room before they reappear in the living room, hand in hand! I look at their interlocked fingers and feel a pang of jealousy. I mentally shake myself, closing my eyes for just a second to compose myself. When I re-open them, Ollie is watching me carefully. This must be odd for him too. Coming into our home for the first time and seeing his daughter's bedroom for the first time. I smile at him and he cocks his head to one side.

"Penny for your thoughts, Luce?" I shrug then decide to tell him.

"I was just thinking how odd this must be for you. Visiting Bella's home for the first time. It feels odd to me." Bella lets go of Ollie's hand and resumes her seat on the sofa, watching Ariel.

I make my way to the kitchen and sense Ollie following behind me. I turn and he's there, watching me.

"Is this too awkward, Lucy? I'm sorry, I never thought." I shake my head and try not to get transfixed on his beautiful face.

"No, its fine. It's just odd. We'll get used to it, won't we?"

He moves towards me and I freeze. My heart has stopped and I can't breathe. This is too close. I watch as he lifts his hand to my face, his eyes glued to mine. He reaches with his thumb and rubs my chin.

"You've smudged your lipstick, Luce." I feel my blush as he stops rubbing. His thumb is still there, I can feel his touch burning my face. His ice blues glisten as he smiles.

"Beautiful." He turns and walks out. I have to take a minute to hold the counter and calm myself. Time for a pep talk.

Come on, Lucy! Pull yourself together and get out of here, fast!

****

I watch the city streets flash by me through the taxi window and I panic that I didn't spend enough time showing Ollie around the apartment. I needed to get out so I rushed around showing him where everything is. Oh hell, he'll be OK and if he's not, I'm sure he'll phone me.

Lisa whistles as I walk towards her at the wine bar we've all arranged to meet in.

"Wow, you look good, Lucy. Who are you trying to impress tonight? It's not Dan, is it? He's been giving you the eye all week."

I look at my friend. Shocked. Shocked, firstly that she thinks I look 'wow' and secondly that Dan, one of the shoot models, apparently hasn't stopped looking at me all week. What planet am I on right now, because it's certainly not the one Lisa's familiar with. She laughs.

"Are you OK, Luce?"

"Hmmm. Well I'm not sure, Lisa. I just left my daughter with her daddy babysitting her and it feels kind of weird." Lisa whistles again but for different reasons. She forces a glass of liquid into my hand.

"Drink this, honey, I'd say you need it, sweetheart." I swish the glass and guess that its either vodka or gin. I like both so I don't question my friend I just take a sip.

"So, what was it like when Oliver came round? Have you started to get over him yet or does your heart still beat out of your chest when you see him?" Lisa's grinning when she asks, me on the other hand, well I'm frowning at my friend.

"So, you still love him?" She raises an eyebrow and I feel my face blush.

"It just won't switch off, Lise. I tell myself every time I see or speak to him that it will get better, but it doesn't."

"So why waste time fighting it Lucy? You love him, he loves you and you have the cutest baby together so why aren't you living happily ever after with this man?" I go to answer when my phone rings in my bag. I quickly search and look at Lisa who's grinning when she sees the caller ID. It's Ollie. For once, my nerves are not because it's him. I'm worried something has happened to Bella and I need to get back.

"Ollie?" I more or less shout down the phone.

"Whoa, Lucy, it's OK. No need to panic, Bella is just fine. I just wanted to check if it's OK to give her a cookie before she goes to bed? Are you OK with that?" I sigh.

"Shit, Ollie, I thought something was wrong. Of course, she can have a cookie if she wants one. You can decide yourself you know, you don't have to ask my permission." Now he sighs.

"Well I don't want to upset you, that's all. I'm sorry to bother you." Now I feel like a cow for snapping.

"Ollie?"

"Yes?"

"I'm sorry I snapped. How's it going, you know, just the two of you?" I can hear the smile in his voice and my heart aches a little.

"Real good. God she's so cute, Lucy, I could eat her. She's just been showing me some photos of you and her, you know that little album she keeps in her bedroom. Every time she turns the page, she kisses you, sweetheart." I feel my eyes awash with tears. I want to go home and watch them together. They sound so perfect.

"You don't mind me looking do you, Luce?" I shake my head.

"No, of course not. I'm glad you're both OK. I miss being there actually. It sounds like more fun than I'll be having with a load of vain fashion models for company tonight." He laughs at my comment. I look at Lisa who has her hand over her heart and is pretending to swoon. I turn my back to her so that I can concentrate on listening to Ollie.

"Well enjoy your freedom, Lucy. What time will you be home?"

"I'll get a taxi back, probably about eleven, is that OK?"

"Yes fine, any time's fine."

"OK, I better go and be professional for the evening. See you later. Oh, and give my girl a big kiss from me."

"I will, bye, Lucy." I wait to hear him hang up. I want to go home more than ever now. I look at my friend and she gives me a wink.

"Come on let's go and have a good time with some perfectly formed male models." She pulls my arm into hers and we walk over to where Will, our boss and a few others have congregated.

****

115

I check out Lisa who is already flirting madly with a dark and handsome model called Jason. Lisa looks so damn sexy, as always. She's wearing black fitted leather trousers with a white halter-top. Lisa is curvy, you know, sexy bottom and boobs that I would die for. I'm not flat chested or anything but I'd like more and Lisa has more!

I watch as Dan walks in and take in his look. He really is a looker but he knows it and that kind of spoils him. He scans the room as he walks across. I guess he's seeing if anyone is checking him out. I'm immediately put off. I think of Ollie, who in my eyes is far better looking than Dan and never seems to notice the effect he has on women when he walks in a room. Now that's sexy. I look up and realize Dan is heading my way. I have to be polite because I'm working so I plaster on a fake smile. Dan leans in and air kisses both my cheeks. I catch Lisa watching and grin at her. She laughs and holds her glass up to me. It will do no harm to have a flirtatious evening with Dan, it might even take my mind off Oliver Ashcroft, and so I take a seat next to him and plan to do just that.

****

When Lisa and I stumble out of a club that I've never heard of and flag down a taxi, I realise that maybe I've had slightly too much to drink. I was fine until I hit fresh air and now everything seems a little blurry. Lisa keeps giggling at nothing in particular which makes me giggle, so the journey home is filled with inane, drunken laughter. I get dropped off first and watch, laughing, as Lisa pulls faces at me through the taxi window as she's driven away.

I try very hard to be quiet as a mouse when I unlock the door. I tiptoe down the hallway, shushing myself as I go. All is quiet, no TV or anything. I have no idea what the time is. I step into the kitchen to check the time on the cooker and gasp when I see it's two in the morning. I turn out the light and head for the living room. The only light is that of the side lamp next to the sofa. I see Ollie sleeping and my heart feels crushed. He looks so damned handsome. I want to just go over and lie next to him, pull his arm around me and snuggle in. I try desperately not to wake him as I walk over and grab a throw from the chair. I gently cover him and lean down to turn off the light. I'm watching his beautiful face as his eyes open. He smiles and I can't help but touch his cheek.

"Hey, did you have a good night after all?" His voice is croaky from sleep. Sexy! I nod my head.

"Mmm hmmm, it was good. Lisa and I went dancing. I'm sorry I'm so late, Ollie, I really didn't realise the time."

"It's OK. Your sofa is actually very comfortable." He moves to get up.

"Hey, you can't go now, it's far too late. If you're comfy, you can stay there if you like. But beware, Miss Bella will not let you sleep in." I laugh and he smiles, sitting up.

"Are you sure, Lucy?"

I wave my arms in the air. "Of course, it's fine. I need to go and sleep now, Ollie. Will you be OK?"

He laughs, nodding his head. "I'll be fine Luce. I think you should get some water though. You'll have a real bad head in the morning if you don't."

I salute him and wander off to the kitchen. I drink a pint of water and pour myself some to take to bed. I head back to the lounge to check Ollie and find him sleeping. Once again, I make my way over to switch off the light. I watch as he gently breathes and wish he were mine. I wish I could give in and tell him I want him. I lean over and very gently kiss his lovely lips.

"Goodnight, Ollie, I love you." My voice is a tiny whisper. He continues to sleep. I smile and leave the room in search of my bed.

****

The sunlight daring to shine through the gap in my bedroom curtains is most unwelcome this morning. I hear the door open and wait for Bella to jump on my bed. Instead I hear her giggle and the whisper of someone trying to shush her. Oh God, that's right, Ollie stayed here on the sofa last night. Shit, he'll see me at my worst today if my pounding head is any indication of how I might look. A gentle little kiss on my cheek makes me smile. Bella always makes me smile. She's perfect and she's mine. I love my Bella.

"Good morning, Princess. Did you sleep well?" My voice sounds hoarse this morning.

"Yes, Mummy, did you?" I open my eyes a little to see her and notice Ollie near the door. He hasn't come into the room, he's watching from the doorway.

"You can come in, Ollie. Just be prepared that I will look like a monster. God, my head is killing me." Bella jumps on the bed and hugs me tight as Ollie moves into the room a little.

"Would you like some coffee, Lucy? I can make you breakfast if that will help."

"Urghh, no thanks. Water will do just fine for now, thanks. Bella needs breakfast though, if you don't mind?"

"Daddy and I already had ours, Mummy." I try to sit up and groan at the pain in my head as I do.

"Wow, Bella, were you up with the lark today?"

"Lucy, it's eleven a.m." I can hear the amusement in Ollie's voice.

Shit! I rub my eyes and look at him. "Ollie, I'm so sorry. Look I'll get up now." He puts his hands in the air.

"Lucy, it's fine. We've had a lovely morning, haven't we, Bella? And I'm glad I could help you out." Bella jumps off the bed and stands next to Ollie, hugging his leg. It's like he's been part of her life forever.

"Can we go to the park, Mummy, pleeeease?" I check out her dimple and look up to see Ollie's too as they both wait for my response.

"How can I possibly say no since you both let me lie in bed so late?"

"Is that yes?" Bella waits for a straight answer. Ollie winks at me and I feel flutters in my stomach as my heart misses a beat.

"Yes, sweetheart, we can go to the park." Bella squeals and I pull the covers over my head to drown out the noise. Ollie ushers her out of my bedroom.

"Let's go and make Mummy some coffee while she gets ready, Bella." I hear her nattering away in the kitchen as I make my way to the bathroom.

I feel slightly more myself after a long, hot shower. I'm dressed in simple jeans and a navy t-shirt this morning. I've pulled my damp hair up in a knot and have only applied mascara to my eyes. The smell of coffee as I walk into the kitchen is actually quite inviting now I'm up and about. Ollie holds up the jug and I nod my response. I pass him my favourite red mug and he pours my coffee. Our eyes meet as he passes me the mug and I sense something is different but I don't know what. The electric current fires through me as his fingers touch my hand so nothing there has changed. I frown and he just grins.

"Why are you grinning, Ollie?" He stops and looks at me with his head tilted.

"You're very cute when you're drunk, Lucy." I scratch at my neck feeling awkward. I don't think I did or said anything embarrassing when I got home and I remember everything.

"Why?" He walks towards me and I hold my breath.

"Nothing in particular, just cute all round really." I breathe a sigh of relief.

"God, for a minute there I thought maybe I'd forgotten a whole chunk of the night or something. I am really sorry I was so late, Ollie. Thanks for staying and taking care of Bella for me." He frowns.

"Please don't thank me, Lucy. I want to do this. I'll be here every weekend and watch her for you if you like." I shake my head laughing.

"You need a life, Ollie." He shakes his head.

"I only have room for you two and truthfully Lucy, you're all I want." I place my coffee cup on the counter and leave the room. I need to separate myself from him before I cave and tell him I feel the same. I know I've told him countless times that I love him but the temptation to drop my guard and run to him is overwhelming right now.

****

We haven't talked about what he said in the kitchen earlier. Even if we wanted to, we haven't had time. Bella is full on today. She is demanding of Ollie and he doesn't seem to mind. I sit on a park bench soaking up the sun amused at the sight of Ollie running around, pushing the roundabout, as Bella squeals with delight. When he takes her down the big slide on his lap I swallow hard. They look wonderful. I pull out my phone and take a photo. It's their first photo together. I call them over and wave my phone at Ollie. He's out of breath as he smiles.

"Look, Ollie, your first photo with Bella."

"No, it's not Mummy. Daddy took lots of photos, didn't you?" Bella looks at Ollie who is pulling his phone from his pocket. He scrolls through and takes a seat next to me. I watch in awe at the series of photos they took last night while I was out. My heart aches wishing I'd been there.

"You OK, Luce?" Ollie is frowning.

"Yes, sorry, I'm fine." I stand up and prepare to leave the play area. Ollie watches me. As I walk away, I tell him.

"I just wish I'd been there, that's all." He stands and follows me, calling for Bella to follow. She's run off and is busy climbing through tunnels in the giant wooden boat. I feel him tug at my sleeve.

"Lucy, please?" I stop and turn to look at him. His ice blues are dancing as he smiles at me.

"Why won't you give in and let me love you? I promise I won't hurt you, sweetheart." I sigh and look away. My mind is telling me to say yes, to let him take me in his arms and make the world feel right but my heart is yelling at me to be careful. He pulls me to him and I let him. As he wraps his arms around me, I let the feelings of love take over me just for a few seconds. This feels so right. I feel his breath as he leans in and whispers to me.

"Baby, I love you so damn much, it hurts. Please give in?" I swallow a sob and feel his lips gently kiss the side of my head. My body is pulsing at his touch. My body has craved his touch constantly. Nothing and no one makes me feel the way he can. It feels like hours but must only be seconds that we stand and I let him hold me. I don't want to pull away.

"Mummy, are you OK?" I look down as Bella forces her way through so that she's standing between us, looking up. I smile at my girl as Ollie kisses the top of my head.

"I'm fine, sweetheart. Daddy was just keeping me warm." I shudder to make out I'm cold and Ollie rubs the tops of my arms, playing the charade well.

"Can we go and feed the ducks?" The moment has gone. We follow our daughter, neither saying a word.

We call at the café in the courtyard at the park. Ollie and Bella go and pick us some sandwiches for late lunch while I stay seated and watch them. I can see so many of Ollie's mannerisms in Bella that I never noticed before. They stand the same and when Ollie speaks to Bella she tilts her head, just the way he does. I'm lost in my world of watching them. I love them both so much. I'm happy, so damned happy that Ollie knows and that he can be Bella's daddy now. He glances over and gives me a wink. I feel my heartbeat quicken and smile. I look over and catch an elderly lady at the next table watching me. She gives me a smile and leans forward.

"You make a beautiful family. You know I love the way you watch them with such love in your eyes. It's magical, dear." I blush and thank her. Am I that obvious that a complete stranger can see the love I have for Ollie?

I eat my sandwiches, knowing that food will do me good. If I'm honest I have no appetite right now but I need to feel better.

"Feeling any better, Luce?" He's watching me. I'm immediately drawn to his ice-blues when I look up. Since he met Bella, he constantly looks happy and I like it.

"I'm getting there. Can I ask you something?"

"Anything, fire away."

"Do you feel happier now you know about Bella?"

He tilts his head before answering. "I've never felt so happy in my life, Lucy. I can't believe a tiny person could have such an effect on me but she does and I love it, I love her. Why do you ask?"

"You just look happier and I wanted to know if it was Bella." He grabs my hand across the table and my heart stops.

"There's only one other thing that would make me happier." I pull my hand away and he looks hurt. I turn to Bella as a distraction.

"What are we doing next then, Bella, sweetheart? Shall we stop at the sweetie shop on the way home for chocolate?"

Her beaming smile answers that question. She looks at Ollie and his smile returns.

"Do you like chocolate, Daddy?"

"Yes, sweetheart, I do." He takes her hand and I feel bad again for pulling away from him.

****

Bella is driving me nuts this morning. Ollie is dropping by to take her out and she's like a cat on hot bricks right now waiting for him to arrive. They're going alone, my choice. Ollie asked me to go too but I think it will be nice for them to have some time on their own, special time without me as a distraction. I plan to meet Lisa for lunch whilst they're gone. Ollie's heading back to Layton later after he drops Bella back. When I hear the buzzer, I can't help but smile as Bella runs for the hallway. She's ready to go, shoes and coat in place. She lets her daddy in the building and calls for me to open the apartment door for him. I must admit I think I feel as excited to see Ollie as Bella. I'm just not dealing with this well, am I?

"Hey, how's my favourite girls this morning?" Bella hugs his legs and I can't hide my smile at seeing him.

"So where are you two heading today?" His eyes are on me and I can't look away. I stand and stare. He looks perfect and I want to reach out and touch him. I turn quickly and walk through to my bedroom. I'm safe here, he won't follow.

"I know how much you like the zoo, sweetheart, so would you like to go there today?" Bella's squeal of excitement tells him he's made the right choice. I stand, stock-still, my eyes closed and try my hardest to quell these emotions fighting their way through my body. I call out to them in the hall.

"Good choice, Ollie, Bella loves the zoo, don't you, sweetheart?"

"I do, so does Mummy." I close my eyes again. My heart is banging loudly in my ears right now. I open my wardrobe and grab a jacket and shoes. When I leave the bedroom, they're gone. I can hear their voices coming from the kitchen so I follow them there.

"You off somewhere nice, Luce? You look good." I look down at my appearance and smile back at him. I'm wearing cut off white jeans and a simple red t-shirt. Nothing special really.

"I'm meeting Lisa for lunch."

"Anywhere nice?"

"She lives in Camden so we'll probably take a browse around the market then head to a bistro we usually visit." As I'm telling him, I'm transported back to the time we went to Camden, together. The best week of my life when I loved him and he loved me and I thought it would last forever. I look up and his face tells me he's right there with me.

"Sorry." I feel uncomfortable. He smiles.

"Don't be sorry. I relive that week all the time. The best ever." He looks wistful as I try to move past him and leave the room. He touches my bare arm, stopping me in my tracks. My body is trembling at his touch and I wonder if he can feel it.

"Lucy?"

"Yes?"

"What time would you like us back?" He looks down at our daughter and she's grinning back.

"So long as madam is back for bedtime, it's up to you." His eyes are on me again, his hand still holding my arm. I look at his hand and suppress the urge to touch him.

"OK." His voice is quiet as he answers. I look at his mouth, those perfect lips that I remember so well. I suddenly remember kissing him the other night. I pull my hand to my mouth in horror. Oh shit, I did, didn't I? I kissed him, oh God! And I told him I love him. Ollie is frowning at my expression. I can't possibly explain this, not now, in front of Bella. I'll try in a cryptic way.

"Sorry, I just had memory recall of something I did and said the other night which I had completely forgotten." He smiles.

"I hope it was nothing too embarrassing, Luce." He raises an eyebrow and I can see the smile in his eyes. Shit, was he awake?

****

The apartment feels lonely now he's gone. It was the first weekend he's visited and it already feels like he belongs here. Ollie stayed for about an hour after he and Bella got back. I was fascinated watching the two of them sharing stories of their trip to the zoo. They were so animated and excited. In all the time I've lived here, I've loved my job and Sunday nights have always been my downtime once Bella's in bed, so that I can get ready for my busy time at the office. Tonight feels different. I don't want to put her to bed and I certainly don't want to think about work. I'm scared. Scared that once I sit down on my own, I will be consumed with thoughts of Ollie.

I take a seat, sighing loudly. Bella was so tired, it would have been cruel to keep her up just to use her as a distraction. I've poured myself a glass of white wine and put on some music. I grab a magazine to read but the music catches my attention, the words to the song actually. Lady Antebellum's *If I Knew Then* is playing. As I listen to the words, I can't stop the tears from flowing. What if love does only come once? What if that perfect week was it?

My phone ringing has me pulling myself together. I pause the music and grab a tissue. Shit, it's Ollie!

"Hi, Lucy." He sounds so happy.

"Hi."

"I just wanted to say thank you for this weekend. It was up there with the best I've ever had." I can't help but smile at his words. I knew he'd love Bella.

"I'm glad Bella makes you so happy, Ollie, really I am. You don't have to thank me. Just promise me you'll always be there for her, that's all." He's silent for a second.

"Lucy?"

"Yes?"

"I meant what I said, sweetheart. I will never hurt you, not knowingly, and that includes Bella. You're her mummy and if I hurt her, I'll hurt you and I promise I will never hurt either of you. I will do my best to love her as much as she deserves and to make up for when I've not been there for her. You do believe me, don't you?"

"Thank you. Will you be in London next weekend?" I can't dwell on what he said.

"Yes, is that OK? Have you got any plans; do you need a babysitter?"

"It's fine. I'm not planning on going out but if things change, I'll let you know."

"Well I'll be there, so I don't mind, Lucy."

"Thank you for being here this weekend Ollie. It was... special. Thanks."

"I'll call Bella tomorrow before bed, is that OK?" I smile at his obvious love for Bella that is already so strong.

"Yes, of course, bye."

"Bye, Lucy." He's gone. I feel distraught all over again. I turn the music back on and resume my melancholy state of mind, tears and all.

Chapter 10

The last few weeks have been somewhat strange. I've spent all week counting the days to the weekend. Ollie has arrived every Friday and gone back to Layton on Sunday evening. The time we've shared has been mixed. Ollie took Bella shopping on a Saturday morning when I had to work then they met me for lunch and we took Bella into the city to Hamleys toy store where Ollie spent a fortune on her. I'm not big on spoiling her, partly because I've never really been able to afford it, but also because it's not how I was brought up. But watching the joy on both their faces as Ollie indulged my baby was special.

Ollie came round a few evenings and we had pizza and watched Disney movies. He's constantly mesmerized by Bella and was in awe of the way she knows all the lines to *The Little Mermaid* and *Cinderella*. Watching Ollie watching Bella is my new favourite pastime. We ventured to the swimming baths where Bella delighted in Ollie constantly trying to drown me. That was by far the worst time. Being so close to him was torture. Every time he touched me, I melted some more and at one point, I very nearly kissed him as he pulled me into his arms.

This weekend is very different and I'm a little anxious. Bella and I have just arrived in Layton and the plan is for Bella to stay here with Mamma and Dad for a few weeks at least while I go back to London. I plan to visit at weekends when possible. This was all arranged months ago... before Ollie got involved. You see, the problem is that Ollie now lives in Layton, so Bella will be here and he won't be far away. Me, on the other hand, well I will be hundreds of miles away in London, far from both of them. Mamma is fussing over our bedrooms and unpacking Bella's small suitcase. I look up as she calls my name.

"What's wrong, Lucia? You look worried sick, sweetheart." Her face is full of concern as she waits for me to answer. I frown, not sure how to put into words how I feel.

"This was planned months ago, Mamma, you know, ages before Ollie knew about Bella. It just feels odd, that's all." She places a pile of Bella's underwear gently in a drawer then turns and walks to me. She pulls me to her talking as she watches my face.

"You're my girl, Lucia and I won't let you get hurt. The plans are that he sees Bella at the weekend when you're here, right?" I nod my head and she smiles sweetly.

"And if there's a time when you can't get here then Emilia will be your stand in, right?" I nod again and giggle at my mother's precise recital of the plan.

"So, stop worrying, please. We will do as you ask. Oh, and of course, Ollie will call Bella in the evening, yes?" I sigh. The thought that they'll be sharing conversations that I can't hear makes me jealous. I look over at Bella who's watching and listening.

"Gosh, Bell, you'll have two calls every day. One from me and one from Daddy, you lucky girl." I take her in my arms as she bounds to me. As we spin round, I catch my Mamma grinning at us.

"See, it will be just fine."

We head downstairs when Dad calls and Bella squeals in delight when she spots my sister Emilia sitting at the large wooden kitchen table.

"Auntie Em, I missed you." Em scrapes her chair out and pulls Bella up so that she's seated on the table in front of her. Em looks Bella over, firstly holding out each arm, then each leg, then her hands, finishing with a close look at her fingers.

"Gosh, Bella you've grown so much, sweetheart. Have you been eating all your dinner like Mummy asked?" Bella nods vigorously as Mamma and Dad watch on, laughing at Bella's cuteness.

"Look at my hair, Auntie Em, it growed too." Bella swishes her hair around as Em coos at her. I take a seat at the table and Em turns to me.

"You OK, Luce?"

"I'm good, Em, what about you?"

"Fine. Glad to have you here this weekend. Can we go out for a drink tonight?" I look over at Mamma who's grinning.

"Go, you go and have a good time together, my beauties. I need cuddles from my perfect Bella anyway."

"Hey, what about me?" Bella giggles as Dad looks forlorn and Mamma slaps his arm.

"No room for boys in our cuddles are there, Bella?" Bella frowns and we all wait, simultaneously holding our breath.

"Well Nonna, I like my cuddles off Granddad, oh, and Daddy, so can we have some boys?" Mamma looks at me, as do Em and Dad. I shrug. What can I say? She loves her daddy. That's how it should be. Mamma makes light of it as Dad touches my shoulder whilst standing behind me.

"Just those two then, Bella." Bella grins and all is right in her tiny world.

****

I'm just finishing my hair in front of the bedroom mirror when my phone rings. I grab it from my bag and swallow when I see it's Ollie calling. Of course, he's calling Bella. He always calls to say goodnight. It's still the same, even if we are in Layton.

"Ollie, hi."

"Hi, Lucy. How are you, and how's my princess?" I can't help but smile.

"We're all good. She's downstairs at the moment with Mamma and Dad, being spoiled rotten. Just give me a sec and I'll call her." I rush to the top of the stairs and call Bella.

"Bella, Daddy's on the phone, sweetheart." She's there in a flash. I watch as she makes her way up the stairs on her tiny legs, her hand held out for the phone.

"Daddy, I miss you. Are you coming to see me today?"

My heart is in my mouth. Poor Bella. She wants to see her daddy. I never thought. I'll speak with him and arrange something for tomorrow. I wait anxiously as she chatters to Ollie about nursery and her week. I whisper to let me speak to Daddy and Bella nods at me.

"Mummy wants to speak to you, Daddy. Night, night, I love you too." Each time I hear her say that, I have to force back the tears. I love that she loves him. I love him too!

"Ollie?"

"Yes, Lucy?"

"I'm sorry. I never thought to make plans with you to see Bella tonight. What are you doing tomorrow?"

"It's OK, I'm going out with my friends anyway. I wanted to ask you about tomorrow, actually. Is it OK if I take Bella to meet my mum, Luce?" I can't breathe. I don't want him to take Bella anywhere without me and I certainly don't want him introducing her to his family. She's mine! My Bella!

"I'm not sure Ollie... I..." What do I say?

"It's OK, Luce. If you're not ready yet it's fine. I do want Bella to meet my family soon, though." I can hear my heart loudly in my ears. Mamma won't like this. Shit! Bella has another grandmother, shit!

"Ollie?"

"Yes?" He sounds pissed off.

"I just want to make proper plans, that's all, you know, tell Bella. Why don't we tell her tomorrow and arrange a date?"

"OK. Lucy?"

"Yes?" Now it's my turn to be huffy.

"Thank you. I know this is hard and I don't mean to make you uncomfortable." I sigh, this time because I know I've been a bitch.

"Oliver?" He laughs at my use of his name.

"Yes, Lucia." Now I giggle.

"I'm sorry." I can just hold back the tears. I love him and I don't want to hurt him but honestly, in my ideal world, there would just be me and him and Bella. Wanting him, needing him, just won't go away.

"Lucy, let's not fall out. No more sorrys, OK? Let's just make plans for tomorrow like you said."

I nod my head and smile with a heavy heart.

****

Emilia and I are heading to the White Hart, our local pub. I'm wearing my favourite LBD. A simple, fitted, sleeveless, black dress that finishes above the knee. The evening air is warm so simple black summer sandals are my choice of footwear. I've tied my hair back in a ponytail. Em is dressed similarly in a short summer dress but her one is bright blue. She always seems to carry off colour better than me. We're arm in arm as we stroll to the pub, enjoying each other's company.

"So, how's things going with Kyle, Em?" She's talked about him when we've spoken on the phone but I sense she's not been too open with me. They've been out quite a lot in the last few weeks and my guess is that Emilia is getting scared. Scared that she might really like him. This is the first man she's been out with more than once since she started dating again after losing Jamie. She sighs and glances sideways at me before smiling tentatively.

"I really like him, Luce. He's just, well we have so much in common and I love being with him." I reach over and kiss my sister's cheek.

"Well, that's good news. Why do I get the feeling there's a big 'but' coming up in this conversation?"

"Hmmm, I just feel guilty, Lucy. You know I never thought I'd find anyone after I lost Jamie. Not someone who could mean as much, and well, Kyle, well he's getting under my skin and I feel like I'm being unfaithful to Jamie."

"Well, you know Jamie would want you to live happily ever after, don't you? And he wouldn't expect you to do that alone, sweetheart. I can't even begin to imagine what it must be like to have lost the love of your life, although I miss Jamie every day, but I think, in time, your heart can love another, Em. And Kyle is such a sweetie." I glance at my beautiful sister and she gives me another tentative smile.

"So, you think Jamie would be OK with me falling in love again?" she looks and I nod my head. I can feel the lump in my throat.

We walk into the pub and are greeted by many familiar faces from the past. There are people I don't know who know Em really well. She started going out again not that long ago. Sarah really helped her, along with Em's friend, Louise. They have been regulars in the White Hart over the last few months. We did call Sarah earlier about meeting us tonight but Ben's out so she couldn't make it and Louise is on holiday until next week. I make myself noticed at the bar and order our drinks. We've decided on wine tonight so I've ordered a bottle. The evening air is warm so we head out to the beer garden at the back of the pub. It's busy, the tourists are out in full force. Em spots a small table and heads over to grab it. We get comfy and I pour the wine.

"There's a band on later, Luce, should be good. They've played here a few times now and the crowd gets bigger every time." I grin. Em and I love a good dance.

"So, where's Kyle tonight?"

"He's out with Ben and a few of the lads. They may come in here later so you can get to know him better." I like the idea of that. I want to get to know Kyle. I'd also like to warn him not to hurt my sister. If she's ready to give him her heart, he had better be good to her. I'm guessing that if she likes him that much, he's not the type to mess her around, but I would like to warn him all the same. Em is a good judge of character. I used to wonder why she thought so much of Ollie when he was horrible to me, but now I know what she saw in him.

"Lucy?" I look up and my sister's staring, her head tilted, a smirk on her face.

"Sorry, Em, did you say something?"

"Yes, I asked how things are with you? How's it going now that Ollie is in Bella's life? It must be strange. Do you ever talk about what happened, you know when he dumped you?" I place my glass on the table and glare at my sister. She smiles.

"I can't believe you could be so heartless, Emilia." She laughs, her head thrown back in amusement.

"Emilia!"

She just laughs harder. I can't help but smile. It's Em's way of talking about a tricky situation. Make light of it first, then it's easier to tackle.

"It's OK." That's all I can say. She stops laughing and frowns.

"Oh, Luce, I'm sorry. Is it that hard?" I nod my head.

"He gets on just great with Bella which is lovely, really lovely. It's just difficult having him in our lives and not being with him, Em. You know I've loved him forever and that isn't changing. I'm trying to be his friend, but honestly…" I look at her face and see the tears in her eyes.

"Why don't you give him a chance to make amends, Lucy? If you love him, don't give up, sweetie. Love like that doesn't come around too often. Make the most of it. He's perfect for you, always has been, and if Baby Bella loves him, then you three should be together." I hug my sister tightly, wanting and wishing I could just let go and do what she said but I'm so damned scared that my heart will be broken again.

"Hey, you two, you having a heart to heart or can we join you?" Emilia pulls away with a very girlie, teenage, blushing grin on her face as I take a look at Kyle who is smiling back in much the same way. Oh Gosh, they have got it bad! I watch as Em jumps up and

Kyle takes her in his arms. They look so perfect together, and honestly, they look like they're completely in love!

"Come and join us, Kyle, we need to get to know each other, I think." I grin at him as he shyly smiles back.

"Hi, Lucy, I will but Ben and the others are with me, can we all join you?" I look over and feel my heart stop. Ollie is standing chatting to his cousin, Adam, the barman from the golf club and to Ben. Jordan and Mark, two of our old mates from school are also with them and they look to be having a really good time. I just hope that seeing me won't spoil Ollie's night. I look at Em, who is waiting for my reaction before she replies. I give her a reassuring smile; how can I possibly spoil her night? She's so pleased to see Kyle! I watch, my heart in my mouth, as Kyle motions for the others to come over. They're all engrossed in conversation as they meander through the sea of tourists and their offspring to get to us. I'm holding my breath as I wait for him to notice me. I can't do it, look at his face, so I look down. Kyle is busy chatting and pulling up more chairs when I look up and see Ollie watching me. He doesn't speak, he doesn't smile, he's just watching. I feel so nervous, and crestfallen, like I just met the man of my dreams only to find he's married. He doesn't look happy. I grab my drink and empty the glass. I reach over to the table to pour myself some more. My hand is shaking, shit!

"You OK, Luce?" Em is watching me with a concerned look on her face. I smile and nod. I've lost the power of speech right now. I close my eyes, listening to the happy chatter going on around me. I cover my face with my hands, rubbing to try and erase the discomfort I'm feeling right now. I smell him before I open my eyes, his gorgeous scent. He's next to me. I can feel the heat spreading through me as I feel his arm touch me.

"Hey." Just that one word has my belly doing flick-flacks and my heart racing. I move my hands away from my face and pray no-one is watching us right now because I have no idea what he's going to say, I'm only hoping he's not too angry to see me here.

"Hi." My voice is wobbly as I look sideways. He's smiling. I breathe!

"You don't mind us gatecrashing yours and Em's night out, do you?" I shake my head and smile, the blush spreading up my neck and across my face. I quickly glance to see if the others are watching – they're all busy chatting, good. I lean in a little, not wanting them to hear.

"I was worried you'd be mad. You look like you're having a good night." He turns to face me and once again, I stop breathing. As I look into his ice blues, I feel the need to kiss him. Now that would cause a scene!

"I could never be mad to see you, Lucy. We come here quite a lot these days. The local band that gig here are really good. How's Bella?" The twinkle in his eye appears and I can't help but touch his hand that's resting on his knee. It's a gesture that tells him I know how much she means to him. I watch as he looks down at my hand then back at me. He closes his eyes and when he looks back, those ice-blues are different. I pull my hand away.

"I'm sorry." He pulls it back, covering my hand with his own. My heart is racing and I feel sick with anticipation.

"Don't be sorry, sweetheart. I love your touch, it just shocked me, that's all." Just as I let myself begin to relax, I hear a voice from the past and just want to run inside.

"Oliver sex god Ashcroft, it's good to see you. Come and give me a hug, will you?" I look at Ollie who hasn't taken his eyes off me until he glances over his shoulder at Debbie. Debbie was one of the three girls that Ollie used to date when we all hung out at the pier as teenagers. Debbie never knew about the other two, she was never very bright. I watch as she grabs Ollie's arm, almost pulling him off his chair. Ollie is reluctant to move so Debbie just leans over him, her vast expanse of bosom right there, in his face.

"So, it's right what I heard then?" she looks at Ollie who's trying his best to look anywhere but at her chest.

"What's that then, Deb?"

"So, I heard you gave up dating since you found out you're a daddy. Is that right?"

He laughs, looks at me, then at Debbie.

"Well, I never was dating, as you put it, Deb. But you're right about me being a daddy. I have the most beautiful daughter called Bella." Debbie stands up, grinning.

"So, who's the lucky mummy then, Ollie? Who finally bagged you?" I notice everyone has stopped chatting now and they're watching and listening. Em steps forward but I put up a hand to stop her.

"Actually, Deb, it's me." I watch as she processes what I just said and her face turns dark red.

"No way... you two? Well, I never. So, all those times when you were mean to her, Ollie, and I thought you really fancied her, you did. See, my instincts are always right. So, what does the lovely Declan have to say about this?"

"That's none of your business, Deb." Deb turns to me and I brace myself for a mouthful, but before she can retaliate, Ollie is up out of his chair and marching her away. I warily look at the others, who are all smiling at me.

"So, you bagged Ollie did you, Luce?" Ben is grinning as the others begin to laugh. I smile and take another gulp of my wine. I'm drinking far too much, far too early, but I think I deserve it just now. I watch as Ollie takes his seat next to me. I breathe in his smell and close my eyes for a second.

"Lucy?"

"Yes?" I look at him and grin. He frowns.

"We're going to have to get used to this for a few weeks, aren't we? We'll be the gossip of Layton once people start seeing us out and about with Bella." He leans in to whisper to me. I instinctively close my eyes. There's something about him being that close that makes me close my eyes to savour the moment, like it's the last time I'll feel him near me or something.

"I can't wait to be seen out with the two of you." I feel his lips kiss the side of my head and electricity powers through me. I look up and notice Em and Kyle disappearing inside. The sound of singing tells me the band has arrived.

"Shall we go inside and watch the band? I haven't seen them before." Ollie stands and pulls me by my hand, his eyes bright with happiness.

I follow him inside and take him in, all of him. He looks gorgeous. He's wearing black skinny jeans and a light grey t-shirt with black converse pumps. As he leads me through the door to the conservatory where the band is playing, I have to squeeze past him. I stop momentarily and just look at him. I feel his breath on my face when he talks.

"Lucy, we're blocking the door, sweetheart. You can stare at me all you like once we're inside." I look back at a queue of angry faces waiting for me to move.

As we enter the room, he pulls me to him as my legs turn to jelly.

"Lucy, tell me what that was about, please? Because right now, I just want to kiss you, sweetheart. I don't want to spoil things though, if that's not what you want. Tell me no and I'll go and get a drink and try to calm myself down." I'm afraid to talk, afraid to tell him, so I nod my head. He looks confused.

"Lucy, what?" I watch as he runs his hand through his hair. I lean up on my tiptoes and whisper in his ear.

"Kiss me." I hear his gasp and look into his eyes. Hoping he wants me, really wants me because this is my first step to letting him in. As his lips crash on mine, I'm lost in my perfect world of Ollie and me. Pulses are running riot through my body as he holds me close and our tongues find each other and we taste every inch of each other's mouths. When we finally pull apart, he takes my hand and pulls me through the crowd to a corner. As we reach the corner of the room, he pulls up two chairs and pushes me down. He sits opposite, pulling up his chair so that we're as close as possible. He opens his legs so that I can fit mine inside his. I lean my hand on his thigh and take a quick gasp of air. For so long, too long, I've dreamed of touching him, really touching him. I want to leave right now and take him home with me. I don't think I can sit here and just look at him. I feel his hands either side of my face and look into those ice-blues. He pecks a kiss on my mouth and grins.

"I love you, Lucia. I love you more than life itself. You and Bella are everything to me. My world. Please tell me that kiss was the start of something, Luce, because my heart is beating out of my fucking chest right now." I can't help but giggle.

"This isn't really the place, is it, to talk about us?"

"Look, I don't care where we are if you're about to tell me you're going to give me a chance. I'll go up there on that stage and announce it to the world if you like, just tell me, please?" I look into his eyes and all I can see is love. I have to go with that and trust that he won't break my heart again. I need to be his, I need him to be mine.

"I love you Oliver, I can't stop loving you, so I have to give us a chance, right?"

He doesn't speak. His mouth is on mine before I can take a breath. He speaks through his kisses and I feel my heart soar to heights I only ever dreamed of.

"Oh my God, Lucia. I will not let you down. I will love you and our daughter forever. Please say you'll let me take care of you both?" I pull back and smile.

"Ollie, let's take things slowly." He sits back, running his hands through his hair.

"Yes, sorry, Luce. I just want to be with you. We've wasted too much time apart. I want us to be a family."

****

The band is good. They sang some of their own songs and a few covers. I've found it hard to really concentrate tonight. Ollie and I are standing to the back of the room. I have my back to him, his arms tightly around my waist. Every now and then, he leans in and kisses my neck, whispering tender words in my ear. I glance over and catch Em smiling at me lovingly. She blows me a kiss. I send her one back and giggle as she pretends to catch it like we did when we were kids. I watch as Kyle leans down and kisses her and can't help but feel giddy with happiness for my beautiful sister. She deserves to be loved and Kyle is perfect. Em and Kyle joined us for a while earlier and I grabbed the opportunity to have a chat with him. He's so in love with Em, it's almost sickening. He kept telling me how lucky he is and how he can't believe she's with him. I trust he's just what she needs and I really do believe that Jamie is looking down on them and smiling.

"Lucy, sweetheart, will you come home with me tonight? I know you said we should take it slowly and we will. I just want to spend some time with you, alone." He's turned me to face him and I can't take my eyes off his ice blues. I said slowly and I meant it. I need to know this will be OK. If I go home with him, I'm not sure I can be as cautious as I'd like. Ollie and I alone together? I'm not sure!

"Lucy!" I turn around as Em calls my name. She's grinning like a teenager as she leans in to whisper to me. "I'm going back to Kyle's tonight; will you be OK going back to mine alone?"

We agreed with Mamma and Dad that I'd stay with Em so that we don't disturb anyone when we get home. I nod my head, grinning at Kyle who looks slightly embarrassed, like I'm Em's mother or something. I give him a wink and nod my head at Em.

"I'll be fine. I'm sure Ollie will make sure I get back safely, won't you?" I look at Ollie for confirmation and he gives Em his biggest smile.

"Don't you worry, Em, I'll make sure she gets home safely." Em gives me a quick kiss on the cheek, hands me her key and she's gone. I don't mention what Ollie just asked. I'm not sure I know what to do, if I'm honest.

"Can we go and dance one last time before we go home?"

The band are doing a really good job of covering Coldplay's 'Fix You' as Ollie and I gently move to the music. I look up into his beautiful face and feel completely contented. He leans down and kisses my neck before whispering "I love you". He wins, I'm his, forever, and that's a promise!

Chapter 11

I'm usually a fairly cautious person and once I've made a decision, there's no going back. Tonight however, is an exception for several reasons. Oliver Ashcroft can be very persuasive. He has convinced me that I need to check out his place so that he can bring Bella there, knowing I'm comfortable with where she's going. I'm also very inquisitive and I desperately want to see Ollie's home, nosey I suppose you'd say. The thing that swayed me the most is the fact that I don't want to leave him tonight. I want to be with him. I want to look at him, to touch him, to listen to him talk. I just want tonight to be never ending and the longer I stay with him, the better. So here I am, about to enter Ollie's home.

All I know is that he has an apartment on a new development that he and Ben have been working on. Ollie has one of the first built, one that was originally a show home. He explained that it worked out well for him as he didn't need to buy furnishings or anything. He just moved into it as it was. The stylish, modern development is in the bay, overlooking the sea. It's to die for!

I follow him into the foyer of his apartment building where we head straight for the lift. Ollie acknowledges the concierge who politely gives me a smile. I'm in awe, wondering how many comings and goings that man watches at a weekend. It must be a fascinating job. I watch as Ollie enters a key to operate the lift and we head up. I have no idea which floor his apartment is on. We're standing on opposite sides of the lift, just staring. I look at him and admire his beauty. He's perfect in every way. I like his hair longer. I watch as he runs his fingers through it. I want to do that! I study his forearms that are muscular and defined. He has a small tattoo of a cross, only about half a centimeter wide on his right inner arm.

Just a single cross, I like it. As I trail my gaze down his face, I grin at his smile. His ice-blues are twinkling as he looks at me. I'm not sure why we're not speaking. Maybe he's as nervous as me! My heart is thumping as I ring my hands together. Maybe this wasn't such a good idea. I have goose bumps and we're only in the lift.

I jump as the lift bell pings our arrival. Ollie smirks. The doors open directly into a hallway. I step forward as Ollie reaches his arm out, leading the way.

"After you, beautiful." I feel pulses dancing through my body as I step past him out of the lift. I take a glance and watch him close his eyes. He's too good to resist. I quickly lean in and kiss his perfect mouth. His eyes shoot open, he gasps. He steps out of the lift, yanking at my arm so that I stop. He pulls me to him and folds me in his arms. I can hear my heartbeat in my ears, loud and clear. We're on dangerous ground here. You see, I've dreamed of this for so long, Ollie and I back together. He's the best sex I've ever had, and the thought of being naked with him again is driving me wild. I knew this was a bad idea. Coming here means there will be no going slow, I can feel that already. He kisses my chin lightly, his eyes transfixed on mine.

"Lucy, I think maybe this was a bad idea. I really had no intention of seducing you here, tonight. As much as I want to, I thought we should spend some time together first, and talk. But…" I smile at his 'but'.

"You're right, this is bad." I lean back a little, wanting to suggest I leave but I can't.

"I can't go, Ollie. Common sense is telling me I should go home, but I want to be with you." I feel his kiss on my neck and my knees just about buckle under me. He groans deeply in his throat then pulls away. He turns and walks down the hallway pulling me along behind him.

"Right then, Lucia, let's be sensible, we can do this." He looks over his shoulder, smiling, and I almost feel disappointed. I want him to sweep me off my feet, to take me in his arms and tell me he can't wait. To make love to me all night, telling me how much he's missed me as we re-explore each other's bodies.

He stops walking. "This is what you want, right?" I frown, nodding my head. He laughs. It's not funny... at all!

The living space of his apartment is open plan. We walk through and immediately to our right is the kitchen area, separated from the living/dining area by a breakfast bar. He leads me past the dining table to the far end of the room where there are two low, beige fabric sofas facing each other. Behind the sofas are floor to ceiling sliding doors with views over the bay. The sight is awesome. I pull my hand to my mouth as I look out. Wow!

"How high up are we, Ollie?"

"This is the penthouse, we're on the top floor of six, do you like the view?" I nod my head as I walk towards the windows. The soundproofing is good which is sad because I want to hear the sea. I turn and look at him, watching me.

"I bet it's beautiful with the doors open, listening to the sea. It's my favourite sound, one of the things I miss most about Layton." I watch as he unlocks one of the doors and slides it open.

"Here you go, the sound of home." I close my eyes and listen to the waves crashing on the shore. I can smell the sea air. This really is wonderful.

"Would you like a drink, Luce?" I open my eyes and find him standing in front of me, his head tilted as he waits for my answer.

"Yes please, what do you have?"

"Wine, spirits, beer, what would you like? Or there's soft drinks if you prefer." My head tells me to go with a soft drink but I need a drink. Tonight, I need to drink alcohol to get through it.

"A glass of wine would be nice."

"Coming right up. Red or white?"

"White please?" I watch him walk to the kitchen, admiring his rear view as he moves.

The sound of the sea catches my attention again and I move closer to the door. I stand, leaning on the doorframe, my eyes closed as the sea breeze blows on my face. Now I know why he's moved back here.

"Lucy?"

His voice breaks my thoughts. I turn and he's there, offering me a glass of wine.

"Thank you, Ollie."

"Cheers, sweetheart." His eyes glisten as we clink glasses. My heart is constantly racing just now, being here with him.

"Would you like to step outside? I know it's a bit chilly now but if you'd like to, I can get you one of my sweaters."

I can't resist. I love the sea, especially at night. It's so romantic. I nod my head as Ollie heads out of the room, I guess in search of a sweater for me. He's soon back, handing me a red hoodie, which I slip over my head while he holds my wine glass.

Stepping out onto his terrace reminds me of being on holiday. Apart from actually being at the beach in the evening when I lived in Layton, holidays are really the only other time I'd get to see the sea this late into the night. I step forward and lean against the balcony as Ollie stands next to me.

"It's nice to have someone here to share this with. I'm usually out here on my own this late at night and there's been so many times I wished I could share it. You know I dreamed that you'd stand here with me one day, Luce, I never believed it would really happen." I turn to look at him as the wind whips some of my hair from my ponytail around my face. He immediately reaches up and pushes the stray hair back. I can't help but lean into his hand. He runs his thumb down my cheek as he says my name.

"Lucy... Lucia Meyer, love of my life." I giggle, he smiles.

"I love to hear you giggle, Lucy. I love the way you crinkle your eyes when you smile. You know Bella crinkles hers in exactly the same way." He raises his eyebrows at me and I smile.

"I love having you to talk to about Bella. It's been hard, having no one to share her with these last few years. You know, all those important things, milestones. I love it that you already know so much about her. It's like you've studied her."

"I must admit, I can't help but stare in awe at her most of the time. I can sit and watch her for hours."

"Me too. When I'm not working, that's what I usually do. I like to take her to the park and watch the delight on her face when she's excited." I feel the power surge through me when Ollie places his hand over mine as I hold onto the balcony edge. I take a large gulp of wine before looking at him. He's watching me, I can feel it. I peek over the top of my glass as I drink and he grins.

"I love to watch you too. You know I've relived that week in London over and over, Luce. When you slept, I'd watch you. You look so peaceful when you sleep and the soft noises you make… well." I finish my glass of wine and place the empty glass on the table behind us. I move forward, shivering. Ollie is watching me still, and I know he's afraid to make any kind of move towards me.

"Ollie, I can't do this." His face drops and I suddenly realize what he thinks I mean.

"No, no, I mean I can't do this." I wave my hands in front of me, directing them at him and me. "I can't be here with you and stay so far apart."

He looks up, his eyes full of sorrow.

"I thought you meant you can't do us." His voice is a whisper, I shake my head vigorously as I move nearer.

"Oliver, I love you. I need you. Please hold me?"

He quickly places his glass next to mine and takes my hand pulling me towards the door. He looks over his shoulder as he speaks.

"Let's go inside, please?" I nod my head and follow him. I swallow hard. I can't do the 'taking it slowly' thing at all!

I follow him out of the living area and down the hallway. My heart is pounding and my groin is already aching. We step into a bedroom and Ollie looks at me questioningly.

"Is this OK?" I nod my head.

We stand still as he plays with a strand of my hair. Our eyes are locked. I glance at his mouth and see it curve in a smile. I lean forward and lick his lips. I hear his gasp as his hand reaches behind my head and pulls me to him. As his lips crash onto mine, he says my name, my full name, just the way I love. I close my eyes and enjoy the sensations running through me as his lips tickle tender kisses up and down my neck. He pulls his hoodie over my head then gently eases my dress off my shoulder as his trail of kisses continues. I run my hands through his hair and say his name over and over.

"Lucia, you have been in my dreams for so long, baby, so, so long. I need you so much, sweet, beautiful Lucia." I let him take off my dress and stand in front of him as he takes in my black lace underwear.

"You are so damn beautiful, baby." His kisses move from my shoulder across to the top of my bra. Pulling at his hair, I gasp as his tongue flicks over the lace, I run my hands over his back, loving that he feels so familiar and so perfect, just like my dreams. I reach up inside his t-shirt, running my fingers over his muscular stomach and chest. I pull at the bottom of the shirt and he quickly leans back to let me take it over his head. I run my fingers down his torso, licking as I go.

"Shit, Luce, this is too much, baby." He takes me by my shoulders and gently pushes me back onto the bed, reaching down to undo his jeans as I fall. I shuffle back as he lies next to me on his side. He trails his fingers across my breast and down the middle of my stomach, running them across the top of my panties then back up. I feel ready to explode right here and now. As his eyes watch my face, he gently continues the pure torture of caressing my body with his fingers.

"You know, you're always better than my dreams, baby. You are so damn perfect. If I don't make love to you soon, it's not gonna happen because I'm already about to explode, Luce." I turn on my side, our noses touching. I run my fingers through his hair as I lean in and whisper to him.

"Make love to me, baby, I need you so bad." He pushes me over as his tongue finds mine, our mouths pressed hard together as we enjoy each other's taste. I gasp as his fingers slide into the sides of my panties and pull them down. He quickly stands, pulling off his jeans and boxers as I watch, completely fixated on his perfect body. He pulls me up to unfasten my bra, then his mouth is on mine again as we fall back down together. I pull my legs up around him, his arousal rubbing me in just the right spot. He pushes up on his arms and gently begins to enter me as I cry out his name. This is heaven, I have found heaven!

"Lucia, I love you, baby."

"I love you too." As we move together, my body is in overload, pure, blissful overload. Ollie quickens the pace and I pull at his hair, calling his name quietly. A tear escapes my eye as we reach our peak together both shouting our names simultaneously.

As we lay still, neither moving, just breathing, I feel complete. Ollie smothers my face in kisses.

"Lucy, are you OK?"

There are tears. I can't help the tears. They're happy tears. Tears because he does love me. He does want to be with me and he always did, just like I do him. I nod my head as he kisses the salty tears from my face.

"Please, don't cry, baby?"

"Promise you won't leave me, Ollie. I love you so much, but last time I felt like this, you left me." I feel his mouth on mine. His kiss is one filled with hidden meanings. His kiss tells me he'll never leave me. His kiss tells me… he's sorry. I kiss him back, sending him all my love, feeling his arousal start to return. I push my groin on him as he moans.

"Lucy, Lucy, Lucy. I love you so much, baby. I'll never hurt you again, I promise."

As we start to move together again, I feel his love pour through me, my soul mate, my dream come true.

****

The morning is here too soon! I don't want this weekend to end. I have to go home to London tonight as I'm flying off to Milan early tomorrow with Lisa and Will. I have to, want to, spend today with Bella. I won't see her until next weekend at the earliest. I'm wide awake, my mind working overtime. I turn and take a look at Ollie, unable to hide the smile from my face. I watch as he sleeps. His gentle breathing is just beautiful.

The bedroom is quite bare, beige carpet and cream walls with very little furniture, but I know that once he opens the curtains, there is a view to die for from this very bed. The sea! This apartment is wonderful. I love the idea of being able to constantly see the sea. I contemplate getting up and having a peak from the window but I just can't bring myself to leave his side just yet. Instead, I place an arm around his waist and cuddle up, kissing his shoulder as I do. I smile again at the soft moan that escapes him as he sleeps.

The bleeping of my mobile pulls me from my slumber. I roll across the bed and fumble on the floor, looking for my phone. I grab it and hastily check for messages. When I'm not with Bella, my first thought is always her when my phone bleeps. It's Em. Oh shit, I didn't tell her I was coming here. She thinks I'm home alone at her place.

"So, where are you, Luce? I'm home and I have no key!" I curse as I sit up, dialing her number. She answers on the first ring.

"Em, I'm so sorry. Are you waiting outside?" She laughs.

"Don't worry, I was blagging. I'm not really at the flat, I just wanted to tease you. I guessed you'd either end up at Ollie's or he'd end up at mine with you. Either way, I knew the thought of me outside the flat would freak you out." I flop back down on the bed, relief washing over me.

"You cow, Em. That was a cruel joke." She's still giggling.

"So, are you at Ollie's then?"

"Yes." I can feel my blush emerge. How silly am I?

"So what time will you be back, just so that I know when to head home?"

"I have to go soon. I need to go to Mamma and Dad's to see Bella. I thought I'd take her to the beach today before I head back to London."

"So, are you going straight there? I can meet you if you like?" I laugh.

"Em, I am not going to our parents dressed in last night's clothes to pick up my daughter. I'll meet you back at yours. Can you give me about an hour?"

"Luce, it's really early. I'll see you there in two, OK? Give you some more time with Ollie."

I smile at her thoughtfulness.

"Lucy?"

"Yes?"

"I'm glad it's finally working out for you two. You're so perfect together." I grin.

"Thanks, Em. You two look rather good together yourselves." I can hear the smile in her words.

"See you later then, Luce. I'm off back to bed." We both giggle as we hang up. I place my phone on the floor and turn to cuddle back up to Ollie. He's watching me, a cute smile on his face.

"Morning, sexy." I lean in and kiss his lovely mouth.

"Morning, Oliver. You really are perfect to wake up with, you know." He pulls me to him, groaning as I straddle him. I sit on top of him, leaning over, my hair tickling his face and neck. His handsome features seem even better in this early morning light.

"I'm so glad this is all real. I was afraid to open my eyes in case I dreamed last night, Luce. Were you talking to Emilia just now?"

"Yes, she was just finding out if I was OK and where I am. I have her flat keys. The spares are at our parents. She'll meet me back at hers in a couple of hours." I laugh as a grin spreads across his face. He pushes me over, leaning over me.

"So, I have you all to myself for a few more hours, then?" He kisses me gently, his ice-blues burning through me.

"Mmmhmmm," my pulses are going wild at his kisses.

"I love you, Ollie." He stops, looks at me, his face full of lust, love, passion.

"God, I love you too, Lucy. Please let me spend the day with you?"

"OK, how does the beach sound with your favourite tiny princess?"

"Perfect. But first, I need to show you just how much I love you, beautiful girl." I don't put up a fight. I'm living my dreams!

****

Em and I walked up to Mamma and Dad's after we both showered and changed. I've arranged for Ollie to come here and meet Bella and me for our trip to the beach. Mamma and Dad seem happy with seeing Ollie. I know they're happy to see how much he loves Bella. I wonder what they'd say if they knew about last night. I think I'll save that snippet of news for another time. Ollie and I need to do some serious talking. Plans need to be made. God knows how, but we need to sort things out, not me and him, the arrangements about Bella. She needs him in her life, not just the odd weekend. We need to talk, that's a sure thing.

"Mummmmmyyyy." God, I love the way my baby always greets me. I take her in my arms as she runs at me, full force. I take in her baby scent and love the feel of Bella in my arms.

"Hello, Princess, did you sleep well?"

She leans back, her hands clasped behind my head as she answers.

"Yes, Mummy. I slept with Nonna, and Granddad slept in one of the guest rooms. Nonna says he snores too much." I walk into the kitchen with Bella in my arms. Em follows me, laughing at Dad and the fact that he's being bullied by a three-year-old.

"Hey, little Miss, I happened to walk past your room last night and you sounded just like Peppa Pig, so I think it's you who snores, Miss Bella." I watch my little princess chuckle at her granddad.

"That was Nonna, Granddad." Mamma gasps and we all laugh. Bella loves the constant teasing from my dad.

We all take a seat around the large kitchen table, making snoring sounds at Mamma who's busy clearing away after breakfast.

"What are we doing today, Mummy? Can we go to the beach?"

"Where are your manners, Bella?" Mamma gives Bella that look, the one she used to give Em and me. Bella gives her a cheeky smile.

"Pleeeease, Mummy?"

Oh, she's so cute.

"Actually, Daddy's going to come and meet us here, then we can all go together." I'm trying to sound natural even though there are four pairs of eyes staring at me. Bella's are glistening with delight at the idea of seeing Ollie. Mamma, Dad and Em are all watching and waiting. I stare back and when I speak, I know I sound like a petulant teenager.

"What?" Mamma and Dad share a look while Em grins at me. "It's just a trip to the beach."

They all immediately stare at me again. Em kicks me under the table. I give her a look that says shut up. She looks at Mamma who's staring between the two of us, taking everything in.

"Just a bit at a time, Mamma, that's all. We need to take things slowly." She touches my shoulder, giving me a loving smile. As she leans down and kisses my cheek, she whispers.

"Take it slow, baby girl, and it'll be just fine" Em and Dad are watching, so I just smile.

When we hear the knock at the kitchen door, I feel my heart miss a beat. Bella is down from the table in a flash.

"Daddy." The cute way she says Daddy melts my heart every time. I realise I'm grinning as I look up and find Mamma, Dad and Em all grinning back at me.

"Looks like Ollie's here, Lucia." Em's tone is teasing, just like when we were teenagers. Mamma taps her arm and gives her a look. I giggle at my sister being reprimanded, she tutts loudly. Dad scrapes his chair and stands as Bella leads Ollie into the kitchen. I watch my lovely dad walk over to Ollie and pat him on the shoulder.

"Come on in, Oliver. Sofia has just made some tea. Would you like a cup?"

My stomach is in knots. He looks adorable and I want to go over and kiss him. I stand up and lean on the back of the chair as he watches my every move. Dad looks at me then back at Ollie.

"Ollie?" Ollie looks at Dad and has no idea what he just said. Em giggles. Now I give her a look.

"Tea, son, would you like some tea?"

Dad is now holding the teapot in the air with an amused smile on his face. Ollie coughs nervously and I push back the urge to go to him and hug him.

I watch him walk towards the table as he nods and thanks Dad. He's wearing worn blue skinny jeans and a white t-shirt with scruffy pumps. His hair is still wet and I can smell his delicious smell from across the table. Bella is clinging tightly to his hand and I feel slightly jealous. I realize I'm licking my lips as I take him in. He tilts his head at me and gives me a wink. Oh my, this is going to be difficult. Mamma is still standing near me and I feel her hand touch my shoulder. She saw that, every bit of that. My lip licking, his wink. Oh, she knows this is not going slowly at all, I just know she does.

I nervously stir my tea as Dad makes idle chitchat with Ollie about work. When I take a glance, his eyes are on me. I shift in my seat, he just keeps watching. Bella is sitting in his lap playing 'one potato, two potato' with a very amused Em. I move to stand up and all eyes turn to me.

"I'll go and get our things ready for the beach." He's smiling. I can't help but smile back.

"I'll come and help you, sweetheart." It's Mamma. Oh no, maybe I'm in for a lecture.

I follow Mamma out of the kitchen, listening to the others chatter away as we head upstairs. I watch as Mamma pulls out everything we need for the beach. Most of it is already in a big hold all that she keeps ready for such occasions. There are towels, sunscreen, a hat for Bella, a bucket and spade and a spare pair of sunglasses. As she passes me the bag, Mamma smiles.

"You love him, don't you, Lucia? You love him more than life itself." I hold back the tears and just nod my head. Mamma pulls me to her and hugs me tight.

"Well just take things slow like you said so that things are sorted properly for Bella, sweetheart. You have a lot of things to consider, don't you?"

"What do you mean, Mamma?"

She tucks some stray hair behind my ear as she talks.

"Well geography for a start, Lucy. You and Bella live in London, how will that work? When is Oliver going to see you both?"

I sigh. She's right. I have thought about it but then I've just pushed it to the back of my mind. I have no idea how we will sort that little problem.

"I know. We need to have a good talk and try to sort everything. Maybe when I get back from Milan, Mamma." She shakes her head at me.

"You shouldn't put it off, Lucy. Sort it out, sweetheart, so that you can be happy."

"Come on, Mummy." Bella has appeared and is trying her best to pick up the beach bag. She's desperate to get going. I smile down at my daughter, then at my mamma. She's right but this scares me. How will we sort things?

****

I watch as Ollie and Bella run back and forth to the water's edge, collecting sea-water for their moat. Bella has the largest, most intricate sandcastle I have ever seen. I smile as I recall times when I'd sit here and feel envy as I watched other children with their daddies, building sandcastles, and now look at my girl and her daddy. I close my eyes in the heat of the sun and think about the conversation I had earlier with Mamma. How will we conquer the problems of where we live? I love my job and I love living in London. My life has been there for so long now. I know I miss Layton but that's because it's where I grew up. I'm not sure I could come back, and anyway, Ollie hasn't mentioned anything like that. Fear runs through me. The thought of this not being a permanent set up frightens me.

I open my eyes to find Ollie watching me. He puts down his spade and crawls across the blanket to me. He sits down beside me and leans his arm against mine. It's the closest we've been since I left him this morning. I close my eyes and enjoy feeling him so close.

"Are you OK, beautiful?"

His voice is a whisper. I swallow hard. Just hearing his endearment melts my heart. I look at him, nodding my head.

"You look worried, Lucy, what's wrong?" he pushes some hair out of my face. I watch as he licks his lips. My mind is all over the place right now. I want, more than anything, to kiss him, to be kissed by him. He leans in to whisper. I catch my breath at the feel of his breath on my skin.

"I love you. So damn much, it hurts. Please tell me if something is bothering you?" I look into his ice blues, glance at Bella who is in her own world of sand building, then I kiss him. Very quickly but very directly, I kiss him. The feel of his lips and the sound of his gasp sends tingles through my whole body. I smile.

"I love you too. I'm just scared about how we can make things work that's all. We need to sort things and we don't have much time, do we? I'm going back to London tonight and then I'm off to Milan for a week. How are we going to live so far apart, Ollie?" He runs his hands through his hair. The look he gives me tells me he's been thinking about this too.

"We can talk, Lucy. We can talk as often as you like. I'm always available on my phone. While you're away, we can make plans and sort this, I promise."

"But how? Bella and I live in London, our lives are there, my job is there. You have a new life here." He looks out to sea, his face etched with worry.

"I know but we'll find a way. Please say you'll try, I promise I will."

I don't have time to answer. Bella is bored with building and wants her daddy's attention again. He looks at me with concern as he's dragged off back down to the water's edge. I watch them, the two people I love the most in this world, and I worry. Should I offer to give up my life and move back here? Do I want to do that? I know I don't want to lose Ollie again, that's for sure.

Chapter 12

Lisa and I clamber into the foyer of the Four Seasons hotel in Milan, hastily following a quick marching Will. He has no time for site seeing or looking at this magnificent hotel we're booked into. The hotel is a converted fifteenth century convent and it is extravagance at its best. Lisa and I share a grin as we wait for Will to check us all in. He makes sure we're all on the same floor with adjacent rooms. He likes to have us on call wherever we are. The fact that we're in this spectacular hotel in beautiful Milan makes no difference, we will be at his beck and call just as if we were in the office.

We'll have our first meeting at dinner tonight. We're seeing the art director, Adriano Giannini, and local photographer, Giovanni Centriti, to go over plans for the week. Will has ideas for a men's fashion shoot at one of the main parks here in Milan. He wants to check out locations and put together ideas with the others. Lisa and I booked the meetings with local professionals and need to be on hand to make any more arrangements as the week goes on and plans forge ahead. We also have to liaise with our London office, making sure anyone needed from there is added into the plans.

Lisa and I are also hoping for some time to shop in this fashion paradise, that's if Will actually has a heart. I love him to bits but he can be so focused sometimes, he forgets that we need down time. Shopping here will be a perfect break for us girlies.

We're sharing a room. Something that Lisa and I asked for. We have been friends for so long and there seems no need for the expense of two rooms when we've spent plenty of time in shared rooms on holidays together. This part of the trip is the only bit that feels like a holiday. Lisa and I take a while to enjoy the balcony that overlooks the landscaped courtyard before we are summoned back to work.

"So how did the weekend go, Luce? Did things work out OK with Bella seeing Ollie?" I know I'm blushing, I can't help it. She's watching as her mouth falls open.

"You didn't! Lucy, did you and Ollie…?" I nod my head and take a sip of water.

"It sounds so cheap now but it wasn't, Lisa."

"Hey who said it was cheap? He's the father of your child and you've always loved him, Luce. So, come on, tell me all about it? How did you two finally get together?"

Lisa crosses her legs and leans forward, ready for my tale of love and passion. I feel excitement run through me just thinking about my time with Ollie.

****

We finally dragged ourselves back inside to get ready for dinner with Lisa constantly gushing about my weekend. I must admit it does sound romantic and I do feel completely bowled over with love. We're already dressed in our best work/evening attire. Lisa is in a knee-length, grey, crepe dress that looks adorable and I'm wearing a light blue, short-sleeved, knee-length dress. We've tried to go for elegance seeing as we're dining in Milan and we're representing the magazine. Fortunately, the dresses are from our wardrobe department so the fact that they're designer has had no bearing on our bank accounts!

I step out onto the balcony to quickly phone Bella and say night-night to my princess.

"Hi, Mamma, is Bella OK?"

"Hi, sweetheart, she's just fine. She's playing a game of cards with your dad before bed. I'll go and get her, hang on."

"Mummmmyyy. I miss you." My heart swells and I feel homesick for my baby. I close my eyes and imagine her smell. I know she'll be all clean and fresh in her pyjamas, just how I like her best.

"Bella, Princess, I miss you too. Are you winning at cards?" She chuckles and I grin. I know my dad always lets her win, he can't help himself, the big softy.

"Granddad is trying, Mummy, but you know he can't play very well. Nonna says he has a very tiny brain like a pea." We both laugh and I know my baby is just fine with my special parents to love her while I'm away.

"Sweetheart, I have to go now so you make sure you sleep well and I'll call you in the morning, OK?"

"Yes, I know. Daddy said that too." My heart just missed a beat. Of course! Ollie will have called to say night-night too. I swallow hard.

"Did Daddy call already, Bella?"

"Yes, and he said he loves us both and blew me a great big kiss. Mummy?"

"Really, sweetheart?"

"I love my daddy, do you love him too?" I close my eyes and try to think what to say. Should I be honest or should I not say just yet?

"Daddy is very special, Bella, and I know you love him and he loves you."

"He loves you too. Do you love him?"

Sometimes my daughter is just too damned clever for her age!

"Yes, baby, I do." There, I said it. Oh, God, I hope she doesn't go tell Mamma that I told her.

"Good. Night-night then, Mummy, sleep tight, don't let the bed bugs bite."

"Night-night, sweetheart." I hang up and feel sad. I hate nights when I don't put my baby to bed. She seemed happy with my simple yes as an answer. Maybe that's all she needed for now.

I contemplate phoning Ollie. I want to talk to him about Bella. I love that we can share her. I love that he loves her like I do. Lisa calls to me from inside. We need to go down for dinner. I don't have time. I feel regretful. I can't think of anything I'd like more than to hear his voice right now. I'll call him later, after dinner. I head back inside, not really feeling the enthusiasm I need for this meeting, at all. I check my appearance in the mirror as I walk by, Lisa chuckles.

"You look beautiful as ever, Luce. You OK, you look worried?" I sigh.

"I'm fine, Lisa, I just don't want to be here right now. No offence meant by that, I love you, you know that. It's just, well there's so much going on right now in my life. I want to be in Layton, with Bella and Ollie. I want to be making plans for our future. We have so much to talk about. This weekend sort of, well we needed to talk, not—" She cuts me off.

"You had the best time, didn't you? Was it perfect?" I nod my head, blushing yet again.

"So, stop stressing. We'll be back by the weekend, if we get our fingers out and make this plan happen quicker than quick for Will, and we can, we did it before when I wanted to go away that time remember?" She pulls me to her and we hug.

"Yes, I do remember, Lise. So, now, you need to help me out. I need this trip to be as short as possible. I can't believe I'm saying that about a trip to Milan but needs must."

"Right, so come on then. Let's get as much sorted tonight, plan our visits for the next few days and make sure that Will is confident with what we come up with. Get your business head on, Lucia Meyer, we need to be on top form." I breathe deeply, pulling myself back into work mode and give Lisa a wink. I grab my bag, dropping my phone in. Oliver Ashcroft, I'll talk to you later. Right now, I need to work hard so that I can come back and be with you and our daughter, then we can make plans.

My phone vibrates in my bag as we leave the lift. I quickly check in my bag, I always panic in case there's a problem with Bella. It's Ollie. I glance at Lisa who's watching my every move.

"Can I just check this text, Lise?" She grins.

"Let me guess, its Ollie?" I nod my head and quickly open the text.

"Hey beautiful, I know you're busy but I just spoke to Bella and I can't stop thinking about you. Let me know when I can call you. I love you, baby xxxx"

I stare at the screen and know I'm grinning like a fool. I wave my phone at Lisa and walk towards the reception area of the hotel. I press his number and listen, hoping he answers.

"Lucy?"

"Hey."

"I thought you'd be busy. Are you OK?"

"I'm fine. I'm just about to go for dinner. It's our first meeting of the week. I spoke to Bella just a few minutes ago. She said you called." I hear him sigh. I hold my breath. Something is bothering him.

"Yes, I did. I know you can't really talk now but I'd like to have Bella over to stay soon. I want to be with her, Lucy. I hate the thought that she's just a stone's throw away and I can't put her to bed. I'd like her to stay here with me. I promise I'll look after her." He falls silent. I feel the thudding of my heart in my chest.

"Lucy?" he sounds worried.

"I know, Ollie. This trip couldn't have come at a worse time. I promise we'll talk later and we'll make plans. We can make arrangements for her to come and stay with you. Can I call you later? It might be after eleven."

"Please call me, Lucy. Oh, and Luce?"

"Yes?"

"I'd prefer it if you both came to stay. I love you and I want to be with you so damn much, Lucy." I smile as I hear Lisa calling me.

"I have to go, Ollie. I'll call you later, though. I love you."

As I walk to Lisa she pulls me by the arm and literally frog marches me to the dining room.

"Come on, Mrs Lovesick Lucy. We have a dinner to get through and you need your head straight for this. We need to make sure Will chooses that park we like for the shoot. You know he was looking at a shopping centre. I know its legendary but really, the man has no taste."

Adriano the art director makes a big fuss of us both as we reach the table. We've worked with him a few times before and spent many evenings entertaining him when he's been in London. We greet each other with the traditional air kisses and Adriano introduces us to Giovanni, the local photographer who we haven't met before.

"Good evening, ladies, it's a pleasure to meet you both." Lisa and I are both swooning at his every word. The way he pronounces everything in his Italian accent is way too sexy! Giovanni is gorgeous. He is about six feet tall, skinny with long, dark hair pulled back in a ponytail. He's wearing skinny black jeans and a designer dress jacket over a dark t-shirt, which looks so damned stylish. His face is perfection and I note the look of adoration on Lisa's face as we take our seats. Will gives me a smile as I look from Lisa to him.

The evening passes quickly with Giovanni agreeing with mine and Lisa's choice of the park for the shoot. He knows Parco Sempione well and thinks the 'Bridge of Mermaids' set in the heart of the park will be perfect. Lisa and I share a smug grin that our choice is right and I catch Will grinning at our childish interactions.

We've made plans to meet early tomorrow. We need to be at the park for most of the day. Will wants to see the chosen settings at different times to decide which is best for lighting etc. Giovanni would like to shoot late morning and then again in the evening but Will wants to check for himself before agreeing.

We're seated in the bar after dinner and are getting along just fine. It turns out that Adriano and Giovanni are old friends and we soon get to know Giovanni. He's single, having split up with his fiancée about six months ago. I sneak a peak at Lisa when he tells us this and catch the glint in her eye. Will is first to leave the group. I know he wants to go and phone home. My thoughts are much the same. I desperately want to go and phone Ollie, I can't leave Lisa alone with the two men though, it would appear rude. Adriano married last year and his beautiful wife Maria is expecting their first child soon. I catch him looking at his watch and smile when he sees me.

"I'm going up now, Adriano, would you like to walk me to the lift?" He gives me a grateful wink and nods his head enthusiastically. As we stand, the others are deciding what to do.

"One more drink, Lisa?" Giovanni holds up his glass as he asks and Lisa gives him her sexiest smile as she nods in response.

"Right then you two, good night. I'll see you in a while, Lisa and you in the morning, Giovanni?" He leans over and kisses my hand. I feel my blush. I can't help it. He's hot!

I walk as quickly as possible along the hotel corridor to our room, pulling my phone out as I enter. I'm already dialing Ollie's number before the door has even closed. He answers on the first ring as I kick my shoes off and dive onto my bed.

"Lucy?" His voice is quiet.

"Ollie, did I wake you?"

"I must have nodded off in front of the TV. It's a good job you called or I'd have been here all night. How was your dinner?"

"It was good, actually. The art director and photographer agreed with mine and Lisa's choice of venue for the shoot, which is great. We have an early start tomorrow. Will wants to check the location for lighting at all times of the day. There will be a lot of hanging around I think. What about you?"

He sighs. "Just TV for me. I have been thinking, though, Luce. How are we going to sort things?"

My heart stops and I swallow hard. I lean up on my elbow, sighing too.

"Well, we need to build things up for Bella. Maybe if we spend some weekends with you in Layton and then you come and stay in London?"

"I'm not sure, Lucy. That won't really solve anything, will it? I want us all to be together permanently. Is that what you want?"

His voice is quiet as he asks. I sense he's a little scared to ask.

"Yes, it is." I'm scaring myself with what I've just admitted. How will we sort this?

"Right so one of us needs to move. I think maybe I should speak to Ben. You can't move with your job, can you, so maybe I need to commute. I have a place in London anyway so I can work from there most of the time. What do you think?" I don't speak immediately. I'm blown away that he's willing to do this for me and Bella. I wipe away a tear. I am so touched by this, I'm finding it hard to say anything.

"Lucy?"

His voice is still quiet. I swallow before answering.

"I love you, Oliver, thank you." My voice is a whisper. The emotion is raw as I speak.

"Hey, I love you two more than life itself and I want to be with you. I will do whatever I have to, Lucy, to be with you."

"What if Ben says no?"

He laughs quietly. "Sweetheart, he won't say no. I've been commuting while we set up the business. It's not as easy as living in Layton, I must admit, but being with you is my top priority now. Ben will understand that, so please don't worry."

"Bella will be so excited, Ollie. Will you come and live at my place?"

"That's up to you. Maybe you should come and see my place first. Do you rent your flat?"

"Yes."

"Mine's paid for so maybe you should move in with me. When you're back, I'll take you and Bella, see what you think. It will save paying rent if you do."

"Well Lisa and I are working hard so that we can be back at the weekend. Having agreement on the location has saved us a day already. If we had to trawl different venues, we could have been held up, so hopefully I'll see you and Bella sooner than we thought."

"If you're back, Lucy, will you and Bella come and stay over at the weekend, baby? I'd love to put her to bed and wake up with her in the morning." I smile at the thought. It's such a romantic idea, the three of us together. I'm nodding my head in response as I smile to myself.

"Lucy?"

"Sorry, yes, Ollie. If I'm back, we'll come for a sleepover. Please don't tell Bella, though. I don't want to get her hopes up in case I'm not back in time?"

"I can't wait. Should I buy anything special? I'll get her favourite cereal and some chocolates and sweets. Which are her favourite crisps, Lucy?" I smile at his enthusiasm.

"Pomme bears."

"What?"

I laugh. "They're teddy shaped crisps."

"Right, pomme bears, will you text me so I know what to look for?"

I laugh again. "She really won't mind what you feed her, sweetheart."

"Well, I want it to be special for my girl."

"OK."

I sit up as the door opens. Lisa has the biggest grin on her face as she walks towards me. She places her finger over her lips to indicate that she'll be quiet as I finish talking to Ollie. I pull myself off the bed and head outside to the balcony. Lisa has disappeared into the bathroom.

"Ollie, I have to go. We've got an early start in the morning and I don't want to keep Lisa awake."

"I can't wait to have you back, sweetheart. Will you be able to call me tomorrow? I can call you but I won't know when it's convenient."

"I'll call. Are there any times you won't be able to speak?"

"Call me anytime. I love you."

"I love you too, night."

"Night."

Lisa and I share mirrored grins as I walk back into the room and she emerges from the bathroom.

"Happy?"

She nods as she replies.

"Very, and you?"

"Very."

"Perfect." We chorus as we both jump into our beds, each lost in a world of men and romance.

****

Although it's the crack of dawn, I can't help but share my friend's enthusiasm as she gives me a second by second account of her hour alone with Giovanni while we munch on our continental breakfast. Will has yet to appear which worries me a little as he's always first to arrive. When he does finally make an appearance, he looks worried and a little pale in the face. I'm not sure he's actually had any sleep. I frown. This doesn't look promising.

"Morning, Will, are you OK, you don't look so good?"

"Morning, ladies, I'm OK. I didn't sleep well, though." He runs his fingers through his hair as Lisa and I wait patiently for him to continue. Will plonks himself into a seat, leaning his dead weight heavily onto the breakfast table.

"My wife, my beautiful wife, is threatening to leave me." Lisa and I gasp simultaneously. I'm not sure what to say. Should I ask for more details or should I just wait for Will to add more to his shocking story? Lisa breaks the deathly silence as she leans over and grabs Will's hand in hers.

"Oh, Will, I'm so sorry. Whatever happened? You and Marianne always seem so happy, so... together." I nod agreement at my friend's analysis as Will looks between us. I hold my breath. I'm sure he's going to cry. He rubs his hands roughly over his face as Lisa and I share a look. The seconds seem to move so slowly as we wait for him to talk. I tentatively look around the room, we're the only ones here, thank goodness.

"You remember how we went through a rough patch about six months ago?"

He looks at us, Lisa nodding and me shaking my head. I had no idea. Lisa is obviously more observant than me, or just nosey!

"Well I had a fling with one of the models on the summer shoot when we were in Mexico. It was stupid, I was stupid. I went home and confessed all to Marianne. She went to stay with her mum for a few weeks but we worked through it and she came back. I thought everything was OK. I thought we were back on track."

"So, what's happened to change things, Will?" I let Lisa do the talking. I just listen, shocked to hear that Will would do such a thing, if I'm honest.

"She phoned me late last night, said we needed to talk. She wanted to wait until I got back but I knew something was wrong, really wrong, so I pushed and pushed her to talk last night. God, I wish I hadn't." I brace myself, fearing the worst. Not really knowing what the worst will actually be.

"She told me that she found out she was pregnant two weeks ago." I sigh with relief. A baby might be just what they need to bring them back together. I know you shouldn't really think like that but honestly, the bloke looks broken and I'm hurting for him right now."

"So, you didn't plan to have kids, then?" that's it, Lisa, keep asking. He shakes his head, his eyes awash with unshed tears.

"No, but you know the idea sort of appeals when faced with it. But I never got to choose, you see, she went and had an abortion yesterday. She planned it for when I was away. And now she's regretting it and blames me. She says she only got rid of the baby because she didn't think I'd stay around and now, she's a mess, a real mess." I can't control the tear that escapes. I love my baby more than life. I can't imagine what Marianne or Will are going through right now. What a mess! Lisa and I share a concerned look as Will covers his face with his hands. I speak for the first time.

"Will, why don't you go home and be with Marianne? You can't deal with this from here. You need to be together. Lisa and I can take care of things here. We'll make you proud, won't we, Lise?" I watch my friend shuffle nervously in her seat as Will looks up hopefully.

"Really, would you be OK?" I nod my head enthusiastically, my smile giving nothing away as to the nerves I'm really feeling at the offer I just made. Lisa coughs and stares at me. I give her, then Will, a reassuring smile.

"We can do it. We've worked with Adriano loads of times before. He knows what you like, we know what you're expecting so I'm sure we can do it." I give Lisa a look that silently tells her to agree with me. She plants a fake smile on her face and nods her head at Will when he glances at her.

"Girls, that would help so much. Maybe if I go home today, I can salvage something and maybe Marianne will be OK. Maybe we'll be OK." His voice is a whisper. It's as though we're not here and he's speaking to himself.

"Do you want me to see if I can get you a flight today then, Will?" Lisa has gone into practical mode, thank God. Will nods agreement and Lisa leaves the table, phone in hand as she tries to sort a flight for Will.

"I'm so sorry, Will. I really am. I don't know what else to say." I look at my boss and he gives me a tiny smile.

"Hey, you girls are the best. I know you'll do me proud and with any luck, I'll be able to sort out my marriage and I'll forever be in your debt, Lucy. Thank you so much for offering to do this. I know Lisa's a little more skeptical than you, so thanks."

"We'll try our utmost to get this perfect for you." Lisa is on her way back, ever the efficient assistant.

"Flight sorted, Will. You need to go and pack and leave for the airport in about half an hour, OK?"

We watch as he jumps from his seat and heads towards the lift. His mind is already elsewhere, bless him.

"Well that wasn't the start to the day we expected, Luce. Let's cross our fingers we don't encounter any more hiccups today or this short trip could take longer than you want." Oh God, I hadn't thought about that. Getting home for the weekend isn't looking too promising.

****

I sigh as I pick up my phone. This week is really not going to plan. The weather has been awful. The first few days went so smoothly, I suppose it was inevitable that something would go wrong. The weather was the problem, it rained all day today so we've missed a day's shoot and now we won't be leaving tomorrow as planned. I have to phone Bella and tell her. Although if past calls are anything to go by, I don't think she'll be too bothered. I also have to call Ollie who I know has plans for our big sleepover weekend.

I was right, Bella is having too much of a good time with Auntie Em to worry about seeing me tomorrow. As long as she knows I'm coming home soon, she's not worried and I'm glad about that. At least I don't have to worry about her being upset, that would kill me. I'm not so sure Ollie will be quite as understanding. He answers on the first ring and I swallow hard.

"Hey, Luce, how's it going?"

He sounds so happy to hear from me. My heart is in my mouth as I think of what to say next.

"Bad news, I'm afraid. It's rained all day so we haven't been able to go out. We have one more day's shooting to do so I'm not going to be back tomorrow." I wait… silence.

"Ollie?" I hear his sigh and my heart misses a beat.

"Right. Well there's nothing you can do about the weather, is there?" He sounds so downbeat and it's all my fault.

"I'm sorry, Ollie. I so want to come home but I have to finish this. Will is going through hell right now and the last thing he needs is a crap shoot to top off the week. We need sunshine in the afternoon and that's what the forecast is tomorrow. So, we'll finish tomorrow and get a flight back on Saturday. I just don't know when yet. We can't book until we've finished so it all depends on which flight we can get a seat on at the last minute." Another silence. I pull my phone away and check that I still have a signal – yep!

"Ollie?"

"I'm sorry, Luce, I'm just disappointed, that's all. I had everything planned for you and Bella coming over to stay and it's a big deal to me." Now it's my turn to sigh. I feel so bad!

"Well how about you have Bella over, anyway? I can phone Mamma and tell her to expect you."

Chapter 13

Choosing to let Bella go and stay with Ollie this weekend seemed like a good idea. Now I feel jealous and that's not good. I phoned Mamma who was only too pleased to pack Bella's bags and let Ollie take her away for the night. I sent him at least twenty text messages with list after list of Bella's routine and her likes and dislikes. My mind hasn't been on my job and I feel bad for Lisa. Somehow, we've got through this photo shoot with Adriano and Giovanni spurring us on. They have been a godsend. Lisa and Giovanni appear to be getting to know each other very well. I'm also jealous of them! What the hell has got into me? I have never been so discontented in my life. It's Saturday afternoon and we have to wait another five hours before we can head home. No bloody flights available and I'm miserable, truly miserable.

Lisa has gone off for a late drink with Giovanni, leaving me to wallow in self-pity in the hotel room. I check my phone – nothing! Bella and Ollie are obviously having a good time without me. I throw my phone on the bed and sulkily open the door to the mini bar. "Fuck it!" I grab a small bottle of wine and pour some into the 'not so clean' glass from the bathroom. I scoff at my elegance and shout cheers to my reflection in the mirror, feeling sad and lonely. I down my glass of wine and top up with the remains of the miniature bottle. My phone starts to ring and I laugh a sarcastic laugh.

Who wants to speak to me? They're all out enjoying life while I'm in this lonely hotel room, alone! I grab the phone and check the caller ID. It's Will. I answer, praying that he's OK.

"Will, hi."

"Lucy, how are you, sweetheart?"

"I'm OK. Waiting for a flight home. How about you? Have you managed to sort anything with Marianne?"

"Well, sort of. We're getting there. Actually, we're heading off to my in-law's place in Cannes tomorrow. That's why I'm calling. Firstly, I want to thank you and Lisa for stepping in and helping me. I don't know how or what I can do to thank you girls but I promise I will." I can't help but grin at this news. Will is a good guy. I'm not condoning what he did, or what Marianne did for that matter, but they are a good couple and they deserve to be happy.

"Oh, Will, I'm so pleased you're sorting things. That's such good news. Hey, and the photo shoot went well in the end. I think you're gonna love the finished pictures. How long will you be away for?"

"Just the week. Will you and Lisa be able to hold the fort for me while I'm away?" I smile into the phone.

"Of course we will, boss." I hear his laugh and it makes my heart swell. He's almost back to the old Will we love so much.

"Weren't you going home this weekend, Luce?"

"Yes but don't worry, Bella is all sorted and that's what matters, so it's all good." I feel my heart physically ache when I think of Bella and Ollie together without me. Will doesn't need to know that right now. He needs to rebuild his life with Marianne.

"Luce, you're a diamond, thank you."

"Hey, go and woo your wife. I want to hear just how good things are when you get back, right?"

"I'll do my best and that's a promise, Luce. See you next week." I hang up the phone sighing. I want to go home to Layton and I can't. Shit!

I have to phone Ollie and let him down again. I really did think that no matter what, I'd arrive in Layton at some point this weekend, but it's not going to happen now. The phone rings a few times before he picks up. I smile thinking how different it is with a little one under your feet. I regularly miss phone calls because I can't get

171

there on time. I wonder if he's had the same problems getting to this call.

"Lucy?" He sounds out of breath as he almost breathes my name. I giggle.

"Did you have to run for the phone, Ollie?" I wait in the silence that tells me he's distracted.

"Hang on, Lucy. Yes, Bella, sweetheart, it's Mummy." Before we have chance to share another word, I hear my baby speak and my heart melts.

"Mummmmmyyyy."

"Hey, sweetheart. Are you being a good girl for Daddy?"

"Yessss. I was just having a wee wee, Mummy. I showed Daddy how I can wash my hands and I wet his trousers and the floor." She doesn't sound the least bit bothered. Poor Ollie!

"Well, who's a big girl then? Are you having a nice time, sweetie?"

"Yes, Mummy. We went to the park and Daddy pushed me really high on the swing. Oh, and Mummy, we fed the ducks at the pond." I smile in spite of the jealousy I feel. I'm happy, really happy that they're getting this time to bond but I want to be there with them.

"That sounds really fun, Bella. Can I speak to Daddy now, please?"

"When are you coming to take me home, Mummy?" I sigh, not wanting to tell Bella before I've spoken to Ollie.

"Soon, sweetie, really soon. I love you."

"Love you more, Mummy." She's gone and I feel my heart wrench.

"Lucy?"

"Hey." I'm grinning when he says my name. I feel all girlie and silly. Oh, I like this man so damn much its mind blowing.

"How's your trip, Luce? You ready to come home yet?"

"Hmmm, that's the trouble. I'm not going to get back to Layton this weekend, Ollie. I'll be back in London late tonight hopefully, if we get on the damned flight. The problem is that I'm needed at the office so I can't travel to Layton tomorrow. Mamma wasn't expecting me anyway when we planned this, ages ago, so there's no problem with Bella, I just…" He doesn't reply and the silence between us seems to last hours.

"Hey sometimes things just get in the way, Luce. It can't be helped." I can hear the disappointment in his voice. That reassures me that he cares.

"Well, this is unusual for me, Ollie. Will had to fly home and he's got huge personal problems that need sorting so he won't be at the office when we get back. Lisa and I need to oversee this project at least until Will returns."

"So, will it be OK for me to drop Bella tomorrow at your parents or do you want me to take her today?"

"Hey, you've got her for the weekend. You go and have fun with our daughter. Is she behaving, Ollie, because she'll get away with murder if you let her?"

"She's fine. Just perfect. I can't believe how clever she is for a three-year-old, Luce. She's gonna grow up to be a genius, you know."

"That's what I tell anyone who'll listen. She really is bright, isn't she?"

"You know she can count to twenty-five now. Oh, and she can count backwards from ten. I'm sure I couldn't do that at her age. I'm going to check with my mum tomorrow. Is it OK if Bella speaks to my mum on the phone, Luce?"

His question instantly puts a stop to the proud grin I was wearing. Oh God, his parents. Bella's other grandparents. This is weird and I'm so far away from it all.

"Yes, Ollie. Just your mum or your dad as well?" the thought of that man makes me feel sick to my stomach. I hear his shocked gasp.

"God, no. I don't really have anything to do with him now, Luce. My mum and dad aren't really together any more. They come together for the occasional family do but other than that, they barely speak."

"Oh, right. Yes, it's fine for Bella to speak to your mum. What does she want to be called, by the way?" I hear his laugh, I smile.

"She hates Grandma, is Nanna OK?"

"Hey, it's your mum's choice, not mine. Nanna sounds perfect. Bella will be so excited you know, when you tell her."

"My mum can't wait to meet Bella. I can't wait to see you again, Lucy, I miss you. Being with Bella is a constant reminder of you. She's your mini me and I love you both so much."

"Hey, we'll make sure to spend next weekend together, OK?"

"OK." I hear Bella calling Daddy continuously and can't help but smile. I hope he's coping OK and Bella's not driving him nuts.

"Ollie, I think you'd better go and sort madam out. She won't stop until you do." We both laugh as I hear him talking to Bella with his hand over the phone.

"Lucy, call me when you're back, OK?"

"I will, but call me if you have any problems with Bella, OK?"

"We're fine but yes, I will. Safe journey, sweetheart."

"Bye."

He hung up and I'm listening to a dead phone. I conjure up the picture in my mind of Ollie and Bella. I bet he's knackered really!

****

Lisa and I have been people watching in silence now for about thirty minutes. The flight that we've managed to get on is delayed so we're sat at the boarding gate with many other irritated travellers, all eager to get on the plane and head off to our destinations.

"Are you going to see Giovanni again, Lise?" I nudge my friend with my elbow as I speak quietly. She turns sideways and grins.

"Urr, yeahhh. He's flying out later this week. He spoke to Adriano and they agreed that since Will won't be around, he'd come and support us. I'm sort of hoping it's just an excuse to see me again but that's just wishful thinking."

"Well, have you arranged to meet up when he's over?" Lisa blushes. I wait in anticipation for her response.

"He's gonna stay with me." We both giggle loudly and cause many irritated passengers to check us out. There's nothing else to do here so the first sign of a drama and everybody is on it. I smile at a few friendlier faces then look back at my blushing friend.

"Wow, Lisa, he's so sexy. You lucky girl."

"I know, I keep pinching myself. Who'd believe I'd find my Italian dream man this week? The only good thing to come out of this shitty week has been meeting Giovanni." I sigh, thinking about what a difficult week it has been.

"Hey, if this all goes well and the magazine feature works, we could get promotions out of this so hold your fire on the shitty week bit, it could be a blessing in disguise." Lisa raises a disbelieving eyebrow at me. I smile, ever the positive one!

****

Walking into my silent, darkened flat, I don't feel happy at all to be home. I missed what could have been a perfect weekend with the two people who are my world and now I'm here, alone. I kick off my shoes and wearily make my way to the bedroom where I drop my bags and switch on the light. I sigh. Yes, it's the same as when I left it, only I don't feel the same. When Bella and I first moved here, I felt like the cat that got the cream. I had a brilliant job that I loved, a beautiful baby and to top it off, we had a lovely home. Tonight, yet again, I feel discontented. I switch on every light as I walk through the flat, checking out each room. As I pass Bella's room, I stop and look but I don't enter. I know if I go in there, I'll crumble. I miss my baby and I want to be with her and Ollie in Layton. For the first time, I realize that maybe London isn't the be all and end all. I need my family to be happy. Bella has always been here with me and so I've been happy but right now, the prospect of being a happy family here in London doesn't sound as good in comparison to a family life by the sea, in my home town, surrounded by my closest friends and family. Ohhhh…

****

I've been busy right through the week. I've made daily calls to Bella at my parents and she's filled me with exciting stories about her time spent with Daddy. Mamma and Dad had Ollie round for dinner, which pleased me until I heard that my sister, Em, was there too. Somehow that didn't seem right. Everyone but me!

Giovanni arrived yesterday and has been such a support to Lisa and me. We decided to shoot some internal shots as an extra feature, which Will knows nothing about. I hope he's pleased with the finished pictures, I'm thrilled.

Adriano is due to arrive at the office just before lunch so we have meetings planned all afternoon.

I look up when Will's assistant, Suzie, taps gently on the office door that I share with Lisa. Lisa is out with Giovanni on some project that I choose not to ask about, it's definitely nothing to do with work, so I'm alone.

"Lucy, there's a man here to see you. He doesn't have an appointment but he says you know him." I frown in wonder.

"What's his name, Suzie?"

"Mr Ashcroft." I grin as my heart flutters. Ollie has come to see me. Oh God!

"Well show him in, Suzie." Suzie grins back, looking happy that I'm so pleased with my visitor. I stand up and straighten my clothes, pulling my skirt straight. I rush round from the desk to the mirror on the opposite wall. I just need to check I look half decent for my man.

"Don't spruce yourself up on my behalf, young lady." I pull my hand to my mouth in shock as I catch his reflection in the mirror. A

176

sickly smile is spread on his face as he gloats at my obvious discomfort. It's Ollie's dad. I spin around and look for Suzie, I need support but she's already left. I watch as Ralph Ashcroft confidently walks across the office and takes a seat on one of the comfy sofas that are situated in one corner of the room. For a second, I think about my manners and ask myself if I should offer him a drink. My first instinct is NO! But then I think how much better than him I am, so I politely offer a beverage to the nasty old man who I hate so much.

I watch my hand shake as I pour his water. I know he's watching my every move and he's enjoying the fact that I'm nervous. I take deep breaths and tell myself to calm down. I smile a sweet smile as I pass him the glass of water and take a seat opposite him.

"What can I do for you, Mr Ashcroft? Your visit is most unexpected." He nods his head and I brace myself for what he has to say.

"I hear you're back in touch with Oliver." I nod my head, not sure what to actually say to this man. He managed to come between us before so I'm pretty sure this visit is not to welcome me to the family.

"And you have a daughter. Is it right that the child is Oliver's?" I nod my head, anger rising through me at his tone when speaking about my daughter. I'm not a confrontational person but when it comes to Bella, I will fight anyone.

"You obviously know the answer to this. I take it that's why you're here. Oliver and I have a daughter, Bella." His expression shows no emotion when I speak. He's hard as stone. I feel a chill run through my body.

"Well, Miss Meyer, I think you probably know that I'm not a fan of your relationship with my son, never have been. The fact that you got yourself pregnant to trap him just proves what a gold digging, low life you are. I've come here to tell you that there is no way on this earth that I am going to let you trap my son. He is heir to my business and my money and I am not letting you and your low life family get your grubby hands on any of it." I swallow the tears that are pushing hard to escape. I look away, unable to look at his stony face for a second longer. His eyes are full of hatred and I feel like I want to run and hide. When I turn back, he's leaning towards me offering me an envelope.

"I've set up a trust fund for your daughter. There's enough for a good education and more to set her up later on. The paperwork here gives you details of how to access the money. I've also set up an account for you with a substantial amount to look after the two of you until the child turns eighteen. The only thing I ask is that you leave Oliver alone, for good. Tell him the child isn't his, he'll soon get over it and move on." I watch as his hand shakes the envelope in my direction. I look straight into his cold eyes, lost for words as this cold-hearted man tries to buy me off. I shake my head and he laughs.

"This is not up for negotiation, Miss Meyer. I'm offering you a good life in exchange for my son's freedom. If you refuse, I will make your life a living hell until eventually, you give in. By then, there will be no money and rest assured there will be no Oliver either. Take the best option now, my dear, think about the child." Standing, I look down at this despicable man and drum up some courage to speak.

"I love your son more than life itself. He loves Bella and I, and nothing you can say or do will stop our love. Money will never be a substitute for us being together. You tried once before to come between us and you failed. I will never give in to your threats, Mr Ashcroft, so I suggest you take your envelope and get out of my office now before I have you forcibly removed." With that, I stride to the door and pull it open, not giving him another chance. I catch Suzie's eye as she looks up from her desk and she rushes over, sensing that all isn't well.

"Suzie, Mr Ashcroft is just leaving, please show him out?" I smile at Suzie before turning to a stiff looking Mr Ashcroft whose face is beetroot red with anger. He pushes past me nearly knocking me off my feet before turning with one last venomous sentence.

"This isn't the end, Miss Meyer. You've picked the wrong person to fight with, I guarantee that." I fall back against the doorframe and watch as he leaves with Suzie running along behind him. I don't move until I hear the ping of the lifts arrival and watch Suzie walk back alone. She rushes towards me and I usher her into the office locking the office door behind us. I find my way back to the sofas, sinking down as the sobs begin. Suzie pats my back and makes cooing sounds as I cry like a baby.

"Lucy, tell me who that man was. Do I need to call anyone for you?" I try and calm down, wiping constantly at my eyes with scratchy tissues from the box on the table. Just then I notice the envelope, still there. The bastard left it!

"That was Ollie's Dad, Suzie. He hates me, thinks I'm after his money and that I got pregnant to trap Ollie. He came to try and buy me off." Suzie gasps as I try and calm myself down.

"Jesus, Lucy, that's terrible. I must say I was shocked at your response when I told you he was here. Such an offensive looking man. I just thought maybe he had a kind side that you knew." I laugh at Suzie's innocence.

"No, Suze. I stupidly thought Ollie was here to see me when you said Mr Ashcroft. I would never have agreed to see that man if I'd known." Suzie gasps again.

"Oh, Lucy, I'm so sorry. I never should have let him in."

"Hey it's not your fault. He'd have found a way to see me no matter what. He's evil and determined not to let me and my daughter be happy with his son."

"Are you going to tell Ollie, Lucy?" I look at Suzie and my heart skips a beat. How the hell can I tell him that? It sounds ridiculous to me and I just witnessed it so I'm sure Ollie will think I'm making a drama out of a misunderstanding.

"Suzie, can you keep this to yourself, please? I'm not sure how or if I want to tell Ollie. God, what a bastard, Suzie!" I look to this poor girl who has been forced into being part of this dreadful situation. She smiles to reassure me but I guess she wishes she hadn't just experienced that little scenario.

"Hey, Lucy, my lips are sealed. I do think you should tell Ollie some time soon, though. You shouldn't keep this from him, you know." I nod my head at this lovely girl who cares even though she doesn't know the whole story.

"Oh, I will, Suzie, I'm just not sure how to, if I'm honest." I sigh. I am so damned pissed off right now.

Chapter 14

As the train pulls into the station at Layton, I peak out of the window, eager to catch a glimpse of those two, special people who I love with all my heart. I'm not disappointed as I catch sight of my beautiful Bella in the arms of the most handsome man I have ever met. I love watching them especially as they can't see me. Watching their interaction and the way Ollie kisses Bella between words as he speaks to our daughter – my heart is melting. I wait patiently as the train slows into the station, watching for the light to glow on the button that operates the train doors. I press to open and feel a little discomfort after what happened a few days ago. Surely that nasty man would change his mind if he only took some time to see his only son with his only granddaughter. I know deep within that this is never going to happen. That man obviously has a plan for Ollie that doesn't include me or Bella. I swallow the tears that have threatened to rear their ugly heads so many times in the last few days. I force the smile of joy on my face and jump from the train. In spite of everything that has happened, I will not let that evil man spoil this reunion with my beautiful daughter and the love of my life.

"Muuuummmmmyyyyy." I watch as Ollie lets Bella down and she runs to me. All bad thoughts leave my head as I relish the love that this perfect little girl has for me. As I lift her in my arms, I bury my nose in her neck and inhale her perfect scent. My baby! No one will ever take her from me. I make a silent promise to myself that I will fight that retched old man if I have to die doing so. He will not hurt the people who I love more than life itself… ever!

He has never looked better, Oliver Ashcroft is most definitely sex personified. My love for him grows with time, that is a definite!

"Lucy." His voice is quiet as he says my name. It almost sounds like he's reassuring himself its really me.

"Hey, you!" I feel shy, like he's not mine, but I'd like him to be. When his arms surround me, I have to try so hard to swallow that sob that desperately wants to say hello. I smell his 'oh so sexy' smell and smile inwardly.

As we kiss, I know that I am right to fight off the enemy that is Ralph Ashcroft. I just need to find the right time to tell Ollie.

I watch like a spectator who has never been up close and personal as Ollie fastens Bella securely into her car seat. I am fascinated by how much they have bonded in my absence. I'm shocked that I don't feel jealous. To anyone who didn't know, they would have no idea, not one, that these two haven't been together forever. I'm grinning as Ollie closes the car door and frowns at me, wondering why I look so ridiculous. Instead of explaining my joy, I pull him close and hug him.

"I love you so much, Oliver." I whisper in his ear as he pulls me tighter.

"Not as much as I love you, beautiful Lucia." I keep my eyes closed and place those words deep in my heart and mind. Just in case I don't win my fight with the devil!

I call Mamma whilst on our journey back to Layton and make plans to see them tomorrow. Mamma knows this is our first weekend at Ollie's together as a family.

"Sweetheart, don't expect too much and it will be perfect, I just know. You three are meant to be together, you're perfect." I hear Mamma's quiet tears and take comfort from her lovely words. Please, God, let Mamma be right!

As Bella leads me into Ollie's beachfront apartment, I suddenly feel like the visitor. These two have spent far more time here alone together, than Ollie and me. I should be jealous but I'm not. I'm happy for both of them. Time together has been just what they needed. If I had been here, I know their bond wouldn't have grown so quick and fast – another reason why that week in Milan was NOT a disaster. I make a mental note to tell Lisa next time I see her.

"Come and see my bedroom, Mummy." I'm guided by Bella, looking over her head as I watch Ollie give me a nervous smile.

I gasp as I enter what I can only describe as every little girl's dream bedroom. A miniature four-poster bed greets me in the centre of the room, drapes and all. There's a glitter ball off set to one side of the candy pink crystal chandelier. The bed is adorned with Disney princess bed covers, which match the tied back curtains. There's a dolls house in one corner that I'm sure I could climb in if I tried hard enough – it's enormous. There are cute rugs and multi-coloured boxes full of toys everywhere you look. It's basically like looking at the perfect bedroom in a magazine – something you'd only ever dream of – and my baby girl has it. I could cry!

"Is this OK, Lucy?" He looks so worried. My heart swells, just at the amount of love that has gone into making this perfect for Bella. I know why he's done it and I love him more if that's possible.

"Yes." I don't say any more than that. Instead, I grab my baby and pull her into a hug on her princess bed as she shrieks in delight. I pull my baby close, enjoying our closeness as she kisses my face and tells me she loves me. I look up and catch Ollie taking a photo on his phone as we play around on my princess's new bed.

Life with Ollie is just too perfect. We are now enjoying an indoor picnic. Bella is loving the process of getting it ready. Ollie has included her in every part of organizing this and has the patience of a saint. I'm in awe! We are now seated on cushions surrounding a large blanket in the middle of Ollie's living room as Bella passes me a bowl of cheesy curls.

"Would you like one, Mummy?" I giggle and take a handful.

"Thank you, Princess Bella" She blows me a kiss then turns to offer her perfect daddy some. I giggle again as he takes some and kisses Bella's hand. Ollie looks over Bella's head and gives me a wink – my heart misses a beat. I look around this large room and take in the view of the sea from the huge picture windows and feel contented for the first time in a while. I feel like I'm where I belong.

Bella looks so disappointed when I announce that its bedtime for our princess. Ollie looks to me, asking me to give in and let her stay up but I shake my head. He gives Bella a sorrowful look and she looks at him conspiratorially as they both give me harsh looks.

"Beautiful girls only grow if they get their sleep, little princess." Bella accepts this and lets her daddy take her in his arms and carry her to the beautiful princess' bedroom. I follow, smiling as I watch the two of them, relishing in the fact that once upon a time this was just a dream – Ollie and Bella… and me!

Together we wash and dress our baby, getting her ready for bed. I watch as Ollie gently brushes Bella's tiny teeth and feel slightly guilty for all the times I've rushed, and brushed far too harshly. Together we take a seat on each side of her princess bed and sing bedtime songs. I swallow back the tears as I feel such elation from these perfect moments. I watch as Ollie gently pulls the bedroom door until its slightly ajar, then we both quietly walk back down the hallway to the living area of his beautiful apartment. Once in the living room, I feel Ollie's arms around my waist as he pulls me to him. He inhales deeply as he speaks into my neck.

"God, Lucy, I have missed you soooo much, sweetheart. You smell so good, I could eat you." I relish his touch and his words.

"I missed you more." He spins me around in his arms, our noses touching as he then kisses my face lightly.

"Not a chance, beautiful." I close my eyes as he pulls me tightly to him. I get the urge to cry and fight so hard not to. I'm not sure I can keep the secret of Ollie's horrid father and his threats for long. I need to tell someone. Maybe I should call Em.

I watch as Ollie takes me by the hand and leads me to the sofa. As we take a seat, he pulls me to him and I find myself straddled across his lap. His hands are at the back of my neck as he gently plays with my hair. I close my eyes, enjoying his touch.

"I love you." My words are quiet as an involuntary tear finds its way free and traces its way down my cheek. I feel his thumb rubbing the salty water from my face.

"Hey, baby, why are you crying?" I open my eyes and find his ice blues staring back at me. Those beautiful eyes are the trigger that starts the ensuing waterfall that I just can't hold back. Between sobs I impart small truths, too afraid of sharing everything.

"I missed you both so much, Ollie. I really couldn't help being away from you both and I am so sorry."

"Hey!" The feel of his fingers running over my face comforts me slightly as I try to suppress memories of that meeting with his dreadful father. What did his threats really mean? How far would he go to stop us all from being together?

"Lucy, baby, it's OK really. I was disappointed but right now, I'm just so happy to be with you. Please don't dwell on it. We're together now so it's not a big deal, is it?" As his thumbs rub across my face and he holds my face in his hands, I feel like I should ignore the bad feelings. I pull back, breathing deeply.

"You're right. Sorry." His head is tilted as he checks me out. I pull myself together, telling myself this is not the time to let him know.

"Shall we have a drink to celebrate me being back?" He pulls me off him and jumps up from the sofa.

"Oh, that sounds good. What would you like? I have champagne, how does that sound?"

"Perfect, just like you." He gives me a wink as I watch him disappear into the kitchen. I feel unsettled and I can't shake it off. At some point this weekend, I will have to tell Ollie about his nasty father.

I'm awake, listening to the contented sound of Ollie's gentle breathing as he sleeps. We spent hours gently making love in the most sensual way ever. I needed to show him how much he means to me and it seems he needed to do just the same. The passion was still there but the need to love seemed to override everything tonight. My mind is racing in these dark hours. I keep going over what Ralph Ashcroft said and wondering just what he meant. The thought that he'd hurt Bella crosses my mind and I feel sick. I jump from the bed and find my way to the bathroom as quickly and quietly as possible. I close the door behind me and hope that I don't wake Ollie as I lean over the toilet bowl and empty my stomach. The sick feeling doesn't subside even after retching for what seems like ages.

"Hey, sweetheart, are you OK?" I didn't hear him come into the bathroom. God, I must have been making such a noise. I wipe the back of my hand over my mouth before answering.

"I'm sorry, Ollie, I never meant to wake you." I pull myself up and fumble about at the sink for my toothbrush. I lean forward over the sink to brush as Ollie gently pulls my messy hair back, holding it out of the way. I feel his fingers lightly stroking my cheek as I spend time making my mouth fresh. As I stand he hands me a towel, I take it and dab at my mouth. Ours eyes are watching as I move silently about. He smirks, making me frown. What is amusing about me noisily throwing my guts up in his en-suite toilet?

"What's so funny, Oliver?" He pushes my hair back, smiling.

"I wasn't laughing, Luce. I was just smiling, honest. Do you think I gave you food poisoning? We only made you sandwiches and you know how obsessive Bella is about washing hands, it can't have been the picnic." I shake my head smiling back at him.

"I think I've just been mega stressed this week and I've not been sleeping well. It's just caught up with me, that's all. Maybe the champagne hasn't helped." He seems to accept this pulling me to him and kissing the side of my head.

"You ready to come back to bed now, baby?" I lean back nodding my head at him.

"Yep. My tummy is completely empty now." Ollie grimaces at my comment and leads me out of the bathroom.

We lay spooned together as he gently kisses the back of my neck.

"I love you, Lucia Meyer, please stop stressing now. You know I'm here for you, Luce. I will share all your problems from now on, baby, promise." I close my eyes as Ollie strokes my hair.

I must have drifted off as I'm now hearing that familiar cute voice calling me quietly. Bella always whispers in my ear when she pads into my room in the morning. She usually says 'Good Morning' then slips beneath the covers and cuddles up with me. I suddenly realize that I'm in Ollie's bed and Bella has found me. "Oh shit!"

I sit bolt upright, nudging Ollie who is still sound asleep. He mumbles and turns over, pulling the covers around him.

"Morning, sweetheart, are you OK?"

Bella grins whilst nodding.

"Can we cuddle up, Mummy?" I sigh with relief.

"Yes baby, climb in." Fortunately, I pulled on pj's after I was sick last night. I pull my baby in close to me and smell her beautiful scent as I close my eyes and enjoy what I hope will be the first of many mornings I will wake with my two favourite people.

The sound of Ollie's phone wakes us as we all snuggle up in his very large comfy bed. Ollie looks over at me and a sleeping Bella in my arms and grins as he grabs his phone and quickly answers.

"Mum, hi. No, it's OK, I was awake but Bella is still sleeping." His whisper makes my heart swell. I lean over and kiss Bella's chubby cheek. She still doesn't rouse. I watch Ollie as he sits on the side of the bed and talks with his mum quietly. I reach out and touch his arm, needing to feel his skin. He turns and looks at me, concerned, so I smile to reassure him all is OK.

"OK, Mum, let me talk to Lucy and I'll call you back. OK, love you too, bye."

He gently places the phone at the side of the bed and turns to me, touching my face.

"Luce, Mum desperately wants to meet up with you and Bella. She wants me to ask you to make arrangements."

187

"Well, I arranged to go and see Mamma and Dad later but we could go round this evening if you like, or tomorrow if that's no good." He laughs.

"I promise she will cancel anything if she has plans. She can't wait to properly meet you both." I watch as he dials his mother. I feel a tiny frisson of fear. Please don't let Ralph Ashcroft hear about this.

I watch as Ollie cheerfully makes plans with his mother, constantly checking with me as we decide to go round this evening about six. I gently move my arm from around Bella and try to move from the bed without waking her. Ollie follows me from the room and as we enter the living room he pulls me around to him.

"What time did Bella come in, Luce?" I shrug.

"I have no idea. It's a good job I put my pj's back on, though. She didn't seem bothered though. Has she come into you when I wasn't here?" He nods smiling.

"She's the best snuggle buddy ever."

"Perfect." I close my eyes as Ollie gently kisses my mouth. Just then, we hear the patter of tiny feet and both look to the doorway as Bella plods through, hair a complete tangled mess as she looks at us grinning.

"Good morning." She sings at us and Ollie chuckles before leaving my side and taking our beautiful daughter in his arms for a cuddle.

Our afternoon at my parents is lovely. The weather is warm so the four of us and Bella are taking a walk around the campsite. It's a large plot of land and my dad usually rides around on a quad bike he bought a few years back. A few of the campers shout hello as we walk by and fuss Bella as she speaks with each and every one we meet.

"Does everyone staying here know Bella personally, Dad?" I smile as my dad looks over at me, then at Bella.

"Mmm, most of them. She helps clear the breakfast tables in the morning but also likes to help check people in, don't you Bella?" He ruffles Bella's hair as she nods at me seriously.

"Granddad lets me hand out the keys, Mummy. He says I'm velly important." I grin as I check out Ollie who looks so in love with our daughter right now. I squeeze his hand and feel my heart flutter when he gives me a wink.

"What time do you have to be at your mum's, Oliver?" Mamma's dark eyes are twinkling with joy as she looks between Ollie and me. Mamma has always been such a romantic and I know she's always had dreams of happy ever after's for Em and me. So far, we haven't really done well on that front and I sense she's over the moon right now that there's a chance Bella and I will be together with Bella's daddy. It's Mamma's perfect ending.

"About six. There's no fixed time. We're just going for tea, nothing too grand or anything."

"And will your father be there?" I can see concern on my dad's face as he asks. Dad and Ralph Ashcroft have met up a few times and I know Dad wasn't impressed with the rude, arrogant man. I feel my heart pounding at the mention of his name. Ollie gives my hand a squeeze. He must sense I'm uncomfortable.

"No, Pete. To be honest, my parents aren't really together any more. It's never been made official. I think my dad likes people to believe he's a family man. Looks good in the business world. Mum rarely speaks to him anymore. I don't either, if I can help it. You know, after what he did, about Lucy and me before Bella was born, well I kind of try not to think about him too often." My dad pats Ollie's shoulder and clears his throat as if he has something important to say.

"Well I'm glad to hear that, Ollie, because to be quite honest, I don't like the idea of that man anywhere near my precious daughter and granddaughter. What he did to you two was unforgivable." Ollie looks to me, his face looks sad. It must be hard to hear this from my dad. I know Dad really likes Ollie or he wouldn't be saying this.

"I know exactly what you mean. I have no intention of letting him near Bella, so don't worry, Pete." Mum touches my arm reassuringly but I don't feel reassured. My heart is pounding and I suppress the urge to tell them all, here now, about Ralph Ashcroft and his threats to me. Instead, I lean in to Ollie and take comfort from his words. He'll protect us, I know he will. I just need to tell him.

Chapter 15

The Ashcroft family home is overwhelming and huge! The very wide gravel drive leads to a turning circle in front of the house that has two wings that I can see. The house is white and reminds me of something you'd see on *Dallas*, the eighties American TV series. As we pull up I feel anxious. I came here a few times as a girl with Declan to call for Ollie but we never went further than the front door. The only times I've spoken to Ollie's mum in recent years has been when I've seen her fleetingly in town. Ollie looks over and touches my face as we park outside the house.

"Hey, don't look so nervous. My mum is lovely, Luce. She's so excited about meeting you two properly. Please don't worry. It will be fine." He turns to Bella who's excitedly trying to unfasten her seat belt.

"You ready to go and meet Nanna, Bella?"

"Yes, Daddy. Does she look like Nonna?"

"No sweetheart, she doesn't. Nanna has blonde hair and blue eyes." He looks amused as he steps out of the car and reaches into the back to help Bella. I tentatively step out of the car and wish I'd made more effort now. I'm wearing white capri trousers and a striped t-shirt with white flip-flops. I tied my hair back this morning. Ollie assures me I look just fine but I'm thinking my attire is not quite befitting of a visit to this rather grand home.

Ollie's mum bursts out of the front door as we approach, the biggest grin on her face as she watches her only son carry his daughter to meet her for the first time. I swallow the tears that are eager to escape and grab my phone to capture some pictures for Bella to keep as memories.

True to Ollie's word, his mum is a complete contrast to mine in looks. She has beautiful blonde hair cut into a perfect bob and the bluest eyes, just like Ollie's. She's dressed immaculately in white trousers and a short-sleeved powder blue top.

"Oh, my goodness, hello beautiful princess, you must be Bella." I watch Bella enjoying the attention and click my camera. Bella turns to look at me for reassurance and I nod my head. She holds out her arms to Ollie's mum and he passes her over. As the older lady embraces my daughter, hugging her so tight, I feel happy that we've finally got to this. Ollie steps back and places his arm around my waist. He leans in to whisper.

"Thank you, Luce. This is a very special day, you know." I nod my head, unsure how long I can hold back the tears at this emotional union.

Ollie's mum carries Bella into the house and I follow Ollie, who's leading me by the hand. I watch as his mum places Bella on the floor and turns to me.

"Lucy, dear." Her arms are outstretched as she walks towards me. She takes me in her arms, talking quietly.

"I can't tell you how grateful I am that you're here. Thank you so much for letting me meet Bella. I want you and Oliver to be happy, sweet girl, and I know he loves you so much."

"Thank you, Mrs Ashcroft." She laughs.

"You can't call me that, Lucy."

"No, Mummy, it's Nanna." I giggle as Bella steps forward, hugging my leg.

"Nanna's a special name just for you, Bella. Mummy should call me Penny."

"I like your name, Nanna."

"Thank you, sweetheart." Penny leans down and kisses Bella's chubby cheek.

"Shall we go and sit outside seeing as it's such a lovely evening?"

"Yes, Mum, that's a good idea." I can't help but notice the look of love that Ollie shares with his mum as I follow them through the grand house. We walk through the kitchen and out onto the large patio area that overlooks a very spectacular looking pool.

There's a marble garden table that's seats about twelve people, which is all laid out with a buffet. There is everything you could imagine, in fact, I think I've been to parties that have been less catered for than this and there's only the four of us for tea – I hope!

"Oh, Mum, this looks lovely. You really shouldn't have gone to so much trouble." Ollie looks adoringly at his mum and she smiles back, looking proud that her son is impressed.

"This is a very special occasion, Oliver, so what else could I do?" Bella is eagerly eyeing up the different choices of crisps and sausage rolls, her favourite. Ollie passes her a princess plate and helps her fill it. I watch on, feeling a little uncomfortable in my surroundings.

"Catherine's gone out with Abbie for the evening, Lucy, but she'd love to meet up with you and Bella properly, when you feel ready, of course."

"Maybe next time we come round, Mum. What do you think, Lucy?" I glance at Ollie and smile in agreement. I remember his sister Catherine from school but we never really had much to do with each other.

****

The tea went well and as time passed, I felt a little more relaxed around Penny. She may live in a grand house and want for nothing but she's very down to earth and was nothing but lovely to Bella.

Ollie and I have just put Bella to bed and we're now relaxing on his balcony, overlooking the bay. I close my eyes and listen to the sea as it crashes against the shore.

"Was it really OK for you at my mum's, Lucy?" I open my eyes and watch his concerned face. I smile.

"Of course, it was. I expected your mum to be a bit more frightening than she was. She's really down to earth, isn't she?" Ollie laughs.

"Mmmm, I suppose so. It's my dad who came from money, Luce. My mum is American, I assume you guessed that from her accent. She was only a teenager when my parents met in New York. She was a waitress he seduced, then whisked away from her family in the States. Mum was a part-time model and aspiring to be an actress. My dad promised her the world. Once he got her back here, he treated her the way he treats the rest of the world, like she owed him a favour. Mum never got to follow her dreams. She never complained though, how could she? He gave her all that, you know, the house and everything. Mum was expected to produce children and heirs for him, so that's exactly what she did. You know, I've never heard her complain in spite of the fact that I've never seen him show her love." Ollie's face looks sad as he's lost in thought. I suddenly feel so sorry for his lovely mother. It sounds like she's never experienced the love we share. How cruel can life be? I decide now is the time to tell him, he needs to know and this is the perfect opportunity.

"Ollie, I need to talk to you about your dad." He turns quickly, his face full of concern.

"Why?"

"Well, he came to see me last week." Ollie stands and I rub my legs in discomfort.

"When, why? What did he say, Lucy?" His voice is raised. I feel nervous. I stand up. Ollie leaning over me wasn't nice.

"Ollie, calm down and I'll tell you. Please don't shout at me?" He runs his hands through his hair, then pulls me to him and squeezes me oh so tight.

"Lucy, I'm sorry. I don't want him anywhere near you or Bella. I didn't mean to shout." He kisses my lips gently. I touch his face, knowing he's not going to like what I have to tell him.

"Let's sit down and I'll tell you all about it. But please don't shout at me, Ollie, it's unnerving." He takes my hands and guides me back to the wicker sofa we were sitting on before. We're seated facing each other and he looks so anxious.

"He tried to give me money, Ollie. Money for Bella, he said for her education and money for both of us, you know, to live." I see Ollie visibly relax, he laughs.

"Oh, right. That's unbelievable, Luce. I thought you were going to tell me something bad. Maybe he's not as bad as we all think. Maybe there's a heart in there somewhere." Now I laugh, sarcastically.

"No, Ollie. The money was to get rid of us. Out of your life, forever. He threatened me, Ollie. I refused his offer and he basically said that I now have a fight on my hands." I watch as Ollie jumps up and shatters the wine glass he's picked up.

"No fucking way. I will kill that man, Lucy. If he comes anywhere near you two, I will kill him." I rush to Ollie and try to hug him to calm him down but he pushes me off.

"When did he come and see you? Was it in London?"

"Yes, middle of last week."

"Why didn't you tell me before, Lucy? You shouldn't have kept this from me." Ollie looks at me with anger in his eyes.

"I didn't keep it from you, Ollie. To be honest, I didn't know how to tell you. It's not something I come across regularly in my life. I don't usually get threatened in the middle of my working day." I know I sound slightly sarcastic but he's making me mad.

I watch Ollie move towards me; I step back.

"Lucy, I'm not mad with you, sweetheart. I'm mad with him. I'm scared too. How am I going to protect you and Bella if he'll come and find you like that?"

I step back into the living room after checking Bella is sleeping. I was a little nervous that Ollie's shouting might have woken her but she's absolutely fine. Ollie is deep in conversation on his phone. I cough to let him know I'm in the room. He glances at me and then leaves the room, heading off into his office, closing the door behind him. I feel a little put out. He could at least have told me he was making a private call before I went to check Bella and not just leave me like that.

I walk back out onto the balcony, shivering at the temperature drop. I head back inside, grab Ollie's hoodie and pop back out to listen to the sea. If ever there was a sound that could calm me, it's the sea, and right now I need to stay calm. Ollie is anything but calm and one of us needs a level head. I pour a glass of wine, tuck my legs under me on the wicker sofa and close my eyes as I feel calm running over me. I actually feel better now that I've told Ollie. I know he's gone into panic mode but at least I'm not keeping this from him anymore. He knows his dad better than anyone and he knows what he's capable of, so I'll let Ollie deal with this if I can.

I've made plans to meet Em at the beach tomorrow for a few hours. I hope this isn't going to be a problem now. I could do with a good old chinwag with my sister. I also want to find out how things are going with Kyle. Last time I saw them, they were getting along very well and I want to find out what's going on with my sister and her new man. I sip my wine as Ollie steps outside, calling my name.

"I'm here, Ollie." He walks over, leaning in for a kiss.

"I'm sorry, Lucy. I haven't handled this very well, have I? I didn't mean to shout, sweetheart, and that call was just, well, I need to protect you so I have to find out what my dad has planned. I called an old friend of mine in London. He's going to do some checking for me." I watch as he takes a seat beside me. The feel of his fingers gently stroking my cheek instinctively makes me close my eyes. I murmur slightly at his touch.

"I'm coming back to London with you tomorrow, Lucy. We all need to move into mine as soon as possible, sweetheart. I need to have you and Bella with me so that I can protect you properly." I open my eyes, feeling anxiety rush through me. This man is as dangerous as I thought. If Ollie's worried, then things don't look good!

****

As we step inside my flat, I feel completely out of control. My life is completely taken over by Ollie and his associates who are busy planning mine and Bella's move. Lisa is picking Bella up from nursery later and taking her out for tea so that we can get sorted without worrying about her. My emotions are mixed. I'm grateful that Ollie is taking these threats from his dad seriously but I feel like I'm watching my life played out on a TV screen. I feel such sadness that, all of a sudden, our life is turning upside down and spinning around. This happy home that my beautiful daughter and I have shared throughout her short life is quickly being emptied and the memories tossed aside like they don't matter. I leave the men in the living room and find myself seated on Bella's small bed. I drop my face in my hands and quietly shed a tear. This was our happy home. The place I was going to make a life for Bella and me. I was going to be rich and successful and bring my daughter up in luxury eventually; that was my dream. This was our first step on the ladder to happiness. Now it feels tainted by the hatred of Ralph Ashcroft.

"Lucy?" Ollie's voice is quiet when he calls my name. I look up and find him leaning against the bedroom door. His hands are deep in his pockets and he frowns as he takes in my sad demeanor.

"I know this isn't what we planned, baby, but are you OK?" I wipe at my face with the heels of my hands. My voice is croaky when I reply.

"I'm fine, I just never imagined leaving here under a cloud. This is mine and Bella's happy home. We've only had happy times here, Ollie, and all of a sudden your nasty dad has come along and spoiled that forever." His blue eyes are sad as he watches. I guess he's trying to find the right words to say and struggling. How can he justify his dad's callous actions? As he walks over to me, I feel

197

so sorry for Ollie. I can't even begin to imagine what it must be like to have a father like his. It seems like he's always been like it but surely that doesn't make it any easier to live with. Ollie takes a seat beside me, sighing loudly as he does.

"I don't know what to say, Luce. I... my dad is a despicable person who has treated everyone and anyone like this whenever they got in the way of his ambitions. My mum was his first victim and it hurts like mad that he's behaving like this with you. I love my mum but she has chosen to stay with him all these years so in some ways she's as guilty as him for letting him behave like he does. But you, and Bella, well you don't deserve any of this. The easy thing to do to protect you would be for me to walk away from you both." I gasp at this. Would he do that? Could he do that? My heart is thudding right now waiting for him to continue.

Ollie turns to face me gently lifting my chin in his hand. I sniff loudly, my tears continuing to roll. He wipes at them with his thumb but the stream is never ending right now.

"Lucy, sweetheart, you are my everything, you know that, right?" He looks so sincere as he watches my face for a response. I shrug and he half laughs.

"I don't know how I got through the years without you. Everything I've done seems to have been in preparation for me meeting back up with you and finding Bella. My life was empty before you two came along. I worked so hard but I had no one to share it with and to be honest I never really wanted to share it. But now I have you and Bella, I can't imagine a life without you. I want to give you the world, and I promise I will. There is no way in this world I would walk away from you two and give my Dad what he wants. We will sort this I promise. I'm sorry you have to leave here, but you know it was never really going to be any different, was it? I told you that when you were in Milan. I have a home that's paid for, ready for you two to move into now. You never have to worry about paying the rent on this place any more." I huff.

"Ollie, I never dreamed of being a kept woman. I dreamed of you and a life with you but not your money. Well I didn't know what you had, did I? I just wanted to be with the Ollie I've always loved. I dreamed of becoming successful in my own right. I wanted to give Bella the world."

"Well why don't we agree that together we'll give Bella the world, how about that?" He's smiling as his ice blues shine. He tilts his head as I sigh.

"OK. Together. But how are we going to sort this out with your dad?"

"Let me worry about him, Luce. I just want to protect you and Bella and make sure he never pulls any stunts like that again."

I make my way through the empty flat, Ollie following closely and quietly behind me. The tears have subsided but the lump in my throat tells me they're on their way back. As I walk from the front door I remember the day I brought Bella home. Em and Jamie were with me. The three of us were so excited. As I peak into Bella's bedroom I feel a wave of sadness when I think of how overwhelmed I was that Em and Jamie had decorated Bella's room while I was in hospital. The pale pink walls are still the same. I walk over and touch the wall, thoughts of Jamie flooding my mind. I speak to Ollie through my tears.

"Em and Jamie painted this for Bella. He was such a good person, Ollie. Soon there won't be any memories left of him, will there?" I feel a pull towards staying. I'm not sure if I'm ready to move on.

"Well the physical things disappear pretty quickly but no one can take the memories in your head away, Luce. You've got loads of photos of the three of you with Bella when you first brought her home, haven't you? You'll always have those to share with Bella." I sigh. He's right I can't cling on to this place just because Jamie painted a few walls.

I open the fitted wardrobe doors just to check they're empty and giggle. At the back, peaking out is one of Bella's baby socks.

A tiny white sock with a bow on the side. I lean in and pick it up, turning to Ollie.

"Look, one of Bella's first socks." Instinctively I pull it to my nose and sniff, grasping for any scent from the past. Ollie takes it from me, playing with the tiny sock that is dwarfed by his enormous hand.

"I wish I'd been here, Lucy. To see her born and share all those memories you have of her first few years." He pulls me to him and we hug silently. I'm suddenly aware that these changes are affecting us both. Ollie has regrets that I wish I could banish. We have to move on so that we can make amends for what Ollie's dad made happen. I pull away and kiss him lightly before smiling.

"So that's it then. Your dad will not win this fight, Oliver Ashcroft. If I stay here, it will always make you feel sad for what you missed so that's the best reason I can think of for going. I want you to start building memories of Bella growing up so let's go and do that in your home." His eyes sparkle.

"Did I tell you today how much I love you?"

"You can keep telling me 'cause it's the thing I like to hear the most from you and our daughter." He leans in, kissing my neck as he speaks.

"I love you so much, Lucy."

"I love you too."

Chapter 16

We're on our way to Ollie's via picking up Bella from Lisa's. I didn't think it was necessary for Bella to see the empty flat but there is something special about us all walking into Ollie's place together. Today is our first day as a family living in London and I want us three to share those first steps. I turn and peak at Bella who is sound asleep in the back of Ollie's car. I don't have a car and never felt the need for one whilst living in London. Ollie drives a black Aston Martin DB9, which is very impressive. There's just enough room for Bella's tiny frame in her huge seat in the back. There's not much room for her to grow though. Ollie assures me that he will change his lovely car for a more practical one very soon. I feel slightly guilty about this. I know he loves this car and don't expect him to change everything to accommodate Bella and me. Maybe I should buy myself a small car. Yes, that's what I'll do, then Ollie gets to keep this lovely car.

I'm awash with such a mixture of emotions right now. I'm sorry to say goodbye to mine and Bella's happy home but I know this is the right move for us.

Ollie's London home is a penthouse at Fulham Reach. I haven't yet visited; things seem to move in odd ways with Ollie and me. Everything's upside down and back to front. Ollie peeks over at me and gives me a wink. He touches my hand for reassurance. I smile back but for once the butterflies in my tummy are through nerves, and not from his touch. I watch the streets pass me by as we drive through the city, lost as I watch the world busily going about its business. How many people are just doing the mundane, everyday things they always do? How many people are making huge changes to their lives today like me?

"Lucy." I'm pulled out of my deep thoughts and glance at Ollie. His eyes are full of concern. I touch his leg and he quickly covers my hand with his.

"We'll be OK. I promise I'll look after both of you and I'll do everything in my power to make you happy."

"You already make me happy, Ollie. Today's just a big day that's all. I can't believe I'm moving to a place and taking my daughter, when I have no idea what it looks like, never mind if it will be practical."

I feel the car slow down as Ollie pulls over to the side of the road. Cars from behind blast their horns at the inconvenience of manoeuvering around us on the busy street. Ollie seems oblivious. As we come to a standstill he turns to look at me.

"Lucy we're nearly there. I promise I will make any changes to my place that you want. If you don't like it, we'll move. I don't mind really. Just for now though I want you and Bella to be with me as much as possible so that I can make sure you're safe. Why don't we just look at this as temporary, hey?" He tilts his head and smiles, his ice-blues watching me intently. I run my hands along my legs and take a deep breath.

"Right, no more worrying. If we were just moving in together without the problem with your dad looming over us I would be so damned excited, Ollie, so I'm going to pretend that Ralph Ashcroft doesn't even exist, just for tonight." I lean over and kiss his handsome face before speaking again.

"I'm sorry, Ollie. I don't mean to make you worry."

"Hey, I just want my girls to be happy that's all." He pulls the car back into the traffic and I silently give myself a good talking to. I need to be positive.

Fulham Reach is set on the north bank of the River Thames. As we pull up to Distillery Wharf I'm blown away by the sheer elegance of this place... wow! I know Ollie owns a penthouse apartment but I had no idea it was at the top of this luxurious multi-storey building. Ollie pulls his car into a private garage where we step out. He runs round to me excitedly, grinning like a child on Christmas morning. He pulls me into his arms, breathing into my neck.

"This means so much to me, Lucy. I can't believe you're both here. I've never bought a girl back here before. You and Bella are the first, my special girls. Do you want to wake Bella or would you prefer we leave her sleep?" We peek in at the sleeping angel. It seems cruel to wake her.

"Why don't you carry her up and we'll see if she stirs. She sometimes does." I watch as Ollie gently takes Bella from her seat and pulls her close to him. I close the door, throwing my bag over my shoulder as I follow Ollie to my new home. We take a lift leading straight to the apartment.

Ollie is oblivious to our surroundings as we step out into the lobby and I gasp. Everywhere I look I see luxury. This is not what I expected. I guessed it would be expensive but this… I'm blown away. The lift lobby itself is totally awesome with silver, natural stone covered walls and a bespoke metallic ceiling. I follow along with eyes as big as saucers. The entrance lobby, which is as big as my old lounge, has its very own feature fireplace, oh my God!

Ollie waits and watches as I follow him into the living space.

"Welcome home, beautiful" He whispers as Bella continues to sleep in his strong arms.

The living area is one open plan space set around a central fireplace. Ollie carries Bella into the lounge area and gently places her on one of the giant sofas. She murmurs then just turns on her side like the sleeping beauty that she is. Ollie walks towards me, his hand out for me to take.

"Come on, Luce, I'll show you around." I pull at his hand to stop him.

"What, is something wrong?"

"No, Ollie. Why didn't you tell me you lived in such luxury?" He smiles uncomfortably, glancing at our surroundings.

"I never really think of it like that. I don't spend much time here, Luce. I prefer to be in Layton if I'm honest. I put my name down and paid for this when I first returned to London and to be honest I've always felt a little bit lost here. It's not exactly a bachelor pad, is it?" He laughs, I grin.

"It's pure, flipping luxury Ollie. I've only ever seen anything like this in magazines. I never thought I'd be living somewhere so grand. It's a bit out of my league." He pulls me to him.

"Like I said before. Everything seems to have led to us being together. Maybe now I'm sharing this place with you and Bella it will feel like home. This is the perfect home for you two, and it is definitely not out of your league."

I try desperately to take everything in as Ollie guides me through the apartment. The living space has panoramic views with floor to ceiling sliding windows everywhere. The view is of the River Thames and is pretty bloody awesome. Ollie waves his hand in front of him as he leads me through each area giving me the briefest descriptions possible, mostly just one word seems sufficient.

"Dining area. That bar area is called the entertainment kitchen and behind that glass wall is the main kitchen." I pull him to stop as I admire the luxurious area he's describing in his minimalist tone.

"Wow, Ollie, this place is beautiful." He kisses the side of my head.

"Thank you. I'm glad you like it. If there's anything you want to change, then just say OK?" I laugh loudly.

"How can you change perfection, Ollie?" He looks back at me as he continues to guide me.

"Just saying, that's all. Guest bedroom." He looks and I laugh again.

"Ollie, at least look like you enjoy living here, 'cause right now you're doing a good job of putting me off. Your sales patter is crap." He stops and pulls me to him.

"I'm in a hurry to get you to the master bedroom so that I can show you where you're going to sleep from now on with me,

beautiful. I promise I will be very enthusiastic when we get there."
My heart speeds up as he kisses me lightly.

"First though I want to know what you think of Princess Bella's
room. I had it designed a few weeks ago. I can't wait to see her face.
I hope you like it, Luce."

Oh wow! I'm lost for words. I thought her bedroom in Layton
was wonderful but this is something else. Ollie frowns when I don't
speak. I giggle.

"This is every little princess's dream, Ollie. In fact, I bet this is
better than most princess's bedrooms."

Pale pink walls show off this little girl's boudoir. On the far
wall is a hand carved antique white bed dressed with a pale pink
canopy. On the opposite wall is a matching hand carved antique
white wardrobe with a mirrored door. The floor to ceiling windows
are dressed with beautiful drapes covered in tiny pink hearts with
matching pelmets. There's a cute miniature armchair to match in
one corner but the thing that catches my eye is in the centre of the
room. There's a central pink and cream rug and in the middle of the
rug stands a miniature hand carved antique white table and two
matching chairs. I feel like I've stepped into Alice's wonderland
right now. It's adorable. I pull my hand to my mouth and force the
sob back down.

"Oliver, this is just... perfect. Thank you." His smile is a shy
one.

"You don't mind that I didn't wait and ask your advice?" I
shake my head laughing.

"I don't think I could have come up with this, Ollie."

"Well let's hope our little princess likes it as much as you." As
if on cue we hear our baby calling out. Ollie runs, both of us aware
that Bella won't have a clue where she is. I decide to wait here for
them. I'll get the best view of Bella's tiny face when she sees her
new room. I'm not disappointed.

"Daddddyyyy, Mummmmyyy!" Ollie and I watch as Princess Bella inspects her room and its contents, gently touching each piece of furniture as she walks around.

"Can I sleep here forever, Daddy?" Ollie nods his head, his eyes awash with tears.

"Yes, princess, apart from when we go to Layton, then you have to sleep in your other room." She spins around delighted with this answer, her cute dimple showing as she grins.

"Shall we get you ready for bed then, Bella?" She's never been so eager to go to bed.

As we leave Bella's room Ollie grabs my hand and leads me in the opposite direction from the living area.

"Where are we going, Ollie?"

"I still haven't shown you our bedroom, Luce" My heart skips a beat. Our bedroom... us... we, me and Ollie, our bedroom. I like that, very much.

The master bedroom is as luxurious as everything else I've seen so far. The huge bed is situated centrally on a raised floor with a perfect view of the River Thames through the floor to ceiling windows. Ollie guides me through to the dressing room lifting his arm as he speaks.

"This is your side of the room, Luce. Is there enough room for your clothes?" I look around me and feel slightly anxious. I don't have enough clothes to half fill the space Ollie has provided. His clothes are all hanging along one side. His shirts are all lined up in order of colour followed by his trousers and jackets. There's a series of shelves, which again are organized in colour ranges of clothes such as t-shirts and jumpers. His shoes are all neatly paired up on racks to the far end. It's like visiting a master tailor's. I giggle before answering.

"Don't worry, there's more than enough room, Ollie. I don't have that much stuff." He takes me to the bathroom where there are side by side sinks. Ollie shows me the cupboard set aside for my toiletries, again far more room than I need. I sigh. This is another world!

The center piece of the bathroom is an oversized oval bath. To one end of the room is a walk-in shower, which I must admit is calling to me. I'd love a shower right now. I carefully stroke my fingertips along the marble surrounding the sinks. As I look up Ollie is watching me. His eyes are full of emotion, I can't make out if he's happy or sad right now.

"Are you OK?" He frowns at my question, moving towards me slowly. He lifts his hand and touches my face, sending heat right through my body.

"Of course I'm OK. I'm so damned happy right now, I could explode, Lucia." As our noses are just about touching, he leans his forehead on mine.

"Are you OK?" He lightly kisses my lips as tingles tickle my insides.

"Mmmhmm" is all I can manage. I feel his fingers touching my hair as he places one hand at the base of my back. We gently sway as he talks.

"What would you like to do now, beautiful? Would you like to eat?" Another light kiss sends my body into turmoil. I can't think as he presses his lips to my neck. I quietly moan, feeling his smile as he kisses me over and over.

As our lips meet all thoughts of food are diminished. I just want Ollie, to be with Ollie, and to be kissed by this man who I love with all my heart. He pulls away and my heart lurches. I frown, he smiles, taking my hand and leading me out of the bathroom.

We walk into the bedroom, no words spoken as we cherish these first few moments of being together here. Ollie steps behind me as I admire the view from the window. His arms wrap around my waist as light kisses on my neck send pleasure shooting through me.

"This view is amazing." My voice is quiet and breathless as I try and talk to him.

"Mmm" Is his only reply as he continues his tender assault on my skin. I feel light headed as he pulls me around to face him. Staring into his ice blue eyes I feel my heart pounding in my chest.

"I love you Lucy, more than you'll ever know." Our lips crash together, gone are the delicate featherlight kisses, taken over with the passion and lust we are both sharing right now.

As our tongues dance I can feel my groin begin to ache. We walk backwards together neither one letting go as we devour each other.

"I need you so much baby." My heart swells at his words. As he pushes me back onto his huge bed I relish the feel of his weight on me. I wrap my arms around his neck kissing him like crazy, wanting to show him just how much I love him. Our kisses go on forever, only stopping when we need to breathe.

Ollie lifts his body slightly his hands either side of my head. I'm melting inside as he looks down on me. The love on his face is mind-blowing.

"I'm going to make love to you now, baby, slowly, ever so slowly, so that I can enjoy every bit of you and this delicious body." Kisses and tiny bites on my neck and shoulders make me cry out. I try to be quiet, anxious that Bella isn't woken. I need to be with him on my own right now and enjoy Ollie, my Oliver!

I close my eyes and enjoy the tantalizing feelings that are flooding through me as Ollie slowly removes my clothes, kissing his way around my form. With each item that he removes he alternates with a kiss or a delicate bite. I touch and feel, lost in the perfection of my man. I run my fingers very lightly down his muscular arms and smile as he gasps.

"God, you drive me mad with just your touch, Lucy." I open my eyes and meet his gaze, my fingers running down his hard, toned back.

"I love to touch you, you're perfect, Ollie." He leans on one elbow, the forefinger of his other hand running gently from my forehead, down my nose and around my lips. I watch as he licks his lips and follow suit, biting at my lower lip. He smiles, a wicked smile before crashing his mouth on mine.

I'm overwhelmed with emotion as our bodies grind together. I wrap my legs around Ollie and relish the feel of his arousal in my groin. I run my fingers down his back, loving the feel when I reach his tense buttocks. He moans softly at my touch. I kiss and gently nip at his neck and his ear, whispering as I go.

"I love you, Ollie, I need you."

"You can have me, baby, all of me."

As he enters me the feeling that I belong washes over me. I know without a doubt that we are meant to be together.

We move slowly together, like he promised. Being so close is driving me wild with emotional turmoil. I want this to go on forever but my body is too excited. I want him so desperately now, forcing him to move quicker and harder. Our love making is frantic, passionate and off the scale. I'm losing control, calling his name.

"Ollie... I..." Words are lost as I find myself climbing, the feel of his mouth on me driving me over the edge.

"Come with me, baby, now." We get lost in our perfect world together as we call each other's names, falling over the edge as one.

I lay in his arms feeling so relaxed I could sleep. The loud grumbling of my tummy tells me I need food. Ollie chuckles.

"I think someone might be hungry. Shall we go and eat?" I watch as he moves away and feel sad. I want to lie here in his arms forever. He holds out a hand and I take it as he pulls me from the bed. He leans in and kisses my neck as he pulls me close. The feeling of our skin touching sends fireworks through my body once again. I moan, he laughs.

"Ollie, shall we just skip food altogether and just go back to bed." I lean my head back as he kisses my neck. He speaks through kisses.

"That's sounds good, Luce, but we have forever now. We can do this every night forever, so let's go and eat. I think you might need the energy baby because I'm not finished yet. This is just a small interlude." He raises an eyebrow and I grin.

"OK, food it is then."

I sit at the counter and watch as Ollie prepares cheese toasties for us. He moves around the kitchen like a pro and I can't take my eyes off his perfect body dressed in just his boxers. Each time he passes I get a wink; I blow a kiss. He's cute! He holds up the Worcestershire sauce and I nod in answer then watch as he shakes the dark brown sauce onto the golden cheese. The smell as the cheese melts has my tummy grumbling once again.

"Ollie?" I want to ask him so many questions.

"Hmm?" He's distracted as he watches the cheese grill.

"Why haven't you ever bought a girl back here before?" He glances at me then back at the grill.

"I never met the right person." I swallow before asking the next question that's burning to be asked.

"So have you had any serious relationships?" He curses as the toasties burn his fingers as he places them on the plates. The look he gives me is serious. I'm not sure I want to know the answer to this but...

"Not like this." He waves his hands between me and him. "But yes, I've had a few girlfriends."

"So, tell me about them." He tilts his head as he bites into the melted cheese. The look on his face tells me he's trying to work out what to tell.

"Well I met a girl when I was abroad. She was working there too so we kind of hooked up. Her name was Carly. We saw each other on and off for about nine months. It ended when she moved away." I feel nauseous at the thought of him with someone else.

"So are you still in touch." He bites more toastie, shaking his head.

"No. She phoned a few times but long distance wasn't my thing. It was really quite casual anyway so I just sort of assumed when she left that would be it."

"Anyone else?" I tilt my head as I ask. He stops eating, placing his half eaten toastie back on the plate.

"Are you going to eat, Lucy or just bombard me with questions all night?" I reluctantly take a bite of my toastie and for a few moments get lost in the salty taste of the buttery cheese. Once I've finished chewing I look up and he's grinning.

"What?" Ollie leans over and runs the pad of his thumb along my chin.

"Melted cheese has a habit of dripping grease on your chin." I feel my blush as I watch him lick the end of his thumb.

"So, tell me, any more?" He tutts loudly.

"Yes, Lucy, there were a few girls I took out, but nothing serious. One was called Mandy who I met through some friends at work. We met at the tennis club. Then there was Serena. We dated for about six months." I kind of wish I hadn't asked but now I want to know everything. Jealousy and curiosity are mixing and fighting their way into my brain right now.

"So where did you meet Serena?" He eyes me suspiciously.

"Haven't I told you enough, Luce?" I shake my head. Why hasn't he told me more about Serena? Oh God, he loved her! I shake my head, he sighs.

"Her father, Bruce Hamilton is a banker and a close friend of my father. They are golf buddies amongst other things. I was introduced to Serena at a charity ball. That's it." I watch as he clears his plate away. He looks uncomfortable.

"Have you finished? He nods his head to my half-eaten plate of food. I stare at the food then back at Ollie, nodding my head. I watch his perfect body as he walks to the bin, the dishwasher, then to the fridge.

"Would you like a glass of wine?" I nod my head, my mind whirring with questions and all of them about Serena.

"Did you love her, or any of them?" He turns and walks slowly to the other side of the counter. We don't speak. His eyes are fixed on me as he walks to a cupboard and retrieves two glasses then walks back. Still no words. I watch him pour the wine, his eyes flitting from the glasses to me and back again. I wait… still no words. He takes a seat, passing me a glass of white wine. He leans forward and clinks my glass.

"Cheers, beautiful, and welcome to your new home. I promise I will try my hardest to make you and our daughter happy here, baby." I mumble my response, at a loss as to why he hasn't answered my question. I feel uncomfortable. Why won't he tell me? If he loved others I will deal with that. I won't like it but I'll deal with it.

"Lucy." I look up from my swirling glass of wine, which is nearly spilling over the sides as I nervously play.

"Yes." My response is quiet.

"Baby, I've only ever loved you. You're my dream girl, you know that. Will you stop asking me about my past now? I want to plan the future with you and Bella, not think about times when you weren't part of my life." The relief washes over me as I smile shyly at Ollie.

"I'm sorry, I just want to know all of you."

"Well maybe then I should ask about your previous relationships but right now I don't want to spoil our first night together in our home." I feel slightly guilty but glad I got that out of the way.

"OK, cheers, Oliver, love of my life, here's to happy times as a family." We clink glasses, our eyes fixed as we both sip our wine. He winks as my body heats with desire. Just one look from this man has such an effect on me! He drives me crazy.

Chapter 17

It's been two weeks now since Bella and I moved into Ollie's London apartment. We've just about got into a routine, Ollie insisting that Bella join the crèche at Fulham Reach where he takes her every morning. I watch the two of them as they head off for their days away from me and feel so relieved that I finally told Ollie about Bella. They adore each other, my two favourite people in the world!

We're back in Layton for the weekend and I'm so excited to see my family. We arrived last night and are heading over to Mamma and Dad's for breakfast. Em is meeting us there, Bella's favourite 'big girl' in the world. She constantly talks about when she's a 'big girl' like Auntie Em, it makes me giggle.

Standing on the balcony, listening to the sea, smelling the salty air, I feel those familiar pangs of wanting to come home. I feel so calm as I watch the sun glistening over the water. I never felt like this until I met Ollie again. Its as if I need to come home now we're together as a family. Perhaps my sub-conscious made me move away when I couldn't be with Ollie? I feel his arms around my waist smiling as he kisses my neck.

"Good morning, Lucia. You enjoying the sea?"

"Mmm, I love the smell and sound of the sea, Ollie. This feels like home." He turns me around, lightly kissing my lips.

"Just say the word, sweetheart, and we can move back here whenever you want. You know how I feel about Layton. I will stay wherever you want, Lucy." I kiss his mouth hard. God, I love this man.

"I can't leave my job, Ollie. There's nothing around here even remotely similar to what I do. I need to change career for us to move back here and I can't for the life of me think of anything else I'd like to do." I smile feeling slightly forlorn at the prospect of not being able to come home.

"Lucy, you don't have to work. If you want to move back, then we can live easily on my salary. You can stay home with Bella." He looks at me hopefully. I shake my head.

"No, I have to contribute, Ollie. I don't think I could be a stay-at-home mum anyhow. I'm sure Bella would hate being cooped up with me all day when she has so much fun at nursery."

"So, Bella can still go to nursery, just not such long hours, maybe just the mornings instead." He tilts his head, his eyes glistening as I think about his offer.

"Hmm, I'll think about it. Come on, we need to get over to my parents for breakfast."

"Can we go and see my mother tomorrow, Luce?" I smile. I really like Ollie's mum and I want to get to know his sister, Catherine.

"Of course, why don't you give her a phone and see what she's doing? I'll get a shower then wake Bella." I hear Ollie chatting happily to his mum as I step into the shower in the en-suite bathroom. I wash hastily, desperately wanting to get going to see my family.

****

As we step into the big old kitchen, Mamma drops everything to take Bella in a hug.

"Oh, it's so good to see my princess. I missed you so much, Bella." Bella laughs as Mamma spins her around, kissing her chubby cheeks.

"I missed you too, Nonna."

"Bella!" My dad appears from the dining room and rushes to take Bella from Mamma. I cough loudly.

214

"Excuse me, you two, what about us?" I point to me and Ollie, left, abandoned while my parents throw all their love into our daughter. Mamma rushes over and grabs me for a hug and a kiss, then takes Ollie in her arms, hugging the life out of him. He grins at me over Mamma's shoulder.

"Ohhh, welcome home, you three." Dad places Bella on the floor, walking to Ollie and clapping his back as he shakes his hand.

"Thanks for bringing my girls home, Ollie."

"It's my pleasure, Pete, really."

"And come here my beauty. Dad pulls me in, kissing my forehead before having a good look at me. "You look so well, Lucy. It's so good to have you back." I feel a lump in my throat. Homesickness overwhelms me right now as I cast a glance at Ollie. He gives me a wink, making me love him more, if that's at all possible. He knows he's made an offer that means I can come home, he's my hero right now.

"Heyyyy, baby Bella!" Emilia appears in the doorway as Bella runs excitedly, throwing herself at my sister. Em picks her up giving her another spin, smothering her in yet mores kisses. Bella laughs excitedly. Oh, my girl loves being here so much!

****

Breakfast was lovely. Chatter constantly filled the air as we all caught up on each other's lives. Mamma and Dad have been offered some help from an old friend meaning they can take a holiday soon. Mamma would love to go home to Sicily and I think Dad's secretly planning this. He gave us a few winks when Mamma mentioned it over breakfast.

Bella's gone off with Ollie and Dad to look at something on the park. Mamma is just busy as usual so Em and me take a walk. I need a good catch up with my sister. I'm eager to find out what's happening with Kyle.

"So, come on then, Em, spill the beans. How's things with you and Kyle?" She blushes. Oh, my sister has it bad.

"Things are going well, Luce. We're hoping to go away in a few weeks. We're going touring round Europe. You know we have so much in common. Kyle loves travelling and you know I do. The only thing that stopped me before was Jamie." She stops walking as I grab her hand.

"Hey."

"No, Luce, I feel bad. I shouldn't have said that."

"You were only stating the truth, Em. Jamie did stop you from travelling. It wasn't his fault he was afraid of flying but you can't feel guilty for pursuing your dreams now he's gone."

"I know, I just feel like I'm betraying him by finding Kyle and loving Kyle."

"So you love him." I glance at her watery eyes as she nods her head. I pull my beautiful sister in for a hug, kissing her hair as I hear her sniffle. I can't even begin to imagine what it's like to lose the love of your life and to find a new love and go through so many emotions, it must be so damned hard. I pull back taking my sister's face in my hands.

"Emilia Meyer, I know Jamie loved you with all his heart and you know he'd want you to be happy, right?" She nods, her face etched in sorrow.

"So why don't you remember that every time you feel happy with Kyle. Remember that Jamie would be pleased for you. He'd be so glad you're not going to be old and lonely since he left you too soon."

"Do you think I should tell Kyle how I feel?" She looks so confused right now.

"Have you ever talked to Kyle about Jamie?"

"Not really. I've never felt the need and he's never asked so I sort of ignored talking about the fact that I was going to marry someone who died." She laughs, an uncomfortable laugh. I sigh, pushing some loose hair behind Em's ear.

"I think it's time you two had a talk then, don't you? I understand why you haven't before, but if you love him then you need to tell him about you and Jamie. He'll understand, Em."

"Hmm, I know. I need to be brave and deal with the past don't I, so that I can move on." I nod my head hugging my sister once more before we carry on with our stroll.

Em and I get back to the house before Ollie, Dad and Bella. Mamma pours us coffee and we take a seat at the garden table situated just outside the kitchen door.

"So, girls, how are things for you both? Everything seems to be changing in both your lives all of a sudden and I don't feel like we have enough time to catch up any more."

Em and I share a look. Mamma wants details. We grin.

"Come on, girls, put your mamma out of her misery. Tell me about the loves of your precious lives."

"Oh, Mamma. Do you really feel like you don't know enough about us?" She nods her head and I feel guilty. I shuffle in my seat to get comfy and smile at my sister and Mamma before I begin.

"Well, do you remember Ollie's dad, Ralph?" Mamma tutts loudly, the grimace on her face telling me just what she thinks of Ralph Ashcroft. Em frowns, she doesn't look sure.

"He's not a nice man, Em. Anyway, he made it clear before I had Bella that he doesn't want me to be with Ollie."

"Right, we know that. So has he been in touch again? I thought Ollie had nothing to do with him." My beautiful sister looks worried sick. I sigh, knowing they're not going to like what I tell them.

"He came to see me at my office a few weeks ago. He basically tried to buy me off. He wanted me to tell Ollie that Bella isn't his and get out of Ollie's life for good." Their gasps make me smile in spite of the sadness I feel at sharing this news.

"So, I refused and asked him to leave. As you can imagine he wasn't very happy and basically told me that he'll do whatever it takes to keep me and Ollie apart."

I watch as Mamma takes a tissue from her pocket and wipes a tear away. Em scrapes her chair closer to me.

"I take it Ollie knows about this?" I nod my head.

"That's why he came back to London with me a few weeks ago. And that's why we all moved into Ollie's place straightaway."

"Now it makes sense why it was all so rushed. Sweetheart, that's just terrible. Your dad is not going to be pleased when he hears this." I sigh loudly again.

"I know Mamma. Ollie is sorting it. He has people working on this, making sure he finds out what his dad has planned next. Bella is just fine. She just loves living with her daddy so there are positives to come out of this."

"So are you planning on staying in London then? I thought Ollie was working with Ben now here in Layton. That must be difficult." Em tilts her head as she comments on this complicated situation we've found ourselves in.

"Well you know we have talked about coming back. The problem is me. What job could I possibly do here?" Mamma and Em both raise their eyebrows at my question.

"You mean you want to continue doing what you're doing now?" Em smiles as she asks.

"Why are you smiling like that, Em?" I feel a little hurt by her obvious humour at my expense.

"Oh sorry, Luce, I was just thinking about that conversation with Summer, Dec's girlfriend. She said you should look at change, didn't she? If you want to move back, see if you can transfer your skills to something else. There must be something." I shrug. I feel completely lost every time I try and think of a career change. I love my job and I can't think of anything else I'd like to do. Mamma giggles.

"What?" I'm beginning to get frustrated at their need to find my situation amusing – I don't!

"Well you always got plenty of praise from Tony when you worked at the ice cream parlour, maybe you should go back to that kind of work." Em snorts with laughter, tipping her chair back on its back legs as she howls. Working at the ice cream parlour was my weekend job when I was sixteen years old!

"Thanks, Mamma, that kind of advice really helps." Mamma and Em are still laughing loudly as Ollie and Dad approach, swinging Bella between them.

"Glad to see my girls are all so happy." Dad gives Mamma a peck on the cheek as he stands behind her, massaging her shoulders as he watches us.

"Hmm, as usual Dad, it's at my expense." I glance at Ollie who gives me a wink. My heart flip-flops and I give him a smile, just for him. Em coughs loudly. As I look at her, she pretends to gag. I grab a biscuit from the plate in the center of the table and throw it at her, just missing as she ducks.

"Girls, stop it." Mamma gives us a look. We stop. Bella crawls up on my lap and distracts me from all previous conversations.

"Can we go to the beach today, Mummy, please?" I look into her dark eyes and feel my heart melt as she smiles and I see her dimple. I look up as Ollie smiles at me and I check out his matching dimple. They are my world and I love them both so much!

"Of course we can, Princess, just check with Daddy in case he made plans." Bella and I both look at Ollie for agreement. He blows Bella a kiss and she pretends to catch it.

"I'd love to go to the beach with my favourite girls."

****

We arrive back at the apartment and I'm shattered. Bella has had a ball this afternoon. Ollie and I have been in and out of the water with her constantly. We've built sandcastles, cars and boats. We went fishing in rock pools with our new nets that Ollie insisted we buy. If you could write the perfect day at the beach for a three-year-old princess then today was definitely perfect material. Ollie chuckles as he watches Bella trying to keep hers eyes open as she eats her dinner. It's painful to watch so I take a seat next to her and spoon feed her the pasta I quickly made.

Ollie sits opposite and watches as Bella slowly opens her mouth for each spoonful.

"Hey, beautiful." Bella looks at her daddy and grins with a mouth full of food.

"Bella! Close your mouth. Princesses don't do that." I smile as she clamps her mouth shut and chews as she eyes Ollie. He gives her a wink and we both giggle as she tries to wink back. It's just the cutest thing ever to watch her blink both eyes closed whilst she lifts her cheek.

I walk into the living room after settling Bella down as Ollie appears from the kitchen with two glasses of wine in his hands. Coldplay is playing in the background as I follow him to the sofas. We cozy up on one sofa, both tired out from our busy day entertaining our daughter. We don't speak, each of us lost in thoughts and contentment. I glance at my dream come true and can't quite believe I'm here with him. He really is perfect and I regularly pinch myself to reassure me that this isn't just one of my girlie dreams. Ollie is wearing navy board shorts and a fitted white t-shirt. He has a perfect body and I can just make out his abs through his shirt as he sits next to me with his legs up of the sofa. I watch as he touches my foot with his toe. Even a touch like that drives me wild. I look at him and he smiles, a slow sexy smile.

"I love being with you, Luce. This is just perfect. Thank you, baby."

"Don't thank me, Ollie, please." He frowns, I tilt my head and sigh.

"Baby, you gave me the most perfect little girl in the world and I will never stop thanking you for Bella." I swallow the urge to cry. At times like this the guilt comes back in waves. I wish he'd been there from the beginning. I place my wine glass on the side table and pull myself so that I'm straddling Ollie. I run my fingers through his hair, leaning in to smell his wonderful scent.

"I love you so much, Oliver." I gently kiss his lips and relish the moan that escapes his mouth.

"I love you more." Our foreheads touch as I shake my head.

"Not possible, Oliver."

We're interrupted by the cry of Bella. It's unusual and I jump up, concerned for my baby. I rush to her princess bedroom as she waves her arms in panic.

"What, baby, what is it? Mummy's here now, what's wrong, Bella?"

"Ly, Mummy, ly." I stand still and listen to the buzzing sound of a blue bottle frantically trying to get out of the window.

"Oh, baby, don't worry. Mummy will let the fly out." I open the window and shoo the fly out. I turn to my baby who is calming now. I take a seat on the bed and cuddle her, taking in her lovely baby smell.

"You OK now, Princess?" She nods her head so I gently lay her back down on her pillow and kiss her gently goodnight.

I smile to myself as I walk back to the living room. I hear Ollie's voice and realize he's on the phone. I can see him pacing to and fro in the kitchen. I choose not to enter, taking my seat on the sofa instead. I take a sip of the tasty white wine and try not the listen to Ollie's conversation. He's talking to his mum. I smile. I bet they're making plans for tomorrow.

"I don't want to see him, Mum. What's so important that he has to get you to contact me to see him?" I'm curious now, not moving so that I can hear.

"So why can't you just tell me? Why have I got to see him? I know it's not your fault, Mum. Yeah, OK, I'll call him. I'll see you tomorrow. OK, Mum, love you too, bye."

I wait for Ollie to return. He doesn't. I place my wine back on the table and make my way to the kitchen. Ollie is standing with his back to me, leaning against the counter, both arms straight in front of him. He looks anxious.

"Ollie." My voice is quiet. I don't want to make him jump. He turns quickly, running his hands through his hair then pinching the bridge of his nose.

"Hey." He smiles, his eyes full of anxiety.

"You OK?" Obviously, he's not. He thinks for a few seconds before responding.

"Not really Luce. That was my mum. Apparently, Dad has contacted her to let me know he wants to see me."

"Why?" I feel anxiety pouring through my body. He shrugs, his face pale as he thinks.

"I don't know, Luce. He wouldn't tell Mum. Just insisted that she tell me he wants to see me as soon as possible."

"Is it about me?"

He frowns. "I hope not, Lucy. I love you, baby, and I don't want to involve him in any part of our lives." He holds his hand out to me and I take it as he pulls me to him. He kisses my hair and I relish his touch.

"You and Bella are my world and he won't come between us, baby. I promise."

****

The afternoon at Ollie's mum's house has been nice. There's the phone call about his dad looming over us like a dark cloud. No one mentions it but we're all aware. Occasionally I catch Penny, Ollie's mum, watching me. When I look, she just smiles. It's a sympathetic smile and I feel awkward. I stand to take Bella to the toilet and feel slightly relieved that I can get away for a few moments. Bella and I head into the house from the garden. I glance back and watch as Ollie and his mum are deep in conversation, no doubt about Ralph Ashcroft and his demanding ways.

"Mummy, my tummy hurts." I ruffle Bella's hair as she takes a pee.

"Well I did tell you not to eat two pieces of cake, baby." She stands as I rearrange her clothing, her face looks so pale all of a sudden. I touch her forehead with the back of my hand. She feels OK. I check her neck. No temperature. That's good. I turn to open the toilet door as Bella vomits all down the back of my legs and over the tiled floor. I scream in shock as Bella bursts into tears.

"Oh, baby! Lean over the toilet, darling, in case you're going to be sick again." I hold her with one hand as I rub at the back of my legs with toilet paper. Fortunately, I have shorts on today. I rub Bella's tummy as she vomits again. My poor baby!

We must have been in here for a while now. In between Bella vomiting, I've been trying to clean up the mess on the floor. Bella has stopped crying and is being very brave, poor thing. She's had two enormous pieces of Penny's homemade chocolate cake and I'm pretty sure that's why she's been sick.

"Lucy, are you two OK?" It's Ollie tapping lightly on the toilet door. I risk leaving Bella for a second to open the door.

"Not really. Bella's just thrown up everywhere. Could you ask your mum for something to clean the floor, please?" Penny is standing behind Ollie.

"Oh, Lucy, don't worry about that, I'll sort it later. Is she still being sick or has it stopped?"

"To be honest, I think she's finished now. Too much cake, I think."

"Daddy." Bella's pathetically tiny voice makes everyone look and say 'ah' simultaneously. Bella holds her arms out to Ollie. He gently pushes past me and takes her in his arms.

"Poor baby. I think Daddy needs to take you home." She snuggles in as Ollie carries her out of the bathroom. I follow them, grabbing my bag, finding some baby wipes to clean the back of my legs.

"Mum, we'll get going, OK?" Penny looks awash with worry.

"I'm sorry, Lucy, I shouldn't have let her have so much cake."

"Please, don't be sorry. She'll be fine, I'm sure." I lean in and kiss Penny's cheek then follow Ollie out to the car.

Fortunately, we planned to go back to London tomorrow so Bella can just go straight to bed when we get back rather than have to travel back. I've taken the day off work tomorrow so that Ollie can catch up with Ben. He's been a bit neglectful of his new business partner since all this with his dad visiting me.

We settle Bella down on one of the sofas, wrapped in her quilt with a bucket next to her, just in case, then we settle down to watch her, both worried in case the vomiting starts up again.

"You OK, Lucy?"

"I'm fine. I might just go and take a quick shower though. I can still smell vomit on me." Ollie grimaces as I head off to the bathroom.

"Will you be OK?" I look back, he smiles.

"I promise I won't take my eyes off her while you're gone." I touch his cheek as I walk past. He grabs my hand, lightly kissing my fingers.

I wander back into the living room with my wet hair pulled back in a ponytail, dressed in a simple white t-shirt and some grey shorts to find Ollie in exactly the same spot as I left him.

"She's fast asleep now, Luce. I think you were right. Too much cake!" He pats the seat beside him. I check Bella's temperature before taking a seat.

"I'm sorry we had to come home early." Ollie pulls me close kissing the side of my head.

"Mmm, you smell good enough to eat now, Luce." I look into his ice-blues before kissing his beautiful mouth. Fireworks shoot through my body as we share a kiss. I pull away, aware that Bella is right by us.

"What time are you meeting Ben tomorrow?"

"About nine thirty. Shall I drop you at your parents on the way?"

"Yeah, that'll be fine so long as Bella's OK."

****

Bella was fine. She slept through last night and has had a ball following Granddad around the grounds as he went about his jobs this morning. We've come for a walk to see Auntie Em who's busy painting in her studio while Todd her student helper holds the fort out front of the shop. Todd is studying fine art at university and helps Em out every holiday. He's lovely and Bella finds him highly entertaining.

"Hey, Bella, how are you, princess? Come and let me see how much you've grown." I watch as Bella heads straight to Todd, her dimple showing as she grins at her friend. Todd makes a big fuss about how tall she is and Bella just delights in his attention. I leave the two together as I head out back to find Emilia who's engrossed in her painting.

"Em." She wipes the back on her hand across her forehead before dropping her paintbrushes.

"Hey, Luce. How's your weekend been?"

"Good except Bella threw up when we were at Ollie's mum's yesterday." Em groans and I grimace.

"Is she OK now?"

"Yep, just too much cake, I think. Anyway, how about you, have you had a chance to speak to Kyle?" Em holds up a mug, offering me coffee, I nod my head, watching closely as my sister proceeds to make us a drink.

"Coffee, Todd?" Em shouts to her assistant.

"Yes, please, Em." Em makes us all a coffee, taking Todd his and fussing over Bella before she returns to me when she can fill me in on what's going on with Kyle.

"We spoke."

"Is that all you're telling me?" I raise an eyebrow at my sister.

"No, silly." She pats my arm and takes a sip of coffee.

"Kyle was fine. Just like I thought. He said he loves me and will just go at my pace. He asked if I want to slow things down, but I don't, Luce. Is that bad?" I shake my head smiling at Em.

"Of course, it's not. If you feel it's right, then it is. So long as you communicate and tell Kyle if something is bothering you then he'll always be able to understand, won't he?"

"Hmm. I decided I really want to go on this holiday with Kyle, so I've squared it with Todd to look after this place for me while we go away."

"When are you going?"

"On Friday."

"That soon?"

"Why wait? Kyle had holiday booked from work anyway and if Todd's here it means I don't have to shut the shop so yes, that soon."

"Oh, Em, I'm so pleased for you. Where are you going?" Em places her mug of coffee down and jumps up excitedly.

"We're picking up a camper van on Friday morning then driving down to the docks. We're starting in France and then we have no plans at all. We're just going to see where the roads take us. I'm sooo excited, Luce." I feel my heart swell as I watch the enjoyment on Em's face at sharing this news with me. She deserves to be happy, so much.

"Oh, Em, that's sounds so exciting. I'm jealous. I wish I could just take off with Ollie like that. How romantic."

"You off back to London tonight?"

"Yes. Ollie had a call from his mum yesterday. His dad is demanding to see him. I assume he'll be seeing him this week."

"Oh, Luce, that's not good news. What's it about?" Em's face is creased in a frown as she asks.

"I don't know, neither does Ollie. I just hope it's not about me, Em."

"Maybe it's business. Ollie worked for him for a long time, didn't he?"

"I hope so, Em." Em rubs my arm supportively as Bella drags Todd through to the back.

"Mummy, I love Todd." Todd's blushing face is a picture as Bella kisses his hand whilst declaring her love for him.

"I'm sure if you ask him nicely, Bella, Todd, will marry you when you're a big girl." Em giggles as she plants the idea in Bella's head and Todd's face reddens some more.

"Perhaps you need to meet Bella's daddy then, Todd." I give him a wink as he sidles back out front of shop – poor boy!

Chapter 18

Bella slept all the way home last night as I filled Ollie in on all my family news. He was as pleased as me to hear about Em and Kyle's plans to go away. That gave us food for thought so we spent the rest of our journey back to London sharing ideas about where we'd like to visit in the world.

I'm back at work and enjoying the fast pace of planning a new shoot. Lisa and I are working on separate projects this time and I kind of miss her. Will decided to let us shine independently after the success of Milan.

I stop for lunch, a quick sandwich at my desk. I check my phone, no calls. I was expecting to hear from Ollie at some point. I wonder if he's called his dad. I decide to give him a call.

"Hey, I was just going to call you, baby. How's your day?"

"Good, really good, but I miss you. Have you called your dad yet?"

He sighs before answering. "Yes, I'm meeting him later. Might as well get this over and done with as soon as possible. He enjoys all this anticipation, Luce, it's part of his plan, you know, to get us guessing? He loves playing games."

"Where are you meeting?"

"He wants me to go to his office. Maybe it's about work, sometimes things crop up from years ago. Maybe he needs my help?" Ollie laughs, I smile at his optimism.

"What time?"

"Two thirty. I'll pick you up as normal, I can tell you all about it on our way home. If I get caught up, I'll let you know in plenty of time so you can pick Bella up. I shouldn't be more than an hour, though."

"Well I'm in the office most of the afternoon so call me any time OK?"

"Will do. Luce?"

"Yes?"

"Stop worrying, it'll be OK, I promise." I smile in spite of my anxiety.

"OK. I love you, Ollie."

"Love you too. Bye Luce." I hang up hoping he's right and it's nothing more than a business meeting. I suspect it has nothing to do with work though and dread starts to seep through my body.

****

The afternoon flew by as I worked on my new solo project. I had a few micro meetings with Lisa where we reassured each other on the ideas we've had for both our projects. Sharing my ideas with Lisa feels normal, I feel more confident now I've discussed things with her.

As I leave the office the anxiety, I felt earlier creeps back. Ollie is waiting outside for me as usual so that's good. He didn't get held up which I believed he would.

"Hey." I step into the car and lean in to kiss Ollie. His smile is there but his ice blues are definitely not sharing joy. I frown. He smiles harder. He's trying too hard.

"What's wrong?" He hasn't spoken yet.

"Nothing, Luce." He pulls me into a hug, inhaling my scent before kissing me hard on the mouth.

"I missed you, baby." His eyes are intense. He stares at me for a few seconds, his index finger running down my cheek.

"Did it go OK with your dad?" I reach to fasten my seat belt as I ask. When he doesn't answer straight away, I quickly look back. He's looking out of his side window, as if he can't look me in the eye. The fear I've had since he got the call from his mum on Saturday is galloping all over me giving me goose bumps.

"Ollie?" He turns to me trying to smile.

"It went OK, Luce. Nothing to worry about, baby. Let's go and fetch our princess, shall we?" As he pulls out into the traffic, I get the distinct impression that all is not well and he's not going to tell me why. I want to challenge him but I'm scared to know, if I'm honest. I spend the rest of the journey home in silence, anger building inside. Anger towards Ollie for not telling me every tiny detail about his meeting with his dad, but more anger towards Ralph for causing all this unsettled shit that's going on.

I silently go about preparing dinner and realize that Ollie is completely avoiding me. He's been intently playing with Bella since we got back and only speaks to me when he really has to.

The three of us sit at the dinner table, Bella enjoying all this attention. She's usually admonished for talking too much instead of eating, but tonight she has free rein to talk as much as she likes – she's the only one talking. I stay seated as long as I can stand the agony of knowing that something is going on and I'm not going to be told, before taking my plate of food and scraping the uneaten meal in the bin. As I turn to place the plate in the dishwasher, Ollie is there, standing, watching me. His eyes look sorrowful. My heart prepares to be broken again, I just know this isn't going to end well.

He walks towards me and pulls me into his arms. His hug is far too tight. I take in his smell and hold back the tears. I run my fingers up and down his back feeling his taut muscles.

"I love you, Lucia, more than life itself." I pull back thinking maybe now I get to hear the bad news because I know there's some coming.

"I love you too, Ollie. Are you about to break my heart again because if you are, can we get this over and done with?" His watery eyes are staring at me and I have to look away.

"Mummmmmyyyy," Bella yells from her place at the table. For once, neither of us acknowledges our daughter.

"You know I promised I would spend the rest of my life making you happy and I will try and keep that promise, Luce, really I will.

Today was hard and I really don't want to talk about it. Needless to say, my father was his usual conniving, spiteful self. But I'll deal with it, Lucy." I pull away, angry with him.

"So tell me what happened, Ollie. If you keep this from me, then your father's battle is already won. He's coming between us and with very little effort, from what I can see."

Ollie looks angry, his ice-blue eyes staring me out.

"NO, Lucy. Now let's just drop this, shall we?" He doesn't raise his voice but the anger is there all the same. I run from the kitchen, unable to hold back the tears.

I lie on the bed for a while and listen to him playing with Bella as if nothing is wrong. When I can't stand it any longer, I sit up and grab my phone.

"Lisa?"

"Hi, Luce. Thanks for today. It feels so wrong not going through plans with you. Once I'd explained my project plan to you, I felt so much better, didn't you?"

"Yes, Lisa, I did. Listen, are you doing anything tonight?'

"No, why? Are you OK, Lucy?"

"Not really, can I come over?"

"Of course, is Bella OK?"

"She's fine. I'll be about an hour. I'll just get her to bed, then I'll leave."

"OK, see you later."

I pull myself from the bed and head to the bathroom for a shower. I'm just about to step in when Ollie and Bella appear before me.

"You OK, Luce?" I look at him crossly. No, of course I'm not OK.

"I'm just taking a shower."

"Shall I get Bella ready for bed then?"

"Yes, please, I'll come and say night-night when I've finished, baby" They leave the room and my heart aches.

He really is going to carry on as if nothing happened today. Maybe I should contact his father myself. If he wants to hurt me, I'm sure he'll share whatever is going on with me.

I'm towel drying my hair as he walks into the bedroom. I'm naked, and for a second I contemplate covering up from him. I feel so hurt right now. He walks towards me and I step back.

"Is Bella in bed?"

"Yes, sweetheart, she went straight to sleep, sorry, I tried to keep her awake for you." I sigh. Something else to upset my evening. I didn't get to tell my baby goodnight!

"I'm going out for a couple of hours. Will you be OK to sit Bella?" He runs his hands through his hair and sighs loudly.

"Of course, I'll sit my own daughter, where are you going?"

"Just over to Lisa's, we need to talk about a project at work."

"Right, you didn't say earlier."

"I forgot, she just called to remind me." Oh, my God, I'm lying now. Maybe Ralph Ashcroft will win without even trying. He's already creating problems. I sigh and sink down onto the bed. I drop my head into my hands, not wanting to be here right now.

I feel the bed dip at the side of me. Ollie places his arm around my naked waist. The feel of his fingers on my skin makes me want to forget all this shit and just get lost in my man. He leans down and kisses my shoulder. I don't move, I can't.

"Lucy, talk to me?"

"Ha!" I lift my head as anger soars through me.

"How fucking dare you ask me to talk to you when you can't even share what's actually going on here." I wave my hands around as I stand up. Ollie stands, grabbing me by the wrists. A tear escapes as I struggle to get free from his hold. He pulls me to him as I continue to struggle.

"Lucy, look at me." I look down, refusing to look at him. He turns us around and pushes me back on the bed. Before I can escape he straddles me, sitting on my legs and holding my arms above my head.

"Do you trust me, Lucy?" I close my eyes tightly shut, ignoring him completely.

"Lucy, answer me, do you trust me?" I stay silent. He sighs loudly. The air of silence hanging over the two of us as he holds me down is deafening.

I feel his lips on my neck and a shiver runs through me. Now he's not playing fair.

"You are so beautiful, even when you're mad with anger, you're beautiful, Lucia." His kisses move across my neck to my shoulder as a moan escapes my mouth. His tongue licks my skin my eyes shoot open.

"Do you trust me?" He looks up and kisses the end of my nose. My body is letting me down here. I'm so damned angry with him but I want him so, so badly. I refuse to answer yet again. He runs his tongue across my lips.

He's going to torture me with sex until I speak! I close my eyes again, hoping I can block him out if I don't look at him – no chance!

His beautiful mouth is playing havoc with my senses right now as his lips tickle my skin, moving across my upper body.

"I will make you speak to me, Lucia, even if it's just to tell me how much you want me baby." I feel his tongue running circles around my nipple and arch into his body. I feel the smile on his mouth and curse his sexiness. He moves to the other nipple as my groin begins to ache.

Oh God, this feels so good. I wriggle around wanting him to free my hands. I need to touch him. He won't let go.

"Look at me, beautiful. If you want me to let go, you have to look at me." I open my eyes and come face to face with his ice blues.

"I love you." The words are out before I can stop them. His mouth crashes on mine as I open my lips to find his tongue. He lets go of my wrists and I run my fingers through his messy hair, then down his back pulling at his shirt. I want him naked. His kisses move down my neck again until he finds my nipple. I cry out his name, lost in a world of lust and love. He quickly removes his clothes before lying next to me on the bed. We're side by side, facing each other as he runs his fingers up and down my body. I touch his lips and he takes my finger in his mouth. The light touch of his fingers set my body on fire as they move down my thigh, my heart racing at his every touch. I'm on fire right now and my need for him has far surpassed my anger. His fingers make gentle circles up and down my thigh to my knee and back. I groan. He finds the top of my legs and I arch into him. I want to feel him on top of me. As he strokes his way through my folds I run my fingers up his forearm quietly calling his name.

"I love you, Lucia, with all my heart, I love you." He pushes me onto my back and enters me slowly and gently. Our eyes are transfixed as we move together, our bodies joining as one. I don't want this to end. I want to stay here forever. His kisses start at my nose and move all over my upper body as he makes sweet love to me. My heart feels like it will explode with love for my man. As my desire takes over I force him to move faster and harder as I bite on his shoulder. As we reach our peak together my world feels just perfect at this second. With my eyes closed I lie still and savour the feel of his body on mine, his gentle kisses as he tells me over and over how much he loves me.

****

We may have just made THE most perfect love but I'm still mad! I'm dressed and ready to leave. I kissed Bella night-night when she was already sleeping and now Ollie is watching me as I prepare to go out.

"Do you really have to go out, Luce?" I stop applying my lipstick and watch his reflection in the mirror.

"Ollie, this isn't over, is it? You can't even tell me what happened today but I have to talk about this situation. Sooo, I'm going to see my friend who will happily chew the cud with me." He shrugs his shoulders and leaves the room. That just makes me madder!

I called a cab and when the buzzer sounds, I rush and answer quickly. Grabbing my bag, I look for Ollie. I can't see him so I shout goodbye. No answer. I shrug, my heart hurting from his actions. As far as I'm concerned, he's being a child and the more he does this, the angrier I get. I slam the nearest door as hard as I can and stomp off to the elevator.

I arrive at Lisa's in a foul mood. He is so damned unreasonable but thinks it's OK to seduce me even when I'm mad as fuck!

"Hey, come on in. What's wrong, sweetie?" We hug quickly and I follow Lisa into her flat. Maroon 5 is playing, enticing a smile from what seems like my permanently grumpy face.

"Oh, Lise, a bit of Adam Levine always makes me smile, thank you." She turns with a grin. "He's gonna marry me one day, just you see." We laugh. Lisa pours me some wine but hugs me before passing me my drink.

"I love you, Lucy." Just those words bring on the tears. She holds me as I sob into her shoulder.

"What is it, Lucy? What's wrong?"

"Oh Lisa, Ollie's dad is back causing problems again." We both sigh loudly as we take a seat on her sofa. I sip the wine she poured and smile as she watches me.

"So, what's the old bastard gone and done now?" I can't help but giggle at her phrase. Chris Martin from Coldplay fills my head as he sings 'Yellow' and for a moment I'm lost in his words, welcoming the distraction.

"Lucy." Lisa is watching me intently.

"Sorry, Lise, that's just it, I don't fucking know!" I look at my beautiful friend as she watches me intently.

"Ollie had a call from his mum demanding that his dad see him. His mum had no idea what it was about. So anyway, he went to see him today but won't tell me what or who it was about. I'm so fucking mad, Lisa, with Ollie for not telling me and with his dad for upsetting our happy life. Oh, and to top it off, I wouldn't speak to Ollie so the bastard seduced me before I came out." Lisa chuckles, kissing my cheek.

"Oh, baby, too much emotion for any person in one night." I'm not sure if her voice is mocking or sympathetic so I go with the latter.

"So, help me out here, friend, what should I do? Should I let him just pretend nothing is going on or should I bloody well phone Ralph Ashcroft myself and find out what's going on?" Lisa is shaking her head frantically, her long, blonde hair swirling around her face.

"Please don't contact Ollie's dad, Luce. Just give Ollie a bit of time. Maybe it's easy fixed and he doesn't want to tell you until he's sorted it." We share a look.

"You don't believe that any more than I do, Lisa. Knowing what his dad did in the past, I'm sure this is just as bad, if not worse."

"So maybe you just have to trust Ollie and let him deal with it. He won't want you worrying, Luce." I sigh.

"Hmm, that's what he kept asking me earlier, do I trust him, but I was too angry to even speak to him then."

"So, give him a chance, sweetie. You live together now as a family and my guess is that he won't let anything come between you, not again." Great! So now I feel bad. I should have spoken with him and not walked out in a huff. Bugger!

My phone beeps a text, I grab it from the table, it's from Ollie.

"I'm sorry, Luce, I love you xx" I look at Lisa who is smiling, her head tilted to one side.

"Ollie?"

"Yep."

"So, all will be fine, my special friend, all will be fine, I just know it."

"I wish I had your confidence, Lisa." I text back a heart and a kiss as I speak to Lisa.

"Just let Ollie deal with this and you concentrate on building your life as a family instead. By the way, how are things at Fulham Reach, you lucky cow?"

"Good, really good. Bella loves the crèche and she also loves that Daddy drops her off every day. They've got their own little club, those two. But seriously, I miss Layton, Lisa, I'm thinking about moving back. I know Ollie would love to. His work is based there now with Ben so living in London creates a few problems for him. He's going to have to start staying away soon, I know. I just don't know what I'd do for a career if I leave the magazine. I love my job, I just don't know." My friend touches my arm. I look up into her pretty hazel eyes.

"We all have to move on you know. We evolve, Lucy, that's good. You know, I've been thinking about moving on." I'm shocked, really shocked.

"What, why?" Lisa giggles.

"Well, you know Giovanni?"

"Yessss." Now I'm excited. I know they've spent a lot of time together. Giovanni was here for ages after Adriano went back to Milan and I know Lisa's been back to Milan for a weekend.

"Well, I think he's the one. I don't want a long-distance relationship, Luce. I want to be with him all the time. He's perfect. I love him." Wow, that's an information overload.

"Oh my! So what are you going to do?"

"Well I'm looking for some work out there. Maybe I'll work with Giovanni for a while, I have some savings so I could work with him and maybe practice some photography myself. You know I did that evening course ages ago so it wouldn't be like I don't know anything." I'm nodding my head and imagining my dear friend getting married in that beautiful setting, Parco Sempione, where we shot the winter shoot that Will our boss loved so much.

"Oh, Lisa, that sounds so exciting. Soo romantic. Gosh, imagine if we both leave, Will won't be too pleased."

"Oh, you have to look out for yourself in this life, Lucy. There are loads of good interns coming through. Will could easily find our replacements."

"Thanks, Lisa." I knock her arm playfully.

"Well, you really didn't think you'd stay there forever, did you? You gain your experience and you move on to bigger, better things, right?" She raises an eyebrow and I have to nod my agreement.

"I know you're right, it's just scary when everything changes. Change is good, but it's going to the unknown that shakes my nerves."

"You will find something and it will be perfect for your new life with Ollie and Bella. It might not be what you planned in the beginning but who follows their plan to the letter these days? There's too many opportunities out there, Lucy, to stand still in life."

"And when did you become so wise?"

"Just living, Lucy, just living."

****

I tiptoe through the flat, hoping I don't make too much noise. It's not too late and I'm guessing Ollie will be in bed. I'm wrong! As I enter the living room, I hear the hushed tones of the TV and find him sleeping on the sofa. He looks divine. He's stretched out hugging a cushion to him, lightly snoring. I turn off the TV, turning to watch Ollie. He is perfect. His long lashes lay perfectly on his cheeks, hiding those beautiful ice blue eyes that mesmerize me. I lean over and lightly touch his kissable lips with my finger. He licks his lips as I smile, feeling very lucky indeed that we eventually found each other. I kneel down beside him and gently touch his hand. He moans and fidgets but continues to sleep. Should I find a blanket and leave him here or wake him? I decide to go get a drink first, heading to the kitchen for some water.

I turn, glass in hand and he's there, watching me.

"Hey." His voice sounds gruff from sleep. I sip my water as my heart swells at the sight of my dream come true.

"Hey. Would you like a drink?" He moves towards me, I don't move. I need to feel him, to make things right from earlier. Lisa's right, I need to trust him. I need to apologise. Ollie takes me in his arms, kissing me softly.

"I'm so sorry, Lucy. I should have talked to you. I just don't want you worrying, baby, that's all." I pull back.

"I'm sorry, Ollie. I should have trusted you. I do. I just have to let you sort this and tell me when you're ready. I'm scared, that's all. Your dad scares me so much after what he did before. He could so easily make this…" I wave my arm between Ollie and I. "Fall apart."

"No, he fucking can't, Lucy. Don't ever think that. He will never, ever, come between you and me again like that, I promise."

Chapter 19

Things are just about back to normal. Ollie and Bella go about their daily drop off / pick up routines. They love it! I love watching them together.

Ollie has to go back to Layton for a few days so we've been out for a special dinner tonight – to Bella's favourite restaurant of course! Bella tucked into her favourite pasta as Ollie watched her like he's never going to see her again. He's going for two days whereas if you were watching him, you'd think he was disappearing for a year. Ollie insisted on sharing a huge ice cream dessert with Bella much to her delight and she's now snoring her head off in her princess palace bedroom.

I open the door and head out to the roof terrace. The night is warm and balmy, the air quite humid. I walk out to the balcony's edge and lean out to watch the image of the world drifting by the River Thames. The view out here is spectacular, the warm breeze invigorating. Ollie is busy packing his bags, which I found really hard to watch so I came out here to clear my head. My project at work is going well but I'm so busy now that I'm working on my own. It's only now that I appreciate how much easier it was when Lisa and I had each other. Work is full on from the moment I get there until I step out of the foyer and spot Ollie's car each evening. I know Ollie has been neglecting his work to look after me and as much as I like it, it can't last forever.

****

So, he went off to Layton this morning and I feel lost already. I miss him, my heart hurts that he's far away and I want him back. I feel like a spoiled child but I can't help the way I feel. I don't voice these thoughts to anyone, not even Ollie when he texts to see how my day is. Instead I sulk in my office like a teenage girl who's fallen out with her best friend.

Lisa called in earlier and we had one of our micro meetings where we show each other what we've worked on so far and then critique each other in the friendliest possible way. I have no idea if Will knows how often we're meeting but so long as we achieve the desired outcome I doubt he'll say a word. I love working side by side with Lisa, I miss her! I place my elbows on the desk and lean on my hands, sulking once again. My hormones must be all over the place, I am so emotionally up and down today it's disturbing for me, so goodness knows what it's like for those around me.

I'm pulled out of my teenage sulk when the phone rings. Suzie cautiously tells me there's a Mister Ashcroft on the line for me.

"Do you want me to take a message, Lucy?" I sigh rubbing hard at my forehead with my fingertips.

"No, Suzie, put him through. I've been expecting his call." This is true. I kind of guessed that whatever happened with Ollie, he would make sure I knew. Does he know that Ollie's out of town or is this just a coincidence?

"Mr Ashcroft, hello." I keep it short. I really don't want to speak to the man. I take deep breaths trying to stay calm even though my heart is currently beating out of my chest. I hear his sly laugh and swallow hard. He's evil, pure evil.

"Did Oliver tell you that we met? Well anyhow, Miss Meyer, I wonder if you'd like to meet, we need to chat." I swallow again. Why does he want to see me?

"If you've seen Oliver then you have no need to see me." He clears his throat loudly. I move the phone away from my ear and pull a face at him.

"Well I think maybe you need to know what we discussed and seeing as I've heard nothing, I'm guessing Oliver hasn't told you so I really think it's in your interest to meet me." I sigh, closing my eyes as I pinch the bridge of my nose. Should I call Ollie first before I agree to see him, should I refuse or should I just hang up? The air is heavy with silence as I think and this evil man waits for my answer.

"Really, Miss Meyer you should know everything, don't you think?" He sounds so damned arrogant and I hate him, really hate him but I know I'm going to agree to see this man because I want to know what's going on. Fuck, fuck, fuck!

"OK, when and where?"

"Come to my office, Miss Meyer, when are you free?"

"How soon do you mean?"

"Well let's get this over with shall we, today would be good. Can you meet me here this afternoon?" I check the time. I have to pick up Bella after work. Usually Ollie picks her up before fetching me but he's away so I have to get a tube back.

"I don't have much time today. I can make it to your office in the next hour but I won't have much time. Is this going to take long?" He laughs. I hate him some more.

"Be here in forty-five minutes. It won't take long." He hangs up before I have time to answer. The phone only just survives as I slam the receiver back with all the anger I feel towards this man. There's a quiet knock on the door. It's Suzie.

"You OK, Lucy? I know last time you spoke to him he really upset you." I smile at her thoughtfulness.

"I'm OK thanks, Suzie. Angry but OK." She tilts her head.

"You sure? You look very pale. Can I get you something?" I laugh sarcastically.

"Hmmm, maybe a gin and tonic." Suzie doesn't laugh she raises an eyebrow and stares at me.

"Lucy, are you sure it's OK?" I nod my head whilst my inner self yells NOOOOO.

I watch as Suzie leaves the room and feel my heart weighing heavy in my chest. I stand and walk over to the cabinet and pour a glass of water. I watch my hand shaking as I pour. Damn that man!

****

I stand outside Ralph Ashcroft's office block and wait just a few seconds before entering the lobby. I know I look fine on the outside but right now my stomach is churning and my head is pounding. What can he say or do to hurt me? What?

I make my way to the lift taking deep, steady breaths in order to keep calm. I step into the empty lift and press the button for the tenth floor. He knows that I know where to find him. The last time I came here was when Ollie told me he didn't want me. When I was pregnant with our child.

I step out of the lift and walk towards the reception desk. The immaculately coiffed receptionist looks up and smiles as I approach.

"Can I help you?"

"I'm here to see Mr Ashcroft."

"Can I take your name, please?" I cough nervously. I want to go, to phone Ollie and tell him I nearly saw his dad. To let Ollie tell me I did the right thing by not going but I don't. I put on my best smile and give her my name. She looks down and checks, smiling as she asks me to take a seat.

My phone beeps a text, it's Lisa. I let her know where I was going before I left. I had to tell someone. I have no idea what I'm walking into today and I needed to make sure someone knew to take care of Bella if I get held up in any way.

"Are you there?" I smile at my friend's text and quickly respond.

"Yes, I'm waiting to be seen ☹ and shitting my pants ☹"

"Be brave and don't agree to anything without telling Ollie first OK!" I nod my head as I type my reply.

"I will and I won't xxx"

"Miss Meyer," I jump as the pretty lady calls my name.

"Mr Ashcroft will see you now." She stands and walks around the desk to me, guiding the way to Ollie's dad's office. My throat is dry and I all I can hear is my heart beat. I'm scared, really scared.

I walk into his office and I'm not surprised at all by the dark oak furniture, thick carpet and the heavy drapes at the windows. It's very old school and so... him!

Ralph Ashcroft is seated behind a large desk, something I'd expect to see in a solicitor's office. He's seated in a large, leather swivel chair, that creaks when he moves. He thanks the receptionist and waves her away. I go cold when I'm left standing alone as I hear the door close behind the kind lady. I want to call out to her not to leave me. I look down and try with all my might to stay calm.

"Please take a seat, Miss Meyer?" He gestures to a seat opposite him. I tentatively walk across the room and take a seat. My hands feel clammy and sweaty from nerves. He looks calm as can be – pig! The room is silent for a few seconds. I don't look up. I have no desire to see this man's face ever again. The longer I can put off staring into his evil face the better. I'm slightly shocked when I hear a knock at the door.

"Come in." His voice is commanding as he calls out. I hear the door open and close. I don't look up. I sense someone in the room and wait for Ralph to converse with the visitor.

"Miss Meyer, I'd like to introduce you to Miss Hamilton." I look up, surprised and curious. Who is this woman and why is he introducing her to me? The woman is taller than me, a good few inches taller. She's skinny and very feminine in her beautifully tailored, deep red dress. She has very short dark hair and the biggest, most beautiful blue eyes that glisten as she holds out her graceful hand to me.

"Lucy, isn't it?" I nod my head, standing to shake her hand, curiosity just about killing me.

"Call me Serena. It's good to meet you." The penny drops and my blood runs cold. Why is Ralph Ashcroft introducing me to

Ollie's ex-girlfriend? I look across the room at him and he's smirking. The smug bastard is smirking.

"Take a seat, Serena dear, Miss Meyer." He gestures for us both to sit. We do. Serena takes the seat next to me and smiles a sickly-sweet smile at me. Now I know I shouldn't be here. This is wrong. I should leave. I turn to Ralph and make to stand.

"Mr Ashcroft, I'm sorry but I've made a mistake, I shouldn't have come today." Anger flashes across his face, quickly replaced by a sly smile.

"Nonsense, sit down, girl. You need to know what I spoke with Oliver about." I look at Serena who is nodding in agreement. I take deep breaths, silently telling myself to stay calm.

"Are you aware that Oliver and Serena had a relationship?" I look to him, then Serena and nod my head in response. I've lost the power to speak right now.

"Well that's a start then." He smirks at Serena and she giggles. I feel my body tense.

"You see, dear. Serena came to me a while ago, a good while after she broke up with Oliver." I'm confused and frown as I look between the two people staring at me.

"What does this have to do with me?" He laughs, she shrugs and looks to him.

"Would you like to tell her, Serena?" She reddens slightly as she looks at Ralph and he nods his head at her. I watch as she rubs the palms of her hands down the perfectly tailored skirt of her dress. Is she uncomfortable? What the hell is she going to tell me?

"You're a mum aren't you, Lucy?" My mind is reeling. Bella! I am not talking about Bella!

"Yes, why?"

"Do you have a son or daughter?" I frown at this question as my suspicions grow.

"That's none of your business. What do you need to tell me Serena?"

"I'm a mother too."

"Congratulations, now can we get to what we need to discuss please?" I'm lost and anxious. I want to get out of here. I hear Ralph snigger. I turn to look at him, my anger moving from simmering to a boil. What the hell do they want with me?

"I have a son. He's eighteen months old. His name is Xavier."

"Lovely." I don't know what else to say.

"Yes, he is. He's my first grandson and I adore him." Ralph's words don't register immediately. I look at him as he grins. I look at Serena who is blushing now. Like ice melting in water the news begins to register, seeping through my body. Ralph coughs. They talk but I don't hear. I stand but my legs are like lead. I can't move. Serena stands and grabs my arm to steady me. She's talking to me but I don't hear her. I slump back down in the seat. Their muffled voices start to make sense.

"Lucy, are you OK?" I look up feeling almost drunk. Serena actually looks concerned. I look between them as I try to find my voice.

"Are you telling me that your son is Ollie's son?" I look at her, my voice a mere whisper as I ask. I don't want to hear the answer and I already know what it is anyhow. She nods her head.

"Yes, Oliver has a son, Xavier. He is eighteen months old." Now I know I must leave. I hear their voices as they call after me. I move as fast as I can. The woman at the reception looks up and is startled. She rushes round to me but I dash for the lift as I hear the bell sounding its arrival.

There is no cool air outside as I stand and watch the world carry on around me. I reach into my bag and grab my phone. I dial Lisa.

"How did it go, sweetheart?" She sounds so chirpy. I begin to sob.

"Shit! Lucy, I'm on my way. Are you at his office?" I nod my head in answer as the sobs rack my body.

"Lucy, answer me?"

"Yes." The voice sounds nothing like mine. It's a shrill cry as the pain forces its way through every part of me.

"Stay there I'll be with you in a few minutes."

My mind is whirring as I think back to the time when Ollie told me he didn't want me, when my world fell apart. I stood right outside this very building. How can this be happening again, and at the hands of that dreadful man? Why didn't Ollie tell me? This news has completely rocked my world and the fact that Ollie chose not to tell me has me seething with anger. Why on earth would he keep something so life changing from me? What did he think he would achieve by not telling me? It's not as if the child is going anywhere.

When Lisa pulls up at the curbside I can't wait to get in the taxi. I know my make-up is running down my face and I must look an absolute sight but, fuck!

"Sweetheart, what the hell has happened?" Lisa pulls me into her as I cry like a baby. I try to tell her through tears and snot, it's not easy! I hiccup my way through the scenario that played out in Ralph Ashcroft's office as Lisa looks on in complete shock.

"I can't believe that Ollie wouldn't tell you this, Luce. Fucking hell, this is off the scale, really!"

My heart aches as reality sinks in. Ollie has a son with another woman. He found out and chose not to tell me. What the fucking hell is he playing at?

"Lisa, I need to go and get Bella. Can we stay with you tonight? I really don't want to stay at Ollie's." My friend looks as heartbroken as I feel. She nods her head in response and gives the taxi driver directions to Fulham Reach where my baby is innocently waiting for me. I close my eyes, leaning back on the seat, my mind racing through everything, from the conversation with Ollie's dad to how I'm going to explain to Bella why we're staying at Lisa's tonight.

****

I didn't make a big thing about us staying at Auntie Lisa's tonight. We've stayed before so I just played it calm and it seems to have worked. The only problem I know I have to face is when Ollie calls Bella to say goodnight. I know I have to speak to him and right now I can't think of anything I want to say, apart from to tell him it's over. I am not going to be pushed aside while Ollie and his dad play these petty, childish games. Ollie choosing not to tell me what's going on makes him just as bad as that evil dad of his.

Bella settled easily in Lisa's spare room. As I walk into the living room my friend passes me a large glass of wine. Her eyes look sad as she smiles sympathetically at me.

"Don't look at me like that, Lise. Please don't feel sorry for me?" We take a seat either end of Lisa's sofa and silence descends.

"Of course, I feel sorry for you. I cannot believe this is happening. After everything you two have been through to be together, how could he keep this from you? Lucy, I'm devastated for you."

"You know it's not right, Lisa, I have a feeling this isn't all. He hasn't phoned Bella, has he?" I feel sick to the pit of my stomach. What the hell is going on?

As if on cue my phone beeps a text. It's Ollie.

"Lucy, I'm sorry I haven't called Bella. I'm stuck at the building site. One of the men had an accident so I'll be here for a while sorting things. Give her a big kiss for me. I love you both. I'll call you later. O xx" I smile. It's as if nothing has changed. How can he carry on like things haven't turned upside down recently? Why?

I show Lisa the text and she shrugs, a deep frown set on her face.

"You know, Lucy, I trust Ollie. Really, I do. His dad is a different matter, but Ollie well, this just doesn't sit right. You're bang on when you say there's more to this." Neither of us speak for a while. I swirl my wine around, sipping every now and again.

"You need to speak to him, Lucy. I know he's tied up right now but when he calls you must tell him what happened today. Have you ever thought that maybe Ollie knows nothing about this? Maybe they're making out that Ollie knows just to cause trouble."

"Oh, I hope so, Lisa." We drink more wine and wait in anticipation for Ollie's call.

I listen as Lisa chats with Giovanni when he calls and miss that. I miss the innocence. Why is mine and Ollie's relationship always so complicated? Lisa doesn't stay on the phone long and I feel guilty. I know it's because I'm here.

"Lisa, can I go and have a shower please?"

"Of course you can."

"You can call Giovanni back while I'm gone, then you can speak properly. I don't want you to cut your time with him short because I'm here." My friend smiles at me gratefully and pulls me in for a hug.

"Thanks, Luce." I head off to the bathroom to wash my day away.

As I walk out of the bathroom wrapped in a towel Lisa is waving my phone at me.

"It's Ollie. I had to answer for you. He sounds surprised. You need to talk. Use my bedroom, Luce" Her voice is a whisper. My heart is thumping as I swallow the lump in my throat. Where do I start? I take a seat on the edge of Lisa's bed, breathe deeply, then I speak.

"Hi." My voice is steady but quiet. It's not giving away the turmoil that's going on in my head right now.

"Hey, baby, why are you at Lisa's? Where's Bella?" His voice is full of concern. There's no suspicion there. Maybe Lisa's right. Maybe he hasn't a clue that he has another child, a son.

"I've had a rough day, Ollie, and I needed my friend so we're staying here the night."

"Shit, what's happened? Are you OK, is Bella OK?" I force back the tears. I love him so much and he sounds so worried.

"Bella's fine, she's sleeping. I'm not so good." I go quiet, thinking of how to word my next sentence.

"Lucy, what's wrong? What's happened, baby? Do you need me to come back tonight?" I shake my head as I answer.

"No, Ollie, you don't need to come back but I do need to tell you about today."

"OK." He sounds so worried.

"I'm going to tell you everything so just listen, OK?" He coughs. I can tell he's nervous.

"Your dad called me this morning." He interrupts straight away, just as I expected.

"Lucy, listen."

"No, Ollie, like I said I'm going to tell you. You need to listen and not speak until I've finished, OK?" He sighs.

"Well OK then." He sounds pissed off. Just how I feel!

"So, he told me he needed to see me today. Asked me to go to his office. Initially I refused as I don't think it's my business to get involved in what's going on with you and your dad, but he convinced me I should go." I take a deep breath before I continue. This is where I find out if he knows or not and I'm dreading his response.

"There was a woman there too. Her name is Serena Hamilton. I think you know her." My voice is sarcastic, I can't help it.

"Lucy, stop. Listen to me, will you?"

"NO, Ollie." My voice is raised and the tears are falling now. I want to tell him every last detail so that he knows just how bad it was for me today. Whatever is going on I want him to know that at least.

"The two of them shared some news with me. I don't know if you're aware or not but they told me Serena has a son and he's yours, Ollie. You have a little boy with Serena." I spit her name at him then fall silent. He doesn't speak. My heart is crumbling. He knew! As the silence lingers and my suspicions are confirmed, I feel ice run through my veins. I cancel the call and switch off the phone. I don't want to listen to his excuses, why he couldn't tell me something so important?

250

After quickly pulling on my clothes and tying my wet hair back, I walk into the living room where Lisa is hunched up on the sofa, biting her nails nervously. She knows just from looking at me how the call went and that Ollie knew. Lisa jumps to her feet and runs to me with her arms outstretched.

"Oh shit, Lucy. Shit, shit, shit!" I regale the phone conversation to my friend, gulping at my glass of wine as I do.

"So, you didn't give him chance to explain?"

"Nope. What's the point?"

"I can see why you're angry but you need to hear what he has to say, Lucy. You can't just ignore him. Remember what happened before. His dad intervened and Bella didn't get to share the first three years of her life with her daddy. You can't let that happen again. You need to speak to him. You need to sort this out properly." I sigh. I know she's right but I'm scared to hear what Ollie has to tell me. She takes my phone from the table and switches it back on. I don't try to stop her. My heart is racing. I know it won't be long before we hear his ring tone.

Chapter 20

I was wrong! The telephone didn't ring at all. Nothing. Not a word. Lisa and I sat for almost an hour in silence watching and waiting. My emotions are completely frazzled. I'm sad, I'm angry and I feel completely lost. I don't know what to do next.

"Should I call him?" I look to my friend as she frowns yet again.

"I don't know, Luce. I thought he would be frantically calling you. Maybe you should." I pick up my phone and roll it around in my fingers. I look at the screensaver and wince. It's a picture of me and Ollie and Bella, all smiling and happy. I feel the pain in my heart as a tear drops to my cheek.

"Don't cry, Lucy, please."

"Oh, Lisa, what a fucking mess." She rubs at my back as I wipe at my eyes. My head hurts and I feel absolutely broken right now.

The loud knock at the door stops us in our tracks. I swallow hard and Lisa raises an eyebrow.

"Maybe he's here, Lucy." I watch my friend stand and walk to the hallway. I follow, my nerves on end as I wait for her to check through the spy hole. She turns to me, a small smile on her lips.

"It's Ollie, Lucy." Her voice is a whisper. I hold my hands to my head, wishing so much that this wasn't happening. That he was just here to pick me up. That he would just take me in his arms and kiss me gently when he sees me. I nod my head to Lisa and she unlocks the door. Ollie pushes past the door and freezes when he sees me.

"Lucy." He voice is choked. I feel my hands shake. Lisa rushes past me and into her bedroom without a backwards glance. I turn and head to the living room. I hear him following behind me. I close the door as we enter and turn to see his face etched with worry.

"Please, let me explain, sweetheart." He steps towards me, I step back. He grabs me by the arm and pulls me across the room. I want to fight but the reality is that I love his touch. I want him to hold me and love all this bad away. I know I need to hear what he has to say. I don't know if I have the energy for this. I am emotionally spent right now. I feel weak.

I take a seat next to him on Lisa's sofa and look into his ice blue eyes that captivate me. They look sad, so damned sad. I watch as he rubs the back of his neck awkwardly.

"I'm so sorry he hurt you today, Lucy. He had no right to call you. This was the news he happily told me when I met up with him." I gasp at the truth. I knew it was coming but it still hurts like mad.

"Lucy, I don't believe the baby is mine. I've told Serena I want her to take a paternity test. That's why I didn't tell you. I wanted to be sure either way, before I had to upset you."

"You can't keep things like this secret, Ollie. Especially when you know how vindictive your father can be. You should have told me." My voice is barely audible. I'm struggling to have this conversation with him.

"I know that now. I never thought he'd contact you, Luce. I'm so sorry."

"Sometimes sorry isn't enough, Ollie. You've hurt me. He hurt me but I expect that from him. I knew when I went to see him that it wouldn't be good but I never expected that you'd conceal something that's potentially so life changing for all of us." I bury my face in my hands and silently cry. My heart is shattered right now and a simple 'sorry' really isn't helping. I feel his fingers touch my hair. I would love to let him touch me more, to comfort me and take the pain away, but this problem hasn't gone away. We're only at the start of what could be a lifelong change in our circumstances. I look straight at him when I speak.

"What if he is your child, Ollie? What then? Have you thought about that? You missed three years of Bella's life and here you are possibly in the same situation with another child. Fucking hell, Ollie, what a mess!" He doesn't answer, he just moves closer as I look into his eyes, wanting him to tell me it's all going to be all right when he has no power right now to do that.

"Lucy, I'm sorry. I wish I could sort this now but it's not that simple is it. First of all, I have to convince her about the paternity test. She's not making it very easy for me. She has my dad on side, which doesn't help. I've taken legal advice and the solicitor is dealing with that side of things. I spoke with my mum as she knows Sara, Serena's mum. I'm hoping Mum can help me out here. Lucy, I don't know what else to say. I love you, I love Bella and I want us to be together forever. Nothing will ever change that, you know that, right?" As he touches my cheek, I move my face to his hand. I need Ollie, I only need Ollie. No one else will ever make me feel like he does. He leans towards me and gently kisses the end of my nose. I don't pull away. I love his touch, it always sooths me. When I don't pull away, he moves closer on the seat and lightly pecks at my mouth. It feels so good, in spite of everything that's happened today he can still make things better with one solitary kiss.

"Oliver." I say his name and feel so in love with him, it hurts. I never want us to be apart again and I never want that evil man to come between us.

"You need to tell me things, Ollie. Don't keep trying to protect me from him because it makes him more dangerous. We need to fight him together or he will win, Ollie."

"So, what shall we do now, Lucy?" He waves his arms, meaning where do we go? We're in Lisa's apartment as she hides in her bedroom and our daughter sleeps in her spare bed. Ollie is supposed to be in Layton and I know he needs to be there.

"Why don't you head back? I'll stay here the night." He shakes his head.

"I'm not going anywhere tonight, sweetheart. You need me, I need you. Come home with me?" He tilts his head, a tiny smile at the corner of his mouth. We both look up as Lisa coughs to let us know she's entering the room.

"Are things sorted now, you two?"

"Well, not really, but things are clearer. I'm sorry, Lisa." She waves her hands in the air.

"Hey, don't be sorry. I'm glad I could be there for you. Are you heading back, Ollie?" He shakes his head as he takes my hand, squeezing lightly.

"Thanks for being here for Lucy, Lisa. I'm sorry you got dragged into this shit with my dad. I'll sort it, I promise." He turns back to me.

"Please come home with me. I can go back to Layton in the morning. It's not a problem."

"Bella is fast asleep, Ollie. I can't wake her to drive home, it's not fair. And she'll wonder why you're here when you said you were going away."

"Why don't you leave her here with me Luce, I can bring her home in the morning if you like?"

"Are you sure, Lisa? It's right out of your way." She's smiling as she answers.

"No problem. I'll start later. We can meet for breakfast if you like. I'll tell Bella you had to nip home for something when she wakes up. She'll be none the wiser." Ollie jumps up and takes Lisa in a hug.

"Thank you so much, Lisa. You're a star." Lisa laughs as Ollie kisses her cheeks.

"Let go of me, and go and make up, will you?" Lisa pulls away as I stand up.

"Seriously though, Lise, thanks for this."

"Stop thanking me and go home will you. Ollie's got some serious making up to do. Go on!" Ollie grabs my hand and leads me out of the room. We head to Lisa's spare room and both kiss our baby goodnight before we leave.

****

The air is foggy with unsaid words as we enter Ollie's apartment at Fulham Reach. In my head it's Ollie's place and that seems all the more poignant tonight. I follow him through from the lift as he looks over his shoulder, constantly checking I'm OK. I'm not OK, far from it actually, but we need some time alone to sort this out so tonight is as good a time as any. As we enter the kitchen he goes straight to the fridge and holds a bottle of white wine in the air, offering me a drink. I nod my head in acceptance. I'm uncomfortable. Thoughts race through my head imagining what life will be like if Serena's child is Ollie's son. I feel a cold shiver when I realize that Bella will have a brother. I feel sick. I don't want Bella to have a brother unless he's my son. Fuck!

"You OK?" I look up as Ollie watches me whilst pouring the wine. I shake my head.

"The more I think about this situation, the more disgusting it sounds, Ollie. I just realized that Xavier would be Bella's brother. I want to give her brothers and sisters. I don't want her to have them with anybody else, except you and me. I know that sounds selfish and spoiled but..." I take a seat at the bar and drop my head in my hands, elbows resting on the top.

The deafening silence makes me look up. Ollie is standing by the large floor to ceiling window, looking out across the river. His hands are frantic, first running through his hair then the back of his neck. He's lost right now, I know that. He has no answers and I hate that for him and for me. We both want to sort this and we can't. He turns to look at me, his face etched in sorrow.

"I'm so sorry, Lucy. I don't know what to say or do, if I'm honest. Nothing can be done until we know for sure about the paternity of Serena's baby." I notice that he never refers to Xavier by name, always just Serena's son, or baby. Maybe it's his way of dealing with it. Maybe if he acknowledges the boy, it will all be too real. I don't respond. I don't know what to say either. When he walks towards me, our eyes transfixed, I swallow hard. Just because we had this news doesn't mean he's stopped being the love of my life. He smiles shyly as he stands in front of me, leaning forward to touch my face gently.

"You are the most beautiful woman I have ever met, Lucia, and I am completely saturated in thoughts of you constantly. When I'm with you, I have to keep checking this is real and when we're apart, I do nothing but think about times I've spent with you. I don't ever want to stop being with you. I love that we have Bella. She is ours and no one can ever change that. I don't want to think about the possibility of having a child with anyone else. I want more babies with you, sweetheart, no one else. Can we just not talk about Serena until I have more details about this test?"

"You have to face reality, Ollie. Xavier isn't going anywhere. Someone is his daddy. Did she say if there was anyone else who could be the father?" He shakes his head miserably.

"Nope, just me. She's adamant he's mine. I just don't get it, Luce. I dated her on and off for about six months. I've always been really careful and used condoms. She told me she was on the pill but because it was on and off. I never really trusted her so I always insisted on condoms. I know condoms aren't one hundred percent but surely if she was on the pill as well, it would be difficult to get pregnant."

"Did she ever get sick while you were together? Vomiting can have an effect on the reliability of the pill." He looks grim as he shakes his head.

"No, not that I remember but then, I suppose she could have got sick when we were apart and if the condom didn't work then, well." We both sigh loudly. There you go! There is a chance Xavier is Ollie's son.

I stand and take my glass, heading over to the window. I pull back the door and step out onto the roof terrace. It's a lovely evening, one where we should be out here enjoying the views and the glorious weather. Instead it feels like a dark cloud has descended on just us and we have no way of escaping. I lean against the terrace's glass walls and look out across the river. I listen to the water and the surrounding noise at the riverside. I close my eyes, my face leaning upwards to the sky. I don't usually pray but tonight I do, silently.

Please let this be a mistake. Please let Serena be mistaken. I wish her and Xavier no harm but I just hope that there is someone else that she's not telling us about who could possibly be Xavier's father.

"Lucy." Ollie's voice is quiet and I guess nervous. I don't think he knows how to approach me or what to say. He walks towards me as I turn to him and sip my wine. I take him in and for a few seconds forget all our worries. He looks so damned sexy in his dark grey slim fitting trousers and white shirt, open at the neck. His shirt is out of his trousers at the back, giving him a very sexy look indeed. He stands before me, a small smile on his face as I just stare at his beauty. His hair is messy, the breeze catching it every now and again giving him that wind swept, just got out of bed look. His eyes are their usual captivating ice blue, his chiseled face and full lips crying out to be kissed. I watch as he licks his lips, biting my lip as he does so.

"Can I hold you, baby?" He holds his arms in front of him as my heart misses a beat. I don't want him to hurt any more than I want to feel hurt myself. I move forward as he holds his hand out, taking my glass. He turns and places it on the table before sweeping me up in his arms. It feels so right to be in his arms. No one makes me feel as secure as Ollie does. I don't move as he gently kisses my neck, talking softly as he does.

"When I found you and Bella, my world was complete, Lucy. I don't need or want anyone or anything else. Please know that will never change." I love what he says but I know that will not be true if he finds out Xavier is his son. He is a perfect daddy to Bella and I know that if it is true, he will be just as good with Xavier. I force back the tears and let him hold me. I don't respond to what he says. I can't!

I feel his hand in the middle of my back, his fingers brushing lightly against my skin through my shirt. I reach up, placing my hands around the back of his neck. As my head falls on his shoulder I let a silent tear fall. Being with Ollie and Bella here, these past few weeks, has been perfect. I don't want my world to fall apart again!

Ollie pushes my hair off one shoulder, leaning in to kiss the bare skin of my neck. I shudder slightly at his touch, loving it in spite of our somber mood.

"I can't live without you now that I've found you, beautiful. Please tell me we can get through this?" I lean back, the tears running freely as I look into his ice blues.

"I need you, Ollie, I love you, but I don't know how this will end. I know I won't stop being there for you, but I don't know if that will be enough when battling with your dad."

When he lightly kisses my mouth, I stifle a sob. He brushes at my cheeks with the pads of his thumbs, his face as close as it can be.

"I promise you, Lucia, that I will not let that evil man come between you and me, ever. He can try but he won't win, Lucy. We can't let him. Our life and our love is far too precious to let his evil win."

His mouth crashes on mine, our tongues dancing as we share our love and passion. His hands run roughly through my hair as he softly moans between kisses. Pulling away Ollie leads me inside. I follow, my heart thumping loudly as his thumb rubs at my fingers, entwined in his.

We walk into the bedroom and I know I need him, I need to show him how much I love and want him. This man is my everything and the thought of losing him pulls at my heart.

We stand in the middle of the room at arm's length, our eyes locked as we sway. A faint smile graces Ollie's full lips as he stares. He tilts his head mouthing 'I love you'. I smile. My body is almost physically shivering in anticipation as we stand and sway as if scared to make another move. I feel heat running through my body as each second passes.

"Ollie?"

"Yes, baby?" He smiles, his eyes glistening for the first time tonight.

"Make love to me… please?" He takes one step forward as pulses race to my groin.

"You know I'd do anything for you, baby." He takes me in his arms as his lips devour mine. The feel of his hands running up my arms makes me shiver through our kisses.

"That good, huh, baby?" He smiles, I nod my head.

"I love it when you touch me."

"Oh, beautiful, I love to touch you" His hand sweeps down my face and gently brushes over my breast. I gasp wanting more. His fingers release the bottom of my shirt and I lift my arms as he pulls it over my head.

"Oh, baby!" He leans down kissing the top of each breast. My body is on fire as he kisses his way around the top of my body. Between each delicate kiss he speaks.

"You. Have. The. Most. Perfect. Body. I. Have. Ever. Seen. I love you." He pushes me back and I fall onto the bed. Ollie takes no time in freeing me from my skirt, pulling gently at my panties. I lean up as he frees my bra, lying naked before him as he grins.

"Perfect. Fucking perfect!" I watch with delight as he strips his clothes from his perfectly toned body. The anticipation of feeling his skin on mine has my mouth watering. He gently lowers his body onto the bed next to me, his eyes never leaving mine.

"Lucia Meyer, I am going to make love to you all night. I am not going to stop showing you how much I love you until you can't physically take any more." His finger runs down my nose, my neck and my upper body, until he reaches my belly button where he gently runs it round and round, dipping down but never actually going any further than my thigh. I arch my body to him but each time he moves his finger away, grinning.

"Patience, baby, patience." His lips trace a trail down my neck, his tongue circling each of my nipples in turn as I quietly call his name. I run my fingers down his side, loving the feel of his taught skin. My head is thrown back, my eyes closed as I enjoy the delights of Ollie's perfect mouth on my skin.

"Lucy, look at me." I open my eyes as he looks deep into them, his face full of love.

"I will spend forever making you happy, beautiful, I promise." He pushes me back as his body weighs me down. I love the feel of his weight on me, opening my legs to pull him as close as physically possible.

"Baby, I need you, now."

"You have me, Lucy, all of me, whenever, however you want, you have me." I feel his arousal on my moist folds, holding my breath as he moves himself over me. This is where I love to be, with my man buried deep inside me.

We slowly move together as our gentle kisses become almost too intense to bear. Grabbing my hands, he places them above my head as his pace quickens and his force becomes much stronger. I am lost in a world of ecstasy right now as I hear him call my name. We move together faster and harder, each thrust better than the last. Oh God, this is good, too good!

"Ollie I'm going to—" His mouth covers mine once again, our tongues fighting each other as passion overcomes every other emotion we feel right now.

"I know, baby, come for me." I feel myself climbing, my body never more alive than when Ollie is mine and I am his.

As I call his name I feel myself climb to the greatest heights ever then freefall with the best feeling ever. I hear Ollie call my name as his warm fluid fills me. Our bodies slow as we whisper our love, my lips covering his neck and shoulders in light kisses. I don't want him to move from here, not now, not ever.

Chapter 21

With hardly any sleep, I know I look dreadful this morning. I check my appearance, glaring at my reflection in the large window of the café I'm meeting Bella and Lisa in for breakfast. I slap my cheeks, trying to bring some colour to my tired skin, it doesn't work. I shrug and pacify myself with memories of why I look so rough today.

"Why are you looking so pleased with yourself, miss?" I bend to kiss the dimpled cheek of my beautiful daughter and give my friend a wink in answer to her question as I take a seat at the table. Lisa giggles and claps her hands.

"Oh, Lucy, I'm so glad you sorted things. You did sort things?" She cocks her head in question.

"Well, yes. The paternity thing is still an issue but we're sorted." I ruffle Bella's hair. She scowls at me, trying to straighten her pretty hair.

"We ordered some breakfast, Mummy. I'm having sausage and beans cause Auntie Lisa said I'm a special girl and special girls have special breakfast." Her beaming smile melts my heart. I think of Ollie and feel slightly sad. He's headed back to Layton this morning and won't be back until tomorrow night.

"What are your plans for the next few days, Lisa?"

"Nothing much. Giovanni flies in at the weekend why?"

"Will you come and stay with me and Bella tonight? I know I said things are sorted but I'm afraid if I spend too much time on my own, I'll have time to think and it scares me, if I'm honest." My dear friend reaches across the table, holding my hand as she speaks.

"So, I get to stay at Fulham Reach, in one of the penthouses, believe me, you don't have to ask twice, Luce. Do I get to use the steam room and sauna?" I can't help but laugh as I nod my head in answer.

"Whatever you like and I'll even serve you champagne if you so wish. Your evening will be better than any stay at Champney's" I order breakfast watching and waiting hungrily as Bella tucks into her sausages and beans.

****

Lisa made sure I got through the day without thinking too long on my own. She scheduled a few micro meetings with me, taking my mind completely off my personal problems by working my brain hard on several projects that our department are responsible for. We also had an office lunch with Suzie where the three of us salivated over pictures of potential male models for a Christmas shoot we're planning.

Ollie texted almost every half an hour, checking and double checking that I hadn't heard from his dad again.

We called at Lisa's on the way home and picked up her overnight things before we took Bella for pizza. Today has been a day of unhealthy take-out food, which has been just perfect for me. Bella has loved all of it and is most excited that Auntie Lisa is coming for a sleep over. She didn't understand why Lisa couldn't share her bed until Lisa physically lay down on it with her and she realized what we meant by 'NO ROOM'.

It's nearly Bella's bedtime and instead of her usual story and a song we are dancing. I just got the new Sam Smith CD and Bella loves 'La La La' so we're all spinning around the room with our fingers in our ears singing loudly. Bella giggles between la la's as Lisa and I take it in turns to spin her around. I only just hear my phone ringing and run to get it from the bar. It's Ollie calling to say 'night night' to Bella. I indicate to Lisa to turn the music down as I walk outside to talk with Ollie.

"Hey, Luce, are you having a party there? I knew you were secretly looking forward to me going away." I feel slight pain in my heart. I miss him.

"Bella wanted to dance with Lisa so we're listening to my new Sam Smith CD. It's got Bella's favourite song on, you know the Naughty Boy track." I laugh as Ollie sings 'la la la' to me.

"Yep that's the one. How are things at work? How's Ben?"

"Good, really good. It's great being here and being hands on with Ben. He's good by the way and sends his love." I feel guilty that he's not there all the time because of me. I decide right now that I'm going to actively look for something I can do near Layton so that we can move back there and soon.

"Lucy."

"Yes?"

"My mum's coming back with me tomorrow night. She'll be staying with us for a few days. Are you OK with that?" My mind is whirring. I know Ollie's mum never comes to London.

"Yes, that's fine, why is she coming, Ollie?" There's a short silence then I hear him sigh.

"She wants to help sort this shit with Serena."

"So, is she going to see her?"

"Yes, and my dad. If anyone can help sort this it's my mum, Luce. It's not often she fights my dad but when she does she's a force to reckon with. He won't be pleased to hear she's in London, I can tell you." I smile. I love Ollie's mum, and hearing that she's going to help is a real comfort.

"I miss you, Ollie."

"I miss you too, baby. Would you like to go out tomorrow night? My mum would love to babysit Bella. We could go out, just the two of us."

"Oh, that's sounds perfect. Do you want to speak to your baby girl?" I hear the smile in his words.

"Yes please." I call Bella as I walk back inside.

"Daddy's on the phone, Bella." She runs to me, her face alight with happiness. She's a little flushed and sweaty from all the dancing as she leans in while I hold the phone to her ear. I savour the sweet scent of my baby.

"Dadddyyy." Just hearing the way she greets him makes me grin. I look up and laugh as I notice Lisa grinning in the exact same way as me, whilst she watches Bella tell her daddy about all the crappy food we've given her today and how she lay on her bed with Lisa. None of it makes sense but she gabbles on in her three-year-old speak and Ollie asks questions every now and again.

"Night, night, Daddy, I love you too, to the moon and back." Bella passes me the phone and rushes back to Lisa.

"Come on Auntie Lise, let's dance." I head back outside as 'la la la' is repeated once again.

"Hey."

"Hey, I miss you two so much, Lucia. I will dream about you baby. I will relive last night, it was awesome, you are awesome." I feel my blush as I giggle.

"So are you. Sweet dreams, Ollie."

"Have a good night with Lisa and I'll phone in the morning OK."

"OK, I love you."

"Love you too, bye."

Walking back inside I can't feel melancholy for long as Lisa and Bella spin round and round in front of me, singing along to Miley Cyrus 'We can't stop'

"One more song, Bella, and then its bedtime." She winks cheekily as Lisa spins her past me.

****

Lisa and I sit opposite each other on the comfy whicker seating on the terrace. The evening is so warm and this feels so good. Bella was asleep in minutes, the excessive dancing helping to tire her out at just the right time. Lisa and I clink glasses and sip our crisp, cool white wine.

"This place is beautiful, Lucy. You see these places in magazines but the reality is so much better. The view here is absolutely stunning. I'd never spend time inside if I lived here." I nod in answer to everything Lisa says.

"I know it really is perfect, but…"

"But? How can you end with a but, Lucy?"

"Well when I moved to London and set up my life here I never thought I'd live anywhere else. I've always loved it here but then I went home and met Ollie and you know I miss Layton. I miss the sea, I miss my family, I miss remembering my childhood with Ollie. I think maybe now we're together I love all the memories, whereas before those memories hurt because I loved him and didn't for one second think he loved me back."

"Oh, sweetheart, that's so lovely. I get it completely. I envy that, you know, the family ties. I wish I had some. Maybe I can start building mine with Giovanni's family when I move to Milan. They are lovely people who have really welcomed me."

Lisa's mum died from cancer when she was only three years old. Her mum was a single parent, Lisa doesn't know much about her father. Her Aunt Becca brought her up. Becca is an eccentric spinster who is absolutely adorable. She's an older version of Lisa, petite like my friend with long white hair that she usually wears tied in a bun. Lisa and Becca also share the same, pretty, hazel eyes. Becca loves animals and Lisa swears she only tolerated her when Lisa was growing up because she had to. I know different! Becca worships the ground Lisa walks on, the adoration is always so obvious. Becca lives in a tiny hamlet outside London where everybody knows and loves her. I spent a few of the holidays there when we were at uni. Becca has always refused to visit Lisa in London, I don't think she's ever left that village since she moved there decades ago.

"What will Becca do when you move to Milan, Lisa?"

266

My friend laughs loudly. "You'll never guess what?"

I frown. "What?"

"She promises she's going to come and visit. Apparently, the love of her life was an Italian lad she met on a school exchange. She's convinced she's going to see him. It's funny but kind of sad isn't it?" I sigh.

"Oh, Lise, imagine. Once upon a time she was in love and nothing came of it. She obviously still dreams about a happy ending. Poor Becca!"

"Oh, and the thing is this lad, Ricco, lived in Rome, it's miles from Milan but Aunt Becca thinks that fate will bring them together."

"I could cry, Lisa. I never knew about this. Have you always known?"

"No, she only told me when I told her about Giovanni. I think she thinks it's a sign, you know, me meeting Gio and the Italian connection. I'm not sure if she's going senile or just living in the past but I just go with it. If it means she'll come and visit me, I'm not complaining."

"Well let's make a toast to young love and hope that fate does find Ricco and take him to Milan." Lisa and I clink glasses, each lost in the world of love and fate.

"Ollie's mum is coming back with him tomorrow Lise. Apparently, she's going to see Serena and Ralph."

"Well maybe she can get it sorted. Why is Ralph Ashcroft involved anyway? This has nothing to do with him. It's between Ollie and Serena, isn't it?"

"Hmm, it is a bit strange, isn't it? I know he thinks he has control of Ollie's life and he's really had his nose put out of joint since Ollie left banking and set up home with me and Bella."

"So maybe Ollie's mum is going to step in and sort the old bastard out 'cause he bloody well needs it." Lisa smiles before sipping her wine.

"Oh, I hope so, Lise. If she could just stop him interfering it would make life so much simpler. We have to deal with this paternity thing and if Ollie is the father then we will just have to get on with it and that would be so much easier if Ralph wasn't lurking in the background."

****

The day has flown by. Lisa and I had a giggle late into last night, the wine having the desired effect: sleep came easy for me. I didn't ponder on the problems that we are going to face when Ollie returns. He'll be here to pick me up from work shortly. He's dropped his mum at the apartment and is heading over to fetch me after he's collected Bella from crèche. I feel the butterflies in my belly when I think about seeing him. I wonder if this feeling will always be here, the teenage rush of love and lust when you think of your loved one. Do people who grow old together, still feel excited about being together? I hope so!

I hurry to Will's office for a run-down of my project plans before leaving for the day, passing Lisa as she exits.

"Hey, have a good night tonight, Luce. Enjoy it sweetheart, and don't waste a good evening talking about that dreadful man, save that for when you're home." I blow her a kiss as I walk through the office doorway.

"Will do, I promise." I'd already decided earlier that we will make our evening out a night free of talk about Ralph Ashcroft or Serena Hamilton. I want to enjoy some special time with my man tonight.

When I eventually emerge into the evening throng of the city, my heart skips a beat when I see his car. I spot my baby waving frantically through the rear window and grin.

"Hey, you two." I take my seat beside the love of my life and turn to check on our baby girl.

"Daddy's home, Mummy. He brought Nanna home too. We're having a sleep over Mummy. Can Nanna sleep in my bed, pleeeeeaaasse?" I glance between Ollie and Bella as she relays her story to me. Ollie laughs as he leans forward, taking my face in his hands.

"I missed you, beautiful." His kiss is tender, my pulse racing as I relish the feel of his lips on mine.

"I missed you too." I turn back to Bella who just keeps calling 'Mummy' waiting for some answers to her questions.

"Sweetheart, Auntie Lisa showed you last night how there's not enough room in your bed for two people. Nanna can't sleep with you, Bella." Bella frowns at me crossly and looks to her daddy for a more positive response. I watch as Ollie tries hard to suppress his smile.

"Your bed is just for you, princess, and anyway I think Nanna snores really loud." Bella chuckles loudly, instantly forgetting her angst.

Ollie gives me a wink before pulling the car out into the evening traffic.

Chapter 22

I feel slightly nervous as I walk into the apartment, well not walk but dragged actually by my darling daughter who is so eager to see her Nanna.

Ollie's mum, Penny, is standing, waiting as Bella crashes through the room towards her, arms outstretched. I watch the scene unfold in front of me and take in the smile of contentment on Ollie's face as his mother takes Bella in her arms, kissing her chubby face over and over.

"Oh, sweetheart, I missed you so much." Penny gives me a smile as she looks over whilst hugging my daughter. Her smile and the glisten of her eyes tells a thousand unsaid words and I know just how much Bella means to her. It really does warm my heart to know that this beautiful lady loves my daughter so much.

"Have you unpacked, Mum, and got yourself settled?" Ollie heads to the kitchen and flicks the kettle on.

I still feel nervous. This still feels like Ollie's home and now his mum's here I feel more like the guest than she is. I want to go to the loo and have to stop myself from asking. Stupid, I know, but this is all too much sometimes. I feel like a freeloader and the feelings are more intensified in the presence of Ollie's mum.

I sneak off to the bedroom and kick off my shoes before heading to the bathroom. I take a few moments of solitude and try my hardest to stop feeling so intimidated, yes that's it, I feel intimidated. This woman is beautiful and clever and I feel so insecure in her presence. Ralph Ashcroft has done a good job of making me feel unworthy of his son's love over the years and it's hard to shake off. I check my appearance in the bathroom mirror, applying a little more make-up so that I don't look tired. I brush my teeth and only emerge from my hiding place when I run out of things to do. Ollie is seated at the foot of the bed, his elbows resting on his knees.

"Hey, are you OK, Luce?" I put on my best smile and nod my head.

"Of course I am, why?" He stands, walking towards me with his hands deep in his pockets.

"Just checking, baby. If there's anything worrying you, please tell me. My dad hasn't been in touch again, has he?" I mentally chastise myself for being so transparent. I thought I could fake being OK, but he knows me too well.

"No, I promise he hasn't. If he ever contacts me again, I will let you know, Ollie."

"So, what's bothering you Luce?" I don't want to tell him now. I really don't want this to spoil our evening.

"Nothing, Ollie, I'm fine. I've had a busy day and I'm tired but that's it." I pull him to me, my hands either side of his lovely face. I lean in and kiss him gently, savouring his lovely, Ollie scent. I moan quietly as he kisses me back. As his hands pull at the back of my head I feel that familiar pull in my groin and smile into our kiss.

"I love you, Ollie, I missed you so much."

"I missed you too, baby. I can't wait to take you out tonight." He pulls me close and I relish the feel of being in his arms again.

As we walk back into the living room, Ollie's mum is waiting, her hands on her hips as Bella giggles, her hand over her mouth trying to hide her humour.

"So, Oliver Ashcroft, what's this I hear that you've been telling my princess that I snore?" I can't hold in my laughter. Penny's shoulders shake as she tries to keep her stern exterior as Ollie checks out Bella. Ollie mimics Bella, holding his hand to his mouth.

"Oh, sorry Mum, was it a secret?" Penny moves forward, playfully slapping Ollie's arm.

"Bella won't let me sleep in her bed now, Ollie." Penny taps her foot on the floor as Bella watches the play in front of her, all seriousness and concentration. She is so damn cute!

"Actually Mum, Bella only has a tiny bed for tiny princesses. Have you showed Nanna your special bedroom, Bella?" Bella looks from Ollie to Penny and grins, holding out her hand to Penny.

"Come on, Nanna, come and see my special room. You'll love it." Ollie seems to have the knack of distraction where Bella is concerned.

****

We step into the restaurant and I can't help but take a sideways glance at Ollie. Every now and again I like to take a look and feel proud, so damned proud that I'm with him. He's gorgeous and sexy and super intelligent… and he's with me! He loves me! Tonight, he looks edible. I have no need to be here really, because if I'm honest I'm quite happy with just Oliver Ashcroft on my menu for the evening. Ollie looks ultra-sexy in his tight black jeans, smartened up with a pale blue shirt, open at the collar. The maître 'd checks our reservation, showing us to our table. Ollie takes my hand and gives me a smile, a very sexy smile as we make our way through the restaurant.

I'm struggling to concentrate on the menu. It's been a while since we got to spend time alone and I seem to have lost my appetite tonight. I love being here but I'm just not that bothered about eating. I tap my fingers on the table and watch as Ollie reads the menu. He looks up, frowning at me.

"You OK?" I nod my head, grinning my reassurance.

"What?" He grins back, his curiosity overriding my reassurances.

"Nothing, Ollie, why?"

"Well, are you even going to look at the menu, or just tell me what's on your mind, then we can eat, Luce?" I shrug my shoulders before answering.

"I just don't have much of an appetite, Ollie. Why don't you order for me?" I tilt my head as he shuffles in his seat, running one hand through his hair.

"Luccccyyyy" I jump as he slams the menu on the table, his ice-blues watching me intently. I smile, a smile that tells him I love him so damn much!

"Yesssss?" I twiddle with my hair, amused as his eyes follow my fingers. I bite my lip and feel the pull in my groin as he gasps.

"Would you like to go somewhere else, do something else?" His head is tilted, an amused look on his face as he waits for my answer.

"I'd like to dance."

He raises an eyebrow. "Dance?"

My response is a nod of my head as our eyes watch each other intently. Picking up my wine glass I raise my glass to him and devour the ice-cold liquid as he watches. I gulp in shock as I watch Ollie stand, his hand held out to me.

"Come on then, Lucia, let's go and dance."

"What about dinner?"

"We can do dinner any time, let's go and dance, beautiful." I take to my feet, excitement coursing through me at the thought of going dancing with Ollie. Ollie briefly and discretely explains to the maître'd, passing him a handful of notes. He gives me an affectionate smile as Ollie takes my hand and leads me from this beautiful restaurant.

I take Ollie's lead and follow him into the club. I'm not familiar with his choice for the evening but I'm not complaining either. It looks very up market and way out of my league. This is definitely not one of the places I frequent with Lisa when we're out in London. Ollie reaches around my shoulders, pulling me to him as he speaks to the doorman who greets him on first name terms. The doorman gives me a friendly smile as he lets us through and Ollie leads me into the club. We make our way to the bar as Ollie turns to ask me my choice of drink.

"Would you like wine, Luce?" I shake my head.

"I think I'll have a cocktail, please?" He smiles, shaking his head as he reaches across the bar for the cocktail menu. I take a look at the barman who is waiting patiently. He gives me a wink. I blush as Ollie catches the interaction between us, mine completely innocent of course. I smile inwardly as Ollie scowls at the barman who quickly makes good work of cleaning the bar area.

"I think I'd like a Cosmopolitan please?"

Ollie leans in pecking my cheek as he whispers. "I love you Lucy" My heart flutters and my world feels totally perfect right now.

Three Cosmos later and I'm like a dancing freak as I move around the floor. Ollie stays close by, pulling me to him if anyone so much as breathes near me. I like this. I love being his, and him wanting me so much. I love that he feels protective of me. I close my eyes moving around the floor to Tom Odell's 'Another Love', every beat coursing through my body. This feels so good, my perfect night out. I shake my head from side to side, singing along to the song as Ollie leans in and kisses me. I stop moving as the song comes to an end and let him take me in his arms.

"I love you, Oliver, you mean everything to me. I don't want to be without you ever again." I pull him close and kiss him hard. I know I've had quite a few drinks but I also know how Oliver Ashcroft makes me feel and right now I couldn't feel better!

When John Legend's *All of Me* begins, I get lost as Ollie sings the words softly to me.

A perfect evening!

Seated in the plush lounge area of the club I sing along to Robin Thicke's 'Blurred lines' as Ollie laughs at my attempt at sexy serenading.

"Let's go away for a few days, Lucy, just the two of us. You know we only spent time alone together for about a week, baby. I want to spend more time with you, I want to be with just you and love just you, Lucia."

"You can take me wherever you like, Oliver. I will go anywhere with you, anywhere." He touches my face as I close my eyes. Just for a few moments I go back and remember my dreams. My constant infatuation with Oliver Ashcroft, that lived with me throughout my teens, right up to the present day. I wouldn't change a single second of loving him, ever.

"Where would you like to go, beautiful?" I sigh as I open my eyes and stare into his ice-blues.

"Anywhere."

"No, really, Luce, where?" I lean in and kiss his perfect lips.

"Well, really, I'd like to be locked up in a luxury hotel room with you for the whole time. No sun, no sea, none of that, just you and me and a great big bed." He pulls me onto his lap, kissing me hard as he speaks.

"Right, that's a deal. I'll organize it tomorrow. I can't wait, sexy!"

I look around as Ollie orders more drinks at the bar. I feel so lucky to be here with him. He is my everything. I watch as he orders our drinks, looking over to give me a wink as he waits.

A girl walks up to him and leans in to speak to him. She looks familiar but if I'm honest I've had too much to drink to really have the concentration levels to bother. I look around and catch the eye of the barman from earlier. He gives me a wink and I look away guiltily, checking that Ollie didn't see him this time. I catch Ollie's eye and feel my blood run cold. The look on his face tells me something is wrong and I don't think it's the wink from the Adonis behind the bar that's bothering him.

I get caught up in the gaze of those very familiar sparkling blue eyes and I freeze. The sudden realization that Serena is the beauty leaning over Ollie and whispering to him hits me hard. Shit! Shit,

shit, shit! Her sickly smile tells me she has every intention of ruining my night. Well she's already well on the way to doing that by just being here in this very room! I don't move, I can't. I wish I had the confidence to just walk over and react as if she really doesn't bother me, but the reality is, I'm frozen to the spot. My heart is already crumbling and my mind is whirring.

She has a child with my man. She is standing there like she has a claim on my Ollie and it hurts so damned much. If she stabbed me through the heart I don't think it would hurt any more.

I watch as if a spectator in a movie theatre as Ollie shrugs her away. Serena is persistent, I'll give her that! I finish my drink, wishing I could magic a fresh one right now. As if from nowhere, the Adonis barman appears with another Cosmo. He gives me a bow as he places the drink in front of me, his eyes full of concern as he mouths, 'Are you OK?'

I nod my head, looking over to Ollie and Serena who are deep in heated conversation. I flinch when I see her touch his arm. He pushes her away but the hurt I feel is a sharp pain in my heart. I take a large gulp of my drink then decide it's time to leave. My caretaker, the Adonis, helps me to my feet, concern still etched on his face.

"Will you be OK, lovely? I can get you a cab, if you like." I smile at his kindness, swallowing the tears that are fighting their way out.

"I'm fine really. Thank you for being so kind." He kisses my hand. I worry momentarily that Ollie may have seen but when I glance over, he's still deep in conversation with Serena. Time for me to leave, I think!

"You know, maybe a cab would be a good idea." I smile as he guides me away. I don't look back and feel my heart sink when I realize that Ollie hasn't even noticed me leave.

A quick and animated call to Penny reassures me that Bella is fine as I make my way to Lisa's in my taxi. I'm not mad, I'm hurt, more than I could ever describe. Why did he think it was OK to continue talking to her as if I wasn't there? How fucking dare he?

As the taxi pulls up outside my good friend's, I have to take a walk about outside in an attempt to curb my anger. I pace up and down, my phone beeping frantically as I try hard to walk off my anger.

"YES?" I answer my phone, the anger not really disappearing.

"Lucy, where are you?"

"As far away from you as I could possibly get, you mindless, thoughtless pig!" A tear escapes and I wipe it away angrily. I will not cry, not now. I am way too angry… bastard!

"Please let me come and get you and explain, baby?"

"NOOO!" I am shouting. I very rarely shout but I am so fucking angry with Oliver Ashcroft right now.

"I don't want to see you. I am glad your mum is there for Bella but right now, I don't want to be near you… AT ALL. I HATE YOU, OLLIE! GO FUCK YOURSELF, YOU SELFISH PIECE OF SHIT!" I hang up and press Lisa's buzzer before falling to the floor and sobbing, loudly.

"How could my wonderful evening end so badly, Lisa? I am gutted she turned up. Do you think Ollie used to go to that club with her?" I watch as my friend ponders my questions.

"Well, I suppose they must have. It's too much of a coincidence that she'd be there otherwise. I'm sure she's not following you or stalking you, Luce."

****

I stopped crying a good ten minutes ago now. My eyes are red and swollen, I know this without even looking in the mirror. My face is sore from rubbing so harshly with tissue after tissue. Lisa has been her usual supportive self, listening to my rants when necessary and soothing me when I became almost hysterical. I'm not sure how much of this I can take. Maybe I'm not strong enough to deal with this situation after all. Ollie called again and I said more or less the same thing, I don't want to see him tonight. He gave in eventually and has only bombarded me with about ten text messages so far. If

I wasn't so hurt and angry, I might be amused by his mobile stalking.

I lie awake in the single bed of Lisa's guest room. As daylight peeks through the window, I wonder what Bella is doing. I hope she doesn't miss me when she wakes up, that she's too excited that Nanna is there to bother about me. I grab my phone from the floor beside the bed and check the time. It's six thirty. I've hardly slept and my head hurts, partly from the cocktails I devoured like a mindless teenager but I'm sure the constant crying throughout the night hasn't helped. I sit up, dropping my feet to the floor and rub my hands over my face. My phone beeps another text. I check the screen and sigh, it's Ollie… again.

"I hope you got some sleep, Luce. Please call me when you're ready to talk. I'll stay home with Bella today. I love you forever beautiful xx" I can't hold in the solitary tear that trickles along the side of my nose and onto my lips. I stand and walk to the window, opening the curtains and then the window. I breathe in the fresh morning air and contemplate how I ended up here, now.

Chapter 23

I'm not really being very pro-active at work today. If I'm honest, I'm bloody useless. I attended the team meeting first thing and basically did just that, attended. I took no part in any of the discussions and when Will asked me a question, Lisa jumped in and answered for me. I don't know what I'd do without my friend. The thought of her moving to Milan is not good. I don't want her to go. We've been through so much together and I want it to stay that way. It hasn't always been Lisa bailing me out. There have been times when she's spent weeks at my place with Bella and me. Bella has been the one who seems to have worked her magic and sorted the pair of us out in our darkest hours.

Lunchtime is one of our team therapy occasions. When I say team I mean Lisa, Suzie and me. A desk full of fatty take-out food, and the three of us putting the world to rights – perfect for my melancholy demeanor right now.

"You know what, girls, I don't know what I'd do without you. These lunches are a godsend. One day when we're old and crumbly, oh and hopefully happily living in bliss, we will look back at these lunches with fondness." Lisa and Suzie grin as we clear away our mess from my desk. None of us is eager to get back to work. Lisa is in limbo right now, waiting for Giovanni to arrive this weekend and make plans with her for their future and Suzie has just about come out the other side of a very bad break up, I'm not sure she's really over it yet but she keeps up appearances, most of the time.

I plough through my emails, not really concentrating on what most of them say. There are a few that peak my interest, reviews of the shoot we did in Milan and some about a show we put on for charity, otherwise the words just roll on and on, and I don't take a single one in! Suzie peaks her head around the door after quietly knocking.

"There's a lady here to see you, Luce. She only gave me her first name, Penny." Suzie frowns, concern obvious after the last few visits and calls I've received. I swallow hard. I don't want to see Ollie's mum, and I hope to God he hasn't sent her to sort out our problems because that will just bump up my anger tenfold. I sigh, rubbing my palms over my cheeks.

"Oh, right, you better send her in."

"Are you sure, Luce?" I completely get why Suzie is so dubious about letting my visitor in. The last time she let Ralph Ashcroft in when I thought it was Ollie. We won't make that mistake again!

I take a look around my office, checking that it looks respectable. Penny Ashcroft is immaculate, a vision of perfection and I am definitely neither. I always look like the mum in a rush. My hair tied back scruffily because that's all I have time for, my clothes occasionally matching – just by luck. I feel intimidated before she even enters my office.

Suzie shows Penny in as I take a deep breath.

"Penny, come in. It's lovely to see you." She tilts her head, frowning in disbelief.

"I doubt that, sweetheart. Ollie told me what happened and I'm sure I'm the last person you want to see today." I feel my blush spreading quickly. Penny offers me a sympathetic smile as she enters my office.

"How's my baby, Penny?" Her smile shows sympathy before she answers my question.

"Bella's fine, sweetheart. Don't worry, she thinks you went to work early and she's pleased as punch that Daddy's taking her out today."

"Oh, where are they going?" I try to hide the disappointment at hearing this.

"Ollie promised her a trip on a boat. I think it's just a quick trip on the river but Bella was in raptures when he told her." My heart sinks. The thought of my baby and my man going on a boat without me hurts like hell. I take my seat gesturing to Penny to take the one opposite. I have no idea why she's here and my mind isn't really in think mode especially now all I can see in my head is a vision of Bella and Ollie having a wonderful time in a boat somewhere, without me.

"Lucy, I came to London to sort out this mess with Serena for both of you. I never come here if I can help it. To be honest, I hate London, not because of the place, once upon a time I loved it here, but not now. This is where Ralph chose to live his life without me and the children. I'm sure you know that our marriage is not good, hasn't been for some time. Ralph should never have married if I'm honest. I'm his trophy wife, the one he keeps locked away except for special occasions when he must be seen with his significant other." I gaze at this beautiful woman who intimidates me in every way and suddenly realize that she leads a sad existence if, as she says, her life is one of pretence, one lacking in love. She deserves more, so much more.

"Why do you stay married, Penny?" Her smile is not a happy smile, more that of someone who has no answer.

"I loved him with all my heart, Lucy. He was my dream come true. When he brought me here, to England, things changed. I had no one to talk to, no one to confide in, I was so young. My parents weren't happy with the marriage so I was scared to go to them. I was trapped so I just got used to existing. When I had Oliver and Catherine I put all my energy into raising them. Life with my children fulfilled most things I'd dreamed of. Ralph hasn't been around much for nearly twenty years and I've grown used to that."

"So why are you here now?"

"I will not let him destroy the love you and Oliver share. Oliver loves you more than life itself, I know you doubt that right now but he does and I will not let Ralph come between you. There's something wrong about this sudden claim from Serena and I will find out what's going on, Lucy. I promise I will help you in any way

281

I can." For the first time in I don't know how long, I feel like I have someone on my side when it comes to dealing with Ralph Ashcroft.

"What now then, Penny?" She smiles sweetly as I pour us both a glass of water.

"Well I'm hopefully going to meet up with Serena this afternoon. She has no idea that I know what's going on. I've arranged afternoon tea with Serena and her mother, Sara, today so maybe I can do a bit if digging." I feel the slightest bit of optimism as I watch and listen to Penny share details of her plan.

"Lucy?"

"Yes?" I fidget in my seat as she watches me.

"Please go home and sort things with Oliver. Give him a chance to explain. He loves you so much, sweetheart. He's gutted that Serena turned up there last night. He never meant to hurt you. Please, sweetheart? Don't make me blackmail you, but if you don't sort it with Oliver, well, Ralph will win and none of us want that do we?" She tilts her head smiling and I can't help smiling back.

"You don't know how much it means to me, Penny, that you came here today. Thank you."

"Oh, sweetheart, don't thank me, just go home and make my precious son smile again. He's in mourning right now, finding it hard to entertain Bella when his heart is breaking." I feel something grip tight around my heart at the thought of Ollie struggling to put on a brave face for Bella. I need to go home... now!

I wave goodbye to Penny outside my office building. I've decided to take the rest of the day off and go home to Ollie and Bella. I'm still mad as hell with the way he behaved at the club but I need to hash it out with him. He needs to know that he can't keep me away from what's happening with Serena. If we're going to have a life together, then he needs to include me in all of this. It may hurt but I'd rather be part of what's going on. Leaving me out of this makes me feel like I'm not that important and I'm sure that's what it looks like.

I make my way through the apartment and feel slightly lost. I'm not used to being here alone. I miss my baby Bella so much right now. I think of her with her daddy and feel jealousy rear its ugly head again. I make my way to her princess bedroom and lie down on her beautiful bed. I take in the scent of my baby, closing my eyes as I think of everything Bella and I have been through in her three years. When she was first born I used to dream of Ollie coming to find us. He'd hear of me and my new baby, put two and two together and come in search, before taking me in his arms and declaring his love for me. Sometimes in the dark of the night when my baby was wide awake I'd sit and tell her stories of her handsome daddy and how he made my heart beat so fast.

I remember those feelings of loneliness as a single mother. No one to share things. Baby's first smile, first laugh, I feel how heavy my heart used to feel and sigh. I look around this wonderful child's paradise and think about how lucky me and Ollie are to have found each other eventually. Ollie because of Bella and me because he's my dream. The sound of Bella's tiny voice echoes through the apartment as I lay silently on her pink covered bed where I've lay in wait for their return.

"There's Mummy's bag, Daddy. Where is she? Muuummmyyyyy." I grin when I hear her shout me. I will never stop loving the sound of that tiny voice call out for me. My heart thumps in my chest as I hear Ollie's voice. He is always so loving and gentle when he speaks to Bella and I am constantly in awe of his patience.

"Let's go look for her, princess. She must be here somewhere." My heart is in my mouth, the anticipation of seeing them both is killing me! I giggle as I hear them moving from room to room. I can't wait to see Bella's grin when she sees me.

Oliver Ashcroft has been my dream for so many years. I can see every tiny detail of his face when I close my eyes. I remember lying in my bed as a teenager. I would live through imaginary scenarios where Ollie would like me and be nice to me. I'd finish with Declan and Ollie would tell me he'd always loved me... we'd finally be together and my life would be perfect. When I allowed myself back into reality, I'd feel sick at the thought of never being his special one.

"Mummyyyy!" I'm abruptly torn from my memories as my baby girl jumps at me. I swallow the tears that would love to make an appearance and use my energy in hugging my tiny princess instead. I inhale her familiar, beautiful scent, my eyes closed as I relish the butterfly kisses she spreads across my face. When I do open my eyes, I look across the room and feel my heart thump hard in my chest. He's there, leaning against the doorframe, watching, his ice blues glistening. I take in my handsome man, yes mine. I must remember he is mine, he loves me and wants to be with me. Oliver Ashcroft looks hot just as he always does. He's wearing tight blue jeans, a white t-shirt and black converses, his hair is messy from his adventures in the outdoors with Bella and he looks good enough to eat.

We don't speak, we just stare. He is smiling, I'm not!

"Hey." His voice is so fucking sexy. One word could not sound so wonderful except when Oliver Ashcroft utters it.

"Hi." I kiss Bella, distracting myself from Mr Perfect who I want to hate but can't. Bella pulls me off the bed, babbling away in her three-year-old speak about the boat trip with Daddy that sounds like an epic expedition. Ollie doesn't speak, he just watches as our baby gives me a blow-by-blow account of their trip along the river in a motorboat. Bella grins her cheeky grin, showing off the dimple that melts my heart as we approach the kitchen and she points to the brown bags waiting on the counter.

"Daddy said I was a good girl so I got nuggets, Mummy." She looks to me for approval. I can't resist, bending down to her level to give her a kiss before picking her up to place her on a bar stool at the counter. Bella loves to swirl around on the stools even when I tell her over and again that she will break them. She spins now watching to see if I'll reprimand her. I guess she's sensed the atmosphere and is trying me out. Perhaps she thinks I'm mad with her.

"Bella don't do that, sweetheart, you'll break the stool." She stops instantly as if she got the confirmation she needed, which is that nothing has changed with me and her. I watch as Ollie leaves the room. I want to follow but I need to be with Bella. This is so difficult. We need to talk but Bella needs attention right now.

"Mummy, we got you a burger." Bella talks through a mouthful of nugget and fries.

"I'm not hungry yet, Bell, I'll eat it later, baby."

****

I'm seated on the bathroom floor watching Bella as she bathes. My heart feels heavy. I want to speak to Ollie but my needs as a mother outweigh anything else right now. Ollie hasn't really spoken, he's spent most of this evening on the roof terrace on the phone. I know he took time off and I appreciate that he still needs to work.

I sing a few songs to Bella as she lays in her pink princess bed, my heart not really in it. I feel guilty for not giving my daughter my full attention but I'm getting more and more anxious as the evening creeps by and Ollie and I don't address our problems.

Stepping out onto the roof terrace, I'm aware that Ollie is on the phone and he sounds angry. He's talking in muted tones but even from behind, his body language tells me something is wrong. I watch as he leans on the terrace wall, overlooking the river. My instinct is to walk up behind and hug him tight, to feel his hard body and smell his lovely smell. I close my eyes momentarily unsure what I should do next. When I open my eyes, I'm met with his ice-blue gaze as he leans against the terrace wall, watching me.

"I have to go, Mum, I'll see you later, love you too, bye" I don't move. If I'm honest, I'm lost. I don't know where to start, what to say, what to do? He walks to me, placing his phone on the table before taking my hand. He rubs at my hand with his thumbs, his eyes fixed on my face. I feel my unwanted blush and look away. He pulls my face to him, my chin cupped in his hand.

"Look at me, baby, please?" I lift my eyes to his lovely face, trying to stay impassive.

"I'm sorry, Lucy. I don't know what else to say, baby. I'm so fucking sorry. One more second in that club and you'd have seen me lose it with her and storm out. I was gutted when I turned round and you'd gone. The barman enjoyed every moment of not telling me where you went, baby." I let him take my hand and lead me to the sofas on the terrace. He takes a seat and pulls me into his lap. I don't fight him, I need to be in his arms, this is where I feel most loved.

Ollie pulls me to him, his face quickly buried in my neck. He whispers, lightly kissing as he speaks.

"I love you with all my heart, Lucia, and I would never knowingly hurt you, baby. I had no idea she was going to turn up there." I sigh, aggravated by the fact that it was obviously a place they had been to together so the possibility of meeting her was always there. I'm also angry that he stayed talking to her whilst leaving me as if I were no one to him.

"I would never, ever speak with someone and ignore you like that, Ollie. You treated me like some unwanted guest when she appeared. I waited for you to call me over but you just..." I find it hard to continue, hurt searing through my body.

"You acted like I wasn't even in the room. How could you?" I look at his face etched in sorrow and I still feel angry. I stand and move to one side, needing just a little space for me, for my dignity, which is somewhat shattered by the man I love.

"Lucy, she's a bitch and I didn't want you anywhere near her." I move further away.

"I am not a child. I don't need you to make choices for me. What I'd like is your respect. I'd like to believe that I can deal with anything if you love me, but you obviously don't think I'm strong enough and that really hurts, Ollie." I watch him run his hands through his hair, his discomfort so damned obvious right now. I turn and head back inside. I need a drink right now, a big fucking drink that will dampen down my heightened emotions with a bit of luck.

"Lucy." I turn, glass in hand. I take a huge gulp of wine and smirk at him.

"What, Oliver?" He smiles, my anger increasing with his humour.

"Please let's talk calmly. I need to talk to you, sweetheart."

"What? Why?"

"I spoke with Mum earlier. She saw Serena and Sara today. Mum thinks Serena is lying about her child. She knows there's something going on but Mum reckons Serena knows who the dad is and she doesn't think it's me. Mum is meeting with Sara tomorrow and is hoping to get more info when they're on their own."

I don't give a fuck any more. I'm mad at Ollie and I'm not even thinking about Serena, the conniving bitch!

"You know what, Ollie, just fuck off. I hate you right now. Nothing you have said in the last ten minutes has made me feel any better about what happened last night. You were a prize pig who only thought of himself. How dare you use your mother as a way of smoothing things over. What you did last night was unforgivable and you still think you were in the right. Fuck off, Ollie, just fuck off!"

I storm outside my anger heating like a volcano's lava. Fuck Oliver Ashcroft and his 'I'm sorry' shit!

Well, what to do now? I've put my baby to bed and completely fallen out with my man, who has now shut himself in his study. I've showered and dressed in trackies and a t-shirt, my damp hair tied back in a ponytail as I decide the time is right for some music therapy. Placing my headphones in my ears, I switch the music on my iPhone to shuffle and recline on the sofa of the terrace. I've come outside to try and gain as much space between Ollie and I as possible. If he wants to ignore me, I can do just the same. I turn up the volume, closing my eyes as Adele serenades me with 'Someone like you'. I feel my heart constrict, I hate fall-outs and this one doesn't seem to be getting sorted. I fear Ollie thinks I should just accept that he's sorry and not question his behaviour. I know he wasn't responsible for Serena turning up but the thing that hurts most is the way he continued to speak with her and just left me on my own to watch. I had no choice but to observe the two of them while I sat alone until I decided to leave.

I listen to one of my favourite songs 'Need You Now' by Lady Antebellum, the song that evokes memories of reading *Fifty Shades of Grey* when I was heartbroken for Ana. My story is nothing likes Ana's but the feelings I have, of being out of my depth with Ollie, remind me of Ana's anxieties.

The breeze on my face feels lovely as I enjoy my music. Ever since I can remember, music has been my solace when I've been upset or stressed. I have an eclectic taste in music and the broad spectrum of sounds being fed from my phone is perfect right now. Moving from slow, sad music to lively tunes, stops me from overthinking and makes me just enjoy the sounds rather than the meaning. I try not to ponder over the lyrics of the songs and just get lost in melodies.

When I feel soft lips touch my mouth, I jump ever so slightly, gasping at the electricity coursing through my body from just one tender touch. An involuntary moan escapes my mouth as I hear Ollie say my name.

"Lucy." I open my eyes to find him leaning over me, staring intently into my eyes. His closeness is overwhelming, just like it always has been!

I should be cross with him and tell him how angry I am, but his close proximity turns me to a jellied mess.

"Yes, Oliver?" He tilts his head at my off-handed response as I pause my music.

"I love you, you know I think you are so fucking sexy when you're mad with me, Luce." I try hard to hide my smirk at his comment.

"I'm mad Ollie, very mad." He smiles, a perfect Oliver Ashcroft smile, one that melts me to my very core. One that reminds me of the times when I longed for those smiles to be directed at me. Will I forever remember the times when I loved someone who I thought hated me?

"Sexy and very fucking mad Oliver." I'm his, and always will be!

"Lucia, come inside, I need to make things right." I let him take my hand and pull me to him. I'm his, just his. No one will ever live up to my Ollie, no one.

As we walk inside, I watch his perfect body. Everything about my man is sexy, and on occasions like this I have to stop and take stock of the fact that he's mine and I belong to him.

I am still mad, but feelings and emotions that always override anything else have taken over me, I don't have a choice here, my body wants and needs Ollie and I don't really want to fight that.

We reach the bedroom and for a second, I feel the need to punish him by turning and leaving… I don't!

I let Ollie take the lead. I don't want to need him, even though I do, and if I take any kind of lead here, I feel I will be giving in and showing my weakness. It may sound crazy but it's my way of coping. I want him to show me that he needs me as much as I need him.

As he gently pushes me across the room, I feel the power surges at his every touch. I'm constantly amazed at how powerful his touch is – I love it!

"You know, you have a real heap load of making up to do, Oliver." We're standing at the foot of the bed as his fingers gently trace the outline of my face.

Looking into his ice blues, I'm transfixed on Oliver and his sexiness. Watching him bite at his bottom lip, then lick across it makes me almost swoon and fall to my knees. I keep my composure, I've no idea how, as he continues to play the game of 'let's turn Lucy on'.

I close my eyes, feeling his tongue gently stroke across my closed lips, my smile appearing as sensations I love, run through my body.

"Oliver…" In spite of my desire to appear unaffected I can't help but whisper his name. He is beautiful and I love him with all my heart.

"Lucia, you are the love of my life. You really, truly are, and I thank God for every day that I spend with you. We will live happily ever after, Lucia, and I will look into your beautiful eyes and only ever see happiness." We continue to stand as our hands gently find each other. I find the bottom of his shirt, tracing my fingers along the skin at the waistline of his jeans, my groin aching as I desperately try to keep control of my need to strip him naked and kiss him all over, right now!

"Lucy, I need you baby. I have loved you forever and I will never stop needing the love that my baby, Lucia, gives me. You mean the world to me and I want you, Lucy." My body has abandoned any thoughts of making him work for this. I will gladly strip myself and let him do whatever he damned well likes for as long as he likes.

"I need you too, Ollie." His mouth is on mine in a second, our tongues meeting, as if for the first time. Yes, it feels like our very first kiss, perfect. It always is!

I let him gently remove my basic clothing, kissing his way around my body as I enjoy every beautiful sensation that runs through me. This man makes me feel so special, it hurts if I'm honest, the pleasure really hurts!

As he pushes me back onto the bed, I let out a loud sigh. Ollie stops and checks my face, looking for signs of anxiety. I smile, a loving smile that I hope gets through to him.

"You OK, Luce?" I nod my head as I pull him, leading his face to mine.

"Make love to me, baby" As his kisses smother my face, I start to feel normal, loved and normal.

"With pleasure, my beautiful girl, with pleasure."

Chapter 24

The week has been quiet. Penny, Ollie's mum, has been busy out and about in London with old friends, lunching and gossiping as much as she can without seeming too obvious. Ralph, Ollie's dad, has contacted her a few times, initially suspicious about Penny being here in London but the story she fed him about wanting to be with her granddaughter seemed to throw him off the scent.

I've noticed Ollie and his mum quietly chatting on a few occasions, which has annoyed me, if I'm honest. I don't want to be kept in the dark, not again.

I'm alone on the roof terrace this morning, enjoying a rare cup of coffee in silence, captivated by the light that catches the water of the River Thames, glistening in the sunshine. I've taken the day off work and Bella is at nursery for the morning. Ollie left for work very early and I have no idea what Penny's plans are for today. I've no doubt she's meeting one of her friends.

"Good morning, Lucy, I wondered where you were, darling." I watch as Penny approaches me. She always looks immaculate, just so. I don't think she spends a great deal of time making herself look so perfect, it just seems that she's naturally like I strive to be, but never quite achieve.

"Morning, Penny, did you sleep well?" Her perfect face tells me she didn't, even though she says she did. I'm guessing she has something on her mind, namely Xavier and who his father is. She obviously doesn't want to talk to me so I'll leave well alone, for now. I'll tackle Ollie later. Since Penny arrived, I haven't heard anything regarding the progress of finding out who Xavier's father is but I'm guessing Ollie knows more and just isn't saying. Maybe it's because he is the father. I shudder, physically shaking the negativity away as I try to push that thought right to the back of my mind. I glance at Penny as she takes a seat opposite me, elegantly brushing her trousers.

"You know, Lucy, I'm quite envious of you, darling." I look up suddenly, shocked by what I just heard.

"Envious, why?" Her smile is a sad smile. Her eyes are tearful and for a second her air of elegance wavers.

"When I married Ralph, I loved him so much and I truly believed he loved me back. I had those usual dreams of living happily ever after with my perfect man but he shattered those as soon as we settled here in England. I see how Ollie loves you, and I know that soon, very soon, you two are going to get your happy ever after. I'm envious but in the best possible way, sweetheart. You see, all I've ever wanted is the happiness for my children that I never had and I actually think it's about to happen for Ollie. I suppose my envy is more about regret, regret that I wasted so many years supporting Ralph when I should have taken my children back to the States and started afresh." I don't comment, I don't know what to say. The perfect façade of Penny Ashcroft is just that, a façade. She masks her sadness so well. My heart aches right now for this lovely lady who really deserves to be happy.

"Have you found out about Serena and Xavier, Penny? Is there news you're not telling me?" She looks away, across the river and breathes deeply before speaking.

"Sweetheart, I have news. I need to tell you and Oliver together. I'm sorry for being so vague but Ollie needs to know first." I nod my head, checking her face for any signs of whether this news is good or bad. Once again, her façade is back up and she's giving nothing away. I stand, grabbing my empty coffee cup and heading inside. I have no desire to sit with Penny knowing that she has something to tell me and she can't, not until Ollie gets back. I slip into our bedroom and call him.

"Hey, beautiful. How are you enjoying your morning alone?" he sounds so pleased to hear from me. My heart swells just hearing his voice.

"Ollie, I just spoke to your mum and she has some news about Xavier." The silence is killing me. I can hear his breathing but that's it, no words, just silence.

"Ollie?"

"Lucy, I have a really important meeting I'm just about to start but once that's finished, I'll be home, OK? Did she give any indication what sort of news?"

"No, she just said she wants to tell us together." Silence once again.

"Ollie?"

"Lucy, I love you and Bella more than life itself, you know that, right?" His voice almost sounds desperate.

"I love you too." I hear his sigh.

"So, no matter what, we will continue to be me, you and Bella. That's our family, right?" I shake my head. He's panicking.

"Ollie, we can't ignore him if he's your baby."

"I don't want anything or anyone to spoil what we have Lucy, I'm scared."

"Hey, I love you no matter what. That won't change Oliver, ever. We can deal with this if we have to." I hear muffled voices. I guess he needs to get to his meeting.

"Sweetheart I have to go. I'll be home as soon as I can. I love you."

"I love you too. Try not to worry too much." I laugh inwardly at my own words of comfort. I'm a mess just trying to picture what Penny is going to tell us. I know she was home late last night but she could have woken us and told us then instead of this.

When Ollie bursts through the door two hours later, I have no fingernails left. I have paced the bedroom God knows how many times. I took the longest shower ever but still the time seemed to go so slow. His face is pale as he walks towards me and takes me in his arms. I'm literally crushed as he holds me tightly, kissing my face and neck as he murmurs my name over and over. I pull away, concern seeping through me.

"Hey, calm down. It will be OK, Ollie. I won't stop loving you, baby. We can deal with this, I promise."

"You have no need to worry, Oliver, Xavier is definitely not your child." Our collective gasp is loud as Ollie and I spin around to see his mum standing in the doorway. Ollie and I share a glance, we know we should celebrate but the look on Penny's face tells another story.

"Are you sure, Mum?" Penny's eyes look so sad as she smiles at her son.

"Oh yes, Ollie, I'm sure. Come and let's talk." Ollie and I follow her through to the living room where we all silently take a seat as Penny openly prepares herself for what she's about to say.

"Mum, what is it? Why the need to talk? I don't want to know any details about who the father is or how it happened. So long as it's not me, that's all I'm interested in." Penny holds up a hand to stop Ollie. I squeeze his hand and tentatively smile at him when he looks at me with a frown.

"Let your mum speak, Ollie." He looks at Penny and for the first time since I met her, the façade has completely disappeared as a tear slides down her perfect cheek.

"Mum?" Ollie's voice is a whisper as he moves towards his mother who looks so damned lonely as she sits opposite us. I watch as Ollie takes a seat beside her and decide she needs both of us right now so I join her on the other side. Ollie and I take each of her hands and wait patiently for her to compose herself. My heart is beating out of my chest. What on earth is she going to tell us?

"Oliver, I don't know how to say this so I'm just going to be blunt and get this out in the open. You're not Xavier's father and I know for sure because I've spoken to Serena. She eventually told me the truth and to be honest, I wasn't as shocked as I should have been."

"So, did she tell you who the father is?" Penny nods in response. Ollie glances at me concern etched on his face.

"It's your father, Oliver." I let go of Penny's hand as I gasp loudly, pulling my hand to my mouth. Ollie doesn't speak. It almost seems slow motion as I watch him stand and walk away. He steps out onto the terrace as his mother calls after him. He doesn't look back. Penny doesn't move.

After what seems like an eternity, I stand and walk across the room towards Ollie. I look back at Penny who has her head in her hands. The faint sound of her crying breaks my heart. I didn't think I could hate Ralph Ashcroft any more but I've managed to find just a little more hatred inside just for him. The mean, manipulative, selfish bastard.

Ollie is leaning against the terrace wall, looking out across the river. I step up behind him and place my hands around his waist. I hug him from behind, feeling his body relax into mine.

"I'm so sorry, Ollie." He laughs. A horrible laugh that makes me squirm.

"Oh, don't be sorry for that old bastard, Lucy." I feel a cold shiver run through me when I think of all the people Ralph Ashcroft has manipulated, me included. Ollie turns, taking me in his arms as he takes deep breaths.

"I'm so fucking angry, Lucy. I could honestly go and kill the bastard right now. I hate him so much. I hate him for hurting you and Mum and trying to keep me from Bella. Catherine is going to be devastated. Shit, Lucy, this is as bad as it gets." Ollie takes me by the hand and leads me back inside to his mother. Penny hasn't moved. She looks such a sad and lonely figure as she softly cries into her hands.

I suddenly feel like I'm intruding as I watch Ollie comfort his mother. I can't even begin to imagine how she must feel right now and how difficult it was for her to tell Ollie about his dad. The news that Ollie isn't Xavier's father should have been something to celebrate, but this situation is something you only read in books.

"Does Dad know that you know, Mum?" Penny shakes her head as she wipes away her tears.

"No, Ollie, only you and Lucy know. I have arranged to meet him later."

"Let me come with you, Mum." Penny shakes her head and the words she speaks are forthright and not up for negotiation.

"No, Ollie. I want to do this on my own. I need to confront him once and for all. I've put up and shut up for far too long and this is my time now. I don't want an audience for what I have to say. The only person who needs to hear my words is your father."

Ollie and I watch as Penny pulls herself together. Standing she looks at us both before touching first Ollie's face then mine.

"You two will get your happy ever after, I'm just sorry that we had to find out about your dad on the back of your good news, Oliver." Penny walks away towards the guest bedroom as Ollie turns to look at me.

His hands cup my face. We don't speak, we just look into each other's eyes. My mind is racing with thoughts of what's going to happen next and I know Ollie must be the same.

"I love you, Lucy, and I'm so sorry for what my dad has put you through."

"Hey, I'm stronger than you think, Ollie. I am worried about your mum though. She loves your dad and he's completely broken her." He leans forward our foreheads touching as Ollie sighs.

"My poor mum, Lucy. What a waste of a life. Loving such a wretch of a man. She deserves so much more. She should be loved." I close my eyes and thank God I found Ollie.

****

Lisa has picked up Bella for me and taken her out for tea, then for a sleepover at hers. I haven't told her everything, I didn't have the heart to reveal the atrocities that poor Penny has had to endure.

Ollie and I have silently moved around the apartment as we wait for Penny to prepare for her meeting with Ralph. When she emerges from her room, she looks beautiful. You wouldn't have a clue that she is a broken-hearted woman about to confront the love of her life.

"How do I look?" Her confidence has obviously taken a trip away and she needs reassurance that she can get through this. I feel anxious for her.

"Beautiful, please let me come with you, Mum? I hate the thought of you seeing him on your own." Penny smiles affectionately at Ollie whilst shaking her head.

"I'm not afraid of him, Ollie. I'm angry and he needs to know just how much. I can only do that on my own, sweetheart. There are things we need to speak about alone. I will be fine."

"Well, can I at least drop you off?" Penny tenderly touches Ollie's cheek as she nods her head.

"That would be perfect." Penny turns to me, touching my face.

"Don't you worry either, Lucy. This will all be sorted once and for all. That man will never bother you again, I promise." I lean forward and kiss Penny affectionately as I whisper to her.

"Thank you, Penny."

As I watch them disappear behind the front door I turn and head to the kitchen in search of wine. I need wine!

No sooner have I found my place on the outside sofa than my phone starts to ring. It's Em, my sister. She must have a sixth sense, I was just about to call her.

"Lucia Meyer, it has been far too long since we spoke, are you OK?" I smile at her fond words, so damned pleased to hear her voice.

"Not bad, Em, how was your holiday?" I hear her contented sigh and smile inwardly. The thought of my sister finding happiness again swells my heart.

"Oh, Luce, it was the best. We drove through France and headed into Spain. We have had such a blast and Kyle…" Her words trail off as she obviously thinks back over her happy holiday.

"Kyle what, Em?" She giggles and I suppress the slight feeling of jealousy at her innocent love.

"Well, he's just perfect. I love him Lucy and, well, I want to be with him. I never thought I'd say that, honestly, I'm blown away, Luce!" I reach out and take a sip of wine. I am so happy for my sister and I don't want to taint this call with my news. I way up the pros and cons of telling Emilia about Ralph Ashcroft. If I don't tell her, she will go mad when she does find out. If I do tell her it will spoil her mood I'm sure. She will start worrying about me instead of planning a happy time for herself. Emilia deserves to be happy after everything she's been through. I want her to plan a future with Kyle. I don't want her to worry about me. I don't want to always be a burden on my family! I choose not to tell my lovely sister and continue the call talking about Em and Kyle's holiday, which sounds perfect.

"So, what have you been up to while I've been away? Have you three got into a comfy family routine?" I put on my best chirpy voice and sift out the good bits from the last few weeks. There's plenty to tell and Em is so excited about seeing Bella's princess bedroom and Ollie's apartment. I get carried away with the positive vibes I'm getting from Em and I almost tell her, tell her about Ralph the pig Ashcroft, wanting her to comfort me. I'm not going to be selfish though so I keep quiet.

I hang up from my sister with a heavy heart. I want to just go about my day-to-day life without so much crap surrounding me. I want to get excited about Emilia and Kyle, I want to go back to Layton for the weekend and spend some time with my sister and her new love. I want to wallow in my sister's happiness. There's no way I can go home until this is sorted. Mum will guess straightaway that things aren't right and until things are sorted in Ollie's family it's not my place to share what's going on.

I need someone to talk to so I pick up my phone and dial Sarah. I'm guessing Sarah will have some idea of what's going on. Ben is Ollie's business partner and Ollie must have explained some of the problems so that he could spend time in London. Ollie has an office in London but prefers to be in Layton, which has caused him a few problems since we got together. Me working and living in London is not making Ollie's life easy at all. Sarah answers straight away and by the sound of her voice she's expecting my call.

"Lucy, how are you, sweetie? How's Ollie and Bella? Is Ollie's mum still there with you?" Question after question, oh Sarah knows plenty! I sigh, preparing to talk about how I feel for the first time in days. I haven't been able to voice my fears to Ollie or my frustrations and anger as it just didn't seem right. Ollie is going through another trauma learning that his dad slept with his girlfriend and has fathered her child. God that sounds bad in my head so saying it out loud scares me.

"We've been better, Sarah. Bella's good though, she loves being with her daddy." I smile at this snippet of good news. What about you and Ben and the girls?"

"Oh, we're all just plodding along here. No traumas, well nothing like you poor things have been going through, Luce. I'm so sorry, Ben told me what's been going on with Ollie and Serena. You must have been going out of your mind. Is Ollie doing OK?"

"He's not bad. Has Ben told you the latest installment of this terrible nightmare?"

"About Ralph being the dad?"

"Yep, so you know everything then. It's like something you'd watch in a trashy soap on TV, isn't it?"

"Jeremy Kyle would have a field day, Lucy." We both giggle in spite of the seriousness of the situation.

"How's Penny, Luce? She must be devastated. I really can't imagine how she feels after giving most of her life up for that horrible man. I have never understood why she stayed with him."

"Well she's gone to see him now actually, to confront him. Ollie gave her a lift so he should be back soon. She wouldn't let Ollie go with her, she wanted to see him alone. Ollie's worried sick, obviously. I can't get my head round how Ollie must be feeling, Sarah. He just found out his dad was sleeping with his ex-girlfriend, as if that wasn't bad enough she's now the mother of his half-brother. Fuck, it's a mixed-up mess isn't it?"

"God, poor Ollie. Does Catherine know yet?"

"No, she's been away with work. I think Penny's heading back to Layton this weekend and she's going to tell her then. I'm sure this will be more of a shock to Catherine than the rest of us. Catherine has no idea what's been going on, poor girl."

"When will you be coming back to Layton again, Luce?" I sigh. This is bothering me just a bit too much at the moment. I think Bella and I need to be with her daddy. I need to move back there so that Ollie can concentrate on his work one hundred per cent.

"I'm not sure, Sarah, but I've been thinking about a career change so that we can move back there for good. I just don't know what else to do." Sarah squeals down the phone making me smile.

"Oh, it would be so good to have you back in Layton, Luce. I'll have a look around and see if I can come up with some ideas for you. Have you any idea what you'd like to do?"

"That's just it, Sarah, I love my job at the magazine and there's not going to be anything like that in or around Layton so it will have to be a complete change. I just don't know. I might have to resort back to my design days, you know before I went to uni?" I did a short interior design course at college before I went to university. I really didn't have a clue what I wanted to do regarding a career so I sort of drifted along until I settled with where I am now.

"Well you were bloody brilliant at that so I'm sure we can find you something. I promise this will be my project and I will give it my all, Lucy. We will find you something and then we'll have a big party to celebrate your homecoming. Oh, and while we're on about celebrating, Luce, what about Em and Kyle?" Of course, Sarah would know, Kyle is Ben's brother!

"She sounds so happy, Sarah, I could cry for her."

"Oh, you should hear Kyle, it's Em this and Em that. He's completely and utterly in love, it's so cute."

"Oh, I want to come home to Layton, Sarah, I want to be a part of all this. I don't want to be far away any more." I look up and Ollie is watching me from the doorway, a small smile on his face.

"Sarah, I need to go, Ollie is back. Yes, I'll call you soon. Love you too, bye." I hang up, my heart in my mouth. I hope Penny is OK.

"Hey, beautiful." I stand and walk to him. He's leaning against the window frame and he looks just perfect.

"Hey yourself. How was your mum?" A small frown appears on his beautiful face.

"She seemed OK but you know my mum, she puts it on. She won't be taken for a fool though, Luce, and that's what he's done. I don't envy him one bit if I'm honest. My mum is the epitome of elegance and she won't let that change but she is also a force to be reckoned with and my dad has pushed her too far this time. I would like to be there to see him leave. The arrogant bastard won't look so cock sure of himself when Mum's finished with him tonight." We both laugh at the thought of Penny wiping the floor with Ralph Ashcroft.

Ollie takes my hand leading me inside with his other hand gently caressing my back.

He leans in to whisper to me and my heart misses a beat when I feel his breath on my skin.

"So, did I just hear you right then, Lucia? Did you tell Sarah that you want to move back to Layton?" I feel by blush at being caught. I cough nervously to clear my throat as we enter the kitchen and Ollie heads to the fridge.

"Wine?" He holds the bottle up and I nod my head.

"Are you picking Penny up later?" He shakes his head.

"She said she had no idea how long she'd be and was adamant she'd get a cab home. She can be very stubborn, you know. I suppose Mum's been so independent for so many years it's hard to get out of the habit." I take a seat at the bar on one of Bella's favourite stools. I smile at the thought of Bella.

"Where did you go just then, Luce? You looked so happy for a second."

"I was just thinking about Bell and how she loves to spin on these stools. I was tempted just for a second to have a go myself."

"Go on, Lucia, live dangerously, do it for Bella." We both laugh loudly as I spin around and round. Ollie joins me on the next stool and together we spin and spin. When we eventually stop our eyes meet as we laugh.

"I love you, Lucia Meyer. You are perfect, you know that?"

"I love you too. I do feel a little bit sick now though"

I watch as Ollie jumps off his stool, his hand held out to me. As I look into his eyes I feel my body react to him in its usual manner. He gives me a wink, I wink right back at him. I giggle as he pulls me to him.

"Are we feeling playful, Miss Meyer?"

"Maybe, Mr Ashcroft"

"Oh, Lucy, I love it when you call me that" I raise an eyebrow and he laughs.

"Come on, Luce, follow me." He pulls me by the hand through the flat towards the bedroom.

"Ollie, your mum could be home any time, we should wait for her. She'll need you, sweetheart." Ollie continues his quick strides towards the bedroom as I pull at his hand.

"Ollie." As we reach the bedroom he pulls me inside closing the door dramatically and pushing me back onto the door.

"She said she'll text me when she leaves. We'll know exactly when to expect my mum so do me a favour, baby?" It's his turn to raise an eyebrow.

"Yes, what?" His forehead is resting on mine as our breaths synchronize.

"Stop talking and get undressed cause right now I want to fuck you hard." I gasp at his words feeling those instant pulses in my groin.

Our clothes are abandoned across the room in an instant. I love this man so much and the thought of him fucking me hard is just heaven! As his tongue finds mine and we kiss like frantic teenagers he talks through each swirl.

"I need you so much, Lucy, it kills me sometimes to be apart from you. I need you so much right now, baby. I need to be as close as I can possibly get and I can only do that if I'm inside you, beautiful." He stops still, his hand behind my head as we continue to lean against the door. Aside from removing our clothes we haven't moved from our spot leaning on the door.

"Ollie?"

"Yes, baby?" His voice is hoarse with lust, it sounds like perfection.

"Are you OK? I mean, really OK?" He kisses the end of my nose and each cheek before answering.

"Not great, but you know you are the perfect cure for a bad day, which is why I need you to stop worrying and play naughty with me, beautiful girl." I look into his ice blues and see his love for me.

"So, take me to bed then if you want to play." His laugh is loud as he takes me in his arms and carries me to the oversized bed and throws me onto it." I lie flat on my back as he straddles me, kissing my body as he talks. I close my eyes as he kisses my lids.

"Beautiful dark eyes that are so full of mystery, Lucia." He kisses my nose.

"A cute button nose, which is perfect for your delicate face." My lips next.

"The best tasting lips I have ever kissed. I will never kiss another's lips after tasting your sweet mouth, Lucia." I open my eyes and catch his stare. I feel so special right now as Ollie worships my body.

"I love you, Oliver."

"I love you too, baby, and I'm about to show you just how much sweet girl." I never anticipated my night would include this perfect interlude and I am definitely not complaining!

Chapter 25

The night seems to be lasting forever! Ollie and I are seated in the living room, a mug of hot chocolate each as we wait in limbo for his beautiful and fragile mum to return home. I can't even begin to imagine what she's been through this evening and I hate to imagine what her selfish husband's reaction was when she revealed that she knew about who Xavier was. I catch a glimpse of Ollie who is lost in his own world as silence surrounds us. His face is etched in worry, his frown deep as he runs his fingertip around the rim of his mug.

"When are you going to see him, Ollie?" He smiles at my question, a smile of knowing.

"Oh, as soon as possible Lucy. I have so much to say to him. I don't want to hear anything he has to say, I just need to get a few things off my chest and I intend to do that soon." I feel confident that Ollie will be fine when he sees his dad but it doesn't stop the anxiety that runs through me. I think it's just Ralph Ashcroft and the mention of him that sets my anxiety on a roll.

"Would you like me to come with you?" My offer is weak. I have no desire to ever see that man again but if Ollie would like me to go with him, I will, for Ollie. I look up as Ollie laughs loudly.

"Sweetheart, I know how much hurt he has caused you and I can only try and imagine how much you hate my dad, so…" He stops and looks me in the eye, his smile one of empathy as he tilts his head.

"No, baby, I don't need you to come with me and I don't ever want you to see him, ever, OK?" His last word is a whisper as he stares into my eyes making me shift in my seat.

"OK." I don't need to say anything else. I have no desire to meet up with Ralph Ashcroft, ever.

When we hear the key turning in the lock, Ollie and I jump to our feet. My palms are damp and I feel sick to my stomach. I hope beyond hope that Penny is OK. I look at Ollie and my heart surges as I see the fear on his face. Oh God he's so damned worried about his mum!

"Mum, how did it go? Are you OK?" Penny walks towards us, her composure ever complete, with just a tinge of something I can't quite make out. I watch as she walks to Ollie, her arms outstretched and take in just how hard this evening must have been for this faithful, loyal, beautiful woman. My heart beats hard in my chest listening to Penny sob loudly as Ollie hugs her tight. I feel like I should leave the room but Ollie looks to me as if he has no idea what to say or do as he hugs his bereft mother.

"Penny, shall I get you a drink?" I wait, my hands clenched together in complete dismay as I listen to Penny's sobs. I know how she feels, to a certain extent. That man is her complete nemesis, mine and Ollie's too! Penny looks up and nods her head, her face the painful picture of grief.

My hand shakes as I pour gin and tonic into a glass, Penny's chosen drink. My mind races as I think of all the scenarios that could possibly take place when Ollie finally meets with his dad and confronts the arrogant, selfish man.

"Lucy." I look up and smile as Ollie enters the kitchen.

"Sorry to take so long. I thought you needed some time on your own, here" I pass Ollie his mum's drink. He reaches up and lightly touches my cheek.

"Thanks, Luce." I watch him leave the room and decide maybe I should leave them alone for a while. I quietly leave the kitchen and head for the bedroom. I feel a little lost at not checking on my baby and dial Lisa's number as I lie on the bed. It's late but I know Lisa won't mind.

"Lucy, thank God you called. Is everything OK?"

"I'm sorry, Lise. I should have called earlier but it's been… well. How's Bella?"

"She's sleeping like a princess. Lucy, what's going on?" Lisa is my rock. I need to tell her. So, I do!

My friend of so many years is thoughtful, kind and says all the right things when I tell her the whole story. She reassures me that she'll look after Bella while we sort through this mess and I feel better. Better that I know someone who truly loves Bella is there for her when I can't be, and better that I've finally told my good friend what's actually going on.

****

I lie in his arms and listen to his breathing. I know Ollie is not going to sleep well tonight. He found it difficult to see how much this has affected his mum and I know he is desperate to see his dad now and tell him what he thinks. We're lying as spoons, Ollie behind me as he lightly breathes in my ear.

"Ollie." His fingers lightly touch my torso, up and down my ribs and across my stomach. I love his touch. I relish every touch from Ollie that I feel, constantly remembering the times when all I wanted was to feel him. The fact that I have it now is something that I never take for granted thanks to Ralph Ashcroft.

"Luce?"

"Are you OK, baby?" He continues to touch me and I find it hard not to get aroused. I register somewhere in my head that its inappropriate and try to be supportive.

"OK, but you know what would make me feel better?" I feel a surge of something I'm trying desperately to suppress.

"I love you, baby." I don't know what else to say.

"Lucy, I need to make love to you, baby. Please tell me that's what you want?" I feel my heart rate speed up and inwardly smile to me! YEP!

"Baby, I've been trying to stop myself from feeling horny, it's killing me." I feel his smile in his kisses on the back of my neck and feel special, oh so special.

"Please don't stop it, baby. I love it when you're horny. My horny Lucy, oh God, I'm coming just thinking of you!"

My mind is lost on Oliver Ashcroft as his lips trace their way across my skin. Every touch from him sends pulses through my body, almost exploding my head as I try to hold in my arousal, which is currently off the scale. All thoughts of what's going on in our lives are lost as I let my body succumb to my man who makes me feel absolutely God damned perfect.

I trace my fingertips over the taught skin of his back, relishing the feel of his tiny shudder at my touch. Kissing his shoulder, I whisper my true feelings, wanting him to know just how special he is and always has been.

"I love you so much it hurts, baby." He pulls his weight up from me, holding his arms straight as he looms down on me, his eyes twinkling as we share these lovely moments.

"Me too, Luce, no-one, and I mean no-one will ever come between us and what we have." I close my eyes and feel his tiny kiss on the end of my nose. His lips find mine as he gently and sexily licks, sending beautiful sensations in every direction through my body. As his tongue trails down my neck I gasp, loving his mouth on my body. Feeling him lightly blow my nipple makes me call his name, inhibitions getting lost somewhere in my moments of perfection.

"Shhh, baby." His mouth covers mine, drowning out any more noise I may possibly make. As our tongues dance his fingers take over where his lips left. Each touch and squeeze of my nipple makes me arch my back only emphasizing his arousal as I press my body to him. I need Ollie more than I need air right now. Fire burns through me as his fingers play me like his personal instrument. Each touch and caress is music running through my head. I'm in ecstasy and I love this.

"Ollie, please?"

"What, baby, what do you want me to do?" His lips travel south, his tongue circling first one nipple then the other, his fingers running up and down my inner thigh turning me into a frenzied mess.

"Make love to me, please?" As his fingers find my core I gasp and enjoy the sensations of his touch, each one sending electricity through my veins.

"You know there is nothing like the feeling of being inside you, Lucia, my favourite place, ever." As he quietly utters that last word he enters me so, soooo gently, the feel of his lips on my neck as he whispers my name. I'm lost, completely lost in Oliver and his feel, his taste, his scent, his perfection.

****

I'm not one to ever call in sick unless I'm incapacitated so I give Will, my boss a quick call and explain that I have some personal things to sort out, so I need the day off. Will knows I would never take time off unnecessarily and my support for him over his marriage problems has earned me a halo in his world of angels forever.

I make my way to the kitchen, noticing how quiet it is around here without our little bundle of love, who constantly chatters at breakfast time. I find Ollie and his Mum out on the roof terrace. I make my way to them, coffee in hand, which is a necessity this morning as we have basically had no sleep. Our discreet interlude of passion did not bring on sleep for either Ollie or me. We were awake into the small hours talking about the past, his parents, their marriage, our past, our love, our break up and our plans for the future.

We have agreed that we will move back to Layton. Watching Ollie's mum, Penny deal with her life fall apart in front of her without any say in what happens made me realise that what we have is so damned special and I want it to stay that way. Ollie staying in London with Bella and I is inappropriate. I need to make a move both personally and in my career. I will find something. I can drive so there's no reason why I can't commute at least forty-five minutes from home each way to work. I need to look further afield and I intend to start today. I will find a job and Bella and I will follow her daddy back to Layton where I know my baby will be so happy.

"Hey." Ollie winks as I take a seat next to Penny. She looks to me, her eyes full of sorrow as she smiles shyly. I give Ollie a smile and take Penny's hand in mine.

"Morning, Penny, how are you this morning?"

"I'm fine, Lucy. I'm sorry if I made a scene last night. I was just a little overwhelmed, sweetheart, I'm sorry."

"Oh, Penny, please don't apologise. I'm sorry you've had to go through all this. You have nothing to be sorry about, especially the despicable behaviour of your husband." I pull my hand to my mouth, ashamed that I just said that. How insensitive can I get?

"Penny, I'm sorry, I shouldn't have said that." I catch a glint in her eye as she looks from me to Ollie and giggles.

"You're right though, Lucy. I shouldn't apologise for that shit anymore, should I? I am not responsible for his awful behavior, any of it." I look to Ollie who shrugs his shoulders as he frowns.

"No, Mum, none of this is your fault." Penny takes her mug of coffee from the table and I'm shocked as I watch her hand shake when she takes a sip. I look to Ollie who raises an eyebrow as he's obviously just observed the same as me.

"Mum, you don't have to put on a brave face here. Please don't." His words seem to be all Penny needs to let go, really let go. She hands me her mug and slumps forward, her face in her hands as she sobs loudly.

"I don't know what to do now, Ollie. He was my world. I know he didn't love me like I love him but still. What will I do without him?" I feel my heart break yet again because of that evil man and watch in anguish as Ollie tries to comfort his distraught mum.

The morning is sad and slow. My mind races in the silence that we share in between Penny breaking down every now and then. I think of Bella and know that she'll be having a ball with Auntie Lisa who has also taken the day off work. Will was completely reasonable when he realized that Lisa had Bella.

I've made endless cups of coffee as we listen to Penny talk us through year after year of emotional abuse she suffered at the hands of Ollie's dad. I'm shocked to the core. I grew up with two parents who love and adore each other. Yes, they have their moments when they don't speak or they rant and rave at each other but nothing in comparison to the emotional torture Penny Ashcroft has been dealt.

I wince when I watch Ollie's facial expressions as he listens. He obviously only knew what Penny allowed him to know which in reality was very little. Being a parent, I understand completely how she felt the need to protect her children from Ralph and his evil manipulation but I can also see how Ollie feels somewhat cheated. What he thought was reality was actually just a farce and I'm guessing from his body language that the hatred he feels for his dad is growing and growing this morning.

Penny looks up in dismay as her mobile phone rings, disturbing another bout of silence.

"It's Catherine, Oliver. What should I say?" Penny is lost. She has no idea how to deal with this and I feel so sorry for her right now. Ollie runs his hands through his hair, sighing loudly.

"You need to tell her something, if not everything, Mum. She can't find out from anyone else. I wouldn't put it past him to make sure Catherine finds out before you tell her." Penny gasps in shock at Ollie's words as she presses her phone to answer the call. Standing, she walks into the apartment, away from us, far enough away that we can't hear as she breaks her daughter's heart with the dreadful news.

As expected, Catherine is devastated by the news of her father's infidelity and completely shocked that she has a half-brother as a result of this.

We all plan to return to Layton this weekend. Ollie wants to be there for his mum and his sister and we want to be together.

I need to tell my parents about this unfortunate situation. I just don't know how to and if I'm honest I don't want to. My news of Ollie and his family always seems to be so negative.

I'm on my way to Lisa's to pick up Bella. The excitement I feel at seeing my beautiful daughter is temporarily taking over the anxiety of the situation back at home. I'm glad to be away from home just now. Penny cries every now and again and Ollie just looks lost. He has no idea how to console his mum and I have no advice to give. This is a shitty mess and I can't see how we will ever overcome the pain and trauma we're going through.

Standing outside Lisa's apartment building as I buzz, I feel almost liberated that I'm here, away from the crap. I'm losing the will to live right now when I think about what's going on. Surely Penny will divorce Ralph Ashcroft but then again, she still loves the man. How will Ollie deal with the mother of his half-brother – his ex-girlfriend? This is surreal, or worse, what would that be? Well whatever it is, we're there and I'm not liking it… at all.

The sight of Bella eases my anxieties although catching a glimpse of the dimple she shares with her daddy as she grins happily at my arrival brings my thoughts back to Ollie and the chaos I left behind.

"Mummy, I slept with Auntie Lisa in her big bed and she let me watch television with her until it was really, really late." I glance at Lisa who gives me a wink.

"It was really late, Luce, and Bella was such a good girl, weren't you baby girl?" I look up as Lisa holds up eight fingers indicating how late. I can't resist a smile as I look at my baby, who believes she has a partner in crime when in reality she's been conned. I lean forward and take her in my arms, kissing her chubby cheek whilst inhaling her familiar scent.

"Well so long as you were a good girl for Auntie Lisa that's OK, Bell." We share a tight hug as my dear friend looks on with affection.

"How's things back at yours, Luce? Anything sorted?" I shake my head.

"Not really, Lise. We're all going back to Layton this weekend. Penny has told Catherine who was shocked and upset. I think Penny wants to be with her. Ollie needs to be at work at some point and its best if he's near his mum and sister too. I'm going to take the week off and go with him, he says he needs me." Bella cuddles up to me as Lisa and I chat. It's as if she senses things aren't right.

"Of course, he needs you, Lucy. This is a shocking time. I still can't quite believe how it turned out. Poor, poor Penny. How on earth will she get over this? I'm not sure how Ollie must feel either, you know Serena being his ex and all that." My stomach churns at the mention of Serena and the thought that she has a son who is Ollie's half-brother.

"I'm not sure how to deal with that myself, Lisa. She is always going to be part of Ollie's life and I don't think it's going to be easy on any of us."

"Well I suppose that depends on how much involvement the family has with Xavier doesn't it?"

"Hmmm, God it's complicated." I follow Lisa into her kitchen and we continue to chat as she makes me coffee. Bella has drifted off back to the living room to watch TV, bored with her lack of attention.

"So, how's things with you, Lisa? Tell me about your uncomplicated life full of love. I need some respite and you're just that. How's Giovanni?" Her huge grin reassures me that there is normality outside of the Ashcroft empire and their troubles.

"He's over in a few days and we're going to make plans for me to move over to Milan. I've spoken to Will and we've agreed that I will work three months notice so that I can train up one of the interns and then I'm off, honey. Off to be with my man and I can't bloody wait, Luce." My heart is in my mouth as I try to hold back the tears. My best friend in London is leaving and I'm gutted. I've spent so much of my time with Lisa since moving here and not seeing her on a daily basis just doesn't bear thinking about.

"Don't look so damned miserable, Lucy, I want you to be happy for me." I pull myself together and pull Lisa in for a hug.

"I'm really happy for you, beautiful, I just don't know what I'll do without my daily dose of you that's all." My smile is barely there as Lisa pulls back to look at me.

"Well I'm guessing you're not going to be staying around here for much longer, Luce, and what would I do, left down in the big smoke when you move back to Layton? It's going to happen, Luce, and I bet this problem you're having right now will push your move to happen sooner rather than later."

"Yeah, I suppose you're right. Oh gosh, Lisa, we're moving apart, far apart. Bella is going to miss you so much." I catch the glint of a tear in Lisa's eyes at the mention of Bella.

"We can share holidays together, just like we have in the past only we'll be staying at each other's. Giovanni will just love Layton and you and Ollie get to spend time in Milan. Gio and I can babysit for you if you stay. Oh, Lucy, it will be just lovely." I try to get caught up in Lisa's excitement but it's difficult. I have other pressing issues to overcome before we can live happily ever after in Layton. My phone bleeping a text pulls me from my thoughts. It's Ollie:

"How's Bella, Luce? What time will you be back? Love you x" I quickly text back, following Lisa into the living room to retrieve my daughter and her belongings.

"Leaving in about ten minutes, love you too x"

"Come on, princess, we need to get your things and go and see Daddy and Nanna." I watch my girl jump up in delight at the mention of her Daddy. I look at Lisa and she smiles.

"I hope I get one like Bella one day, Luce." I'm speechless. Lisa has always snubbed the idea of being a mummy saying she prefers to babysit other people's so that she can give them back.

"Lisa Marie Bevan, I am shocked. Where has this come from?" I watch as my friend hugs herself swaying from side to side with a strange glint in her eye as she looks at me with a slight blush on her face.

"Well I met Gio and... well, I changed my mind. I want his babies, Lucy, lots of babies. I know, I know, it's a complete turn-around but I said all that before Giovanni." I'm laughing excitedly, all thoughts of problems and anxieties diminished temporarily as I share this news. This very, very exciting news.

"Oh, Lisa Marie, I cannot believe you're going to have a baby when you've moved away from me and Bella." Lisa hits my arms.

"Stop using my full name, Luce, only Aunt Becca can get away with that and anyhow, imagine the fun we'll have on our holidays if me and Gio have a playmate for Bella." I pull my friend in once again and hug her tightly. This time the tears run free, tears of joy for my friend and her happy news.

"Don't cry, Luce, you'll set me off and Bella will wonder what the hell's wrong with us." I wipe away my tears grinning like a fool at my friend.

"Can I tell Ollie, he could use some good news, Lise?"

"Of course you can. We need a night together, the four of us and soon." I nod my head in agreement.

"How long is Gio here for?"

"Only the weekend but he'll be back at the end of next week."

"We'll be back next weekend. Why don't you come for Sunday lunch at ours?"

"Perfect. Gio can practise playing the daddy role with Bella." I laugh.

"I doubt he'll get a look in with Ollie but yeah, he'll see how we never have any time to ourselves. Second thoughts, Lise, it might put him off." We laugh as we wander off in search of Bella who's gone to Lisa's bedroom to collect her things.

****

Bustling through the doorway with Bella and all her belongings I'm awestruck at the sight of Ollie pulling her into his arms and kissing her little face frantically.

"Oh, baby girl, I missed you so much. I love you, Bell." Bella giggles and wriggles in her daddy's arms, delirious at his over-the-top greeting.

Dropping the bags on the floor I follow my favourite pair into the living room and feel so glad to have brought Bella home when I see the smile she brings to Penny's face as she runs to her Nanna.

"Hello, Princess Bella, we missed you sooo much."

"I missed you too Nanna. Is my bedroom still there?" Ollie and I watch as Bella drags Penny off to check that she still has a bedroom. Penny looks only too pleased with the distraction. Ollie pulls me into his arms.

"God, Luce, it's good to have you home." His kisses on my face and neck are just what I need.

Chapter 26

As we step inside the penthouse now that we're back in Layton, I head straight for the living room doors, sliding them open so that I can breathe in the sea air, looking out across the bay. The deep breaths of sea air have the calming effect I knew they would and I feel so much better now we're home. I hear the distant voice of Bella as she checks out her other princess bedroom, smiling at the tinkle of her sweet chatter. I feel Ollie's hands as they find my waist and pull me to him. I relish the feel of his nose in my neck as we stand silently, looking out to sea.

"It's good to be back isn't it, Luce?"

"Mmm, it really is home. Do you think your mum will be OK, Ollie?" We dropped Penny at home and she insisted we didn't go in with her. Catherine was waiting with Abbie and Penny wanted to see them alone.

"I understand she wants to speak to Catherine alone. This seems like the final hurdle for Mum. Once she's told Catherine, I think she'll be able to deal with this and move on."

"Has she talked about moving on?"

"She mentioned divorce but said she needed to see Catherine before she could make any plans."

I need to tell my parents. I want to go and see them but Ollie and Bella will be with me and I need to forewarn them and not make Ollie feel uncomfortable while I talk about his family in front of him.

"Ollie, I need to tell my parents about what's happened. I think I should give Mamma a call rather than tell them everything when we go round, what do you think?"

"Oh God, Luce… I suppose you have to tell them. It's so fucking embarrassing though." I place my hands over his and lean into his body.

"None of this is your fault so you shouldn't be embarrassed. I just need to fill them in, that's all. If I do it over the phone it'll be less embarrassing for you."

"OK. You gonna call them now?"

"Well I'd like to go and see them soon so yes I suppose I need to call." He sighs, resigned to the fact that this family saga is going to be shared.

"I'll go and see what Bell's up to while you call. I don't want to listen." His grimace makes me wince. This is so difficult for him.

"Mamma, hi it's me." I hear her laugh and smile at my mother's happiness at hearing my voice.

"Lucia sweetheart, how are you? Are you back in Layton yet?"

"We just got back. We're all fine, Mamma, how about you and Dad?"

"Oh, just the same old same old, Luce."

"We'll come and see you in the morning, is that OK?"

"Of course it is, you don't have to ask sweetheart."

"I know, Mamma. I need to tell you something."

"What, Lucia, something good or bad?"

"Bad, but it's nothing to worry about I just need to tell you before we see you."

"What's wrong, is Bella OK?"

"Yes, Mamma, she absolutely fine. There's been a few problems with Ollie's dad." Before I can carry on with my story she's making comments.

"Well that man is a bad lot Lucia, we know that after what he did to you and Ollie."

"Mamma, listen, will you?"

"Sorry, sweetheart, go on then."

"Well he's been worse than ever this time. He introduced me to Ollie's ex-girlfriend and she told me she has a son and that he's

317

Ollie's." Mamma gasps so I proceed quickly before she thinks too much.

"Anyway, I'll fill you in on all the details later but it turns out she was lying and the father is actually Ollie's dad." I'm sure Ollie and Bella can hear her gasps from inside.

"Lucy, that's awful. How's Ollie and his mum? That Ralph Ashcroft is something else, I don't mind saying. Sweet Jesus!" I can hear Dad asking what's wrong and Mamma whispering in quick speak whilst holding her hand over the phone.

"Mamma."

"Yes, sweetheart, sorry, your dad was worried."

"It's OK. I thought I'd tell you now so I don't have to embarrass Ollie and tell you in front of him when we see you. We just dropped Penny off at home. Catherine was waiting for her."

"Oh, that poor woman. This is dreadful news. Well you give Ollie my love and I won't mention it when you come over in the morning."

****

Mamma and Dad never said a word about Ollie's dad or the sordid story of Xavier's conception when we visited. Dad spent his time fussing over Bella whilst Mamma fed Ollie cakes and pastries she'd made earlier. Mamma's way of dealing with a drama has always been to feed the victim. Emilia and I were fed endless sweet things at each teenage break-up whilst Dad chastised Mamma for feeding us crap.

I can't hold back the grin when Ollie groans as he takes a seat on the sofa when we return home. I have to admit he does look a little pale faced. Memories of too much cake as a small child spring to mind as he fidgets trying to get comfy with a belly full of sugary, unhealthy delights.

"You OK, Ollie?" He groans before answering.

318

"Oh, Luce, we have to go and eat dinner at Ben and Sarah's later. I don't think I could eat another thing for at least a week. Your mamma force fed me all that cake you know." I laugh loudly as I head to the kitchen to grab him some fizzy pop to help his digestion.

"Oliver Ashcroft, she fed you because you kept telling her how lovely her goodies were. You need to learn that you just eat and then keep quiet or she will keep putting more and more in front of you."

"You could have given me the heads up, Luce. I was being polite and now I feel sick as a fat, greedy dog." I laugh as I pass him a glass of lemonade.

"Here, fat boy, try this it might help. What time are we at the Watson's for dinner?" Ollie groans again at the mention of our dinner date with Sarah and Ben.

"I have about four hours recovery time. Should I phone and cancel, Luce? I really don't think I'll be able to eat another thing for at least two days."

"No way, Oliver, I am not turning down a dinner date with my bestie from school because you don't have the nerve to say no to my mamma and her cakes."

"Now I know where you get your persuasive tendencies from, Luce. I could never say no to you and your mamma is just the same." We both laugh as I drop down onto the sofa beside Ollie and fall back onto his body. His groan brings out more laughter as he feels my full body weight on his cake filled belly.

****

I sit back, full to the brim with Sarah's lovely food and look at Ollie who groans yet again today.

"Shit, I don't think I can eat for a week now. What with Lucy's mamma's cakes and your beautiful dinner, Sarah, I'm good for a while I'm sure."

"Oh God, did Mamma fill you with sympathy baking, Ollie?" Em giggles, only too aware of the effects of Mamma and her sympathetic tendencies. Ollie nods and Kyle leans forward with a quizzical look on his face.

"Is this something I should know about?" Ollie, Em and I laugh loudly at Kyle's question, each looking to the others, questioning whether we should tell Kyle or just make him wait until the time comes when Mamma feels the need to bake for him. Emilia gives in and tells Kyle about the cakes. Sarah and Ben share in the hysterics as we watch Ollie try and get comfy with his overload of food on board.

"Seriously, mate, don't visit their parents if you're suffering from any type of trauma. It's definitely bad for your heart." Emilia and I share am affectionate smile as we both think of our caring mamma and her traditions.

"So how is life in London, you two? Is that what all the trauma is about?" The news of Ralph Ashcroft hasn't been shared with many people. I haven't told Em as I don't know how to if I'm honest. Ben knows and so does Sarah. I feel a slight pang of guilt that I still haven't told my sister, but right now I just like watching her be happy with Kyle. I look to Sarah and Ben and they both give me the nod that they know and realize that Em and Kyle don't.

"We're moving back here. Is that a big enough trauma for you?" I use this other morsel of information to distract from the real, disgusting trauma that some of us know about. Emilia squeals in delight as Sarah looks on stunned.

"Are you really doing it, Luce?" My old friend has tears in her eyes as she reaches out for her wine glass and takes a gulp.

"Yes, we really are coming home aren't we, Ollie?" I look to Ollie and he takes my hand.

"The sooner the better. Oh, and Bella can't wait Auntie Em." I forget all the shit and revel in the joy of my family and friends that we're coming home. Honestly, I never thought I'd come back to Layton for good, but now I have Oliver I can't think of anywhere I'd rather grow old.

"Have you sorted anything with work, Luce?" Sarah wipes at her tears as she asks. I know it will be just great seeing her all the time when I do move back.

"No, I need to get active and sort something soon. I'm going to look further afield. I know there'll be nothing too near here but I can drive so I'll commute." I feel Ollie's hand on my knee. I look sideways and he gives me a wink.

"She doesn't need to work does she, Ollie? Why don't you stay home and have more babies, Luce?" I blush as I give Em a look that tells her to shut up and hear Sarah giggle.

****

A week in Layton seemed to disappear before we knew it. Mamma and Dad are off to Sicily, leaving their good friends to look after the campsite for them. It's the end of the season so there aren't so many holidaymakers around. I look to Ollie as we make our final checks before setting off back to London. This has to be the first time I'm not looking forward to returning. In bygone times I couldn't wait to get back to my faster paced life but not now I have Ollie to share things with. The slower pace near the sea is definitely the perfect place for our family life.

When we got home from Sarah and Ben's a few days ago, Ollie mentioned having more children. He would like nothing more than to get me pregnant and me never work again. I don't think it's so much the misogynist in him, it's more the need for us to be together after everything we've been through and now that we're here as a family. I check Bella who's all strapped into her car seat and she gives me her attempt at a wink. I can't help but giggle as she gives me the thumbs up. Maybe another baby would be right for us, maybe?

****

The weeks move fast when we're back in the big smoke. We go about our daily routines and enjoy every moment of being a family together. We spend hours at the park enjoying picnics whatever the weather. Bella thinks it's awesome to sit in the bandstand while it rains outside as we eat our sandwiches.

I enjoy these times and know that changes are on the horizon and although change is healthy I'm nervous.

Lisa's making plans for her move to Milan to be with Giovanni and each time she tells me more I feel sick. I don't want her to move away even though I'm planning on returning to Layton. The thought of her so far away is unnerving.

Ben has asked me to do some interior design on a new development they're starting soon. I haven't so much as looked at a mood board in years but I'm going to give it a go and see what Ben and Ollie think. If I finish early enough and they don't like it, then they'll have time to get a professional to do the work.

Ollie's mum has started divorce proceedings and seems quite positive now she has plans for her future. She's selling the house in Layton and buying something much smaller. Ollie is taking care of that for her. Ralph Ashcroft has not objected to any of Penny's plans. Whatever she said to him is keeping the nasty old man quiet while she goes about making big changes to her life.

Ollie went to see his dad and has not uttered a word about what they said. I asked him once how it went and he just looked and smiled before shaking his head at me. I will ask again but not now. I don't know when, maybe years from now. I don't know if I want to know what was said because I know for sure that the old man would have said pretty harsh things about me and Ollie will not want to tell me that.

****

I think we were all lulled into a false sense of security. I should have known that he'd be back. We've spent the last few weeks pretending that everything is normal, that we live normal lives and don't have all this hanging over us. I should have known that he wouldn't let this go. He wants me out of his family's life. I knew that years ago yet I fooled myself into thinking I could exist without him interfering any more. Wrong!

"Good morning, Miss Meyer." I nod to the temp who's showing him into my office, reminding myself that it's not her fault that she doesn't know he shouldn't be let in here. I cough to clear my throat and mentally kick myself for showing nerves in front of him.

"Good morning." I don't say his name. It hurts deep inside to say it aloud. There isn't anything that can change my opinion of this evil man. I know deep down that he's here to hurt me. That's all he's ever done, hurt me.

I make a point of not offering him a seat. Why should I? I owe him nothing. Instead I stand, trying with all my might to look strong. I will not let this man get to me. I need to keep calm so that he can't see how scared I really am.

"What can I do for you, why are you here?" He smirks, his eyes full of hatred as he stares at me.

"I promised to make your life a living hell the last time I came here and as you know, I am true to my word." I look towards the closed door, willing it to open. Hoping against hope that the temp who's covering for Suzie is telepathic and will come bursting into the room any second now. No such luck!

My mouth goes dry and I struggle to swallow as he walks towards me, the smirk still firmly in place on that evil face of his. He grins and I gasp as I notice for the first time that they share his dimple. Their dimple that I love so much is featured on the face of the man I hate with all my being. I want to cry. I'm devastated. The two people in my life who I love more than life itself share something so prominent with this evil creature.

"Miss Meyer, I have not come here for pleasure and I don't intend to keep you. You have caused me so much pain, young lady, and I intend to pay you back. My son shouldn't be with you and your offspring. He deserves so much better. You are trash and you need to learn that you have no place within my family, now or ever." His words go unheard as he continues to verbally abuse me, all the time moving closer. I step to one side and attempt to move towards the door. How stupid was I to stand at the far end of my office? I know the safety drill. Stay close to the door when you're unsure of your safety.

In one quick movement, his hand is round my neck as he pushes me back, forcing my body against the wall with a thud.

"What is so special about you, Lucia Meyer? What does my talented, intelligent son see in you?" I cringe at his use of my full name, feeling violated.

He forces the weight of his body against mine as he covers my mouth with his large, heavy hand. I feel my tears force their way out and drench my face. I push at his heavy frame knowing that I have no chance of getting free from him. The scent of his aftershave nauseates me; recollection of that same smell from our last encounter fills me with fear.

"Are you a good fuck, Lucia? Is that what keeps you in his life?" He forces his hand up my skirt, pushing so hard on my groin, I cry out. His hand muffles my voice. No one will hear me.

"Let's see shall we, you whore. Show me what thrills my boy gets out of you." I squirm, trying to break free. Fear has taken hold of me and I couldn't cry out if I wanted to. I smell his minty breath on my face as he leans in and bites my neck. I squeal, but again he pushes hard on my face with his hand, halting my cry for help. I close my eyes wishing and hoping that this is a bad dream, a terrible nightmare that I will wake from and sigh with relief. As his fingers push on the flesh of my inner thigh, I feel pain and know this is not a dream. This is so real and I fear for my life right now. How far will this man go to get me out of his son's life.

"You bitch, you filthy, dirty, money grabbing bitch." His fingers tighten on my thigh in a vice like grip, my cry hoarse and guttural under his hand as this evil man assaults me in such a violent intrusive way. I'm aware of a voice and realise that the temp is calling through to me on the intercom. My body suddenly feels light as he swiftly moves away.

"Lucy, your next appointment is here. How long would you like me to delay them for?" I don't move, I can't. Instead I watch as he straightens his bedraggled clothes and smooths his hair, his eyes never leaving me. I'm too scared to move. He terrifies me.

As he moves to the sink and washes his hands, I gag and have to swallow hard so as not to throw up right there and then. I feel my warm tears, closing my eyes temporarily, wishing I could be anywhere but here feeling like I do.

"This isn't over, whore. I promise you that." As he disappears through my office door, I sink to the floor pulling my knees up as I quietly cry.

What do I do? Do I tell anyone? Will he kill me? Oh my God, my baby. He'll get her, I know he will.

I sit and cry for what seems like hours but in reality, is only a few minutes. When Jocelyn the temp gently taps on my door, calling my name I realize that I need help.

"Jocelyn, could you go and get Lisa for me? I'm not too well and she can take my meeting for me."

"Of course, I'll be right back, Lucy."

The next sound makes my heart thud out of my chest as I jump in fright.

"Luce, it's me, are you OK?" I hear the door gently open and know that Lisa, my dear friend will not expect to find me like this. I hear her gasp as she closes the door and obviously catches sight of me in my terrified heap on the floor.

"Fucking hell, Lucy, what happened? Sweetheart, are you OK?" I shake my head and look up at my special friend who's supported me and my baby through so much trouble in my life.

I wince as she kneels down and tries to pull me close. He hurt me. I'm sure the bruises will verify that when they appear but my fear is from actually being touched.

I know right here and now that my troubles have just quadrupled with his visit. My life has changed forever and I'm not sure how I'm going to get over this unwelcome interlude.

"Sweetheart, what happened?" Lisa's voice is gentle, like a mother talking to a tiny child. She strokes my hair, pushing back stray, wayward pieces that have been disturbed by that evil man's brutish hands. I tentatively look up and catch her eyes as she frowns at my sorry state.

"He came to see me, Lisa." Her face changes from confused to one of horror when she realizes who I'm talking about."

"Noooo, not again. Did he hurt you, Lucy?" I nod my head at my friend. I'm ashamed to the core about what just happened but I trust Lisa and I know my friend will help me, and FUCK do I need help right now!

When I eventually step out of my office no one would know what occurred just a few short hours ago in this very building whilst they went about their busy day. Lisa hugs me tight to her, shielding me from the big bad world as we step outside to grab a cab back to hers.

It's mid-afternoon and I'm not due home yet which is a good thing because right now I need some space and I need to decide what I'm going to do about him.

Watching London town speed past me as we head to Lisa's place I know one thing for sure – I want to leave here and never come back.

I'm safely contained in Lisa's flat as she flaps around me, not really knowing what to do. She nervously takes a seat next to me on the comfy sofa.

"Lucy, we should call the police, sweetheart. You need to report him. He should be locked up. At least let me call the police, Lucy?" I look into my friend's hazel eyes and I know she's right. I just don't know if I can do this. I need to look after my family, protect them, don't I?

"What about Ollie, Lisa, he needs to know. How the hell am I going to tell him what just happened, how?" My pitch is high as I ask the question. My friend looks away, her face etched in sorrow as I see her trying hard to deal with the afternoon's catastrophe.

Lisa called the police then Ollie, relaying more or less the same story. The knock at the door brings our conversation to a halt. Who is it, Ollie or the police? I don't know who I'm dreading seeing more. An overwhelming feeling of sickness envelops me as I watch Lisa leave the room to answer her door.

I instantly recognize the hushed tones of Ollie and instantly feel tears wash over my face. I love him so much, I always have. What will he think of me when I tell him what happened?

I don't get a chance to have that conversation with Ollie. The police are just a few seconds behind him and they swiftly tell me they'd like to take me to the police station to be interviewed and examined as soon as possible.

"Bella, I need to be there for Bella." I look to Ollie and Lisa, both faces grey as they look back at me.

"I'll take care of Bella, Lucy, please don't worry about her, I promise." A tiny bit of relief washes over me knowing that my good friend will take care of my baby. She's always been there for Bella and I, and today is just another day when I couldn't do without Lisa.

"Do you want me to come with you, Luce?" Ollie looks almost scared to ask me. I shake my head. I don't want him to come with me. If he comes with me now, this will be another bad memory to add to the ones we already share at the hands of that man.

"No!" It's almost a shout. He flinches. I stifle a sob and look to the sympathetic female officer.

"I'm ready to go. It won't take too long, will it? I have a little girl who needs me. I need to make sure he doesn't get near her." The officer gives me a tender smile before speaking quietly.

"Hopefully Mr Ashcroft will be detained right now, Lucy, so he won't be able to go anywhere near your daughter. We will deal with that side of things as soon as we get back to the station though so don't worry, we have it in hand."

"Lucy." I look at Oliver's horrified face.

"I won't let anything happen to Bella, I promise, sweetheart." I shrug my shoulders at him and watch him flinch again.

The drive to the police station is a blur. The two police officers carry on a quiet conversation about nothing in particular as we hastily make our way to our destination.

Once there, I tell my story as directly as possible, switching off emotion as I go over what happened just a few short hours ago. I'm taken through to a comfortable looking suite and wait with the female officer who tells me she's called Hayley. I have to be examined by a doctor. Hayley tells me this is standard practice. She explains that they will photograph any marks on my body. I have no idea if I have any marks. I haven't looked and I don't want to.

I soon realise that I am marked as another officer takes quite a few photos while the doctor points out mark after mark on my inner thighs, my neck and my face.

"How will I explain this to Bella?" I see her pretty face in my mind's eye and feel the tears begin to flow. Rivers of tears flow for what seems like hours as Hayley makes sympathetic noises and passes me tissue after tissue.

"Lucy, we've finished now." They've taken my clothes for forensic examination so I quickly change into the clothes I borrowed from Lisa before I left. I feel lost. I don't feel like me. I'm in someone else's clothes and my body hurts so much. I don't want to be me right now. I want to crawl away and die. I nod to Hayley and try to smile. I wince at the pain that shoots through my jaw. I swiftly touch my face and realize that I'm more bruised than I thought.

"I think you're gonna have a few aches and pains over the next few days, Lucy, you need to take it easy." I look at Hayley as she passes me the prescription for painkillers from the doctor.

"Will you need to see me again? I'd like to go home to Layton." Hayley looks at me quizzically.

"I thought you lived in London."

"We have a home in Layton on Sea where I'm from as well. My family live there. I'd like to go home and be with my family. Can I?" Hayley reaches up and gently touches my shoulder. I wince. She apologises. I shrug.

"Go and be with your family. We've dealt with the most important bits today so if we need you we can give you notice, is that OK?" I nod, relieved that I can go and see my Mamma.

I called Lisa and arranged a lift back home. Lisa has been my rock since I moved to London and I really, truly don't know what I'd do without her. As I walk out of the police station, I turn to my friend and pull her close for a hug. I sob as she holds me silently.

"I'm so sorry this happened, Lucy, so damned sorry."

"How's Bell?" Lisa smiles at the mention of my baby girl.

"Oh, she's just fine. Busy packing since I told her you're going to see Nonna and Granddad, she can't wait."

"How's Ollie?" I'm scared to ask but I need to know. Finding out what his dad did to me must have hurt, bad!

"Hasn't said anything to me. Basically, spending time with Bella, but when he does look at me, the hurt is right there in those beautiful blue eyes of his, Luce. He looks broken, if I'm honest. How the hell is he going to deal with this?"

The tears flow again as I find my seat in Ollie's car. It takes a few seconds to register that it's Ollie's car. I touch the seat and look at Lisa.

"He insisted I use his car, Luce. He's gutted you didn't want him to come with you."

I look ahead trying to find the words to explain to Lisa how I feel. I sigh and glance sideways. Lisa is watching and waiting.

"I don't know what to say to him, Lise. I don't know how to be around him. I'm lost, if I'm honest." I hear her sob and instantly look to my friend who is leaning forward over the steering wheel, her body shaking as she sobs. I find myself comforting my friend and feel this is somewhat strange.

"Are you OK, Lise?" She looks up, tears streaming down her make up stained face, and laughs.

"I'm sorry, Lucy, it's just so fucking horrible and I feel so bad for all of you." I touch her pretty face as she leans in to my touch.

"Come on, Lisa, let's go and see Bella."

When I arrived at the office this morning, nothing seemed out of the ordinary and I never expected to see Ollie's dad. Suzie our admin support called in sick earlier in the week and we have a temp in covering for her. When she let Ralph Ashcroft into my office, the poor girl had no idea of the devastation this would cause my family.

I'm a mess and the pain from the bruising reminds me of my visit from that evil man. I stop myself from wondering how far he would have gone in his assault on me if the temp hadn't interrupted. It doesn't bare thinking about.

Chapter 27

I slowly pack my things ready to head back to Layton, feeling sorry for myself. I hear Bella chattering to her daddy and smile at her innocence. I have no idea how Ollie and I will get through this and if indeed we will. I hate Ollie's dad with my whole being but I love Ollie with all my heart. It just isn't right.

"What time do you want to leave, Lucy?" He doesn't even sound like my Ollie now. His voice is strained and I wonder if maybe he's had enough. I don't blame him. His father doesn't want us to be together and he will obviously do anything to stop it. I look into his ice-blues and they just look sad. I don't even know if I can see any love there. I turn away, holding back the sob that is fighting to escape.

"Lucy?" The question in his voice reminds me that he did indeed ask me a question. I breathe deeply swallowing my sorrow and turn back to look at Ollie.

"Sorry, I'll be ready soon. I've nearly finished packing my things. I'll just sort through Bella's then we can go. Have you packed?" I feel like I'm talking to a stranger as he almost looks through me when I speak. I watch and feel my heart being squeezed as he closes his eyes then falls to his knees. As his hands cover his face, I vaguely hear his words.

"I am so sorry, Lucy, my Lucy. I can't believe I let this happen to you. I will go after him, Luce, and I promise I will kill him for what he's done to you." I quickly move forward and join him on the floor pulling him to me, my arms around his shoulders. My sobs come fast and strong as he holds me and we sway, neither speaking. Bella's distant calls bring me back to normality. I pull away fast as Ollie wipes at my face with his thumbs. His gentle kiss eases my pain slightly. Ollie stands holding out a hand to pull me up. When I'm on my feet he pulls me in and hugs me tight. His whispers in my ear are a tonic that I need more than anything right now.

"I love you with all my heart, Lucia, please don't leave me. I will make this right and I will try and make you and Bella happy." I pull back, kissing his perfect mouth that I love so much.

"I wasn't planning on leaving you, Ollie. We just have a great deal to sort out, don't we? This will either make or break us don't you think?" A solitary tear trickles down his cheek as he shakes his head.

"I won't let him take you away from me, Luce. He did that once before and it won't happen again." I take in his familiar scent as he pulls me in tight.

"Muuummmmyyyy, Daaaaddddyyyy!" That cute voice pulls us apart as we both smile down at our beautiful baby.

"What's wrong, Bella?" She doesn't answer but takes me by the hand instead and leads me to her bedroom. Ollie follows holding tightly onto my other hand, squeezing the life out of it as we move along. I look back over my shoulder and see the pain in his face. I stop and pull him closer, kissing him lightly before uttering words that make him visibly relax.

"I love you." I realize that I haven't told him that since I got back. I love him more than life and that won't ever change. I just don't know how much we can take as a family. Emotionally we are being tortured and it's not healthy.

The drive back to Layton is torture too. For the first hour, Ollie only speaks to Bella. I turned the stereo on and have spent my journey so far getting lost in the music. I put my phone on shuffle and the tunes playing are spookily topical. I look to Ollie as he clears his throat as if to speak. He turns the music down low and takes a look at Bella in his rear-view mirror. I turn and see that Bella is fast asleep, her tiny rosebud mouth tipped open as she gently snores.

"What happened at the police station, Lucy?" I don't want to do this but it's only fair to share this with Ollie.

"I gave a statement and was checked by a doctor. I had my injuries photographed and they took my clothes for forensics. That was it." Ollie slows the car and pulls in at the side of the road. I swallow hard, nervous as he turns to me. I flinch as he reaches out and takes my hand. I watch his face contort in sorrow.

"I'm sorry, Ollie, you made me jump, that's all."

"He made you like that, Lucy. I will never be able to make up to you for this, for him, will I?" I lean back in my seat and close my eyes. I keep my eyes closed as I speak, afraid of the truth and hoping if I can't see him it won't hurt.

"You can't do this, can you? I understand, Ollie. I love you and I always will but I understand if you want to walk away. This torture is aimed at both of us but if you walk away, he'll leave both of us alone, won't he?" Eyes tightly shut, I hold my breath in anticipation of the bad news.

"Hey." His voice is gentle. I still can't look.

"Sweetheart, look at me." I feel his breath on my face as he speaks. I tentatively open my eyes and he's there, in my face.

"I'm not going anywhere, baby girl. Not unless you don't want me. I intend to sort this. I will sort him, that bastard of a father that curses my life, your life, our family life. Do you want me to leave you, Lucy?" I furiously shake my head as tears cascade.

"No, Ollie, please don't leave us. Bella and I, we need you. We love you so much." He pulls me close kissing the top of my head.

"I won't leave you, Lucy, I won't."

No one is expecting us back in Layton tonight so we've decided to keep quiet and just take a breath and try to be as normal as possible. Bella asked why I have bruises on my face and I felt so bad lying to her. I know she's only a tot and she won't remember in a couple of weeks but the fact that she's seen the bruises on my face is traumatic enough. I told her I had a fall at work in my heels. She giggled as we all remembered how she falls over in her princess shoes every time she wears them.

I watch Ollie carry her tired sleeping form to her bedroom and feel sad. Sad that I can't just be happy for us all to be together. Sad that I'm going to have to tell my family what happened and that Ollie is going to have to tell his poor mother.

I jump as Ollie says my name. I'm taking in the sea air, trying to feel happy to be home like I was not so long ago. It isn't working. On one hand I'd like to go and see my Mamma, I need her comfort right now but I'm frightened to tell my parents what happened today. I feel like I'm going to disappoint them all over again, like the day I told them I was pregnant and refused to disclose who the father was. I have never made parenting easy for them and this is yet another problem to take home.

"Lucy." Ollie sounds almost frightened to say my name.

I turn to look at him and feel anxious. Today was pretty awful and I need to talk about it but I'm not sure I can with Ollie. It seems wrong. Ollie holds out a hand to me and I take it. He leads me back inside, my anxiety getting stronger as we leave behind my comfort blanket of the sounds and smell of the sea.

"Would you like a drink, Luce? I know I need one." He leads me to the kitchen never letting go of my hand. I pull away to let him get a drink. He looks to me, his head tipped to one side.

"I'd like a large glass of wine, please?" His smile is sympathetic.

"Are you OK to drink with the painkillers?" I shrug.

"I don't really care, Ollie, I need a drink as much as you do." He pours the glass of wine without further comment. I watch and notice his hand is shaking.

"What's wrong, Ollie?" He takes a large gulp of his drink, whiskey I think.

"I need to know every detail about what happened today. I need you to tell me, baby, but I know I'm going to hate every word of what you say and I don't know how I'll react. It scares me, Luce."

"We could leave it until tomorrow if you like. I'm not so sure I know how to tell you really."

"Let's just enjoy our drinks then maybe later we can talk." I nod in agreement, happy for my temporary reprieve.

I'm tired, very tired and I ache everywhere. Fighting off that beast of a man earlier in the day has taken it out of me. I rest my head on Ollie's shoulder as we sit quietly, the hum of the TV covering our silence.

"Would you like me to run you a bath, Luce? It might help, you know, with the bruising." He goes to touch my hand then pulls away. I reach out quickly and grab it back. We need to be normal with each other. He can't be scared to touch me or Ralph Ashcroft will be on the home straight to winning this battle.

"Please don't be scared to touch me, Ollie. I'm not made of glass; I won't break. I may flinch because I'm hurting a little but I need you to be my Oliver." He leans in and gently kisses my lips. It's lovely!

"Come on, Lucia, let me bathe you and make you feel like my princess again." He stands and gently helps me up, leading me to the bathroom.

As I step out of my clothes, I hear Ollie gasp as he takes in the sight of my body. For a second, I forgot that the bruising is visible. He holds his head either side as he speaks.

"Luce, I'm sorry."

"Don't be, Ollie. Just let me take my bath and wash this day away, OK." I take his hand and he helps me step into the large bath. He's filled it nearly to the rim and the mountain of bubbles is very inviting.

I lay back, letting the warm soapy water envelope me. Closing my eyes, I try and forget the day and focus on the here and now.

"Is that good, baby?" I open my eyes and smile at my man. He's perched on the side of the bath, swishing his hands through the water.

"You know in some cultures women have personal bathers. Would you like to bathe me?" He takes the sponge, his eyes sparkling for the first time today. This is not a sexual moment, it's intimate. Probably the most intimate I have ever felt if I'm honest. After being so violated today, letting Ollie wash my body is showing him how much I trust him in spite of his evil father. He gently takes each arm, rubbing the sponge up and down, his eyes constantly on mine.

"You are perfect, Lucia, my Lucia. Sometimes when I look at you, I can't quite believe you're really mine. When we were kids, I used to flaunt that stream of girls past you and go home feeling so disappointed that it never appeared to affect you. I used to dream about you, kissing you, touching your beautiful long hair and telling you how I really felt. You know some days I really hated Declan for having you."

"Ironic really that I felt the same. I'd discretely watch and hate every one of those girls. When I watched you kiss them I'd wish it were me. You know the thing I wanted more than anything was for you to hold my hand. I wanted to feel what it was like to be touched by you." He gently reaches up and touches my lips.

"Oh, baby, let's make this right so that we can live happily ever after." I close my eyes as he gently kisses my lips and his hands take care of washing my bad day away.

"Why don't you join me in here? We can wash the evil away together then when we emerge, we can be stronger."

I watch as Ollie removes his clothes and feel happy that he's here with me. I need him more than ever and tonight has been perfect in helping me recover.

"You checking me out, Miss Meyer?" He raises an eyebrow and I giggle.

"I can't help it. You're one sexy man Mr Ash…" I stop at the mention of that name and Ollie quickly moves towards me, understanding completely what is bothering me.

"Hey" He steps into the water quickly and slips down behind me. I lean back against his firm body and close my eyes as the tears stream down my face. I'm silent for a good few minutes then an uninvited sob fills the air.

Ollie's kisses on my face and neck are kisses of comfort as he sooths and shushes away my sorrow.

My fingers are wrinkled when we eventually leave the bathroom. My body is so tired and the aching hasn't really subsided. Ollie leads me to the bed and helps me in. He tucks me in the way he does with Bella, bringing a smile to my face.

"I love you, Ollie, thank you."

"Hey, I love you too and if I could swap places with you, I would, Luce. Please don't thank me." Ollie lays beside me on top of the covers and ever so gently pulls me to him. With his arm firmly around my waist, I hold onto his hand and let sleep take a hold of me.

As I feel his hand covering my mouth and the full weight of his body on mine, I know I need to make myself heard. I feel the fear run through me as I fight to get him off me. He's too strong, I can't breathe. I try to scream but it won't come.

"Lucy, baby, please wake up." His voice doesn't sound the same. He doesn't sound evil. As I slowly wake, I realise I was dreaming. Ollie is gently stroking my face, wiping away the tears as I try to catch my breath.

"Oh, Ollie, I was dreaming. He was here. I couldn't get free. He had his hand over my mouth and I couldn't breathe." Ollie pulls me up and into his body, cradling me like a baby. As he strokes my hair I slowly calm down.

"I'm sorry I woke you, Ollie."

"Lucy, please don't be sorry. Was your dream about what happened today? Did you just relive it, Luce?' I nod my head and flinch at his gasp.

"He had his hand over your mouth, is that how you got the bruises on your face?" I nod my head in response and watch his usually happy eyes cloud over.

Ollie pulls away, crouched over like a child, his elbows resting on his knees as he covers his face. I try to pull his arm but he won't let me.

"Ollie, please don't be upset. I don't want him to upset you. I'm fine. I'll be fine. It was just a bad dream. It only happened today so I'm not surprised I dreamed about it. I'll be right as rain in a few days you see." He looks up, his face lightly smeared with tears. His eyes glisten with tears instead of their usual sparkle. I sigh. He sighs. Can we get through this?

Sleep doesn't come easy for either of us. We lay for hours wrapped in each other's arms, each lost in their own thoughts and insecurities.

The feel of Bella's tiny body lying next to me makes me feel so safe. I can transport myself back in time to the days when we'd snuggle together at weekends and pretend we lived in fairyland. A time when the only worries I had were the day-to-day ones like paying the bills and making sure Bella ate her vegetables. I lean over, breathing in her familiar scent before kissing her pudgy cheek as she sleeps in my arms.

I don't remember Bella coming into our room but I'm glad of her comfort right now. We lie as three spoons, Ollie with his arm stretched over both of us. In my not so deep sleep I occasionally feel his kiss on my face and hear him tell me he loves me. Right now I think we're both broken and don't know how to get fixed. I close my eyes again wishing sleep to take me away, knowing that today is already here and we have to face what happened yesterday and tell those who are most precious to us. This isn't going to be easy.

I move onto my back, leaving Bella to sleep peacefully. I turn to look at Ollie who's watching me.

"Morning, beautiful." His whisper makes me smile. I love waking up with these two, special people and today is even more poignant. He didn't win. We're still all here, the three of us waking up together.

"Good morning, handsome. Did you get any sleep?"

"Nope."

"I thought not. Today isn't going to be the best, is it?"

"Nope." He smiles, a tiny amused smile.

"We're still here, together, Lucy, so we're still not letting him beat us."

"I know and we won't, will we?"

"Most definitely not." I watch as he drags himself out of the warm bed.

"I'm going to call my mum, Lucy. She needs to know as soon as possible. The police are involved so she needs to know." I nod my head knowing that I need to contact my parents too.

I watch Oliver leave the room and say a silent thank you as Bella wakes just at that moment. I won't have time to listen to Ollie break his mum's heart, instead I'll fill my time with entertaining Bella. I quietly sing to my tiny princess, watching her face delight in my flat renditions of her favourite nursery rhymes with a few pop songs thrown in. Bella squeals with joy when Ollie finally returns, her happy noises wiping the worry from his face when he hears her.

"Good morning, Princess Bella, and how did you sleep?"

"I slept good, Daddy and I dreamed of rainbows and elephants." I laugh, never sure if Bella actually knows what a dream is or if she just makes something up on the spur of the moment. Either way her replays of dreams are always a joy to hear. Bella jumps into her Daddy's arms and he spins her around as she squeals with excitement.

"Faster, Daddy, faster." We all laugh as they collapse on the bed. Bella covers Ollie's face with kisses and for a second or two I just enjoy the three of us, shutting out everything else.

"Hi, Mamma. It's me." Just hearing Mamma's voice on the telephone brings tears to my eyes. I swallow hard trying to disguise my sadness.

"I know it's you. How are you, Lucy?"

"I'm OK. Are you home this morning?"

"Yes, why?" Mamma sounds cautious when she answers.

"Well we're back for a few days, maybe longer. Can I come and see you and Dad?"

"Lucy, what's wrong? You never ask unless something is wrong, you just come. Is Bella all right, are you and Ollie OK?"

"Mmm. Bella's fine Mamma. I need to come see you. Please don't worry but I can't talk on the telephone."

"Oh, Lucia, what is it?" Mamma is already crying. I cry. We don't talk, we just cry.

****

I'm ready to go. It took ages to say goodbye to Mamma. She didn't ask again. She knew it wasn't something to talk about by phone; which meant it wasn't good news. Mamma knows it's about me and I sort of think she has an idea what it is. Ollie is watching Bella while I go alone. He's not happy about me telling my parents alone but I'd rather he be here with Bella out of the way. I don't want her to ever overhear any of this. It was an effort to get dressed this morning, old jeans and one of Ollie's hoodies are the best I could do. I honestly don't give a flying fuck what I look like and the effort to brush my hair and tie it back was overwhelming. I don't feel like me today and I'm scared. Scared that I will never be me again.

I pull on my converses and look up at Bella and Ollie who are watching me. They are silent and that scares me too.

"Are you coming back, Mummy?" It's a strange question and it shocks me.

"Of course I'm coming back, baby, why?"

"I love you, Mummy." She holds her arms out to me and I take her in a hug. Bella kisses my face and holds my cheeks like a parent does with a child.

"I won't be long, princess, will you and Daddy be good while I'm gone?"

"YESSSS" Phew! Bouncing baby Bella is back. I'm guessing she has some sort of instinct that tells her all is not right but she doesn't know why so she's checking I'm still going to be around in case that was it. A little piece breaks off my heart and I mentally curse Ralph Ashcroft for bringing insecurity into my daughter's tiny life.

As I turn the key and start the engine of Ollie's car, I feel dread run through me. I close my eyes taking deep breaths. The radio springs to life bringing a whole new meaning to grief. Christina Aguilera singing 'Say Something' greets me and for a few minutes I don't move. I lean my head on the steering wheel and let the tears roll as I listen to the lyrics of this sad, sad song about giving up on someone. As I listen to the words I sob. I let everything out and I just sob.

I wipe away the tears angrily and promise myself, and Ollie, I will not give up on him or us, ever!

The drive to Mamma and Dad's is filled with memories as I follow the familiar route through Layton. I purposely detour, driving past Em's shop, checking if I can see any sign of life. I see a light on upstairs and smile as I think of my beautiful sister finally finding happiness with Kyle.

As I pull up in the driveway, I'm slightly shocked to find both my parents waiting in the doorway to the kitchen. Their faces are etched with worry. My heart weighs heavy knowing I'm going to ruin their day completely.

I check my reflection and sigh when I see the bruises that are even more prominent today. Their colour is a deeper shade of purple and less red today. I touch my face and wince. I'm still so sore, a constant reminder of yesterday and Ralph Ashcroft.

341

I hear Mamma sob as I near the doorway and I know she catches sight of my face. Dad puffs up his chest even though I see the watery unshed tears waiting to escape his eyes.

"What happened to you, baby girl?" Mamma is ever so careful as she places an arm around my shoulders and ushers me into the kitchen and pulls out a chair for me to take a seat. Dad takes my hand and stops me.

"Come here, my girl, I need a hug. Come give your daddy a hug." I rush into his arms and cry like a little girl as he holds me tight. After what seems like forever we take a seat each at the large kitchen table. I'm guessing from their sad faces that they think Ollie may have done this and that hurts. I'm hurt for Ollie that his bastard of a dad makes Ollie a target for possibly behaving like him.

"This wasn't Ollie." Mamma sighs in relief. Dad shrugs his shoulders as if not believing me and I know then that I'm going to have to tell them everything.

Mamma cried throughout and Dad just looks like he's off to kill Ralph Ashcroft any second now. Telling my parents here, alone, has felt like a betrayal of Ollie. He wanted to be here to support me. To show my parents that he's not in any way like his dad but I needed him to be there for Bella. Mamma and Dad understand when I explain. Mamma looks at Dad, then at me, and I shudder. There's something wrong and I don't know what. Mamma begins to cry again and Dad looks from her to me.

"Lucia, we need to talk." I watch as Mamma goes about wiping away her tears. Dad gets up and flicks on the kettle. I watch silently as my parents appear to be preparing for a military operation. Mamma places the teacups on the table, fetching milk and sugar as Dad pours the boiling hot water into the teapot. As he walks to the table his sad look sends shivers through me.

"What's this about, you two? I thought I was the only barer of bad news today. Oh, God, are one of you sick?" Both quickly shake their heads as they continue to look sad and sorrowful. I watch them re-take their seats and Dad give Mamma the nod. She clears her throat and I try to prepare for God knows what!

"Sweetheart, I was hoping this would all fade away and that wretched man would just leave you two alone but obviously he holds a grudge longer than we thought."

"What do you mean, Mamma?"

"Well, Lucia, when I was a young girl and my parents first brought me here to Layton, I was a bit of a spectacle. You know being the foreign girl with the darker skin I was quite a novelty, you know with the boys wasn't I, Peter?" Dad smiles at Mamma lovingly, then at me.

"She was, is beautiful, Lucia, and all the boys wanted to take her out. I stepped back hoping that once it all died down that she'd come out with me and she did."

"Oh, you were the best by far, you were the best-looking boy in the school and I was so lucky to get you." I look from one parent to another. Having never been privy to this information before is a bit of a shock. They've never really talked about when they first met. I knew they met at school, in the last year but that was it really. They've never 'gushed' over each other like this before. I cough loudly, lost as to why they should choose now to tell me all this.

"Sorry, love." Dad looks momentarily embarrassed.

"It's OK. Why are you telling me this now?"

"Well the boy who pursued me like no other was Ralph Ashcroft. He desperately wanted me to go out with him and I always refused. He cornered me one night at a local disco and tried to kiss me. Your dad got hold of him and knocked him out, didn't you, Peter?" Dad nods his head and I snigger.

"Well that's good, Dad, isn't it? You got to punch him. I wish I could right now." Dad's smile is a sad one. Mamma wipes away a tear.

"Well he bothered me until I finished college and married your dad, sweetheart. He was a creep and if it happened today it would be called stalking. Everywhere I went he'd follow. He thought he was being chivalrous but it was scary, Lucy." A shiver runs through me at the thought of that evil man stalking my Mamma.

"My brothers threatened him, so did your dad but nothing deterred him. He called me after we got married and said he'd win me over one day. One day, I'd belong to him." I look at my parents and feel hatred and fear run through me all at once.

"He's never going to give up, is he? He didn't get you and he won't let Ollie have me. Oh God!"

"Well you know what, Lucy? He's not going to bother you again. I'm going to make damn sure of that sweetheart. This family has had enough of that man. Enough is enough."

"What do you mean, Dad? Please don't do anything, he's dangerous."

"Don't you worry about me love but I am going to deal with this. I'm not a violent man but he's overstepped the mark now. He needs to leave us all alone."

Driving home I feel my heavy heart and realize that Ralph Ashcroft is causing bigger problems than ever now. I've heard Ollie threaten to kill him and Dad telling me he's going to sort this out. I'm worried, really worried. These are very angry men and I don't want them to do anything that will get them in trouble. I have never seen my dad so angry and have never heard him make threats, ever. No matter what I said he would not discuss it any further once he'd said he was sorting it. Mamma seemed unperturbed by Dad's outburst too, which also worries me.

As I pull up in the garage ,I take a few silent moments to think about what will happen next.

I gave a statement to the police and I'm determined to press charges against Ralph Ashcroft for his vicious assault on me yesterday. I don't need anyone to take the law into their own hands. This can only cause more pain for both families.

Chapter 28

I love my sister dearly and only held out on telling her everything because she's had so many tough times and has finally found happiness. News of our traumas was not what she needed when she was just getting into a happy place with Kyle. Trying to explain this to a very angry Emilia right now is difficult.

"I can't believe you didn't tell me, Luce. I'm hurt, if I'm honest. I thought we were close, that we shared everything. And look at your beautiful face. How dare that bastard do that to you." I look up, stunned as she begins to cry.

Standing on the balcony with my older sister who arrived in a rush after she spoke to Mamma, I feel guilty. I had Em's best interests at heart when I didn't tell her but now I'm watching her break down over this I'm not so sure I did the right thing. I pull her in to hug her hoping she'll let me. She does!

"Em, I'm so sorry. I just thought maybe you needed a break from bad news. You're just getting things together with Kyle and I want you to be happy, not worrying about me."

"But I do worry and I want you to be happy too, Luce. It goes both ways you know."

"Oh, Em, I'm sorry, really. I wasn't trying to keep you out. It's killed me not being able to talk to you about this."

"Right so you need to tell me everything and if I get upset, well, I'm allowed to, it's a sister's prerogative, OK?"

Talking through the happenings of the past few months with Emilia has really helped. There is always an element of humour in any trauma we deal with and this has helped no end. Ollie joined us at one point but retreated when he realised that we were indeed going over absolutely everything. Ollie struggles to deal with this whole thing and going over his father's terrible actions is not easy for him. In all honesty, I didn't want him to listen to this. I've told him what happened yesterday and I don't want to subject him to that more than once.

Emilia is as angry as I expected. The air is blue with her bad language, which at times has made me laugh. Ollie has peaked his head out a few times and frowned when he's seen me laughing loudly.

Saying goodbye to my sister when she leaves to go home hurts. Now she knows everything, I need her more than I thought.

"You OK?" I look up after leaning on the doorframe for a good few minutes once I've closed the door behind Em to see Ollie watching me. His face is full of concern and again, I feel guilty. These past few days have been a strain on everyone I love and I feel so damned guilty.

"Yes I am. I feel better now that I've told Em. We never have secrets and she helps just by being my Em."

"Good. Come here?" He steps towards me and pulls me into his body gently. His feel and scent are a comfort. Closing my eyes, I feel secure in Ollie's arms.

"Do we have to go back to London, Lucy, can't we just stay here now, for good?"

"Oh, Ollie, I wish we could. I need to go and work my notice. I can't just leave Will in the lurch like that. It's just not fair and it's certainly not very professional, is it?"

"Lucy, Will knows what happened. That fucking magazine is partly to blame for what happened to you. My father should never have been let in to see you. You owe them nothing."

"Well you may think that but I love Will. He's coached me to where I am now in my career and I will always be in his debt. I won't let him down, Ollie. I will work the minimum notice I can but I have to do it."

"You know there is nothing I don't love about you, Lucia Meyer. You are so loyal, so caring and just perfect do you know

346

that?" His forehead is leaning against mine as he speaks. I stare into his ice-blues and get lost in my Ollie. I relish his love for me and feel overcome with love for him at this moment.

"Let's have a baby, Ollie, another baby?" I'm not sure if it's a question or a statement. He doesn't move, his eyes stay staring into mine and for a second, I think maybe I've said the wrong thing.

"Really?" His voice is a whisper.

"Really." I whisper back. I feel his hands on my waist and my feet leave the floor as he picks me up, spinning me around ever so slowly.

"You and me and Bella... and a baby." As we spin, I see the tear drip from his eye.

"Yes, we three and a baby, what do you think?"

"I think I love you even more than I did just five seconds ago, Miss Meyer."

"So, is it something you'd like then Ollie, a baby?"

"Are you kidding, I'd love another baby with you. I want lots of babies with you, Lucy. I want us to live in a great big house and fill it with mini me and yous. I want to grow old with you, watching our huge family live their lives and enjoy every perfect moment of their lives. I want to love them all, with all my heart like I do you and Bella. I want to share our children with my lovely mum who deserves to see happy children who are loved and love. I want to give your dad a grandson, he would love that so much. Not that he doesn't love Bella, but imagine him with his own little man to take around the site, Luce. He'd love it." As we continue our gentle spin, I'm gobsmacked.

"Wow you really have thought about this haven't you, Oliver?"

"Mmmhmm, I was just waiting for a sign that you might like something similar before I told you." I giggle. He kisses my mouth hard. The first real kiss since yesterday's horrors and it feels right and good, real good.

****

347

We've enjoyed a quiet lunch, just us three. Ollie suggested we go out to eat but I'm not ready to go anywhere unless I have to with the marks on my face still very visible.

"I need to go and see my mum this afternoon, Luce. Do you want to come with me?"

"We gonna see Nanna, Daddy?" Ollie looks to me and I sigh. Bella is grinning with joy. Damn!

"Well you didn't handle that well did you, Ollie?" He runs his hand through his hair.

"Sorry, I didn't think. I can go on my own, Bella will get over it if she can't go."

"I want to see Nanna, Daddy, I wanna see Nanna." I'm more than a little cross now. I swing my legs round from the stool where I'm sitting and leave the room without a backwards glance.

"Lucy, wait!"

"No, Ollie, piss off." I know that was cruel but really, did he think he could mention anything about visiting his mum in front of Bella and not get her excited!

I storm out onto the terrace and spend a few solitary moments calming down. I look out to sea and try to remember how it felt that week when I first told Ollie that I loved him. The time when we knew nothing of the stormy ride we would face over many years together at the hands of his evil father.

"Lucy." I spin around still feeling anger towards Ollie and his family. Rage is pulsing through me as I silently find reasons to dislike every single member of his family. My face must be etched in hatred because he physically winces.

"I'm sorry, really."

"You know what, Ollie, I'm sick of hearing you say sorry for your wretched family. I don't want you to be with me and constantly be sorry. I want us to be like other couples, you know just enjoy being together and doing boring things like going to the supermarket. Your dad is evil and you know what, you really have no idea how far this goes back."

"What do you mean?" He sounds a little cross and for a second, I feel bad.

"When I told my parents this morning about what happened yesterday, it turns out there's far more to this story than just me and you. This isn't just about him not liking me."

"Why?" Ollie is holding my upper arms, his face tense as he waits for my reply.

"When Mamma first came to Layton, he started to stalk her. He wanted her to be his girlfriend but she wasn't interested so he stalked her. When she married my dad, he told her that one day, she'd be his. So, you see this isn't about me and you, Ollie. He couldn't have my mamma so he wasn't going to let you have me." He lets go of me and looks down. I watch as he shuffles his feet around. After what seems like an age, he speaks.

"I'm going out now, Luce. I need to get out of here. I won't be long."

"What, where are you going? Are you leaving me, Ollie?

"No, of course I'm not leaving you, Luce. I need to get out of here though. I'm not sure how much more news I can take of my father and his evil ways. I'm going to see Mum then I'll be back, OK?" He tilts his head and I feel dread run through me at the thought of being here on my own with Bella.

"I'll be fine, go." I sound angry when I answer, disguising my fear well. It's the only way I can speak without begging him not to leave me on my own.

When I hear the front door close behind him, I instantly feel sick. I lock and double lock the door checking time and again that it's secure.

"Mummyyyy." Bella has been really good most of the day and I feel bad when I look down at her cheeky smile.

"Yes, beautiful?"

"Can I have a biscuit?"

"What's the magic word, baby B?"

"Pleeeease?" She leads me to the kitchen and I let her.

We settle on the sofa and watch *The Little Mermaid* followed by *Frozen* and *Toy Story* and only then do I start to feel anxious. Three Disney films and I've heard nothing from Ollie. Would it take that long to tell his mother? I know I was only gone for about an hour and a half this morning so he's definitely taking a long time. I press start for the fourth DVD and smile as Bella gets excited to watch *Monsters Inc.*

I leave her watching her scary movie and head to the kitchen. I quickly text Ollie asking if he's OK and grab a drink. I sip my fizzy drink and wait eagerly for a reply. I expect him to text straight back but I hear nothing.

I need advice. I know I could just call him but I don't want to intrude while he's with his mum. I call Emilia.

"Luce, you OK?"

"Hmm, well no I'm not. I told Ollie what Mamma told me this morning about his dad stalking her. He went off to see his mum but it was ages ago, Em. I've texted asking if he's OK, and he hasn't responded."

"Call him." Her suggestion is the obvious one.

"I can't, I don't want to intrude while he's with his mum."

"Why not? Lucy, he'll answer his phone to you. He'll be worried there's something wrong so he'll definitely answer. Call him and stop being silly." Em's abruptness makes me see sense. She's right. There's nothing wrong with calling to check he's OK.

"You're right. Sorry, Em. I'll call him."

"Hey, don't be sorry. That's what I'm here for, to make you see sense, Dumbo! Now go call your man and stop worrying." I smile as I hang up dialing Ollie's phone and expecting him to pick up instantly. Wrong! It goes straight to voicemail. Shit!

"Em, it's me again. Ollie didn't answer, it went straight to voicemail."

"OK, OK keep calm. Just call his mum. Maybe he left his phone in the car or something. Call his mum Luce." I'm sure I detect a note of worry in Em's voice. I try to ignore it, hanging up yet again, and this time I dial Ollie's mum.

"Hi, Penny, it's Lucy."

"Hello, sweetheart. How are you? Lucy, I am so sorry." I hear her voice break and then… silence before Penny sniffles into the phone." I don't reply. I listen and wait for her to compose herself.

"I'm OK, Penny. Is Ollie with you? I tried calling him but his phone went to voicemail."

"He left here a good while ago now, Lucy. Was he coming straight home or going somewhere after?" She doesn't sound concerned as fear runs through me, chilling me to my core.

"I thought he was coming straight home. I'll call him again."

"Well tell him to let me know when he's home so that I know he's safe will you?"

"Yes, I will, thanks, Penny."

"Lucy, sweetheart, take care and please try not to worry. This will all get sorted, I promise you that."

"How can you promise that, Penny? Just when we think it can't get any worse he ups the ante and look where we are now."

"I know and I'm sorry but I promise you that I will sort that man once and for all. He will not hurt you and Ollie again, ever."

"Well, how will you do that Penny? He's dangerous and the only way he can't hurt us is if he's not around anymore and let's face it, you're not the murdering kind, are you?" I laugh, a laugh of near hysterics as I think about Ollie's threat and my dad's threat. Now Penny, who next?

"You're right, but you have to trust me this time. I will sort that evil man who I foolishly thought had a heart in there somewhere."

I sigh when I hang up and feel sorry, sad, angry and more anxious than before. I grab my phone when I hear its ringtone, convinced it's Ollie. It's Emilia.

"Lucy, did you speak to his mum?"

"Yes, he's not there. He left ages ago and should have been home."

"Right, don't panic but Kyle just got back and he said he passed Ollie going through Layton a few hours ago."

"What, heading this way?"

"No, he was heading out towards the motorway. Ollie didn't see Kyle." Em goes quiet as she speaks in mumbled tones, I assume to Kyle.

"Kyle reckons it was more like three hours. He just checked his phone 'cause he remembered a call before he saw Ollie so he just checked the time." I feel sick, slumping onto the sofa next to Bella who is too engrossed in her film to notice my anxiety, thank God!

"Oh God, Em. He threatened he was going to kill his dad yesterday. I don't think for a minute that he meant it but do you think he's gone to see him?"

"Yes, I do. Lucy. Do you want me to come over?"

"No, really, I'll just wait here and hope that I hear from him soon."

"Look why don't Kyle and I come over? Kyle can keep Bell entertained so that you don't have to keep putting on that brave face."

Two more long hours have passed. Kyle has been a godsend keeping Bella entertained while Em tried to reassure me and quell my anxieties. It's not working. I feel sick with worry.

"What if he's had an accident, Em? Should I call the police?" Memories of Jamie's fateful day comes flooding to mind. The look on Em's face tells me she's having similar recollections.

"Let's give it a while longer then you might need to call his mum and his sister in case they've heard something."

"Right, girls. Bella and I have had a chat and we think we should go and get take away for dinner, is that OK?" I look to Kyle, then to Bella. He's holding her tiny hand as he smiles sympathetically at me, his warm eyes full of concern.

"I bet baby B would love a burger and fries for her dinner, Uncle Kyle." I see the tender look on his face when I refer to him as Uncle and enjoy the brief feeling of joy we all share as Em, Kyle and I smile at each other, then at Bella.

"Yes, Unca Kyle, I'd love a burger." Kyle ruffles Bella's hair and leads her away from Em and me.

"Come on then, sweetie, before Mummy changes her mind." Kyle looks back giving a wink as he leads Bella towards the front door.

As if on cue we all stop and look as we hear the key rattling in the door.

"Daddyyyyyy!" Ollie looks a little bewildered as Bella calls out to him whilst clinging onto Kyle's hand.

"Hi, sweetheart, have you been a good girl for Mummy while I was out?" Bella nods looking at each adult in the room for confirmation that she has been good. We all nod enthusiastically as she grins proudly at her daddy who looks pale and somewhat distracted.

"Unca Kyle is taking me for burger, Daddy, you want to come?"

"Not just now, is that OK?" Bella is not giving up her trip with Uncle Kyle, not even for Daddy.

"OK, Daddy, see you later. Come on, Unca Kyle, let's go?" I wave for him to go. Kyle looks anxious as he lets Bella pull him out of the door.

"Hey, now Ollie's back, maybe I should join Kyle and Bella." Emilia looks to me, checking that I'm OK with her suggestion. I smile nervously, not sure if I'm ready to hear what Ollie's been up to.

"I do need to talk to Lucy, Em, thanks." Well that was Em's answer then. I have no choice, he wants to speak to me. I sigh, a long drawn out sigh. Em frowns as Ollie runs his hands over his face as if to wipe away his anguish, which by the look of him hasn't worked. He has dark rings under those beautiful ice-blues and I'm sure there are permanent frown lines that have never been there before.

"Where the hell have you been, Ollie? I've been out of my mind worrying. I've only put off calling the police cause Em suggested I wait a little while longer." My voice is raised which is not like me. I'm not a shouter but at this moment, I'm livid and I certainly intend for Ollie to realize just how mad I am with him.

"Please don't shout, Luce, I'm sorry." That final sorry is like a red rag to a bull. I walk towards him, my finger pointing angrily. If it were possible, steam would be streaming from my ears too.

"NO MORE FUCKING SORRYS, OLIVER." I'm in his face as I shout louder. He doesn't move, his face almost impassive as I unleash my anger on him.

"Your dad has dealt us enough shit and if we're ever going to survive we need to be honest with each other and stick together. So what do you do? Oh yes, you piss off and tell no one where you are. I have imagined every type of scenario possible and none of them had a happy ending, Ollie. This afternoon has been far worse than yesterday. Why couldn't you just phone me, why?" The last word is quieter as tears break my voice.

"I went to see him, Lucy, I had to. I didn't think you'd like the idea, which is why I didn't tell you. I tried not to be too long."

"And do you feel better after seeing him? Have you dealt with this because I haven't Ollie? I've been the one sitting here imagining all sorts of bad things happening to you. I even worried that you might hurt him. You didn't, did you?"

"Believe me, I came close. I had him up against the wall by the scruff of his neck but then I thought of you and Bella and I knew if I hurt him he'd make me pay so I did nothing." I feel my body relax at this news. Ollie's hand reaches the back of my neck, his thumb gently stroking as he leans in and our foreheads touch.

"I don't feel better, Lucy. I never will after what he did to you. I just got to tell him exactly what I think of him and that kind of helps. My mum is devastated so he's hurt her again too. Catherine is in shock. The list goes on and on. He has no shame Lucy, he doesn't give a shit. He's evil and I'm so ashamed to be his son."

Reaching up, I touch his cheek. His face, the face I love so much, looks so sad.

"Well we have to make damn sure our children never get to know just how bad he is. We need to make sure they have the best time ever growing up, and then we'll be sure that he's had no influence whatsoever on our lives, Ollie." Ollie sighs as our eyes meet. His ice-blues are full of sadness. I feel my heart ache as I know his is broken.

Chapter 29

We arrived at Ollie's mum's about half an hour ago. So far, we haven't even mentioned his dad, which I'm relieved about. It's been four days since it happened and the only subject of conversation whenever we meet up with anyone. I know people care and are only being thoughtful but I don't want to go over and over it. I wish it never happened and would love to pretend it didn't. In reality I'll be lucky if I get away with the denial of my situation for more that another half an hour.

"Mummy look, Nanna bought me a magazine. It has a fairy we can cut out and colour. Can we do it now?" I smile at her sweet, innocence and the way she almost gets the word right.

"Maybe we should wait until we get home. I'll help you."

"Oh, Mummy, I want to do it now." I watch as Bella stamps her tiny foot in defiance and struggle to hide my smile.

"Well you can't, Bell. Why don't you look at the other pages first? I bet there are some stories we could read."

"Shall I read with you, sweetheart?" I watch with fondness as Penny leans over, gently kissing the top of Bella's head. Bella looks up at her Nanna, a grin spread across her chubby face.

"Can we cut out the fairy, Nanna?" Penny looks to me, her face showing no emotion as Bella watches and waits. My amusement is growing as I look between Ollie's mum and Bella, both eager to play, but neither daring to do so without my permission.

"Go on then." I delight in Bella's squeals of joy and Penny's brilliant smile, which we haven't seen much of lately. Ollie leans over, kissing my cheek. I look to him, his head tilted as his ice blues shine. His voice is a whisper as the other two ladies in his life plan their activities, oblivious to us and our conversation.

"I love you, Luce, so damned much it hurts."

"I love you too, handsome."

Our afternoon at Penny's has been a much needed distraction. Ollie and I have watched as Bella enjoyed playtime with her Nanna. Catherine popped her head in for a while and seemed as down as the rest of us. She apologized to me for what's been happening over the last few months and I have to say that she looks haunted when she speaks of her dad and his behavior. I know Catherine has always been his little girl and she seemed to be the only one in the family that ever got any attention from him according to Ollie so this must be more of a shock to her. The thought that your dad, who you worship and adore, could be such a monster must be hard to endure.

Bella is sleeping like an angel on the oversized sofa in the very large lounge whilst Penny and Ollie make plans to meet up in London next week. We're going back to London at the weekend. I will hand in my notice at work and we will start to make plans for our move back to Layton. Penny is well underway with her moving plans. She's off to the States in a couple of weeks and has an open ticket with no fixed plans for when she'll return. I know Ollie is really disappointed that she'll be away for so long just when we plan to return to Layton.

Penny excuses herself to answer her phone as I look to Ollie.

"I think we need to get our baby home to bed, don't you?"

"Yes. I'll put the bags in the car. We'll go as soon as Mum's finished on the phone." I stay calmly seated and stroke my baby's chubby cheeks as Ollie takes my bag and Bella's box of toys with him to the car.

Watching Bella sleep is a luxury and something I will never tire of. Watching her lips move slightly as she dreams I lean in and kiss her lightly, smiling at the beauty of my tiny princess.

I'm distracted by voices in the hallway adjacent to the lounge. I can make out Ollie trying to comfort his mother and frown as I wonder what's going on. Catherine makes an appearance and it sounds like something serious is happening. I hear Catherine's sobs and make my way out to find the others, anxious to find out what's happening. I stop in my tracks as Ollie, Penny and Catherine huddle together, each one of the trio appearing to comfort the others.

"What's wrong?" I keep my voice down, afraid to intrude but also aware that Bella is just across the hall. Ollie extracts himself from the group hug and walks towards me, a solitary tear tracing its way down his cheek. I look past him and watch Catherine being held up by her mother. I feel sick, guessing that there's bad news to be heard. Ollie places his hand around my waist and walks me to the kitchen, away from his mother and sister and out of earshot of everyone including Bella.

"What on earth is wrong, Ollie?" I turn to him as we reach the centre of the kitchen. Ollie's face is almost grey in colour as he approaches me.

"My father has been murdered, Lucy. He's dead!"

I recall his words again and again and can't quite believe what I heard Ollie say. His father, the man I hate more than anything in this world has been murdered. He's dead!

I should feel relief, relief for Bella, for Ollie, for me. I don't! I feel sickened to the stomach. Sickened that he was so bad that I'm certain he was murdered by someone who hated him as much as I.

I've spent hours listening to Ollie make endless telephone calls, trying to make sense of this horrendous news. I watch and wince at the pallor of his face. The dullness of his eyes is shocking. He looks completely horrified by the news and no matter how many times he goes over the story he was told by the police, he sounds shocked. I have no idea how he feels right now. That man was hateful towards him yet I know that Ollie craved his love, wanted his father to love him like he loved Catherine. I don't think Ollie has ever understood what he did wrong, why his father loved Catherine so unconditionally yet despised him so much.

"Oliver, the police are on their way here now. They need to take statements from each of us. I'm not sure what their plans are." Penny is like a robot as she speaks. Her monotone speech is chilling.

It's as if Penny left the room but her body remains in person only. There is no emotion in her voice when she speaks. Her eyes are glazed, almost masking her feelings.

I leave Ollie for a few seconds to check on Bella who is still sleeping, oblivious to what is going on right now. I bend and kiss my baby, taking in her scent as a form of comfort. I walk back to Ollie who looks like a lost child as he watches me approach.

"Ollie, shall I call my parents and get them to come and pick up Bella? I don't want her here when the police come."

"Oh God, Bella. Yes, Luce, we need to get her out of here. I don't want her to hear any of what happened or to be frightened by the police. Why don't you go? Take Bell to your parents and wait there for me." I smile at his naivety.

"Ollie, baby, don't you think the police will want to speak to me after what happened with your dad, you know, the attack?" I'm hesitant as I speak, feeling bad for bringing up the bad side of Ollie's dad. He sighs and rubs at his face with both hands.

"Yeah, you're right. Call your parents, Luce." He sounds so defeated. I feel soooo sick!

****

We're home, finally. I'm not sure of the time but I can the see the sun making an appearance as I stand on the balcony and look out to sea. I breathe deep, inhaling sea air as I try and untangle the fuzzy mess that's in my head. I feel the gentle pounding of the headache that's been present for most of the evening, rubbing at my temples with my forefingers. I allow myself to think of Bella, my sweet baby who's fast asleep at my mamma and dad's now, hopefully lost in a world of beautiful childlike dreams where the world is all good.

We're all aware that although we spoke individually with the police at Penny's that they are going to want to see us all again and go over our last few days actions. Ralph Ashcroft was shot. His cleaner found him dead in his London apartment. The police didn't give away too much information and are busy interviewing many people.

Penny had to call the GP who sedated poor Catherine who hadn't even come to terms with my attack, never mind her father's murder. Penny seems oddly calm and emotion free, which worries me. Maybe she'll suddenly realize the enormity of all this and we won't be there for her. Catherine will be of no help. I rub at my forehead, anxious about everyone just now.

"Lucy, would you like a drink? I'm just making a coffee?" Ollie seems rather matter of fact. It's as if he's received news of the death of a long lost relative not the actual murder of his father. I nod my head in response.

"Yes please, a coffee would be lovely." I watch as he disappears inside and feel worried.

The sun is rising and sounds of a new day are finding their way up to me on the balcony. I watch the world go about its usual routine below and sigh. I catch sight of a couple saying their goodbyes as she jumps into a taxi outside the building. The taxi pulls off only to stop a few metres away. The rear window descends as the girl peeks out and beckons her beau. He steps forward and kisses her, one last kiss before the taxi heads out into the early morning traffic. Oh, to be them just for one minute of this awful day, to be in love and full of hope instead of ravaged by the hatred of one dead man.

"Lucy." His voice is quiet as he hands me a steaming mug of coffee. I watch as the steam permeates the cool morning air, not sure what we should talk about.

"I don't know what to say, Ollie. I don't know how to react. I'm lost." I choose to be honest. If I learned something recently, it's that we need to be honest if Ollie and I are to stand a chance in this world.

"Me either, Luce. I hated him yesterday, really hated him. You know I even thought it would be best if he were dead after what he did to you. But now, now he is dead, I feel sad. I'm sad that I never had a dad like yours. I feel sad that I'll never have a chance to make amends with him and sort this out properly so that we could get along. I'm sad that Bella won't ever get to meet him and for him to fall in love with her like I know he would, if he only got the chance. I feel guilty, Luce. I'm not angry with the person who killed him and I should be, shouldn't I?" He laughs a sarcastic laugh as he asks me.

"I can't answer that, Ollie. I don't feel sad that he's dead and I'm ashamed to say that. I can't even begin to imagine how you feel." We stand silently, side by side and listen to the world start its day as the sea washes ashore, attempting to crash through our thoughts with every broken wave.

****

Seated at the large table of my parent's kitchen I take some comfort from just being in their house, my childhood home. The place where I grew up with the least possible worries imaginable. I sigh as I swish the cold tea around my cup. Mamma is busy with the usual breakfast rush, catching glances at me when she can as I sit and talk, then cry, then talk. Mamma doesn't say much, she just listens, and that's just what I need right now.

I've talked through everything that's been going on. It's been a week since Ralph Ashcroft died and we've been on a hell of a rollercoaster ride. Bella has been with my parents for all of that time with Ollie and I popping in whenever we could get the chance.

The worst time so far was when Ollie was taken in for questioning. The thought that he may have killed his father never crossed my mind until I watched him leave with the police officers that day.

When we got the news that they'd arrested someone for Ralph's murder I watched the love of my life crumble and I don't think I will ever get over it. As I talk Mamma through the tale, I feel sick when I think of Ollie and the emotions he's dealing with as he tries to go about the practicalities of his father's death. Mamma stops in her tracks when I tell her. She has every reason to hate Ralph herself but to hear the news of his killer is still a shock.

Bruce Hamilton, father of Serena, Ollie's ex, made a full confession to the police yesterday. Revenge for abusing his beloved daughter was his reason. Penny didn't look at all surprised when we were told. Catherine was a mess again, and Ollie... well Ollie broke down, finally. I think it was going over everything, the deception around the birth of Xavier, the threats to me, to Bella, and the attack on me by his father. I almost feel akin to Bruce Hamilton and I'm guessing that Ollie feels guilty because he too shares the kinship whether he chooses to or not. Someone so hateful as Ralph Ashcroft cannot treat anyone in the way he did without there being an element of relief when they are no longer here.

I'm distraught as I discuss with Mamma whether or not I should go to the funeral. I hated the man and can't see how I can possibly stand in a church and say goodbye to him. I would be such a hypocrite. But how, how can I not go and be there for Ollie? Mamma takes a seat opposite me at the large wooden table that has shared so many sad times with us all. She straightens her hair, which is perfect anyway, before she speaks.

"Lucy sweetheart, sometimes we do things for others against all our better judgement, and the only reason we do is because we love them and they need us. I think deep down you know what you're going to do, don't you? Please remember that this is for Ollie, sweetheart." I swipe at the tears that seem to be forever present on my face these days.

"I know, Mamma, I need to go, don't I?" She nods her head as she pats my hand.

"Just for Ollie and Penny, sweetheart, not for him." I smile at my wise Mamma who always makes sense of things and knows exactly what's going through my head.

"Hey, how's my favourite sister?" I smile at her cheek and feel lucky to have my family around me. Emilia takes a seat at the table and looks to Mamma who automatically pours her a cup of tea.

"She's going." I should feel cross that they've been talking about me but I'm touched that they care. I giggle. They stop talking and stare.

"Yes, Em, I'm going to the funeral and then I'm drawing a line. No more Ralph Ashcroft. No more threats to mine and Ollie's happiness. No more worrying about Bella. Just our family, me Ollie and Bella." Em moves closer in her seat and pulls me to her.

"I love you, Lucy, you'll get your happy ever after, you will." I look to Mamma then to Em who both nod enthusiastically. We all giggle quietly. Hoping that Em's predictions come true.

Epilogue

So, we're here, in Layton, our final destination and it feels right. I never imagined that I'd return with plans to stay forever when I packed myself off to London years ago. I watch Bella run through our new house to the stairs and hear her laughter as she finds her new over the top princess bedroom.

Ollie decided that we should have a house by the sea with a garden if we were moving here for good. He made all the plans and took care of practicalities whilst I used this opportunity to design the interior of our new house. I knew if I got it just right, then Ollie and Ben would hire me as the project designer for their latest development.

I grin as his arm takes me round my midriff, pulling me to him from behind and he whispers into my ear.

"Welcome home, Mrs Ashcroft, love of my life, welcome home."

Oh yes, we got married. A small affair involving just the closest people in our lives at a small ceremony in Sicily bringing great joy to my mamma.

Ollie and I only stayed in London for a month. Will proved to be the best of friends I always knew he was, as well as my boss, by hiring my replacement as soon as practically possible.

Lisa, my best friend in London is still there, working her notice and making plans to move to Milan where she's hoping to live happily ever after with the love of her life, Giovanni. Her Aunt Becca is moving over too after Lisa's settled. She's selling her house and buying something small near to Lisa and Gio. I'm pleased for Lisa, she'll have the only family she's ever known close by. I know from my experiences over the last year that family are so damned important and I can't imagine being away from them any more.

I did go to Ollie's father's funeral, a sad sorry affair which was only attended by a few friends and the family. Nothing grand like I'm sure he hoped and expected. Ollie's mum, Penny has made her move to the States and is settling well. We speak most days and Skype all the time so that she gets to see Bella who misses her terribly. We plan to visit very soon. Ollie needs to see her living happily for his own peace of mind. Catherine is coping better and has decided to take a year off work and travel the world with Abbie.

My beautiful sister Emilia is pregnant and I couldn't be happier for Em and Kyle. It transpired that when they were travelling Em got food poisoning and was sick for a few days and their miracle was conceived sometime after that when Em's pills weren't working as they should. Baby bean, as he's known was a shock but a wonderful surprise and I have never, ever seen my sister blossom with such happiness which is so deserved. She struggled through guilt initially over Jamie, and in the end, Kyle took her to the cemetery where he gave a speech, which broke my heart when Em relayed it to me. He thanked Jamie for letting him love Em and promised to cherish her forever and never forget that she was only on loan from Jamie. He told Jamie about baby bean for Em and informed both Jamie and Em at the graveside that bean would indeed be given the middle name of James in his memory. Since that day Em has been at peace and is enjoying pregnancy and preparation for the birth of her son.

Talking of babies, my friend and ex-boss Will and his beautiful wife are now expecting a baby and are ecstatic. The past and their problems are all forgotten as they plan a move to the suburbs and life with a family.

Everywhere we seem to go there is talk of babies and I have to smile as Ollie looks to me, that glint in his ice-blues as I know he's hoping it happens for us sooner rather than later.

The doorbell rings and I can't help but smile. I know that whoever our visitor is they are most welcome in our new home. It can only be family or friend. I follow Ollie across the large square hallway to the double oak doors and wait as he pulls them open. Em is first through the doorway holding a huge bouquet of flowers out in front of her like a trophy.

"Welcome home, you two, I can't begin to tell you how lovely it is to have you back in Layton." I feel the tears pushing their way through as Em pulls me to her and I watch the line of people walking through my front door. I am overwhelmed with love at this moment.

Kyle, Mamma, Dad, Ben, Sarah, Ollie's sister Catherine and her partner Abbie. Everyone is here in our new house and it feels so right. Bella soon appeared at the sound of all the voices and is now centre stage and playing her part as diva perfectly.

The evening is balmy so we've all descended on our new back garden, which has a perfect view of the sea much to my delight. Kyle opens a second bottle of champagne and we all clink glasses making toast after toast as we all have so many good things to celebrate right now. I take a small sip of my drink and catch Ollie watching me. I tilt my glass to him and smile. He tilts his head and nods towards the house. I watch as he stands and makes his way inside. I look around at our guests and smile, as everyone seems lost in happy chatter. I quickly place my glass on the table and follow my husband into our new home. I make my way across the kitchen wondering where Ollie is. I call his name as I find my way to the living room jumping when he pulls me inside the door.

"I just need a kiss from my wife, Lucia Ashcroft, and I can't wait until everyone goes home." I hitch my breath at the sensations running through me as he pulls me to him kissing my neck.

"I love you, Ollie."

"I love you more, beautiful"

This just seems right. The right time to tell him.

"Ollie, I'm pregnant." I'm straight to the point as he holds me at arm's length, a look of shock on his face. It feels like forever as

I wait for him to say something. His eyes are glistening as he clears his throat.

"Really, oh my God, Lucy, a baby, oh my God!" Each word he speaks reaches a higher level, until the others in the garden must have definitely heard his final word.

I laugh loudly as he pulls me into his arms and spins me around before quickly placing me on the floor and apologizing.

"Oh God, I shouldn't have done that should I? Are you OK?"

"I'm fine, Ollie." He strokes my cheek with his forefinger as he speaks quietly, his finger tracing my lips.

"I promise I will be there every step of the way, baby, I don't want to miss a second of this pregnancy. Oh God, Luce, what do you think Bella will say?" His mind is whirling like mine has for the last few days as I've deliberated over whether or not to do a test. I finally took the test this morning and stared for what seemed like hours at those two pink lines, elation soaring through my body.

Finally, our happy ever after is on the horizon!